THE
ADVENTURES
OF
JAMES RUSSELL

JOHN MILTON LANGDON

EU Conformity Declaration

This product complies with the following safety regulations and standards to ensure consumer safety and product quality: Regulation (EU) 2023/988 of the European Parliament and of the Council on General Product Safety (GPSR): The Consumer Product Safety Improvement Act (CPSIA), Section 101. The Californian Safe drinking water and toxic enforcement act. (Proposition 65) EN71-Part 1: Mechanical and Physical Properties EN71-Part 2: Flammability EN71-Part 3 Migration of certain elements.

Published and Manufactured by Softwood Books
EU Responsible person: Maddy Glenn
Office 2, Wharfside House, Prentice Road, Stowmarket, Suffolk, IP14 1RD
www.softwoodbooks.com
hello@softwoodbooks.com

EU Rep:
Authorised Rep Compliance Ltd., Ground Floor, 71 Lower Baggot Street, Dublin, D02 P593, Ireland
www.arccompliance.com
info@arccompliance.com

Author's Note

In the 1920s, which is about the time this story is set, there were no surfaced roads in Egypt. The bulk of inter town/inter village transport was conducted on the River Nile, on the railways, or on tracks suitable only for foot traffic, camels, or donkey carts.

The magazine, Al-Ahram, reported in 1920 that there were less than 2,000 cars in Egypt and these were mostly owned by foreigners.

It was possible to get from one bank of the River Nile to the other by using one of the Nile Barrages, e.g., Aswan or Eswan, or by crossing the waterway on a felucca. In Cairo, a crossing was possible on one of the bridges.

The Suez Canal was already in use, and it was only possible to cross this waterway by using one of the small vehicle ferries.

There were no roads in the desert to the East of the Suez Canal, just the trade routes, followed by the camel trains from oasis to oasis. From Aden, a trade route ran parallel to the Red Sea and passed through Mecca and Medina before turning north to join the Silk Road at Damascus.

The first surfaced road in Egypt ran from Cairo to Suez and was not opened to traffic until about 1925.

CHAPTER ONE
A Chance Meeting

It was early January in 1920, and the weather in London had been appropriately unpleasant for this time of year. It was now colder and damper than it had been at midday when the sun had made an unexpected and fleeting appearance. Those who saw its short-lived emergence realised that it was too brief an appearance to do more than hint at the pleasures of the summer warmth to come. As the day progressed, it became colder and damper and greyer. Drops of dirty water dripped off the telegraph and telephone lines, which were strung overhead along the streets, and spattered onto the pavements.

By four in the afternoon, a chill mist was rising, and it very soon started to obscure the widely-spaced gas-lit street lamps that were located on the street corners. In the surrounding offices and shops, the gas lights had been burning for some time, and squares and oblongs of warm, yellow light were visible through the gloom.

Some of the rectangles of warm, inviting light came from a Lyons Corner House that was a haven of warmth. Many people sought to escape another chill winter afternoon by basking in the genteel atmosphere; drinking tea and eating one of the myriad delicacies for which the establishment was rightly famed.

There was a comfortable background noise composed of music, conversation, and the subdued clatter of cutlery and crockery.

A little more than half of the tables were occupied, and generally, the people who were sitting at them were small groups of well-dressed and voluble women. There were two men at separate tables reading newspapers, and at another sat a family group composed of a disengaged man, a harassed woman, a squalling baby, and a disobedient small boy.

For those who found the conversation of a companion of only passing interest, they could pretend to concentrate and allow an hour or two to be whiled away listening to an accomplished young woman playing on a grand piano, music gentle enough to accompany afternoon tea.

Of course, if one was alone, then the music could be enjoyed to the fullest.

Not everyone was fortunate enough to while away the hours in such a comfortable fashion of course, and one of those poor souls was the young man who had just come in from the cold, damp street to buy something to eat and drink before driving home. He had realised that he needed a small interval of time in which to recover from a surfeit of meetings in plush City of London offices where he had been discussing with financiers some investments that were of little personal interest but essential to his mother's future wellbeing.

He smiled wryly as he remembered that he never ceased to be surprised at the enthusiasm with which some financial advisors discussed the profligate expenditure of someone else's money.

He looked around the interior of the café and then strode to an empty table.

The ladies who had heard the doorbell chime as he entered, and looked up hoping to see an acquaintance, stopped whatever they were doing and fervently wished that they *were* acquainted.

It was not that he was an Adonis.

It was just that the combination of manly attributes was too overwhelming to be ignored.

He was a clean shaven, tanned, strong-jawed young man about six feet tall, well-proportioned and crowned with recently cut fair hair. He wore, as if he had been poured into it, an exceptionally well-tailored dark suit that had been cut to the height of current fashion. But what attracted the attention of the ladies (whether they were unattached, spoken for, or even married) was the unconscious aura of command that surrounded him.

Here was the handsome epitome of power and money, but not one of the ladies knew who he was, and what was much worse, they had no means for finding out without expressing an open interest and risking embarrassment.

A pretty, young Gladys, as the Lyons waitresses were known, dressed in the customary black dress and long white pinafore, came back to the young man's table to take his order after hanging up his overcoat. In a clear and cultured baritone voice, he ordered Lyons green tea and toasted tea cakes and made some remark to the waitress that made her laugh. Not with embarrassment or concern, you understand, but with genuine amusement, and so we must conclude that he was also a gentleman as well as a good catch, because he could have taken advantage of his undoubted attributes and propositioned the pretty young woman. The Gladys hurried away to prepare the young man's order.

Also in the café, and seated on a table within earshot of the young man, were two well-dressed and very attractive young ladies who had just been to someone's birthday party. One of the young ladies was a blonde, the other a brunette, and both were dressed in the height of 'flapper' fashion. They were exchanging their differing views of the party over cups of Lyons red label tea but stopped chattering to listen to a newspaper vendor in the street outside with expressions of concern on their faces.

"Accident at Southall," he shouted, "No West Country trains tonight."

One of the young ladies, the blonde one, signalled to a Gladys, and when she came to their table, she gave the waitress a few coins and asked her to buy them a newspaper. When it came, they read the relevant columns and then started wondering out loud what they could do to get home.

"My mother will be very concerned and terribly worried if I am not at home by ten," the pretty, blonde-haired young woman said seriously.

"My father and mother will both be angry," the other young lady exclaimed. "But what can we do if there are no trains? We could find a hotel for the night, but they would be worried to death if they do not hear from me."

"We could send telegrams," suggested the blonde.

"We *could* pay for telegrams," her companion responded scornfully, "but there is no guarantee they will be delivered tonight. We live too far away from a town for that." Both the young ladies lapsed into silence as they grappled with their problem.

Unfortunately, neither was able to shout Eureka or offer a copper-bottomed solution to their dilemma.

The young man had been listening to this exchange quite attentively. He wasn't eavesdropping, of course. The young ladies were sitting close to his table and speaking too loudly in their agitation for him to totally ignore what they had been saying. And it was none of his business anyway. He beckoned to the Gladys,

7

and when she came, he asked for his bill, which he paid, together with a generous tip that he justified by saying to himself that the teacakes were excellent and the waitress attentive. Naturally, the fact that she was also extremely pretty was not a consideration, of course.

When the waitress returned with his coat, he gestured to the adjacent table and said, "Those two young ladies are stranded here because of a rail crash at Southall. I am driving home along the A4 this evening. If either or both of them would like to come with me, I am willing to take them. But I think it might be easier for them to decide what they wish to do if *you* ask them, and certainly it will be easier for them to refuse the offer if you agree to carry the message. What do you think?"

"I think it's very thoughtful of you, sir, and I'll certainly ask their opinion," the waitress said as she handed the young man his coat and then walked the few steps to the adjacent table.

The waitress was very discrete as no one heard what she said to the two young ladies, but clearly one was for the proposition while the other, the blonde one, was shocked and very much against the idea. The waitress spoke again, and both young ladies nodded in agreement and smiled at the young man who bowed a little stiffly in acknowledgement.

When the waitress returned, the young man asked her what she had said to change their minds.

"Well, sir," she said, "They don't know if you can be trusted."

"That's not very flattering," he responded. "Don't I look honest?" Then he added, "I suppose if I was in their situation, I would be careful also, so I shouldn't be too offended. What did you say to change their opinion?"

"I didn't try to change their opinion," she said. "How could I? I don't know you either. I told them to stay together and sit in the back of the car. One lives near Upton and the other in Taplow. By the time you have reached Upton, they should have formed an opinion about whether you are to be trusted or not, and then they will decide whether to stay together or separate."

She thought for a moment and then said again, but with more concern evident in her voice this time, "I don't know you, sir, but you behave like a gentleman, so I imagine they will be alright."

"Thank you for your commendation," he said seriously. "Do you know their names?" he asked.

"No, sir," she said and turned away to return to her duties, leaving the young man standing beside his table.

After a few moments of hesitation, he walked the few paces to the table where the two young ladies were just paying their bill and carefully laid his overcoat on the back of an adjacent empty chair.

He said, "Good evening, ladies. My name is James Russell. May I ask," he said, "who I shall have the pleasure to share the drive with and where you both live?"

The blonde-haired young woman said, "I'm Sabrina Severn and my friend is Millicent Malcolm. I live near Taplow and Millie lives in Upton."

"Ah!" he said with the ghost of a grin lightening his face. "The place where you must decide if I am trustworthy or not."

Both young women looked quite embarrassed, and Sabrina Severn said, "She told you?" in a rather shocked voice as if the Gladys had given away a state secret.

"Yes, of course," he responded. "She feels responsible for you because she introduced us, in a manner of speaking, and is a little worried that her good intentions may lead you into difficulty."

"I see," said Miss Severn.

"Shall we go?" James Russell asked as he reached out to take his coat from the back of the chair.

"Yes, of course," the young ladies said in unison as they stood up and reached for the wraps that the Gladys had brought them.

The three of them walked in an ill-coordinated group to the door, which James Russell opened, and then followed the ladies into the cold, damp, mist-wreathed street, and for the first time that evening, they were in complete harmony as they felt the chill in the air and shivered.

"Where is your motor?" Miss Severn asked.

"I parked it along the street about fifty yards from the entrance to the café," he said and then pointed as he added, "There it is, over there."

"It's huge," Miss Severn said. "What is it?"

"It's only a Bentley," said Russell, overlooking the fact that to own one signalled considerable wealth.

Neither of the young ladies commented further but exchanged a few meaningful glances behind James Russell's back.

Russell opened the back door and invited his companions to get in. As they settled into the tan leather upholstered seats, he went to the back of the vehicle and opened the boot. He took out two thick woollen blankets and walked back to the open rear door.

"It's already cold and the mist is getting thicker, I will have to drive with the window open for a time," he said. "I would advise you to wrap yourself in these blankets and keep as warm as you can." He handed the blankets to them.

Miss Severn said, "Thank you, Mr Russell, that is very thoughtful of you. What colour is your motor car?" she asked.

"Dark green," he said, "Some people call it 'British Racing Green'. It looks much better in the sunshine." He then closed the door and walked around the back of the car and then to the front to get to the driver's seat.

The motor car lurched slightly as Russell climbed in, fiddled with various switches and levers, and climbed out, calling over his shoulder, "I'm going to start the engine." There were a number of rattles and metallic clanks from the front as Russell inserted and then swung the starting handle and then a steady rumbling noise accompanied by a gentle vibration when the motor started. The car lurched again as Russell climbed back in and settled himself into the front seat.

He half turned to the rear of the car and looked at two shapeless blanket-clad lumps reclining on the broad, leather, back seats and said, "If you ladies are ready, I'll start?"

One of the lumps moved slightly and said, "We're ready, Mr Russell."

He switched on the big Lucas headlamps and almost immediately switched them off again because of the dazzling reflection of the light from the mist. He put the motor into gear and, using the poor illumination from the side lights, he started his journey across West London towards the A4. The first hour was very hard driving due to the thickness of the mist, and Russell had his head out of the side window, checking his way, more frequently than he had it inside. Several times he had to get out and check the name on a street corner with his torch, and when he saw a policeman, he stopped and consulted him about the best way to proceed. But as they progressed further west, both the visibility and progress improved.

When the mist lifted and he was able to relax for a few moments, he eyed the slumbering bundles on the back seat and wondered how they could possibly decide if he was trustworthy. *They'll probably both get off in Upton,* he thought, *and then I can go straight home and have enough time for a bath before dinner.*

He was quite startled when one of the bundles said, "May I ask you a question, Mr Russell?"

"Of course," he responded. "I thought you were asleep."

"No. Millie is asleep but I'm not tired enough, although the seats are very comfortable and it's nice and warm when the window is shut. It must have been quite difficult to find your way since the mist was so thick."

"I don't know that area very well," he responded, "and it's very easy to mistake where one is when the visibility is so poor. We didn't get lost, which is a blessing."

There was a silence for a few minutes whilst Russell manoeuvred his big motor car through some sharp bends, then he said, "What was your question, Miss Severn?"

"I hope you will not think me impertinent," she said, "but I would like to know what profession you follow." She paused momentarily then added, "If you don't mind telling me, that is."

"I don't mind in the least," he said. "It's not a state secret. I was a major in the last war and now I am the Military Attaché at our embassy in Cairo."

"My word," she exclaimed. "My chauffeur is a diplomat," and then, after a sudden intake of breath, she added contritely, "I'm very sorry, Mr Russell. That was a very rude thing to say when you have been so kind to us. My mother keeps telling me I should control my tongue better."

"I'm not offended," said Russell, managing not to laugh but at the same time failing to keep his amusement from his voice. "Your remark was extremely accurate, but I think your mother might have found it a little undiplomatic."

"Very true, Mr Russell, she probably would." Changing the subject completely, she asked, "Was the war very hard?"

There was such a long pause that Miss Severn couldn't make up her mind if Russell had not heard or was so offended by her question that he wouldn't answer, and then he cleared his throat noisily.

"Sorry," he said, "Your question provoked so many different answers, I didn't know where to start. 'Hard' is not the adjective I would use, Miss Severn. War is madness! It is usually started by political or regal leaders who have said they will go to war if a deadline is not met. To continue to talk when the deadline has passed is seen to be a loss of face, so they go to war. If they faced the first bullet, it would be a little different, but they remain safely in a palatial office, enjoy pampered serenity a long way from the fighting, and let their fellow citizens die for the honour of the country instead. Unfortunately, the citizen soldiers generally have only a very hazy appreciation of the ideals for which they have been put into uniform, and most die without finding out.

"I was lucky. Some of my fellow officers and thousands of our men died. More of them lost one or more arms or legs, and some became insane from fear of death. I repeat, I was lucky. I haven't lost a limb, and for some reason, my mind remains intact, although I have seen sights that have driven other men into an asylum."

After a long silence, she asked, "If the war couldn't be avoided, could it have been finished more quickly?"

"There are a lot of 'if this and if that questions' associated with a complete answer to your question, Miss Severn, but the primary resource an army needs is good leadership. My commanding officer summed up the situation quite well after a particularly bloody defeat. He said, 'We are blessed with some excellent generals and also some not so good generals. The trouble we face at present is due to the fact that none of the excellent generals have been given commands.'"

He stopped with a squeal of brakes, crunched into reverse gear, and backed down the road to look at a road side fingerboard he had only noticed at the last moment. After he had read the rather dirty print on the sign, he said, "Upton is about five miles that way," and he pointed to the left and drove off in the direction indicated.

"Perhaps you could wake Miss Malcolm, Miss Severn, so that she can direct me to her home."

"Yes, of course, Mr Russell," she said and promptly shook her slumbering friend until she sat up.

As Miss Malcolm returned unwillingly to consciousness, she started to take note of her surroundings, and her eyes widened in panic as she realised that she was in the back of a motor car going she knew not where.

As Miss Malcolm's mouth opened to scream, Miss Severn put a finger over her lips and said in her ear, "It's alright, Millie. Mr Russell is taking us home. Remember? You've been asleep, and we're very close to Upton. You must wake up and tell Mr Russell how to get to your home."

Miss Malcolm sat up and slowly rubbed her sleepy eyes. "Where are we?" she asked, and after she had looked out through the windscreen said, "Oh. I see. Please turn left here." But she was too late, and Russell had to stop, reverse back along the road, and then make the left turn. After another hundred yards or so, Miss Malcolm asked Russell to stop beside a big house surrounded by a tall hedge. Russell obediently pulled over to the side of the road to stop where he was requested. The road was quite steeply cambered at this point, and Russell had started to help Miss Malcolm climb out of the car when she realised that her companion was not following her, and she stopped.

"Are you going on with Mr Russell?" she asked in a worried whisper.

"Yes, of course," Miss Severn responded, having totally forgotten her earlier misgivings. "I feel quite safe with Mr Russell, and if he is willing to take me home, I should be pleased to accept his assistance."

Russell said, "Of course I will drive you home, Miss Severn. Taplow is not far from here."

"Very well," said Miss Malcolm. "Goodnight, Sabrina," she said as she climbed out with Russell's assistance. "Thank you for bringing me home, Mr Russell." After shaking his hand, she said, "Goodnight, Mr Russell," and walked away through the entrance gate to the house and disappeared from view.

Russell said, "It's a pity she left as quickly as she did. I was going to ask her the best way to get back to the main road. I'll just have to turn around now. Please excuse me, Miss Severn, but I must see if it is safe to turn here." He took his torch out of the glove box, got out of the car, and disappeared into the darkness on the side of the road, with only occasional flashes of torch light to indicate where he was located.

After a few minutes of silence, Miss Severn decided to get out and ask if she could help.

It was not a sensible decision.

Miss Severn turned on her seat to face the door and released the door catch with her left hand. The rear door of the Bentley was large, quite heavy, hinged at the rear, and the leather seats were ever so smooth. Because of the steep camber in the road, the door immediately started to swing open, so, grasping the door handle even more firmly in her right hand, she threw herself backwards to try to arrest the movement of the door, and her feet were lifted off the floor. She was pulled across the seat and out of the car as the door continued to swing violently open, and her feet just missed the edge of the running board. But instead of landing on the verge of the road as she expected, she found herself falling and had just enough time to give vent to an unladylike screech of fear when her feet splashed down into the mud and water in the drainage ditch beside the road.

Russell came back to the car at a run, stepped across the ditch, and shone his torch on the figure of Miss Severn standing in ankle deep muddy water in a ditch that came higher than her knees.

"Are you hurt, Miss Severn?" he asked, slightly breathlessly.

"Only my pride," she said. "I thought I would get out of the car and see if I could help you," she said in explanation.

"That was very good of you, Miss Severn. May I assist you to get out of your predicament?" When she nodded her agreement, he put the torch down on the ground and said, "Please give me your hands, and I will lift you."

She did as he asked and was amazed at the ease with which he was able to lift her. Russell helped her walk along the edge of the ditch beside the hedge and then cross it to regain the road beyond the front of the car. In the illumination of the side lights, Miss Severn examined her soaked shoes and mud-spattered clothes and then walked with squelching steps to sit on the running board.

Russell said, "I am so relieved you are not hurt, Miss Severn," and a smile started to appear on his lips as he remembered the comical sight of such an elegant young lady standing in a ditch.

She noticed and said with some asperity, "If you laugh at my predicament, James Russell, I shall never speak to you again."

Russell's smile disappeared, and he said in a voice that was so unexpectedly serious and contrite, "I would never wish to bring that fate down on myself," that she chuckled herself.

"I must have looked quite comical nearly up to my waist in a muddy ditch," she said quite cheerfully.

"A sight to draw a veil over perhaps, Miss Severn, but I think we should carry on with our journey now," he said and stepped back across the ditch so that he could reach and close the rear door. He came back around the car and helped Miss Severn get into the back seat.

"There's a side road a little way ahead. I can turn the motor there."

"That's good," she said, then asked, "When you have turned the motor around, perhaps I could come and sit in the front with you?"

"Of course," he said, "I won't feel so much like a chauffeur then," and they both chuckled in remembrance of her previous comment.

Once they were back on the main road, he said, "I live quite near here. If you have no objection, I would like to make a detour to tell my mother that I will be late for dinner. I'll go through Eton Wick and Dorney on the way to Taplow. I hope that is acceptable to you, Miss Severn."

"Yes, of course," she responded and was quite surprised when she realised that she would be quite pleased to spend a little more time with James Russell even if it would only be for an extra half an hour.

All the more surprising, she mused, *when my usual reservations about male company are taken into account.*

Russell slowed down, turned off the road, drove through an imposing gateway, and onto a well-maintained gravel drive.

Miss Severn gasped with surprise and asked, "Are you allowed to drive here, Mr. Russell? It looks like private property."

"I am and it is," Russell informed his companion.

In the bright beam from the headlights, Sabrina Severn could see that the drive was lined with mature beech trees and said, "It must be very pleasant to walk along here when the trees are in leaf."

"Yes, it is," he agreed as he drove around a long right-hand bend, and suddenly the drive way opened out, and Russell brought the big car to a gentle halt at the foot of an imposing flight of steps. He climbed out and walked around to the passenger's side of the motor and helped Miss Severn to alight.

"I thought you were going home," she said. "Whose mansion is this?"

"This *is* my home," he said simply and ushered her towards the steps.

"Are you serious, Mr. Russell?" she asked in a shocked whisper as she walked beside him.

"Yes, of course," he answered as the front door opened. A tall man in evening dress stepped through the entrance, stood on the top step, illuminated by the light that spilt from the hall, and shone down the steps.

Sabrina Severn gasped out loud when the man said, "Good evening, Sir James."

"Good evening, Benson," said Sir James Russell. "This young lady is Miss

Severn. She has had the misfortune of getting herself splashed with mud. Please ask Edith to look after Miss Severn whilst I go and see my mother."

Benson said, "Of course, sir."

To Miss Severn, he said, "I shall only be with my mother for a few minutes, but I expect it will take longer than that to deal with the mud. Ask Edith to send someone to tell me when you are ready to go home."

"Yes, Mr – I mean, Sir James," she said in a voice overawed by her unexpected surroundings.

"Is my mother in the library, Benson?"

"Yes, Sir James," Benson responded. "Will that be all, sir?"

"Yes, thank you, Benson. I'll see you later, Miss Severn. Please go with Benson and he will introduce Edith to you." Sir James Russell turned away from them then and went to tell his mother why he would be late for dinner.

It was a little more than twenty minutes later, and Sir James was still in his study reading the correspondence that had come for him when there was a knock on the door. Benson came in and announced, "Miss Sabrina is ready to leave at your convenience, sir."

"Thank you, Benson," he responded as he picked up the papers he had been studying, squared them into a neat pile, and placed them on the desk in front of him. He stood, walked from the room, and went to the entrance hall where Miss Severn stood waiting.

"Mud all gone?" he asked.

"Yes, Sir James. I must thank you and Edith for making me presentable again. No one would know that I had been paddling in a ditch except that my shoes are a little damp still."

"Very good," he said. "Then let's set off and take you back to your mother before she starts worrying about you."

He led the way outside, held the front door of the motor car open for her to get in, and closed it when she was sitting comfortably. The car engine was still warm from the previous journey, and Sir James was very pleased and relieved when it started on the first swing of the starting handle. It was quite a short drive to Taplow, and once they were in the town, Miss Severn gave timely and accurate directions to her home.

As they pulled up outside her home, Miss Severn said, "If she doesn't meet you herself, my mother will never believe that I have been driven home by a knight. I hope you can spare a few minutes and come in. It's a very small house compared to your mansion, Sir James, but it is adequate for our needs."

He studied the house for a few moments and immediately liked the large stone-built building the girl lived in.

"It's Tudor, isn't it?" he asked.

"Yes," she said.

"It's a lovely house with a sensible garden all round. You shouldn't get the wrong impression about the mansion I live in, Miss Severn. It was built by a wealthy ancestor who wanted something bigger than anything his neighbours had in order to demonstrate how very rich he had become. It's far too big for my requirements, but the mansion and the estate provide employment for many local people, so I do what is expected of me and live there when I am in this country. My small villa in Cairo is much more to my liking, and I don't need an army of servants to look after it or me. Now then, Miss Sabrina Severn, are you going to introduce me to your mother or are we going to stay out here all night, chatting?"

"Much as I would like to continue our chat," she responded seriously, "I think we should go in before my mother's curiosity overcomes her sense of discretion."

He climbed out of his seat, walked around the front of the motor car, and helped Miss Severn alight. They walked side by side to the garden gate, which he held open so that she could precede him. She waited a moment whilst he closed the gate and then walked beside him along a winding paved path to the entrance door.

She unlocked the door and pushed it open, and as she entered the hall, she called out, "Mother. Where are you? I want you to meet my friend." She turned to Sir James and said more quietly, "I may call you my friend, I hope?"

"I should be honoured to be your friend," he said very seriously.

A door opened at the opposite end of the hallway, and a tall, slim, grey-haired lady hurried towards them. She was neatly dressed in a brown skirt with a fawn-coloured twin set over a white blouse and facially could have been Miss Severn's twin.

"Mother," said Miss Severn, "The trains have been cancelled because there was a crash at Southall. This gentleman was kind enough to offer Millie and me a lift home as he lives near here. Mother, I would like to introduce you to my friend, Sir James Russell. Sir James, this is my mother."

"I'm very pleased to meet you, Mrs Severn," he said.

Mrs. Severn opened her mouth to say something but words failed her for a moment, and then she said to her daughter, "Did you say Sir James Russell?"

"Yes, Mother," said Miss Severn, quietly enjoying her mother's momentary confusion. "You don't need to curtsy, just shake his hand and say welcome or something like that."

"I am very pleased to meet you, Sir James," said Mrs Severn, putting her confusion behind her. "It is an honour to welcome you, and I am very grateful to you for escorting Sabrina home as you have."

"It was my pleasure," he said, and he sounded as if he meant it.

"I hope you will stay a while and have something to eat and drink with us, Sir James," said Mrs Severn, recovering her mantle as a good hostess after the shock her daughter had given her.

"I regret that I cannot, Mrs Severn. I will be late for dinner with my mother as it is, and I really should return home."

"What a pity," said Mrs. Severn, thinking *that's a relief as I have nothing I can offer a knight except homemade cake and a cup of tea.* "Perhaps we can entertain you on another day, Sir James."

"I would like that," he said, looking intently at Miss Severn, "but it will depend on your daughter's wishes."

Miss Severn, who had been listening intently to the short interchange between

Sir James and her mother, suddenly realised that Sir James had implied that he would like to meet her again. She definitely wanted to meet this handsome and attractive man again, and as her thoughts cartwheeled out of control, she blushed to the roots of her hair.

Sir James Russell noticed, smiled at Miss Severn, and then, turning towards her mother, said simply, "Mrs Severn, I think your daughter and I are of one mind about meeting again, and when we do, I should be very happy to have homemade cake and a cup of tea with you. But tonight, I really must return home, and I hope you will forgive me."

"Of course, Sir James," said Mrs Severn, wondering if her visitor had read her thoughts about tea and cake.

"I'll walk with you to your motor car, " said Miss Severn with a calmness of voice and features that totally belied the passions raging under her bodice.

They walked along the garden path together, and at the gate, she held out her hand and said, "Thank you, Sir James. I am so pleased that we met."

"As I am," he responded, taking her hand and not immediately releasing it. "And I hope our next meeting will not be too long delayed."

"As do I," she said.

"Would you think me presumptuous if I asked to meet you tomorrow afternoon?"

"No, I would not. I would simply ask you what time is convenient for you to call."

"May I come at three, then?"

"That would be very pleasant, and I'm sure my mother will have a freshly baked cake for you to try. She bakes very good cakes."

"I will look forward to that," he said and added, "But not as much as I look forward to seeing you again, Miss Severn." He started the engine, climbed into the motor car, and drove away with a wave of his hand.

Miss Severn watched until the rear light disappeared around a bend in the road and then slowly walked back towards the house, musing about what had happened. Well, what she had encouraged to happen, she had to admit. Normally, she would have run a mile in the opposite direction if there was any possibility of a meeting with any young man, yet here she was, actively hurrying to meet one. *Amazing*, she thought, *Millie will never believe it.*

Her mother was waiting at the door and said as Sabrina re-entered the house, "What a pleasant young man. I do hope you will be able to meet him again."

"I will, Mother! Tomorrow at three." Then after a short pause, she cried out in alarm, "What should I wear?"

"Clothes!" said her ever-practical mother. "But what can I bake?"

"A cake," said her equally practical daughter, giving her mother a hug.

Mother and daughter spent the next hour together. Mrs Severn listened to her daughter reliving the experiences of the day; five minutes or so to describe the party and the remainder of the hour to describe in minute detail her meeting with Russell and the drive home to Taplow. Poor Millie, Miss Severn's best friend and confidant, was not even mentioned, and that above all things indicated how seriously her only daughter had been smitten by Sir James Russell. *He will be a very good catch*, Mrs Severn mused, *and far better than anyone I could have imagined Sabrina would find.*

Next morning, the Severn household was a beehive of industrious people busily dusting, polishing furniture and floors, and washing the best crockery. And after many discussions and changes of mind about recipes, there was the preparation and mixing of ingredients and then the baking of a cake that was to be the centrepiece of the afternoon's reception.

There were many discretely crossed fingers as the cake was removed from the oven, set in the side of the range, and then turned out onto a grill to cool, but the aroma was delicious and the golden-brown appearance perfection.

The ladies chose and then discarded so many dresses, skirts, and blouses between one thirty and two thirty that their maids had full time occupations simply putting everything back on hangers in the wardrobes. Eventually, and mainly because time for further procrastination was running out, they settled on clothes that they decided would do at a pinch, but by no stretch of the imagination could they be construed as anything approaching the perfect solution.

Mrs Severn had looked longingly at an outfit similar to the one she had worn the previous day, but in the end, a desire for elegance had overcome thoughts of comfort and she had decided to wear a silk and lace tea gown she had bought a few years previously. The dress was of deep blue silk satin with an off-white lace bodice. It was decorated with satin bows and a ball tassel trim. Miss Severn wore a form-fitting gown in rose wool flannel, decorated on the bodice with clusters of pink and white glass grapes attached to pink chenille vines. It was a few years old also, but still elegant for all that.

At five minutes to three, Mrs and Miss Severn came downstairs and entered the sitting room, where they had decided to entertain Sir James. It was not a particularly big room, but it was light and the pine log fire was burning well, filling the air with the scent of hot resin. It was comfortably furnished with upholstered chairs and a chaise longue in green velvet, amongst other pieces of elegant furniture. In the centre of the room was a highly polished, round, mahogany gate leg table with three mahogany balloon-back chairs arranged symmetrically around the perimeter of the table. The floor was of wax-polished oak strips with a number of small Persian carpets scattered about to relieve the sombre colour of the polished wood. The walls were decorated with a rose patterned wallpaper and the ceiling was distempered plain white. The room was set in the corner of the ground floor and had windows on two sides. Opposite the door, the window looked out on the lawn at the side of the house, and to the right, the view took in the front garden and the entrance to the property from the road.

It was an ideal location for Miss Severn to look out with ever increasing impatience as three o'clock approached and no green Bentley appeared. Her eyes flickered between the grandfather clock slowly ticking in the corner and the view from the window.

Her anxiety became so apparent that, in the end, even the very tolerant Mrs Severn found it necessary to say, "For heaven's sake, Sabrina, sit down and stay still. Try to read your book. Your agitation is giving me a headache. He will arrive in due course, and all the hand wringing you are doing will not accelerate his arrival by one fraction of a second."

"I'm sorry, Mother," she said contritely as she resumed her seat and was reaching for her book when the sound of a motor car pulling up outside propelled her out of her chair with unladylike speed. Fortunately, she was far enough from the window to be able to see without her curiosity being seen from the street outside.

She expected to see the manly form of Sir James Russell alight from the driver's seat and was astounded when a short, thin man in a chauffeur's uniform climbed out, pulling on a peaked cap. He hurried around to the rear of the car, opened one of the doors wide, and stood to attention, his right hand quivering beside the peak of his cap as he saluted.

"Mother," she said with surprised amazement apparent in her voice, "Look!"

Mrs Severn stood up and joined her daughter just in time to see a uniformed army officer alight and put on his cap.

It was Sir James Russell.

He straightened himself, said something to the chauffeur, who saluted again and then hurried to the gate and opened it for his master to pass through. While Sir James walked up the path, the chauffeur closed the gate, climbed back into the car, and much to the surprise of the watching ladies, drove away.

"I thought he was only coming for afternoon tea and a piece of cake," said Mrs Severn, jumping to a conclusion as the car drove away.

"He doesn't have an overnight bag ..." said Miss Severn, trying to be a little more objective than her mother but still failing to think of a reason for the chauffeur having driven off and left Sir James behind..

The ladies resumed their seats and composed their features as they heard the doorbell ring. The maid opened the front door promptly and shortly afterwards knocked on the sitting room door, opened it, and with awe apparent in her voice said, "Sir James Russell, madam," and retired, closing the door behind her.

Sir James was the epitome of a well-groomed army officer. His uniform had been pressed to perfection and the buttons and rank badges polished until they gleamed. The leather of his belt, shoulder strap, and boots had been buffed until the light reflected from them. He stood momentarily at the door with his uniform cap tucked under his arm and then stepped forward to greet his hostesses.

He said, and his baritone voice delighted the ears of his listeners, "Good afternoon, Mrs Severn. Good afternoon, Miss Severn. I hope you are both in good health today. I must apologise for arriving in uniform, but I have been called to an urgent conference at the Colonial Office early tomorrow morning so I must go to London this afternoon immediately after I leave here. Tompkins," and he intercepted the puzzled looks exchanged by the ladies and explained, "Tompkins is my chauffeur. He's just gone to check over the car, pick up my bags, and should return in about an hour. I hope I will not be outstaying my welcome if I stay here an hour?"

"Not at all Sir James, although I had hoped to monopolise you for a little longer than an hour," said Mrs Severn.

Not to be outdone, Miss Severn asked, "Can you not stay a little longer than an hour, Sir James? There is a freshly baked cake to eat and plenty of tea to drink. I think you should expect to stay for at least two hours," she added hopefully.

"I totally agree," said Mrs Severn as she picked up a silver bell from a side table and rang it with a delightful, musical ding-dong. A few minutes later, the door opened and a maid appeared.

"Please bring the tea and cake now, Elsie," Mrs Severn said.

To her guest she said, "If you would like to sit here, Sir James," and she indicated a chair looking out towards the garden at the side of the house. Sir James stood beside the chair Mrs Severn had indicated, and after the two ladies had seated themselves, he sat down himself.

The maid returned with a big silver tray loaded with crockery and everything else required for an elegant afternoon tea party, then quietly and carefully laid the table and withdrew.

Then there was silence apart from a number of muted, "Please," and, "Thank you," comments as the ritual pouring of afternoon tea and cutting of the cake proceeded, but eventually, all three had a full cup and a slice of cake. After she had allowed a decent interval for her guest and daughter to try the cake, Mrs Severn decided it was time to start a conversation, as neither her daughter nor her guest seemed inclined to initiate any sort of discussion.

After eyeing the row of medal ribbons on the left breast of Sir James' tunic for a few moments, she said, "When I look at your medal ribbons, Sir James, it is clear that you have had a very busy war. Can you tell us what they were awarded for?"

"They are mainly campaign medals, Mrs Severn. Most soldiers who survived the war will have the same medal ribbons," he responded, carefully omitting mention of the MC and DSO he had been awarded. To avoid further questioning about his war service, he adroitly changed the subject by saying, "This cake is delicious, Mrs Severn. Would you be offended if I asked you to give me the recipe? Our cook at Brantley Hall is always pleased to receive new ideas."

Mrs Severn beamed with pleasure and said, "I'm so pleased you like it, and I should be delighted to write out the recipe for you."

"How long will you be in London, Sir James?" asked Miss Severn.

"I don't know at present," he responded. "I don't even know the subject of the conference yet, but that's not unusual. I expect it will have something to do with the Arab world as I have spent the last year in Cairo. I expect Winston Churchill will have a hand in it, and Lawrence may also attend as he is one of Churchill's advisors."

"I read an account of an army officer who had spent a great deal of time with the Arabs, but I cannot remember his name," said Mrs Severn.

"I expect you mean Colonel Lawrence," answered Sir James. "Lawrence of Arabia as he is more popularly known."

"Yes," she said, "That's the man. Do you know him?"

"I attended a lecture he gave and then met him socially afterwards, but I do not know him. I've read his Twenty-Seven Articles, of course."

"What are they?" asked Miss Severn.

"Lawrence spent a great deal of his time living very closely with the Arabs, and the twenty-seven articles draw on his experiences and describe how a newcomer to the Arab world should behave if he wants to win the trust and cooperation of his Arab friends and colleagues. They are very useful guidelines," Sir James answered.

"Why did he spend so much time with Arabs?" Miss Severn asked. "It doesn't sound a normal thing for an Englishman to do."

"It would be impossible to answer your question in one or two words, Miss Severn, but if you and your mother would like to know a little more about Lawrence, I should be happy to tell you what I know."

"Please tell us what you can," Mrs Severn said immediately, and her daughter nodded her head in agreement. They both made themselves comfortable and leant back in their chairs ready to listen to something new and interesting.

"Well," said Sir James, "Lawrence was born in Northwest Wales. In a small town called Tremadog, actually. His mother was English and his father was from the Irish aristocracy. He went to Oxford University, where he was awarded a First-Class Honours Degree, and then he gave up his postgraduate research to become a practising archaeologist in the Middle East. He studied Arabic at Byblos and worked on excavations in northern Syria. He travelled extensively in Arabia, often on foot, and wore the same clothes as the Arabs. He learnt their culture, language, and local dialects, and consequently, when war was declared, he worked for British Military Intelligence in Cairo. He became the liaison between British and Arab forces and fought with the Arab irregular troops under the command of the son of Sheikh Feisal of Mecca. You will know, of course, about the attacks he organised on the Hejaz railway because they were extensively reported in the newspapers at the time."

Mrs Severn nodded to signify that she did indeed remember.

Sir James went on, "After the war, Lawrence worked for the Colonial Office and attended the Paris Peace Conference as a member of Sheikh Feisal's delegation. At the moment, he is an advisor to Winston Churchill at the Colonial Office."

Sir James started to drink his tea but noticed it had gone cold while he was speaking and put the cup down again.

He concluded his description by saying, "I have given you a very brief summary of the life of an extraordinary man. It would take a very long time to describe Lawrence's life in detail."

"Thank you for taking the time to tell us what you did," Mrs Severn said as she rang the bell once more then asked, "What do you think of Mr Churchill, Sir James?"

"His ability to change allegiance from the Conservatives to the Liberals and back again reminds me of the song about the Vicar of Bray, Mrs Severn. I prefer someone who is more constant," he responded seriously.

"Vicar of Bray?" asked a puzzled Mrs Severn.

"You must remember the song, Mother," said Miss Severn. "It was about a clergyman who changed from catholic to protestant and back again to keep in tune with the dictates of the monarchy."

"It was probably a better option than being burnt at the stake as a heretic, but not a good example to his flock, I fear," said Sir James seriously.

The conversation stopped when Elsie arrived with more hot water and fresh cups and saucers.

Sir James received his fresh cup of tea with a "Thank you, Mrs Severn," and announced, "I must soon depart I'm afraid," as he checked the time on his watch and confirmed that Tompkins the chauffeur had arrived.

"Surely not so soon," Miss Severn cried. "You have been here no time at all, Sir James."

"Nearly two hours, " he said. "And much as I would like to continue our soiree, I will have to take my leave and set off for London."

"Where will you stay tonight?" asked Miss Severn as Sir James had made no attempt to stand and bring the tea party to an end.

"I'll go to my club," he answered. "I can be assured of a good dinner and a comfortable bed, and it is conveniently situated in relation to the Colonial Office. I can walk there in five minutes so I don't have to get up at the crack of dawn in order to be on time."

"I imagine your conference will be a very grand affair," Mrs Severn postulated. "As it's at the Colonial Office, there will be Dukes and Earls and such like, all in fancy uniforms and feathery hats."

"No, I don't expect so," Sir James responded with a smile. "It will probably be a meeting of civil servants in black jackets and grey pin stripe trousers. There may be other army staff there, but their uniforms will be much the same as mine and not very fancy. Please excuse me if I sound a little cynical, but I am sure it will be like other meetings to which I have been called. It will last less time than it takes me to get to London and be largely an attempt by the civil servants attending the meeting to push responsibility for something unpleasant onto someone who has not been invited to attend."

"Why should that be?" Miss Sabrina Severn asked in a slightly puzzled tone.

"If it was good news," Sir James explained, "The civil servants would be queuing up to accept whatever plaudits they could solicit. When it's bad news, they want to distance themselves from any responsibility. It's bad for their future careers, you see. So, a scapegoat has to be found, and preferably one who is not at the meeting and could defend himself if he was."

"How deceitful," said Miss Severn, looking quite shocked about the description she had just heard.

"It's the way government is run, I'm afraid," he said, "And now I really must take my leave. It has been a delightful afternoon, and I'm sorry that the conference in London has to bring it to a premature close. If you have time to write out your recipe in the next few days Mrs Severn, I should be happy to collect it when I'm next near Taplow."

"I don't want to put you out by coming all the way here, Sir James. I can easily send it to your cook by post," she said.

Miss Severn's face exhibited a mixture of emotions as she realised that her mother's attempt to be helpful was actually having the reverse affect upon her wish to see Sir James again, and preferably quite soon. Collecting the recipe would have been an ideal excuse for Sir James to come to her home, and now what could she do without looking too keen?

Like all diplomats, Sir James could, when necessary, utter a barefaced lie with his face a mask of cherubic innocence.

He said calmly, "I often pass near here, Mrs Severn, and it would be no trouble at all to stop and collect the recipe if it's ready, and if you haven't had time to complete it, I can call again at some other time."

"Well, if you're sure, Sir James," Mrs Severn said dubiously. She glanced at

Sabrina, saw in her face what she was thinking, and said emphatically, "Well, that's settled then."

"Most definitely," Sir James responded with relief.

He put his plate, cup, and saucer down on the table with an air of finality that couldn't be ignored, and as he stood up, he said, "I regret leaving such delightful company," as he looked directly at Miss Severn. "But I really must go now as I have stayed much longer than I intended. I have enjoyed your hospitality immensely, Mrs Severn, thank you very much."

He shook hands with both ladies and then walked to the door.

"I'll see you to the front door, Sir James," said Miss Severn, wishing it was ten thousand steps and not just ten.

"Thank you, " he said, and at the front door, he reached out to shake her hand again as he said, "Good afternoon, Miss Severn. I must also thank you for a lovely afternoon. I could not have wished for more congenial company. I expect to be away only two or three days, and when I'm back, I will come and see if the recipe is ready. It would be a great pleasure for me to meet you again, if you are at home."

"For me also, Sir James," she said with a beaming smile of pleasure.

"Thank you, Miss Severn, and goodbye for the present," he said as he raised his right hand to the peak of his cap in salute and turned away.

As Sir James started to walk to the front gate, Tompkins started the engine and then hurried to the back to hold open the rear door. Sir James climbed into the rear of the Bentley and sat down. Tompkins closed the door, and as he hurried to the front and climbed in, Sir James laid his uniform cap on the seat beside him and waved another farewell to Miss Severn. Tompkins let in the clutch and drove away in the direction of London and Sir James' conference at the Colonial Office.

Miss Severn went back into the house, and her mother said, "You must remind me to write out the recipe, Sabrina."

"Yes of course, Mother," said her dutiful daughter, who had every intention of doing no such thing. If her mother had forgotten to do it by the time Sir James returned, he would just have to come back on another day, and that meant the chance to speak with him twice instead of only once.

She turned towards the door and said, "Isn't he a lovely man," and, "Excuse me, Mother," and she retired to her room to mull over every nuance of every word Sir James had uttered.

CHAPTER TWO
The Colonial Office

In the back of his motor car, as it hummed along the A4 towards London, Sir James also mused over his chance meeting with Miss Sabrina Severn. He realised that his Guardian Angel had been very considerate when arranging for him to choose that particular Corner House out of several in the area, enabling his chance meeting with Miss Severn. The journey floated past in a rosy glow as Sir James Russell, the war-weary and confirmed celibate, contemplated future meetings with the lovely young lady from Taplow.

He went directly to his club and, after dinner, immediately to his room and bed.

In the morning, whilst he was having breakfast, the bell boy brought his uniform to the room. During the night, it had been carefully pressed and all the buttons, badges, belts, and boots polished. Russell dressed carefully, and then, allowing himself ample time to cover the short distance, he walked around to the Colonial Office. He arrived at the designated conference room and found that an army colleague had arrived just before him.

They exchanged the usual pleasantries, but when Russell asked about the reason for the meeting, his friend said simply, "No idea, Sir James, but from the size of this meeting room, it must be important."

It was an observation with which Russell could find no fault.

As nine o'clock approached, the conference room started to fill up, and about two minutes before nine, the room was called to order and everyone sat down at the place designated for them. Russell found he had been placed about two seats from the chairman, with high grade civil servants on either side of him. Opposite were more civil servants, and his army friend was a long way away, near the foot of the table. On the stroke of nine, there was a stir in the doorway and a big, burly, square-jawed man marched in and took his place at the head of the long oval conference table.

Russell recognised the man whose inconstancy he had criticised the previous afternoon and hoped the chairman was not gifted as a thought reader.

The newcomer took the cigar from his mouth, examined the glowing tip momentarily, blew out a huge cloud of blue aromatic tobacco smoke, looked slowly at each individual, and then addressed the suddenly silent assembly.

"What we are about to discuss affects, to a major extent, the interests of His Majesty's Government and the sovereignty of one of our colonies. It is so sensitive an issue that it must be considered highly confidential and not discussed except in private and then only with one of the other committee members. As you would expect given the necessary secrecy that surrounds our discussions, there will be no minutes of this meeting or of any subsequent meetings. You gentlemen have all been called here this morning as you have knowledge and expertise that will be relevant to our discussion."

He looked around the table once more, then said, "I assume there are no questions so far," in a tone of voice that indicated he was making a statement and not asking for comment. None was forthcoming in any case, and in the few moments of silence that followed, Russell realised that the forecast he had made about the meeting when he had been with the Severns was turning out to be far from accurate.

This was something altogether different, and he wondered what possible role he could have.

"To ensure that everyone knows everyone else, I will go around the table and introduce each of you in turn," said the chairman, and turning to his right, he indicated the civil servant sitting between Russell and himself. "This gentleman is Sir William Ellis. He is Under Secretary of the Middle East Section and will chair this meeting after I conclude my introductory remarks and leave you. He will also be the liaison between you gentlemen and my office."

The chairman then turned to his left and introduced the civil servant sitting next to him on that side of the table and then proceeded from man to man around the table, introducing 'Sir Somebody This' and 'The Honourable That', all of them quite high-ranking officials in various Government Departments.

Suddenly, only Russell was left, and he was conscious of all eyes being focused on him when the chairman said, "The final and probably the most important member of this committee is Sir James Russell. You will see from the ribbons on his chest that he is a brave young man, but he is here today not because he has been brave, but because he has been the Military Attaché at our Embassy in Cairo for the past year. He has contacts amongst the diplomatic community in Egypt that will be invaluable as we pursue our investigation."

He stood up, and then, as everyone else stood up, he said, "There will now be a short interval for refreshments, and then the meeting will reconvene under the chairmanship of Sir William Ellis. Thank you, gentlemen," and he turned away from the conference table and marched from the room.

Sir William Ellis turned to Russell, held out his hand, and said, "I look forward to working with you, Sir James."

Russell shook the proffered hand warmly and said simply, "And I with you, Sir William, but I confess that I will be pleased when I know what the problem is and how I can assist you."

"The seeds of the problem were sown in one of your last reports, Sir James, and whilst you have been on leave, we have made some discreet enquiries and determined that your hints are actually more substantive than you imagined."

"I have no idea what you can be alluding to, Sir William," Russell responded with a puzzled expression on his face.

Sir William looked around to make sure no one was close by then leant forward and whispered something in Russell's ear.

Russell said in a rather surprised voice, "Oh! Really?"

Sir William said, "Exactly," then added, after looking at an enormous, gold, hunter watch, "Perhaps we should get some coffee before it's all gone?"

"I agree," said Sir James Russell, and he followed Sir William to the table at the side of the conference room, where a uniformed male attendant was distributing cups of coffee. Another attendant was walking around the room collecting empty, used crockery on a tray.

Five minutes and half a cup of coffee later, Sir William called the meeting to order.

Sir William, it should be pointed out, was a career civil servant and looked the part in his pin stripe trousers, black jacket, and immaculately groomed grey hair. He wore half-moon glasses and peered over them with raised eyebrows at whoever said anything he didn't agree with, as if they were congenital idiots. Few civil servants survived for very long after receiving his stare. Sir William looked forward to continuing his unblemished career until he retired and would move heaven and earth to prevent anyone spoiling his record. Unfortunately, this assignment was one that could certainly go sour and spoil his record if it was allowed so to do. Fortunately, he had a tyro diplomat to push the blame onto if everything should go belly up at the last moment, so the presence of Sir James Russell was a great comfort to Sir William.

With that reassuring thought firmly rooted in his subconscious mind, Sir William started to address the conference.

"Gentlemen. Gathered here today are many experts in their own fields of endeavour, but we are exceptionally fortunate to have Sir James Russell with us. He was the first person to alert His Majesty's Government to an impending problem, following his conversations with various people in Egypt. Consequently, we have taken his advice-" here, Russell tried unsuccessfully to catch the chairman's eye in order to explain that he hadn't given any advice. "- and set up the committee that I have the honour to chair. We are here in order to consider what can be done to prevent the catastrophe that Sir James felt inevitable."

Sir James' further polite attempts to intervene and put the record straight were successfully ignored by Sir William, who simply patted Sir James on the arm and said sotto voce, "Later, Sir James, later," and everyone eventually left the meeting with the unassailable opinion that the whole business was something that Sir James Russell had initiated.

And that was exactly what Sir William had intended.

If they were successful, Sir William would ensure that he was the beneficiary, and if they were not, then Sir James Russell would be a useful scapegoat and Sir William's pension and other benefits would be unscathed.

Sir William quickly opened his notes and said, "Reduced to its barest detail, Sir James has reported that a precious metal has been discovered in the mountains not far from Aden, which is in a British Protectorate, and that a neighbouring country might try to annexe the area in order to exploit the reserves and monopolise the markets. Perhaps you will explain what you know, Sir James?"

"I know nothing that has been proven to be factually correct," Sir James said bluntly as he stood up to address the meeting and heard gasps of surprise from some of the other committee members. "I will relate what I reported to the High Commissioner and the tenuous link I drew between two disconnected pieces of information. I was in Aden recently on Embassy business, and when I attended a reception on a visiting battleship -" and he saw in his mind's eye a kaleidoscope of images from that evening; the colourful uniforms and bright ball gowns; the discreet diplomatic negotiations and the not so discreet flirting, "- I chanced to overhear part of a conversation between a diplomat from another embassy and a local man. The local man said, "I worked for Rutherford and I know the value," and then they moved away from my location. I found out later that the local man's name is Jalal Al Hafrey and he is the Cambridge educated son of Sheikh Al Hafrey, who is the ruler of a large and very poor desert kingdom in the south of Nejd. I came across the other piece of information in a confidential report that was circulated amongst the diplomatic staff. It recorded the accidental discovery of uranium in the mountains north of Aden by geologists who were looking for gold. The tenuous link I drew was this. If Al Hafrey had worked for Rutherford in Cambridge, then he could have been associated with the experimentation that led to the splitting of the atom in 1919. Consequently, he could know about uranium and be aware of its scarcity. He could have knowledge of possible future uses and equate that to a scarcity value. By annexing the area where this source of uranium has been discovered, he could become a very rich man. The High Commissioner sent my report to London. The chairman said that checks have been made and my supposition was well founded." Sir James sat down.

"Mr Chairman?" said a voice from the end of the conference table.

"Yes, Mr Davies?" Sir William responded.

"What evidence is there that this deposit is big enough to attract an invasion by a neighbouring country?"

"After receiving the report from Sir James, we contacted the geologist who was leading the exploration and he confirmed in confidence that there were large exploitable deposits," the chairman responded, "but there is no written record of his statement. It was given verbally and in confidence."

"What is this government doing with uranium that makes it so important?" another member asked.

"As you should have realised, that information will be covered by the Official Secrets Act," Sir William responded bluntly, and his questioner stared at the table in embarrassment.

"Why hasn't the government warned Sheikh Al Hafrey that we will take strong action if he invades our territory?" asked another civil servant.

"For two reasons," responded the chairman. "First of all, we do not wish to advertise to the whole world that we have a strong interest in securing supplies of this mineral. Secondly, there is a dispute about the position of the border. In Sheikh Al Hafrey's view, the border is located much further to the south than we believe to be the case. If Al Hafrey can prove that his version of the border location is the correct one, we will be accused of having occupied the area illegally and be invited to leave peacefully or be thrown out. I'm sure he will find a neighbouring colonial power more than willing to supply weapons and manpower to put a crimp in the British Lion's tail. The deposits of uranium are then out of our reach unless we are prepared to pay whatever price Al Hafrey dictates."

Sir William surveyed the members of the committee and said, "We are here to apply our individual expertise to the problem and suggest a solution."

"The pivotal problem," Davies said, "Is to have the location of the border we have defined ratified by an international body like the League of Nations. If that can be achieved, then the other problem can be dealt with from a position of strength."

"What do you think of that suggestion, Sir James?" asked Sir William, avoiding the possibly damaging necessity of making a comment himself.

Sir James straightened in his chair and said, "Mr Davies is essentially correct in suggesting that the border position be finalised. However, it is not as simple as one would imagine. Disputes between adjacent tribes about the positions of borders are commonplace in that part of the world, and these disputes escalate into bloody conflict more often than not. As far as I am aware, there are no written records of border positions, and if one tries to solve a border dispute, one can receive as many opinions about the location of a particular section of border as the number of tribesmen one asks. And even a peaceful enquiry can escalate into violence in moments as a tribesman will not lose face by accepting a contrary opinion."

"You sound as if you have some firsthand knowledge of the problem, Sir James," Davies stated.

"Yes. I have limited experience of border disputes," answered Sir James Russell honestly, suspecting as he said it that he was about to become the saviour of the committee.

"Mr Chairman," said Davies, "I propose that this committee instructs Sir James to investigate the border dispute and provide a report that can be forwarded to the League of Nations for ratification. Perhaps the League will be able to stop wrangling long enough to adjudicate on a simple border dispute."

There was such a chorus of "Seconded" from around the table that a vote was unnecessary. It was quickly agreed that Sir James would be temporarily reassigned from his duties at the Embassy in Cairo so that he could explore this new problem as quickly as possible.

Sir William said, "We will require regular reports, Sir James, but as you are still on leave and have to travel to the area, I will not expect your first report for two months, but you should submit them on a monthly basis thereafter."

"Thank you, Sir William. I quite understand," Sir James responded.

Sir William Edward Ellis stood up. "Thank you, gentlemen," he said. "You will be advised of the venue for the next meeting in due course. This meeting is closed," and he turned and walked from the conference room with a self-satisfied smirk wrinkling his lips.

The next meeting would not be until after Russell reported in two months' time and, most satisfactorily, Russell had been sent to resolve the problem he himself had identified.

CHAPTER THREE
Betrothal and Separation

Sir James Russell said a cordial "Goodbye," to all those members of the committee who had not rushed off in the wake of their mentor, Sir William Ellis. He collected his uniform cap and walked back to his club, deep in thought. He was not cogitating the task he had been set by Sir William's committee, as you might assume, but was trying to assess whether or not he could have luncheon and also manage to get to Taplow at a time that would allow him to call at the Severn's.

He decided with much regret that he would have to forgo his lunch and make up for the loss at dinner.

At the club, he sent for Tompkins and said, "I wish to leave for Brantley Manor as soon as possible. Have you had lunch yet?"

"No sir, but I can get a sandwich and eat it as we go."

"Very well, Tompkins. As soon as you are ready for us to leave, come and see me."

"Yes, sir," he said, and fifteen minutes later, Sir James was safely ensconced in the back of his Bentley and Tompkins was manipulating the steering wheel, gear lever, handbrake, giving hand signals, and also eating a sandwich with the aplomb of someone with at least two pairs of hands.

In fairness to Sir James, it should be noted that he gave serious thought to the problem he had been set by the committee in the five minutes it took him to eat the sandwich he had been given by his chauffeur. But then he drifted off into a delightful and all absorbing daydream about his impending meeting with Miss Severn. Consequently, he was not at all pleased to be woken up by Tompkins calling from the front seat until it registered that the object of his dreams was less than five minutes distant, and he realised that Tompkins had unexpectedly headed for Taplow and not to Brantley Manor.

"Stop, Tompkins," he said.

When the motor car stopped, Sir James climbed stiffly out and started to walk up and down the road near the motor car in order to loosen his legs, which had grown stiff from too much sitting, and his brain, which was still inert from too deep a sleep. He straightened his uniform, checked his watch, and decided that three in the afternoon was not too late to call on the Severn's in order to collect a recipe, so he climbed in to the rear seat again and ordered Tompkins to proceed.

"I didn't tell you to come here, Tompkins," he said.

"No, sir," Tompkins answered happily. "You didn't need to. She's a lovely young lady, if you don't mind me saying so, sir."

Sir James was so torn between agreeing with the sentiment expressed by his chauffeur and disciplining him for taking advantage of his position that in the end nothing was said. And then it was too late anyway as the car was slowing down in order to stop at the gate to the Severn's house. Tompkins jumped down and hurried to the back of the motor car to open the door for his master.

Sir James climbed out of the car, looked his chauffeur in the eye, and said quietly, "Thank you, Tompkins. I don't expect to be long."

"Thank you, sir," Tompkins responded, and he walked happily around to the front of the motor car, climbed into his seat, and settled back for a short snooze.

With great self-control, Sir James managed to prevent himself running up the path, but he was not able to stop an exuberant rat-a-tat-tat on the knocker that echoed through the house and garden.

After a short delay, Elsie answered the door and said, "Good afternoon, Sir James."

"Good afternoon," he responded. "If it is convenient, may I see Mrs and Miss Severn?"

"I'll enquire, sir."

She stepped back from the doorway so that Sir James could enter the hall as she said, "If you would please come in, sir."

She led the way a few steps along the hall and opened a door on the left side and said, "Please wait in here, sir," then closed the door behind him.

Sir James stood and looked out of the window as he heard the sound of Elsie's footsteps diminishing and then the sound of a polite knock, followed by a door opening and closing. There was silence for a few moments, then the door opened again and footsteps could be heard hurrying along the hall and then going upstairs. He heard another set of footsteps approaching along the hall, and these stopped outside the door of the room in which he was waiting. There was a polite knock, the door opened, and Elsie stood in the opening.

She said, "Madam will see you now, Sir James, if you will come this way," and she stepped back into the hall and led Sir James to the sitting room.

"Sir James Russell, madam," she said.

"Thank you, Elsie. Please wait a moment. Good afternoon, Sir James. You will have a cup of tea, won't you?"

"Yes of course, Mrs Severn, I should be delighted to join you," he said.

"Good," she said, then turning back to Elsie said, "Please bring us some tea."

"Yes, madam," she responded and left the room, closing the door behind her.

"You didn't spend very long in London, Sir James. We didn't expect to see you again for several more days," Mrs Severn said.

"You are correct, Mrs Severn. I have returned much sooner than I anticipated. But if my unexpected arrival is in any way inconvenient for you, I will leave and return on a more acceptable occasion."

"Oh, no! Sir James, your visit is most welcome, and we are all agog to hear your news. Miss Severn will be down very soon, I think. I certainly hope so, in any case. She thought she was not suitably dressed to entertain a knight and has gone to change, although I told her that the dress she was wearing was quite acceptable."

"I'm sure your daughter looked lovely as she was, Mrs Severn, and she certainly didn't need to change on my account," said Sir James gallantly.

Mrs Severn sat down, and as she did so, she indicated a chair by the table to her right, and she said, "Please sit down, Sir James."

There was a knock on the door, and in response to Mrs Severn's, "Come in," Elsie opened the door and carried in a tray laden with plates, cups, saucers, milk, sugar, and a large freshly-baked cake. She put the tray down and laid the table for three.

"It was lucky I made that cake this morning, Sir James. It's a different recipe, so I hope you will like it."

"If it is only half as good as the last cake you baked for me, it will be delicious," Sir James responded truthfully.

"Oh, dear!" she exclaimed. "I have completely forgotten to write out that recipe for you. I asked Miss Severn to remind me, and she has forgotten also. I am sorry!"

"It is not a matter to distress yourself about, Mrs Severn," he said quietly. "I can come back on another occasion, and perhaps I will be fortunate to be offered a slice of cake from a third recipe at least as delicious as the first one."

The door opened, and as Miss Severn entered, Sir James sprang to his feet. She closed the door quietly and walked gracefully across the room to where Sir James was standing and held out her hand in greeting. He took and held her hand, gently squeezed her fingers, and said, "I'm very happy to greet you again, Miss Severn."

He was thrilled to feel the answering pressure as she said, "As I am to see you, sir."

They sat down, and for a moment there was silence as each waited for the other to speak, and Mrs Severn busied herself pouring and handing out tea and slices of cake.

When she had served everyone, she said, "Now, Sir James, we would love to hear about your journey to London and your conference at the Colonial Office."

"Well," he said, "As far as the conference is concerned, I will be unable to tell you anything about the discussion we had, as everything that was said is covered by the Official Secrets Act. For the same reason, I cannot divulge the names of any of the participants, but there were some very important government representatives present. The meeting was called in response to a report I wrote in Cairo, and the result of the meeting is that I will not go back to Cairo but to Aden instead, and that is a much less attractive place to live and work. I'm very sorry I have to disappoint you by giving such limited information, but government work is often secret, and it would be better if you mentioned nothing about our conversation to anyone outside these four walls."

"If you had a wife, what would you tell her?" asked Miss Severn, the practical side of her nature coming out.

"Nothing!" said Sir James emphatically then went on. "And that is particularly difficult as married people should not have secrets from one another in my view, especially if the assignment carries a risk to life with it."

"I agree," said Mrs Severn, who was disappointed because not only did she not have a good story to tell her friends, but she could not even allude to it because it was secret.

"Will you be at risk?" Miss Severn asked with concern apparent in her voice.

"No more than I usually am," he responded cheerfully, "and that is a lot less than I was during the war."

"Will you have to be away for long?" she asked.

"I expect to be here for most of the next month and will then go to Aden. I will be away for about a year and then have leave again," he responded seriously.

"Do you have an understanding with -," Mrs Severn started to say.

"Mother!" interrupted Miss Severn as she blushed red to the roots of her hair. "You can't ask Sir James a question like that."

"Why not, pray? I'm your mother and entitled to know all there is to know about the young men who visit my daughter. Even if they do pretend it's my cake recipes they want."

Sir James chuckled a little at that sally and then said, "I don't mind the question, Miss Severn, and the simple answer is that I do not have an understanding with anyone. My mother has tried hard enough to marry me off but without success. During the war, it was not sensible to become a married man, and since the war, I have failed to find anyone who attracts me." He paused momentarily then added, "Until now."

Miss Severn's expression had become rather pensive but brightened at his last two words as if the sun had come out from behind the clouds.

She managed to say, "Thank you, Sir James. That is a nice compliment."

"I must go soon, as my mother has no idea that I have come back from London, but perhaps I can call for a recipe tomorrow?" he said.

"That would be a very good idea, Sir James. What time can you come?" Miss Severn said, then added, "I have no engagements tomorrow."

Mrs Severn's face registered shock at her daughter's forwardness. *Such a comment would have been unthinkable when I was her age*, she thought.

On the other hand, Sir James was very encouraged at Miss Severn's display of interest, decided to ignore the subject of a recipe, and immediately said, "Perhaps I could call for you at about ten in the morning if that will not be too early and we can go for a drive?"

"That's a lovely idea," said Miss Severn. "Where will you take me?"

"Perhaps I shouldn't tell you where we are going, and then it will be a surprise, but I will arrange for my cook to pack a hamper so that we do not have to return for lunch. I imagine you will bring your maid with you, Miss Severn, but do you wish to come with us well, Mrs Severn?" he asked politely, whilst fervently hoping that Mrs Severn would decline the offer.

And after a certain amount of 'shall I go?', 'shall I not go?' discussion with her daughter, she decided she was much too busy to be gallivanting around the countryside and hoped the 'young people' would enjoy themselves.

Both 'young people' breathed enormous but silent sighs of relief.

Sir James then said, "I regret that I must take my leave of you and look forward to seeing you tomorrow. Goodbye, Mrs Severn."

"Goodbye, Sir James," said Mrs Severn and then turned to her daughter and said, "You will see our guest out, Sabrina?"

"Yes, of course, Mother," she said, trying to sound as if it was a commonplace task, and led the way to the front door.

They stood side by side for a moment on the front step, then Sir James turned toward his companion, and as he enclosed her dainty hand in his much bigger one, he said, "I should consider it a great complement, Miss Severn, if you would call me James in future. Sir James is so unnecessarily formal between friends."

"Thank you, James," she said. "It is an honour for me to accept your offer, and I hope you will not think me forward if I suggest you use my Christian name in future also."

"I certainly do not think your suggestion at all forward, and I am flattered by your offer, Sabrina." For a long moment, they looked at each other with smiles of pleasure.

Sir James said, "I really must go to Brantley Manor and let them know I've returned, but I look forward to meeting you again tomorrow." He released the hand he had been holding for a little longer than society would have agreed was proper.

She smiled and said, "Until tomorrow, James," and turned and re-entered the house. She didn't close the door and stood in the doorway so that she could wave goodbye as James was driven away. She continued to stand in the doorway with a dreamy expression on her face until Elsie came to see where she was.

"Madam was beginning to think you had eloped with the young man," she said, and Sabrina laughed, although her cheeks became a little pinker.

The next morning, as the local church clock struck ten, a highly polished green Bentley pulled up outside the Severn's house. The front door opened, and Miss Severn waved a greeting to Sir James, who was just alighting from the rear of the motor car. She set off down the path, closely followed by Elsie, and was watched from one of the front windows by Mrs Severn.

At the gate there was a discussion between Sir James and Miss Severn about who was to sit where. It was a short discussion that Miss Severn resolved with a few imperious waves of her hand as she consigned Elsie to sit beside the chauffeur and Sir James and herself to sit in the back.

Mrs Severn looked quite shocked.

She had totally forgotten about the chauffeur and had expected Sir James to drive, with Elsie sitting on the front seat and her precious daughter sitting in the back, but there was nothing she could do about it now except worry and pray that nothing untoward would happen to her precious child.

Sir James decorously assisted Miss Severn into the back of the motor car as Elsie climbed into the front seat with an unrecorded remark that made Tompkins laugh out loud. Sir James waved a cheerful goodbye to Mrs Severn and climbed into the car behind her daughter. He didn't notice Mrs Severn raise her eyes skywards and say a short prayer for the safety of her little girl before she retreated from the window.

Sir James, "Drive on, please, Tompkins," which he did whilst still chuckling from Elsie's comment.

Sabrina asked, "Where are we going, James?"

"As you live in this locality, I expect you will guess soon enough, but until you identify where we are going to stop for lunch, it will have to remain a secret between Tompkins and myself."

"I'm not sure I like Tompkins knowing before I do," Sabrina said a little tartly.

"In that case, I must tell you where we are going, as I would not wish to upset you. We're having lunch at -"

"Don't you dare tell me," she said quickly. "It will spoil the fun."

"Women!" he said with laughter in his voice. "I'll never understand them."

"You're not supposed to," said Sabrina, but she took his hand momentarily as she joined in his amusement with a chuckle of her own.

"May I ask you a personal question, Sabrina?"

"Yes, of course," she responded, wondering what he would ask.

"I am intrigued by your Christian and surnames and wondered why your parents chose Sabrina."

"My father was an Oxford Don. He was an enthusiast about anything Roman and was particularly interested in the Roman invasion of Britain. He liked the name Sabrina, and as it was the Latin name for the River Severn, it had a connection with his favourite subject, but whether that was the reason my parents chose the name, I don't know. Perhaps you should ask my mother why I am called Sabrina? In school, I was known as 'Two Rivers', which made me sound like an Indian Squaw," and she laughed again as she put her hand behind the back of her head with two fingers raised to simulate feathers.

Sabrina looked out of the window of the car and said after few moments, "We are going in a northerly direction at the moment and should come to a big old house called Cliveden. Do you know anything about it, James?"

"No," he said, "Do you?"

"A little," she responded. "It was built as a hunting lodge by the second Duke of Buckingham in about 1666 as a place to entertain his mistress, amongst other diversions. It has been burnt down twice, and each time it has been rebuilt on a grander scale than previously. It has been the home of three Dukes, one Earl, and Frederick, the Prince of Wales. I read somewhere that since it was first built, every British monarch who has ruled has stayed there at some time."

"That's very interesting," said Sir James. "Do you know the area around your home very well, Sabrina?"

"Not really, and I only know about Cliveden because a friend told me about it. We don't have a car now so we cannot go far from home."

"I see," he said, not really understanding but not daring to ask the questions that came into his mind in case he scratched sensitive nerves, so he asked instead, "The next village we come to on this road is Wooburn. Have you ever been there?"

"No, never."

"There's a very old coaching inn there," he said. "Seventeenth century, I believe, but that's all I know about the village."

"And how is it that your sole knowledge of this out-of-the-way village is the inn, may I ask?"

"My father and I stopped there for something to eat and drink one night on the way back from Aylesbury, where we had gone to visit one of his cousins," he said in matter-of-fact way. "We could have had something to eat at Brantley Manor, but Father did not want to wake up the staff when we could just as easily get something on the way. It gave us a chance to have a quiet talk together before he returned to his command in France the next day. He was killed a few days later."

"I'm so sorry, James. I was being flippant about something that brings sad memories back to you," Sabrina said sadly.

"You were not to know, Sabrina, so don't blame yourself. My father was a good and kind man, so my memories of him are all happy ones, but it still saddens me when I remember that his death, like millions of others, served no good purpose."

"Just like my father," said Sabrina sadly and was comforted when James put his big hand over her delicate one.

"Would you like to tell me what happened?" asked Sir James. "Or would it be too painful for you? I will understand if you would rather not talk about it."

"I have to face up to the facts, James, and not talking about it does nothing to heal the hurt. My father was an academic, an educated man, and he thought he could help his country best by using his intellect. He volunteered for duty in Military Intelligence, but in their infinite wisdom, the army sent my middle-aged father to the front, where he was killed within a few days. The real sadness is that he didn't need to join the army at all, but he was a patriot and believed he should do his bit to support the young men who were fighting and dying as some of his students had. There were too many memories in Oxford, so we came to Taplow not long after my father was killed."

"I'm very sorry to learn that you have had much the same misfortune as me," said Sir James and stroked the back of her hand.

They sat in silence for a few minutes, savouring the unaccustomed comfort that came from the touch of someone compatible, then Sabrina noticed that Elsie had half turned in the front seat and was looking at her with a disapproving expression. Sabrina gently withdrew her hand from Sir James' grasp and clasped her hands demurely in her lap.

They motored on for a little longer and came to Henley-on-Thames, where Tompkins drove off the road and stopped under a big willow tree beside the river.

He climbed out, stretched, and then walked to the back of the car, where he opened the rear door to let Sir James and Sabrina alight. He then opened the boot and started to unload the contents.

"Shall we have our lunch over there?" Sir James asked, indicating a shady spot on the close-cropped grass near to the edge of the riverbank.

"I think that would be an ideal place," said Sabrina. "Should Elsie assist Tompkins?"

He smiled. "If she is able to stop watching her mistress for a few minutes, I'm sure Tompkins would appreciate her help," he responded, "and we can walk a little way along the riverbank whilst they do it."

Sabrina nodded her agreement, and so it was arranged. Sir James told Tompkins where to set up the picnic, and Sabrina said to her maid, "Sir James and I will walk a little way along the river bank," and she pointed to an open area where Elsie could see her at all times. "And I would like you to help Tompkins set out our lunch."

"Very well, Miss Sabrina," Elsie agreed.

Sir James and Miss Sabrina Severn set off to walk a little way along the riverbank whilst luncheon was set out and maintained a decorous distance between each other by mutual but unspoken consent. They commented on the blue of the water and the green of the grass and carefully avoided the presents left by the sheep as a trap for the unwary. The sky was a brilliant blue, the sun was warm on the skin, and the birds sang as enthusiastically as if they were competitors at a choral festival. It was a beautiful day, and it is fair to record that both young hearts were full of joy in each other's company. After about ten minutes, they stopped and turned back towards the car.

Between them, Tompkins and Elsie had worked a miracle. Where there had been bare grass a short while before, Tompkins had laid out a large sheet of canvas as a carpet and then unfolded and erected a table in the centre. Two chairs with canvas seats and backrests had also been unfolded and set at either end of the table. Elsie had opened the hamper and found a neatly ironed table cloth under the lid, which she spread on the table. Crockery and cutlery for two people were then laid out. These were followed by the food that the cook at Brantley Manor had considered to be just adequate for two people but would have satisfied the hunger of a squad of soldiers. There were big slices of ham, pork, and beef, with a selection of cheeses and pickles. There were bowls of lettuce and sliced tomatoes and a large loaf of crusty homemade bread.

Sabrina gasped with pleasure when she saw what had been prepared whilst she and Sir James had enjoyed their walk. She said, "Thank you, James. What a lovely surprise, and the food looks absolutely scrumptious."

"It certainly does," he agreed.

"What will Elsie and Tompkins do? There's more than enough food for all four of us."

"Tompkins will have brought his lunch with him, but I think Elsie will have to have some of ours. Perhaps we should have our lunch and then go for another walk whilst they eat and then clear everything away."

"I agree," she said, and Sir James pulled out the chair facing the river for her. After Sabrina had sat down, he sat in the other chair. Elsie served the food and Tompkins poured the couple a glass of white wine each.

Sir James raised his glass and said, "Thank you for coming with me today, Sabrina. I hope this will be the first of many journeys we make together."

"I hope so as well, James," she said without thinking and then blushed a delicate shade of pink as she realised how much she wanted to spend more time with this lovely man.

"I hope you enjoy the food," he said as he picked up his knife and fork. Sabrina picked up hers at the same time, and they both started to eat and enjoy the food and each other's company. After they had eaten as much as they wanted, they got up from the table and walked slowly along the riverbank away from the picnic table.

"Have you heard about the regatta that's held here?" he asked.

"What is a regatta?" she asked in turn.

"'Regatta' is a general term used to describe boat races that are held on a river or a lake or even on the sea. In this case, it's for rowing boats, and it is an important social event, as well as a sporting occasion. It's known as the Henley Royal Regatta since Prince Albert became its patron in 1851. The finishing line for the races is just along there." He pointed downstream.

"Have you ever rowed here?"

"Yes twice, and we lost our first race on both occasions to the crew who won the event." He smiled happily at the memory.

They had walked a little further when Sabrina suddenly stopped and turned to Sir James. "It's such a lovely day, James, and I don't want to spoil it, but may I ask you an important question?"

"Yes, of course," Sir James responded, wondering what she could need to know.

"How long can you stay in England?"

"Only for about another three weeks," he answered. *Yesterday*, he thought, *it had seemed quite a long time to wait before I sailed back to Egypt. But since I met Sabrina, it has become a desperately short time.*

"It's not a very long time, and if you are willing,, I would like to spend as much of it with you as I can."

"I would like that very much indeed," she answered with a smile that brightened an already sunny day.

Back at the car, everything had been packed away, except the folding chairs, and these were being put to good use by Elsie and Tompkins.

They were sitting quite close together and were so deep in their conversation that they didn't notice the arrival of Sir James and Sabrina until James coughed discretely whilst they were still several yards away. Elsie jumped up, and Sabrina wondered what she and Tompkins had been discussing when she noticed that Elsie was blushing. Although she was extremely curious, Sabrina managed to prevent herself from asking questions and causing further embarrassment but noticed that Sir James had also perceived the blush. He was looking from Elsie to Tompkins and back with a quizzical smile on his face. Sabrina assumed that Sir James would have a private word with Tompkins in due course, as she would do with Elsie.

They climbed back into the car and drove out of Henley. They didn't return along the same route but drove on towards a little village called Wargrave. In Wargrave, the road lay between the River Thames on one side and Wargrave Manor, an imposing old building set on a hill, to the left of the road. Just beyond the manor, Tompkins suddenly slowed the motor car and stopped just beyond a junction on the left.

"What is it, Tompkins?" queried Sir James.

"Well, sir," he said, "I can go straight on along High Street until we cross the A4 or I can turn left off the High Street here and go over Mumbery Hill to the A4. It will cut off a big corner."

"Do you know this area?" Sir James asked.

"Yes, sir. I was born near here and was christened in St. Mary's. You can see the church tower just over there." He pointed ahead and to the right.

"The tower looks quite old, but the rest of it looks new. Do you know anything about it, Tompkins?" Sabrina asked.

"The tower was built in the 1600s but there was a fire in 1914 that destroyed much of the building, and that's why so much of it looks new. It was founded in the eleventh century, I believe," he said.

"I see," said Sir James, and then he turned to Sabrina. "Shall we explore and take Tompkins' diversion or carry on along the main road?"

"I think we should explore," said Sabrina.

"Very well," he agreed. "We will follow your suggestion, Tompkins. Please drive on."

"Yes, sir," he said and reversed the car back past the junction. He drove forward, turned into School Lane, and then shortly afterwards turned right.

"This is School Hill," Tompkins said. "The school is here on the right, and if I remember correctly, Mumbery Hill starts along there where the road curves to the left."

Shortly afterwards, Tompkins turned the car onto the main road and drove steadily to Taplow, where he stopped outside the Severn's house, and everyone alighted.

"Thank you for a lovely day, James. I have really enjoyed it," Sabrina said happily.

"It was certainly a very nice day, and it has been a pleasure for me to have your company," Sir James responded seriously.

"Thank you, James."

"Are you free tomorrow?" he asked. "If you are and the weather remains good, we could have another outing."

"I think that would be a lovely idea. Where shall we go?"

"Would you like to decide?" he asked.

"That would be very nice. I'll talk to my mother and see what she can suggest."

"That's good," he said. "I wish you a pleasant evening, Sabrina," and he took her hand. In fact, he was able to hold Sabrina's cooperative fingers for several minutes as Elsie's attention was focused more on Tompkins than on chaperoning the daughter of her mistress.

Sir James climbed back into the motor car, and as they drove off, he waved to Sabrina and saw out of the corner of his eye Tompkins wave to Elsie.

Sabrina had also noticed the wave from Tompkins, and as she started to walk up the path to the front door, she said with a broad smile, "Do you think I should start chaperoning you, Elsie?"

"No, miss," she said and blushed as she added, "But he's a real handsome man now, isn't he."

"I agree, Elsie. He certainly is," Sabrina said as they entered the house.

With Tompkins and Elsie in close attendance, Sabrina and Sir James spent the daylight hours of almost every day for the next three weeks in each other's company. They explored the local countryside when the weather was good, and when it was poor, they stayed together either at the house in Taplow or at Brantley Manor. It was during the first of the visits to Brantley Manor that Sir James introduced Sabrina to his mother. He was delighted at the way the two so very different ladies developed such a rapport that it was like watching mother and daughter interacting together. During these happy hours they discovered more and more about each other and, perhaps more importantly, what one liked and the other disliked.

There was nothing of major importance, but they discovered many of the little things that can cause friction between two people if they're not known. For example, one didn't like cats and the other soft-boiled eggs with toast soldiers.

Some days before Sir James was due to leave for Egypt, he announced that he would have to go to London early the next day for a meeting at the Colonial Office but expected to return before evening. That evening, and just before he left the Severn's house in Taplow, Sabrina had to go upstairs to her mother's room to get a woollen cardigan for her mother to put around her shoulders. Sir James took advantage of Sabrina's temporary absence to discuss with Mrs Severn a subject that had been of concern to him for some time. Nothing was said to Sabrina on her return with the cardigan, and shortly afterwards, Sir James said goodnight and went home to Brantley Manor.

The next day, Tompkins drove him to London, where Sir James spent a relatively short time at the Colonial Office and a much longer time scrutinising the wares of several expensive jewellery shops before selecting and purchasing a gift for Sabrina.

As a result of his careful planning, Sir James was able to start his return journey long before lunch time.

Sabrina, on the other hand, had a very frustrating time of it.

It was the first time for three weeks that she didn't have Sir James' companionship, and the hours passed very slowly indeed as she wandered aimlessly from room to room and back again. She started to haunt the living room, which had windows facing the road, long before there was the remotest possibility that she would see Sir James return, but eventually, her lonely vigil was rewarded when a mud-spattered Bentley stopped outside the gate.

Sir James alighted from the Bentley and started to walk up the path to the front door but hadn't reached halfway before Sabrina threw convention out of the window and opened it. She could see over Sir James' shoulder the figure of Tompkins a short distance behind his master and registered only that Tompkins was carrying a rectangular wicker basket under his arm that clinked as if it contained bottles before she focused her attention solely on Sir James Russell.

As he arrived at the front door, Sir James said, "Good afternoon, Sabrina. I hope your day has not been too dismal."

"Oh no!" she lied, "I have had a pleasant day reading and talking with my mother. How was your meeting?"

"Not worth the effort of driving to London," he answered, feeling a little perturbed that Sabrina did not seem to have missed him at all. *After all*, he thought, *I have certainly missed her.*

He followed Sabrina along the hall and into the living room, where Mrs Severn was sitting reading.

"Good afternoon, Mrs Severn," he said. "I'm very pleased that you have had a happy day with your daughter today."

"Whatever gave you that idea, Sir James?" she asked. "Sabrina has been wandering around the house all day like a lost soul. I'm very thankful that you have returned. Now, if you will excuse me, I'm sure you young people have much to discuss," and she left the room and carefully closed the door behind her.

"Reading and talking, were you?" he said, "What a story!"

"I'm sorry, James, but I didn't want you to know how much I missed you today."

"Why ever not?" he asked. "I certainly missed you."

"I'm pleased to know that," she said and sat down in one of the arm chairs and gestured for Sir James to sit in the chair beside hers.

He didn't sit and continued to stand in front of her, fidgeting and looking uncharacteristically ill at ease.

"What is it, James?" she asked with concern in her voice.

In response, he knelt in front of her, took her hands in his, and said with his voice full of emotion, "Please, Sabrina, will you marry me?"

Apart from a gasp of surprise, Sabrina didn't wait a moment before saying joyfully, "I should be honoured to be your wife, James, and I accept with the greatest of pleasure. Nothing could make me happier," she added as tears started to cascade down her cheeks.

"I feel like that too," he said as he felt in his pocket and took out the ring box. It took only a moment for him to extract the ring and slide it onto the third finger of Sabrina's left hand.

She looked at it with awe and said, "It's a beautiful engagement ring, , and it fits perfectly. How did you know what size to get?"

"I spoke to your mother yesterday evening and asked her permission to propose to you, and when she consented, she gave me a ring she knew was the correct size."

"She knew!" cried Sabrina. "No wonder she's been going around looking like the cat that's got the cream. I'm so happy, James. I cannot believe so much has happened in the past three weeks. Millie will be green when she finds out," she added gleefully.

"Perhaps we should tell your mother that you have accepted me, ," he suggested tactfully as he stood up. "But first," he added as she stood also, "Perhaps my fiancée will permit me to embrace her?" Suiting actions to words, he put his arms around her and they kissed. And then they kissed again. It was a much longer and more passionate kiss the second time and it left them slightly breathless and very, very happy. They walked to the door holding hands, and Sir James opened it to find Mrs Severn standing in the corridor with her hand poised to knock.

There was a moment of silence as Mrs Severn looked at her daughter's face and then at the ring she was displaying on her left hand.

She stepped forward, hugged her daughter, and said, "I am so pleased for you both." She then hugged Sir James as well.

There was a loud bang and they turned as one to look along the hall and saw Tompkins standing in the hall with a freshly opened bottle of champagne and Elsie beside him with a tray of glasses.

"Come along, everybody," said Mrs Severn as she led everyone into the living room. Tompkins filled the glasses with golden, effervescent liquid, and Elsie served Mrs Severn, then Sabrina, and finally Sir James.

Sabrina and her fiancé exchanged glances, nodded, and Sabrina said, "You must have a glass, Elsie, and you as well, Tompkins."

When all five had a glass in their hands, Mrs Severn said, "Sabrina, I hope with all my heart that you and Sir James will have a long and happy life together," and she raised her glass to the happy couple and drank a little of the wine, as did Elsie and Tompkins.

Sabrina and Sir James simply said, "Thank you," as they were too overcome by their emotions to be able to say more.

Elsie asked if she could see the engagement ring, and Sabrina proudly held out her left hand so that Elsie and her mother could admire it.

It really was a beautiful ring and consisted of a round, half carat, brilliant cut diamond on a white gold filigree mount. All three ladies went into raptures over the ring, and whilst they were discussing it in minute detail, Sir James and Tompkins stood to one side and drank a little more of the champagne.

"Sir James," Tompkins said, "If I might be so bold as to say so, I would like to say how happy I am to see you engaged to such a lovely young lady, and I wish you a long and happy life."

"Thank you, Tompkins," Sir James responded, and then, putting the master-servant relationship on one side for a moment, he asked, "And when can I expect to pay you and Elsie the same compliment?"

"I haven't had the courage to ask her, sir," he said. "Because I'm afraid she might say no."

"I can understand how you feel, Tompkins. It could only have been a few seconds before Miss Severn said yes to me, but it felt like years. I just do not know what I would have done if she had refused me. But on the other hand, I wouldn't have asked if I had thought she might refuse."

Sir James looked at the ladies for a moment then said, "I don't want to interfere in your private life, Tompkins, but if you agree, I could ask Miss Severn to speak to Elsie privately. She might be able to find out what Elsie is thinking."

"That's a wonderful idea, sir, and I should be very grateful to you both if Miss Severn could find out which way the wind is blowing," said Tompkins.

"Leave it with me for a day or so," Sir James said.

"Yes, sir."

Sir James noticed that Elsie had moved away from Mrs and Miss Severn and assumed the ladies had completed oohing and ahhing over the ring and moved on to other, but associated, matrimonial subjects.

He decided to rejoin his fiancée and took her hand. "Mrs Severn," he said, "If you have no objection, I would like to take Sabrina to Brantley Manor so that we can tell my mother about our engagement."

"Yes of course, I don't mind you going," she said.

"Would you like to come as well?" he asked, and Sabrina gave his arm a gentle thank you squeeze for his thoughtfulness.

"I won't come with you on this occasion, but I would like to meet my future son-in-law's mother quite soon. Have you and Sabrina decided when you will get married?" She then answered her own question with, "Of course you haven't. There has been no time to even think of that yet."

Sabrina and Sir James said their goodbyes and walked down to the motor car, openly hand-in-hand for the first time, and climbed into the back. Tompkins closed the door, then hurried to the front to restart the engine with the starting handle.

"My mother's question about a date for our wedding was a little premature," said Sabrina, "but I think it's something we should give some thought to."

"I agree," Sir James responded, then asked, "If you will permit me, dearest Sabrina, I would like to make a suggestion."

"Please do, husband-to-be," she said happily.

"Clearly, there is no time to get married before I go to Egypt, so if my future wife agrees, I suggest we plan for a wedding on my first home leave."

"When do you expect to come home next?" she asked.

"Usually, one is expected to remain on station for a year—"

"I have to wait a year before we can marry?" Sabrina interrupted with more than a bit of an edge to her voice.

Unruffled by his fiancée's comment, he said, "Please let me finish, Sabrina," and when she nodded, he went on. "I was going to say that I would either arrange to come back in six months or resign my commission if no other course is open to me."

"Sorry, James, I shouldn't have interrupted you," she said contritely. "If we can plan for a wedding in about six months' time, the weather should be nice, and it gives me plenty of time to arrange my trousseau. Where will we live?" asked the practical-minded young lady.

"I think there are two answers to that question, Sabrina. If I continue to work abroad, it would be nice if you consented to come as well when the weather is not too onerous. When it is too hot for comfort and you decide to come home, I suggest you live at Brantley Manor. We can convert one of the unused wings into a private apartment. It will require a woman's touch to make it a home, but it would be quite convenient for you as your mother is not very far away. What do you think of the idea, Sabrina?".

"I quite like it. Perhaps we can go and see the rooms you want to convert before you leave and then I can apply my 'woman's touch', as you describe it, whilst you are away."

"Good idea," he said, "We'll do that."

By the time they had finished discussing Sabrina's various initial ideas about colours and curtain fabrics and so on and so forth, they had arrived at Brantley Manor. When they went to the library, they found Sir James' mother fast asleep in her chair with an open book on her lap. They tiptoed to the other end of the library and sat down on a big old sofa beside the log fire.

Sir James said quietly so as to avoid disturbing his mother, "Whilst you were talking with your mother about your engagement ring, Tompkins offered his congratulations, and I took the opportunity to ask him when he was going to ask for Elsie's hand. He wants to propose but won't because he is afraid she might say no and then he would lose her. Do you think you could find out discretely how Elsie would react to a proposal from Tompkins?"

"I can certainly do that this evening, although I'm sure she will jump at the chance," said Sabrina quickly. "I'll tell you what she says tomorrow,," she added, and then their conversation focused quite naturally on more intimate subjects.

Sir James' mother woke up, heard distant, quiet voices, and walked down the library to investigate. She saw her son and the young lady from Taplow sitting close together on the sofa and then noticed a wink of firelight from the diamond the girl was wearing on her engagement finger. *My word*, she thought, *my son's proposed, and about time, too.*

"Congratulations," she said before they noticed her presence, "I hope you will be very happy."

"Thank you, Mother," said Sir James.

"Thank you, Lady Mary," said Sabrina.

Lady Mary sat down on an upholstered chair on the opposite side of the fire place and looked searchingly for a few seconds at the two young people sitting opposite.

She asked, "I expect it's too soon to ask, but have you considered when you will marry?"

"We talked about it in the car whilst we were driving here, Mother," Sir James responded. "And we have decided to marry when I return from Egypt in about six months' time. Of course, we haven't set a definite date yet nor discussed where the ceremony will take place; there hasn't been time for that. I have suggested to Sabrina that we convert the west wing into a private apartment for us to use when we are in this country."

"That's a good idea. Would you like to come and see it, Sabrina?"

"Yes please, Lady Mary. If you have time, I should be very happy to look at it with you," Sabrina answered, wondering why her fiancé had not been included in the invitation.

Lady Mary obviously read her thoughts because she said, "James can come with us of course, but he knows the rooms very well, and he wouldn't have the first idea about furnishing," and she added a little disparagingly, "He's only a military man after all."

"Mother," he said in carefully feigned indignation, "That's not correct, as you well know. You shouldn't give my future wife a false impression of my abilities."

"We talked about furnishing and decorating the rooms on the drive here," said Sabrina in defence of her betrothed. "And I had the impression that James knows a great deal about it."

"And when, may I ask, did you acquire any knowledge of furnishing, James?" Lady Mary queried with scepticism audible in her voice.

"Actually, while I was in the army," he said. "My regiment was moved to a base near Aldershot after peace was declared. The officers' mess was a shambles, and for some reason, the Colonel thought it would be a good idea to task me with the renovation. I think he simply followed the age-old army practice of giving jobs to those least qualified to carry them out. Anyway, winter was approaching and I was given a budget and a date when the officers would start using the mess. With the wholehearted support of a local builder, the task was completed within time and budget, much to the surprise of my fellow officers, and I learned a great deal about the art of renovation. So, you see, Mother dear, the army is not all blood and bullets."

"Wonders never cease," Lady Mary said unoriginally. "Come along, then," and she led them from the library to main staircase, which lead them to the first floor of the west wing. It had been built in a westerly direction from the main body of the house by an unimaginative builder who had constructed ten almost equally sized rooms on either side of a central corridor. They were intended to serve as guest bedrooms in those far off days when large house parties were a normal part of aristocratic life.

Sabrina's heart sank when she saw the rooms and realised the magnitude of the task that lay ahead of them, but then she had an inspired thought. She turned to Sir James and said, "I think we need the help of your friendly builder from Aldershot."

"That's a very good idea," Sir James agreed. "I'll contact him as soon as I can."

After a few moments' thought, Sir James dispatched Tompkins in the Bentley with a note for the builder, requesting him to come to Brantley Manor in the Bentley immediately if at all possible. About an hour later, Tompkins returned and Benson brought Charlie Hod directly to the library, where Sir James and Sabrina were discussing various ideas with Lady Mary whilst they waited.

Charlie Hod was a balding, red-faced, stocky individual who was dressed in heavy-duty, dark-coloured clothes and clumpy nailed boots more suited to a building site than a genteel library with a carefully polished mahogany floor.

Sir James wasted no time.

As soon as he saw the builder entering the library, he jumped to his feet and said, "Good evening, Charlie. It's extremely good of you to come at such short notice, but I have to go to Egypt in two days and I want to get as much arranged as possible before I leave. I would like you to meet my mother, Lady Mary Russell, and my fiancée, Miss Sabrina Severn."

After the usual introductory ritual of hand shaking and How do you dos, Sir James said, "We would like you to help us with the alteration of the first floor of the west wing. We want to convert it into a private apartment for Miss Severn and myself to use after we are married in about six months' time. But perhaps we should go and see the west wing first and talk later?"

"That's a very good idea, Sir James," said Charlie Hod, and they all adjourned to the west wing, where Charlie walked around some of the rooms. He then said, "I think my best course of action would be to measure up the existing layout and then draw up some sketch plans for you to consider."

"How long will that take?" asked Sir James with a premonition that Charlie would suggest "Till sometime next week".

Consequently, he was agreeably surprised when Charlie said, "I'll measure the rooms now and come back in the morning just after breakfast, if that's convenient?"

"Perfectly," said Sir James, and then realising that Charlie was alone and had no one to hold the free end of a tape measure, he asked, "Do you need any help?"

"No, Sir James, I brought paper, a pencil, and a folding rule with me, but I would appreciate it if you could arrange for Tompkins to drive me back to Aldershot when I have finished."

"Yes, of course," Sir James answered. "And he will be available to bring you back to the Hall tomorrow if you tell him what time to collect you."

"Thank you, sir," said Charlie. "Now, if you will excuse me," he said in a polite but unmistakeable dismissal as he started to measure and note and sketch.

Lady Mary, Sabrina, and Sir James looked at each other and then at Charlie Hod industriously measuring and writing, shrugged, and by common unspoken consent, started to drift away, initially towards the staircase and then to the library, where they resumed their conversation about possible alterations until Benson enquired about dinner.

Lady Mary took the initiative, as was her custom, and, with scant attention given to the wishes of her son and future daughter-in-law, decided that they would have a cold buffet in the library and wait for Charlie Hod to complete his work. Benson, accompanied by a maid pushing a trolley, arrived not long afterwards and laid the food, cutlery, and crockery on a table near the fire. Charlie Hod arrived before they had finished eating, and after cutting two doorsteps of bread, he made a cheese, ham, and pickle sandwich to eat on his journey back to Aldershot.

Sabrina and Sir James finished their meals shortly after Charlie had left. As it was already quite late, Sir James decided that it would be better if he drove Sabrina home in the second car rather than wait for Tompkins to return and sent a servant to bring the Rolls from the stable yard at the back of the Hall.

"You have a Rolls as well as a Bentley?" queried Sabrina in a slightly awestruck voice.

"Oh yes ," Sir James answered. "It was my father's pride and joy. We should dispose of it but we haven't had the heart to do so yet."

"I can understand that feeling," said Sabrina as she squeezed Sir James' hand in understanding.

Sir James drove quite slowly to Taplow. It had been a momentous day and he couldn't quite believe how marvellously content he felt as a result of Sabrina's acceptance of his proposal.

Three weeks ago, he thought, *I could never have anticipated that my status would change from bachelor to betrothed before I returned to Egypt*, and he savoured the prospect of caring for the lovely and intelligent young woman who sat by his side.

Sabrina sat equally quietly beside her fiancé, mentally counting her blessings.

Like Sir James, she was stunned by the change in her fortunes. Expecting to be left on the shelf, she had suddenly become the fiancée of a rich, handsome, and very personable man. It was like a dream, and she hoped she would never wake up from it.

When they arrived at Sabrina's home in Taplow, Sir James walked around the front of the car and helped Sabrina to alight. They walked arm-in-arm up the path to the front door, which was opened by Elsie in response to Sir James' rat-a-tat-tat on the big brass door knocker, and then along the hall to the living room, where they told Mrs Severn what they had been doing.

After agreeing to meet Sabrina at about seven in the morning the next day so that they could have breakfast together at Brantley Manor before Charlie Hod arrived, Sir James said goodnight to Mrs Severn. He was then escorted to the front door by Sabrina, who was holding her fiancé's hand as if she was afraid Sir James would disappear in a puff of smoke if she let it go.

Sir James said, "Goodnight, my wife-to-be," and bent forward to kiss Sabrina on the lips. Some minutes later and following a series of kisses that had each been more passionate than the one before, Sabrina pushed Sir James away and said quite breathlessly, "You must go home, my dearest man."

Breathing equally quickly, Sir James said, "Goodnight, my love. It's a long time until tomorrow," and kissed her again, then turned and strode away down the path to the gate and the Rolls. He started the engine with the starting handle, climbed in, and waved as he set off back to Brantley Manor.

Next morning, Sir James arrived at the Severn's front door at exactly seven in the morning, and a minute later, he had embraced Sabrina as if he hadn't seen the young lady for ten years and not just for ten hours. They walked, well, more accurately, almost skipped they were so happy, down the path to the Rolls, and Sir James helped her into the front seat. At Brantley Manor, they left the motor car on the drive outside the front door and went to the breakfast room.

On the sideboard in dishes heated by candles were bacon, eggs that had been fried, scrambled, or boiled, sausages, and various other dishes. There was toast, butter, and marmalade, with coffee or tea to drink. It was a breakfast feast, and both young people had healthy appetites and selected a hearty breakfast to suit.

During the meal, Sabrina said, "I spoke to Elsie last night after you left, James."

"Thank you, Sabrina," he said. "That was thoughtful of you. What did you say?"

"Elsie remarked how happy I looked and how lucky I was to find such a nice man."

"That was kind of her," he commented.

"Yes, and I think so to. That you are a nice man, I mean," Sabrina said with a big smile, and he kissed her on the cheek.

"I thanked her of course," said Sabrina. "And then after a minute or so of silence, Elsie said, a little wistfully I thought, how much she would like to be as happy as I am. Her remark gave me the opportunity to ask about Tompkins. I said what a nice man he appeared to be and how relaxed and happy they seemed to be in each other's company. She said I was correct and admitted that Tompkins was by far the nicest man she had ever met, but they haven't had time to get to know each other because of their duties."

Sabrina ate some more of her breakfast and then said, "Elsie's last words before she said goodnight were, 'I am sure he would be a good husband and father, but he would never look at me because he sees a better class of servant girl at the Hall'. I said that was nonsense, but she wasn't convinced."

Sir James thought over what he had heard and said, "I think it is fair to say that if Tompkins made a proposal, it is probable that Elsie would accept. Do you agree, Sabrina?"

"Yes, I do," she said.

"Good! Whilst the alterations are going on, I expect you will wish to visit Brantley Manor quite frequently to make sure everything is going well."

"Yes, of course," Sabrina responded with a slightly puzzled note in her voice because she couldn't see a connection between Tompkins' probable proposal of marriage to Elsie and the alterations at the Hall.

"And when you come to visit, I expect that you will bring Elsie as your companion," Sir James said.

"Normally that would be the case." Sabrina still sounded a little puzzled.

"Well," he said, "If Elsie is here, and Tompkins is here, there should be plenty of opportunity for them to meet and learn about each other, and then a proposal and its acceptance should not be too difficult for them to organise. Don't you agree, Sabrina?"

"That's very true, James," Sabrina answered. "You are a very thoughtful man. But will you say anything to Tompkins?"

"No," he said after considering the matter for a few moments. "I think we should let nature take its own course now that we know they can spend more time together in future."

Further conversation on this very important subject was brought to an abrupt end by the arrival of Charlie Hod.

"Have you breakfasted?" asked Miss Severn politely.

"Would you like another breakfast, Charlie?" asked Sir James who was well-versed in the ability of the English working man to eat more than the customary three meals a day.

"Yes, and yes please," said Charlie, and he needed no second bidding to pick up a plate and fill it with food. He pointed to some rolls of paper with his fork and said in a voice muffled by a mouthful of sausage and egg, "I have brought some rough plans with me. Perhaps you could look at them whilst I eat and then we can talk later?"

"We'll do that, Charlie. We'll be in the library when you've finished your breakfast," said Sir James, and he and Sabrina walked to the library and spread the plans on the table, using books from an adjacent shelf to weigh down the corners.

Charlie's use of the phrase 'rough plans' was quite apt as there were many places on each sheet where the original idea had been crossed out or amended in some way. But it was possible to discern the original layout of the first floor of the west wing and also identify the proposed new layout that Charlie envisaged. Sabrina and Sir James leant over the plans side by side and slowly deciphered Charlie's notes and headings.

Sabrina said, "What's that room, James?" as she pointed at a particularly unclear room title.

He studied it for a moment, turned it through ninety degrees to look at the word from a different perspective, and said, "'Nursery', I believe."

"Yes of course, it's 'nursery'! Thank you, James," said Sabrina in a matter-of-fact voice and then blushed scarlet as she realised all the implications that the word 'nursery' had.

And then a well-fed Charlie Hod arrived, and the awkwardness dissipated in a rattle of questions and the rustle of plans.

At the end of an hour, they had reviewed all of Charlie's ideas and approved them, sometimes with amendments but generally without. Charlie had then gone away with Tompkins in the Bentley to prepare more detailed plans and to ensure that his workmen were briefed on the first stages of the work.

Suddenly, they found that they were alone. Much worse was the fact that they had no pressing task to distract one from the other.

Charlie had only left them alone for a few minutes, but it was enough time for nature to take its course, and they were in each other's arms and kissing passionately as soon as the door closed.

Where their passion could have taken them is easy to anticipate, but Lady Mary chose that moment to enter the library, and her sudden appearance prevented it from boiling over.

They were very embarrassed by her sudden appearance and even more so when she said bluntly, "There will be plenty of time for that sort of hanky-panky after you're married! Where is Charlie Hod?"

"He's just left, Mother," Sir James answered.

"Pity!" said Lady Mary. "I wanted to look at his plans."

"Sabrina and I went through them carefully, and most of his ideas are very good. There are a few small changes that Hod agrees with, and Tompkins has driven him back to Aldershot so that he can redraw the plans," Sir James explained.

Changing the subject, Lady Mary said, "James! As tomorrow will be your last day at Brantley Manor before you sail, I propose to hold a small family dinner tomorrow evening to wish you God Speed and to celebrate your betrothal to Sabrina. It's very short notice, Sabrina, but I do hope your mother will be able to come."

"I'm sure she will be able to, Lady Mary, but if James will drive me to Taplow, we can give her your very kind invitation and make sure. Can you take me back, James?" she asked.

"Of course I can. Shall we leave now?"

"Yes please," she responded.

Five minutes later, they were motoring steadily towards Taplow. Sir James was concentrating on driving along the winding roads and Sabrina was deep in thought about a subject dear to every lady's heart; the arrangements for her wedding.

She broke out of her reverie suddenly to ask, "James, do you think we could drive to Upton and see Millie after we have seen my mother?"

"Yes of course. What do you want to do there?" was the immediate response.

"I would like to ask Millie if she will be my bridesmaid," Sabrina said.

"That's a good idea," he responded, "but I imagine she will be quite surprised when you appear on her doorstep with a ring and a fiancé."

"Oh, yes!" Sabrina said, and Sir James chuckled quietly at the schoolgirl glee that was apparent in Sabrina's voice.

Shortly after this conversation, they arrived at the Severn's home, and Sir James delivered his mother's invitation. Mrs Severn accepted immediately, and then, totally disregarding the wardrobe crammed full of her exquisite apparel, decided that she had absolutely nothing to wear and couldn't possibly attend a function that had Lady Mary as hostess.

Fortunately, Sabrina was more than capable of calming her mother's attacks of panic, and within a few minutes, calm had returned to the Severn household.

They left Taplow for Upton about ten minutes later and didn't converse very much during the journey as Sabrina had resumed her role as wedding planner. The planning stopped as soon as Sir James turned into the road where Millie lived with her parents.

Sabrina looked at the road for a second, shuddered at the memory of her last visit, and said, "Please don't stop so close to the edge this time, James."

"Perhaps I should drive in through the gateway," he suggested and then wished he hadn't as he remembered how narrow the drive had appeared in the dark.

"That's a lovely idea, James," said Sabrina enthusiastically. "There's nothing like arriving at someone's door in a Rolls."

Fortunately, there was no other traffic, and Sir James Russell pulled over onto the wrong side of the road in order to give himself a better chance of meeting the gateway straight on. He swept through the entrance as if he had done it a thousand times and stopped in a shower of displaced gravel, inches from a very substantial gate that stretched across the drive.

Sir James breathed a sigh of relief because he had thought for a moment that he was going to hit it, and that would have done the angel on the front of the Rolls no good at all.

"What do you want me to do now, wife-to-be?" he asked.

"You could go to the front door and ask the maid to ask Millie to come here," she said and then added, "That's probably not a good idea as she won't know you from Adam and will probably disappear back into the house in a panic. I'll go."

Sir James helped Sabrina out of the car, and she walked the short distance to the front door of Millie's home and watched as she pulled on the bell pull.

The door opened, and Sabrina exchanged a few words with the maid, who clearly recognised Sabrina as they disappeared back into the house together, not quite closing the door behind them.

Sir James stood by the side of the Rolls and resigned himself to a long wait. In fact, he was very agreeably surprised when the door reopened a few moments later and Sabrina beckoned to him from the doorstep.

As he reached her, Sabrina whispered in his ear, "I've only said to Millie that I want to introduce her to my friend. She hasn't noticed my lovely ring, so she will have quite a surprise."

"I should imagine so," Sir James said with a smile as they walked along the hall towards the back of the house and a partially open door, through which sunlight escaped into the hall. As they reached the door, they could hear the muted sound of two women talking. Neither Sabrina nor Sir James could make out any of the words, it was so faint, and the conversation came to a complete halt as soon as Sabrina tapped politely on the door and pushed it open.

The two ladies looked towards the door, and Sir James assumed the elder lady was Millie's mother.

Millie looked directly at Sir James and said, "I know you from somewhere." After a short pause for thought, she continued, "I remember now. You were the gentleman who gave Sabrina and me a ride home from London when there had been a train crash. I'm really sorry, but I've forgotten your name."

Before Sir James could comment, Sabrina said quickly, "That's alright, Millie. It will give me great pleasure to introduce him to you and your mother," and she turned to Sir James and took his hand.

She said, "Mrs Malcolm, it gives me great pleasure to introduce you to my fiancé, Sir James Russell."

Before Mrs. Malcolm could respond, Millie's excited and incredulous voice drowned out everything else. "Your fiancé?" she almost shouted as she jumped out of her chair. "You're engaged? When did this happen?" she demanded, still in quite a loud voice.

Mrs. Malcolm was now standing and said severely to her daughter, "That's enough, Millie. We will know the answers soon enough," and Millie subsided into her chair. Her mother turned to Sir James, held out her hand for him to shake, and said, "It is an honour to welcome you to my home, Sir James, and a great pleasure to congratulate you on your betrothal. Sabrina is a lovely young woman, and you are a very lucky young man."

"I know I am, Mrs Malcolm," he said quietly.

"James and I became engaged two days ago, Millie, and we expect to marry in about six months when James returns from Egypt. Do you like my ring?" she asked as she held her hand out.

"It's beautiful," said Millie, trying not to sound as envious of her friend's good fortune as she felt. *It's a good thing I'm not a chameleon,* she thought, *I would be a vivid green if I was.*

"The main reason for coming to see you this afternoon was to beg you to be my bridesmaid, Millie. You will, won't you?" Sabrina asked and crossed her fingers whilst she waited for her friend to answer.

"I would have scratched your eyes out if you hadn't asked me," said Millie. "Of course I'll support you."

And the two friends fell into each other's arms and wept tears of happiness because of the forthcoming wedding which were tinged with sadness at the realisation that they would not be able to spend so much time in each other's company once Sabrina was married. . Sir James and Mrs Malcolm could do nothing more than watch silently until Sabrina and Millie regained their normal calm demeanour.

When the young women had recovered their composure, Millie sat down again, and Sabrina returned to Sir James and slipped her hand into his.

Mrs Malcolm sat down also and rang the small silver bell she picked up from the highly-polished low mahogany table beside her chair.

She said, "An occasion like this can only be saluted properly with a glass of champagne in one's hand. Don't you agree, Sir James?"

"I do indeed," he responded.

"Good," said Mrs Malcolm as the maid came into the room, received her instructions about champagne and glasses, and left again.

As soon as the door closed on the retreating back of the maid, the three ladies commenced a general discussion about dress styles for the bride and bridesmaid that left the reasonably amiable Sir James Russell thankful that most of this discussion would have been completed by the time he returned home from Egypt. He started to take more interest in proceedings when Mrs Malcolm asked where they would live.

Sabrina said, "Sir James is converting the upper floor of the west wing of Brantley Manor into a private home for us to live in when we are in England."

Mrs Malcolm, who found the idea of voluntarily living anywhere except in her beloved England slightly idiotic, said, "But surely you will live in England all the time?" in a voice rich with incredulity.

"No," said Sabrina, "When we are married, I hope to live at whichever embassy my husband is posted to."

"Are you a diplomat?" asked Millie, sounding impressed.

Before he could reply, Sabrina remembered that she had joked about James being a chauffeur as well as a diplomat on the drive from London and related it to Millie and her mother. The reaction was a mixture of horror at what she had said and mirth at the quick-wittedness of Sabrina's comment.

"If you are to be a diplomat's wife, Sabrina," Mrs Malcolm said bluntly through her laughter, "You will have to learn to control your tongue if you do not wish to hinder your husband's career," and the laughter stopped.

Sabrina said sadly, "My mother says the same, Mrs Malcolm, but it's not deliberate. The words tumble out of my mouth before I realise what I have said. I suppose I shall have to keep silent if we are in public," she added sadly.

"Don't do that, Sabrina," said Sir James. "Your quick wit is something that attracted me to you in the first place, and anyone who is offended by one of your accurate comments lacks a sense of humour and a bit of humility."

"Thank you, James," she said and squeezed his hand as she said it.

Not long afterwards, Sir James and Sabrina took their leave of the Malcolms and drove back to Brantley Manor, where they were delighted to find Charlie Hod with a couple of men already hard at work removing furniture and other fittings preparatory to commencing the alterations.

"We are very pleased to see that you have already started, Charlie," said Sir James.

"Thank you," he said, then added, "I can bring the new plans tomorrow morning if that's convenient, Sir James?"

"If you come about ten, I will arrange for Lady Mary to join us. She wasn't very pleased when she learned that I had let you go this morning before she had seen them."

Charlie Hod simply said, "I'll come at ten then, sir," and went back to his men.

Sabrina and Sir James left the Hall and started to walk hand-in-hand across the landscaped lawn at the front of the building. It was a very pleasant late afternoon with puffy white clouds drifting on the breeze and patterning the countryside with small patches of shade.

Sir James said, "After we have seen Charlie's plans, there will be nothing for us to do until it is time to dress for dinner." He paused.

"Do you have a good idea to propose, James?"

"As the weather is fine, perhaps we should arrange another picnic? We could go back to Henley or find somewhere else on the river for our lunch. What do you think?"

"A picnic is a nice idea," she agreed happily, "but perhaps we could go somewhere else if you can suggest somewhere?."

"I have some ideas, but perhaps you would rather have a surprise again?"

"Yes, please," she said.

***

Next morning, Sir James drove to Taplow, and after giving his lady a loving and tender kiss that made her pulses race, he escorted her to the motor car and drove back to Brantley Manor in time for a good breakfast. Elsie sat like royalty in the back as Sabrina wished to sit with Sir James.

Charlie Hod arrived promptly at ten and was shown to the library, where he spread his plans out for inspection. For Sabrina and Sir James, it was a simple matter to inspect the drawings they had studied the day before and verify that the alterations they wanted had been done. Naturally, Lady Mary took much, much longer than Sabrina and Sir James because she hadn't seen the drawings before, but she also wished to comment on and question every detail. However, it seemed to Sabrina that rather than offering constructive comments, Lady Mary was intent on criticising every aspect of the plans. Nothing in Charlie's excellent designs was good enough for Lady Mary and she began to insist on additional changes that would take much longer to implement than their timescale allowed.

Before long, placid Charlie Hod had become red in the face from suppressed temper and Sabrina seemed to be close to tears, but somehow, Sir James managed to maintain a calm exterior.

But even Sir James' polite and deferential demeanour had its limits, and eventually he said emphatically, "Mother! That's enough. You're splitting hairs over trivia, and I am not prepared to subject Sabrina to any more of your procrastination. I am the responsible member of the family since my father died, and what is to be done or not done is my decision. I value your advice, Mother, but today you are simply being obstructive."

Lady Mary stood up. There were flaming red spots of temper on her cheeks, and she said angrily, "You forget yourself, James!"

"No, Mother," he responded more calmly than he felt. "I am very unwilling to take a position that opposes yours, but, in the circumstances, I must remind you who is master here."

As she heard Sir James' words, Lady Mary turned on her heel and flounced out of the library, slamming the door behind her.

"Oh, James!" said Sabrina, white-faced and aghast at the awful turn of events. Sir James put a comforting arm around his fiancée's waist.

"Charlie!" he said.

"Yes, Sir James?"

"Sabrina and I are satisfied with the plans you have drawn up. Please complete the work as soon as possible, but it must be ready within six months when Sabrina and I get married."

"Yes, sir," said Charlie with his fingers firmly crossed behind his back and after saying, "Excuse me, sir, and excuse me, miss." He also left the library.

Sabrina and Sir James stared at each other for a few moments.

"I'm sorry that had to happen on my last day, but it is a confrontation that has been long overdue. My mother has not yet realised that she can express her opinion and that it will be listened to, but she cannot dictate what action is to be taken. That's my responsibility. Please excuse me for a little while, and I will go and talk to her."

"Very well, James. Please talk to your mother," Sabrina said. "As you say, it could not have come at a worse time, and when you have gone to Egypt, I'm sure Lady Mary will exact her revenge by plaguing me with alterations when things are already half done."

"No. She won't do that," Sir James said confidently and kissed his future wife on the cheek before going to his mother's room.

The content of the conversation Lady Mary had with Sir James Russell was never revealed, but Sir James returned with the confident air of a man who believed he had been very effective in his advocacy of his rights as the 'Lord of the Manor'.

He embraced Sabrina and held her tightly in his arms for a few moments, then said, "Everything is alright. My mother accepts she was in the wrong to interfere as she did this morning. I know it's a little later than we planned, but perhaps we should go on with our picnic. What do you think?"

"Yes of course, James," she said in a very subdued voice as she was still feeling the effects of the disagreement. She had never before experienced an open display of naked, adult anger, and she didn't know how to deal with the conflicting emotions invading her normally calm demeanour. Her courtship had lasted three cheerful, affectionate, happy weeks, and suddenly the mood had totally changed.

She tried to smile at her fiancé, but it was a very poor display compared to the sun-dimming smiles she had bestowed on him previously.

Sir James said, "Everything will be alright, you'll see."

"I do hope you're correct," she said in a very serious voice. "Because if everything is not alright, you will be many thousands of miles away and powerless to help me."

She turned away, walked to the motor, and waited until he caught up, opened the door, and helped her into the back seat. After Sir James had entered the car himself, he nodded to Tompkins who drove off.

Sabrina said, "Where are we going, James? I don't think I want another surprise this morning."

"It will be a nice surprise, Sabrina," he responded. "But since you ask, we will go to Marlow, if you agree, that is. Do you know the town?"

"No, I don't know Marlow. I've heard the name of course and know approximately where it is, but I have never been there."

"Shall I tell you the little I know as we drive there?" Sir James asked.

"Yes please."

But before he could start, she half-turned towards Sir James and took his hand in hers. "This morning was a terrible shock, James. One second everything was calm, even though your mother was being rather difficult, and then suddenly she was terribly angry because you corrected her. I hope I never see that again."

"I'm sure you will not," Sir James said with as much confidence as he could generate. "I really am most dreadfully sorry that it happened, but I couldn't let my mother go on being so dictatorial when I was about to leave. I think it could have been much worse for you if I hadn't taken a stand and stood up for our rights."

"Our rights?" she queried.

"Yes," he said. "Our rights; when we are married, you will be the first lady at Brantley Manor and you must help me fight the old dragon." He laughed. After a moment, Sabrina smiled and chuckled at the sudden image she had of herself dressed as Saint George.

"Do you want me to say something about Marlow now, Sabrina?" he asked.

"Yes please," she said and slid a little way across the back seat so that she could lean against her man for a moment. Sir James breathed a great silent sigh of relief as he felt her shoulder against his upper arm, and succumbing to temptation, put his arm around her shoulders and hugged her close.

"Marlow," he said, "is a very old habitation. In the eleventh century it was ringed by monastic foundations and there are buildings still standing that were erected in the fifteenth century. You know the poet Percy Bysshe Shelley?"

"Yes of course," said Sabrina. "I met a traveller from an antique land ..."

"Who said: Two vast and trunkless legs of stone ..." Sir James continued.

"Stand in the desert ..." They said in unison, then laughed together for the first time for some hours.

Sir James took a deep breath and continued his impromptu lesson. "He lived in Marlow for a few years, about 1818 I believe, and TS Eliot lived there comparatively recently. An old army man called General Sir George Higginson is living at a house called Gyldernscroft. He's nearly one hundred years old, so I imagine he has seen some changes in his lifetime. Quite a number of famous people have lived there, but there isn't time to mention them all."

They drove into Marlow from the south, and after crossing the suspension bridge over the Thames, they turned left off the road opposite All Saints Church, passed between some buildings and the river, and stopped on an open area of meadow. Sir James alighted and hurried around to the other side of the motor car to open the door for Sabrina and help her out. By this time, Elsie and Tompkins had both climbed out and then hurried to the back of the Bentley, where Tompkins opened the trunk, ready to unload the hamper. Sir James quickly looked over the area and selected a suitable place for their picnic under a big willow tree and about fifty yards away from where the car was parked.

"That's a likely looking place, Sabrina. What do you think?"

"Ideal, and it's just on the top of the bank. Perhaps I can paddle if you will not be offended?"

"Of course you can paddle if you desire to, and I will try not to let the sight of your naked toes make me too passionate," he joked.

"I think I had better not paddle after all," she said. "I don't want Elsie to be upset by your hot glances," and they laughed together.

"Tompkins. We'll have the picnic over there," Sir James said as he pointed. "While you and Elsie prepare everything, Miss Severn and I will walk to Boulter's Lock."

"Very well, sir," Tompkins responded, and Elsie curtsied.

Arm in arm, Sir James and Sabrina walked across the grass to the riverbank and then, going with the flow of the river, along the side the Thames towards the suspension bridge. At the bridge they stopped, then walked out along the bridge to the centre where the chains were just about waist high, and there they stopped to look back up stream towards the tree where the picnic was being laid out.

Sir James said, "I know a little about the man who designed and built this bridge if you would like to hear it?"

"Of course" said Sabrina, who was always very happy to listen to Sir James' voice, even if he was only talking about some boring old bridge, although she had to admit, it was quite an elegant structure.

"The designer was a man named William Tierney Clerk. He was born in

76

Bristol in 1783 and was trained by two eminent civil engineers," said Sir James. "He built four suspension bridges, and three of them are in Britain. The fourth bridge is the reason I know something about him, because I have walked across it, and because it was the longest suspension bridge in the world at the time it was opened. It was also the first permanent bridge across the Danube below Vienna since Roman times. It joined the cities of Buda and Pest in Hungary and is called the Szechenyi Chain Bridge after the count who commissioned it."

Despite her initial misgivings, Sabrina had found the account quite remarkable and said, ". That's very interesting, but what were you doing in Budapest?"

"Touring Europe with my mother and father," he said, but didn't elaborate.

"One day, you must tell me about your journeys, James," she said.

"I think it would be much better if we made the tour together, and I would very much enjoy showing you all the famous places I saw as a lad. Would you like me to arrange for us to tour through Europe?" Then he added with his enthusiasm evident in his voice, "It would be a great pleasure to escort you on such a journey."

"Yes," responded Sabrina very seriously, "I certainly would."

And there the matter was allowed to rest as they turned and retraced their steps along the bridge, ready for their luncheon by unspoken mutual consent.

"I hope Tompkins and Elsie are able to get to know each other better today," Sir James said.

"It would be nice if they could be as happy and settled as we are, ," Sabrina said with a cheerful smile that faded. She continued sadly, "I have been so happy since we met, and when you are away, I am going to miss you more than I bear to think about. It's difficult to believe that tonight will be the last time we will meet for six months, so please come back to me as soon as you can."

She stopped walking to be able to turn and look at her fiancé with a loving expression on her face.

"I shall miss you as well, Sabrina, but I will write often to tell you what I am doing, and maybe that will help the time pass more quickly. I hope you will write to me, as well."

"Of course I will," she responded. "All about Elsie and Tompkins, the alterations at Brantley Manor, and the most important subject of all, the preparations for our wedding." She stepped closer to Sir James and buried her face in his shoulder. Totally oblivious of their surroundings, they stood closely together with their arms about each other for several minutes until Sabrina pushed herself away from her fiancé, dabbed at her eyes, and delicately blew her nose. After a few moments, they resumed their walk back to the picnic site.

When Sabrina and Sir James noticed that Elsie and Tompkins were sitting very close together and talking animatedly to each other, they stopped as they were reluctant to intrude on a private moment. Fortunately, or unfortunately, Elsie noticed them, stood up, and was followed a few seconds later by Tompkins.

After lunch, or more accurately in the middle of the afternoon when they had all eaten a sufficient repast, Tompkins drove back to the Severn's house in Upton, where Sabrina and Elsie alighted, and then he drove Sir James to Brantley Manor.

Several hours later, Tompkins drove back to Upton to collect Mrs and Miss Severn and transport them to the Hall in time for dinner.

When Tompkins arrived, he found that his passengers were ready to leave. He had expected to wait at least half an hour for them and imagined he would have time to talk to Elsie and maybe propose to her if her mood was propitious. The new situation was not at all to his liking, but Tompkins had no option. He was a well-trained and obedient fellow and drove his passengers sedately to Brantley Manor. At the foot of the entrance steps, he dutifully opened the doors and helped his passengers to alight. While Sabrina flitted up the steps join Sir James, he offered his arm to Mrs Severn to assist her as she climbed the stairs to the front door. There she was welcomed initially by Benson and then by Sir James and Sabrina.

**

Tompkins withdrew calmly and climbed into the motor car. He drove sedately along the drive until he could see in the mirror that all the guests were inside the Hall and the door had been closed, and then he stopped. *Pity the Master came back when he did*, he thought. *Elsie was so encouraging, I would have proposed if we'd had a few more minutes.* He said under his breath, "Well, nothing ventured, nothing gained." He then checked his pockets, uttered a silent prayer for a silver tongue, and then pressed the accelerator steadily to the floor. He made record time to Upton without frightening anyone and came to a tyre-screeching halt outside the Severn's house. He hurried up the path but went around to the back door. He paused to steady himself, then banged on the door with the knocker. Elsie came to the door, and if she was surprised to see Tompkins outside, she didn't show it and cordially invited him in.

After an appropriate period, Tompkins made his proposal of marriage to Elsie and was immediately accepted, as was the ring he produced from his pocket. As it happened, they were not only unchaperoned, but as the other maid was on holiday, they were also alone in the house. As both of them had only experienced a life of celibacy, it was not long before their exploratory kisses became passionate caresses, and very little more time had elapsed before their fervour enticed them onto Elsie's bed. The result was a foregone conclusion, and by the time Tompkins set off on the return journey to Brantley Manor some two hours later, Elsie had conceived her first child, although neither of them had any idea that this was the situation.

Tompkins drove sedately back to the Hall and parked the Bentley at the back of the building before using the servant's stairs to get to his room. When he was safely alone, he allowed a huge grin of pleased satisfaction to break out over his face and couldn't stop himself dancing a few steps of joy.

***

In the dining room, the dinner to celebrate the betrothal of Sabrina Severn to Sir James was proceeding in a sedate and ordered fashion at a beautifully decorated round table. Sabrina sat on Sir James' right and her mother on his left. Lady Mary sat opposite her son and conversed so calmly with Sir James and the Severns that no one could have guessed there had been a major contretemps earlier in the day.

Between the soup and the fish courses, Mrs Severn asked, "What time do you have to leave tomorrow, Sir James? I hope you will have time to visit us once more before you sail away."

"Alas, no," he said. "I regret very much that I will leave too early in the morning for a visit to be possible."

"I'm very sorry to hear that," Mrs Severn said. "Are you sure you cannot change your plans a little?"

"Unfortunately, duty calls; I have to go to the Colonial Office before driving on to Southampton. The boat sails just before midnight tomorrow night, so I will have little or no time to spare as it is. Tompkins will drive the Bentley back here after I have boarded the ship. As Sabrina knows, Tompkins will be at her disposal whilst I am away so that she can visit the Hall and see how Charlie Hod is getting along. Then when she writes to me, she will be able to tell me how he is managing. He has a difficult task to complete everything in six months."

Sabrina looked at her fiancé's mother, decided it was better to put the morning's upset behind them, and said with obvious sincerity, "When I come to see Charlie Hod, Lady Mary, I hope I shall be able to have the benefit of your great experience."

"Yes, of course," said Lady Mary in a rather surprised tone, then added rather acidly, "Provided my son will not think I'm interfering."

"No, of course not, Mother," he said. "I think it is a capital suggestion. I only wish I had thought of it and not my diplomatic future wife," he added with obvious relief.

The meal proceeded through its various courses. The toasts were drunk to the engaged couple and to Sir James' safe and speedy return, and then it was all over and time for the Severns to return to Upton. Lady Mary stood, and Sir James, with a quiet, "Excuse me a moment, Sabrina," turned to Mrs Severn and helped to move her chair back so that she could stand more easily.

Lady Mary said, "You go on with Sabrina, James. I wish to show Mrs Severn your father's portrait."

"Very well, Mother," he said, and to Benson, who was hovering nearby, he ordered, "Send someone to tell Tompkins to bring the Bentley around."

"Yes, Sir James," he replied and hurried away.

Suddenly, Sabrina and Sir James were alone, and they did what every loving couple does when they are about to be parted for a lengthy period. They hugged each other as tightly as possible and kissed with the fervour of unrequited, youthful passion until they were breathless. But for the fact that Lady Mary made a terrible noise clumsily opening the dining room door, they would have still been embracing each other when the mothers appeared in the hall. As it was, they were able to put a respectable distance between themselves, but there was no disguising their sparkling eyes and other signs of passion they exhibited; but neither mother seemed to notice anything unusual.

The Severns said their goodbyes to Lady Mary in the entrance hall, but Sir James escorted the ladies down the steps and helped them into the car.

With a last, "Take care of yourself, my dearest lady," from Sir James to Sabrina, the Bentley sped away and the lovers started their six months separation only scant weeks after they'd met for the first time and an even shorter time since they'd become engaged.

Sir James climbed the steps to the front entrance as if all his energy had gone in the Bentley with Sabrina.

To Lady Mary he said, "Goodnight, Mother. Please don't wait up. I'll just finish packing and try to catch a few hours' sleep."

"Very well," she said as she kissed her son on the cheek. "Take care of yourself and come home safely. You have chosen a lovely young woman to be your wife and I look forward to your wedding."

"Thank you, Mother. I think so also. Goodnight," he said. He then turned to Benson. "Please arrange for someone to wake Tompkins at four, then to wake me and carry my bags to the car."

"Yes, sir," he said, and they all went their separate ways.

Shortly after four in the morning, a servant brought Sir James' luggage to the main door and helped Tompkins load the cases into the car boot. Once Sir James was safely seated in the back of the Bentley, Tompkins started the engine and drove away from Brantley Manor at the start of a journey that would take Sir James Russell many thousands of miles away from his home and his future wife and lead him into danger.

CHAPTER FOUR
Cairo and Aden

The events of the next six months are best recounted by reproducing in the date in which they were written the letters that Sabrina and Sir James exchanged. They were not only faithful correspondents, but each kept the other's letters. Sir James kept Sabrina's letters in an old leather dispatch box, whilst Sabrina kept her fiancé's letters in a drawer in her dressing table in neat, sorted by date bundles, tied up with red ribbon.

Brantley Manor

9 September

My dearest James,

We were together last evening at dinner and today it is not yet midday but I feel as if you have already been away for years. How will I manage to endure a separation of months when I can barely sustain an hour or two? I hope my mother is correct when she says I will become accustomed to your absence in time. It's true that I may become used to your absence, but I cannot believe I will ever accept it as normal.

As I write, I know you are on a ship somewhere at sea, and I do hope the weather is kind to you, but, in any case, I shall pray for calm seas for the next two weeks. I have never been on a passenger liner, so I hope you will tell me all about it when you have time.

It is quite strange to write a question as if the answer would arrive with your next breath when I know it will be weeks before you read this and even more weeks before I receive your reply. That's something for me to look forward to, my love.

The important news I have to impart is that Elsie and Tompkins have become engaged. Elsie is over the moon, as you might imagine. I hope you will not be cross with Tompkins, but whilst we were at dinner last night, he drove to Upton in the Bentley and proposed. The ring doesn't fit very well, but he didn't have Elsie's mother to guide him as my man did.

Charlie Hod is in his element. I think he enjoys making a lot of noise demolishing things. Lady Mary said his parents should have given him a drum when he was a child and then he would be quieter now. Anyway, there is no new work to write about, so I will not bore my man with many repetitions of the phrase 'bang, crash!'

I will write again soon, my dearest man,

All my love

Sabrina.

✳✳✳

Brantley Manor

16 September

My Dearest James,

I imagine that you must be well over halfway to your destination by now and somewhere in the Mediterranean, perhaps near to Malta. I wonder if your ship stops there. How exciting if it does!

Perhaps you will be able to post a letter there? I do hope so, but I must not calculate when I might receive your first letter just in case my dreams are not fulfilled.

Your mother is well and we seem to become better friends by the day, which is a great relief after the upset during the morning of your last day. I was so afraid she might consider me to be to blame because I had come between you and her, but to my great relief, that doesn't seem to be the case.

Charlie Hod has finished the crash bang phase, which is a relief for everyone, and has started erecting the new walls in accordance with the plans we agreed. It's less noisy, of course, but wet and mucky under foot from the bricklaying. One has to be very enthusiastic to venture into the west wing at present, and Lady Mary is quite prepared to let me get my shoes dirty so that she can supervise from a safe distance.

Charlie sends you his greetings.

Whenever I come over to Brantley Manor, Elsie comes with me as a matter of routine. She sits in the front with Tompkins, and although I try not to eavesdrop, I cannot help overhearing a little of their conversations. I gather that several of the maids at Brantley Manor are not at all pleased that Tompkins has become engaged as they had their eyes on him themselves. I wonder if Tompkins knew he had some admirers in Brantley Manor. Probably not, I imagine. The happy couple have not even started to consider when and where they will marry. Plenty of time for that, Elsie told me.

The weather remains good, but nothing is as green and bright as it was when you were with me, my dear James.

I know it is much too early for me to expect to receive a letter from you, my love, but that doesn't prevent me from looking every day.

I will write again soon, my dearest man,

All my love

Sabrina.

***

Brantley Manor

23 September

My Dearest James,

You have been away for little more than two weeks now, although each week feels like a year, and I have started to hope that I will receive a letter from you quite soon now. The comforting thought is that each week that passes brings you and our wedding one week closer.

The weather has been constantly bad since I last wrote. It's been rainy day after rainy day. And not just gentle, good for the crops sort of rain, but real torrential downpours. The rainwater is simply running off fields that are already saturated. The ditches and streams are already full to the brim, and it will not be long before the Thames overtops its banks if this goes on.

Charlie Hod is going around like a bear with two sore heads. Nothing has dried out properly yet, and he thinks he will have to put some heaters in the rooms if he is going to have any hope of finishing on time. He says he doesn't really want to take this step as he is afraid of cracking.

Your mother hasn't been to the west wing this week. She says, with some justification, that there is no point in getting cold and dirty when there isn't any progress to see. I understand her point of view, of course, but strangely I feel closer to you when I am there, my dearest man. Perhaps I feel that way because it will be our home quite soon.

Elsie and Tompkins spend as much time in each other's company as their duties allow, but they are so happy and content all the time it makes me feel very sad.

Perhaps I should send Tompkins on an errand to the other end of the county for a week and then Elsie will have some idea how I feel?

If all has gone according to your schedule, my love, you will see the High Commissioner tomorrow and start severing your ties with the embassy so that you can go on to Aden. I fear there will be few letters from you when you get to Aden as it's even further away.

Please look after yourself, my dearest man. I think of you constantly.

All my love dearest

Sabrina

PS. My mother remembered to copy the cake recipes and I have given them to Mrs Benton. She was very pleased. S.

***

S.S. Golden Star

Mediterranean

15 September

My Dearest Sabrina,

I hope you are well, my darling wife-to-be. I had no perception of the depth of loneliness I would experience until it was a physical fact and I had watched you drive away home after dinner. It felt as if half of me was suddenly missing, and now I long for the day when I receive your first letter.

As is often the case in this life, one man's misfortune is of benefit to others, and events today are a good illustration.

We have reversed course and are heading back to Gibraltar as we have to send one of our passengers to hospital there. It seems he enjoyed too much brandy after dinner last night and then managed to fall down the stairs between 'B' and 'C' decks and broke his left leg.

So, I have been presented with a golden opportunity to post a letter to my love a week earlier than I expected.

But as you would expect, I have very little news.

I spent an hour with Sir William Ellis, and he talked at length about my assignment in Aden, but more of that later. I collected a small mountain of boxes containing papers and documents for the embassy in Cairo. Naturally, we could not get all the boxes into the Bentley, and Sir William had to send one of the Colonial Office drivers with us in another vehicle. And he was such a slow driver, I only just managed to board the ship with the boxes before it cast off. As the boxes are my personal responsibility until I can hand them over in Cairo, they are stacked in my cabin wherever there is a space. It's not very convenient, as you might imagine. Some of it I have to read before I get to Cairo, so I am occupied all through the day. A good thing, really, or I should just sit and mope.

The ship has a small area set aside for those who have a desire to pray. The captain held a short service there on Sunday morning, and I was pleased to be able to say a prayer for the health and happiness of my future bride. There is a family group on the ship and they have three children, including a twelve-year-old boy. He was persuaded to sing at the end of the service and chose the Crimond setting of 'The Lord is my Shepherd'. He had a beautiful voice and sang like an angel. It was very moving, even for a hardened old soldier like me.

The steward has just come to say we are transferring our injured passenger to a navy ship to save us going all the way back to Gibraltar and if we have letters they can be sent with the sick man.

Goodbye for the present, my dearest.

James

***

Upton House

Upton

24 September

My Dear James,

I cannot describe the joy I felt when Elsie came into the living room yesterday afternoon with a great beaming smile on her face and presented me with your letter. It was quite unreasonable of me of course, but I had been hoping for a letter to arrive long before common sense told me I should expect one.

And here it is.

I have read and re-read your words and carry the letter with me wherever I go. I put it under my pillow last night and found the slight crackling noise when I moved my head very comforting. To you, my dearest, I expect it will seem a little silly to behave so, as it is only a piece of paper. But it's a piece of paper you have touched and recorded your thoughts upon, and it is very dear to me as a result.

I wrote only two days before, so there is nothing new to impart. The rain continues, Henley is flooded, or so a carter told the cook, and Charlie Hod has a face as long as a fiddle.

I will write again in a few days, and hopefully the weather will be better.

Goodbye for the present, my dearest man.

All my love is sent to you.

Sabrina.

***

Brantley Manor

30 September

My Dear James,

I am sad to say that everything is routine, and apart from one topic, it is difficult to find a new subject to write about that you will find either instructive or interesting.

That one topic concerns the continuing very damp state of the alterations. The rainfall has reduced in intensity but that hasn't helped poor Charlie Hod.

He decided that he couldn't wait any longer for the weather to improve and has brought two cast iron stoves to the Hall and set them up at each end of what used to be the corridor in the west wing. He explained to Lady Mary and me what he intended before he did it, of course, and it does seem to be a good idea. He believes he will get a benefit from the heat, which should not be too intense and cause cracking as the stoves are relatively small, and also from the cross draft as the flue goes out through a window on one side and the air comes in from a window on the opposite side. He has people here all the time to tend the fires, and after two days, there is already a noticeable change in colour as the walls start to dry.

Charlie is happier; if one can describe a bear with two sore heads in such terms.

Lady Mary has invited my mother to come to the Hall in two days' time. I think my mother will find it a little strange to eat a cake made to her recipe by another cook, but she seems to be looking forward to a novel experience.

Elsie doesn't seem to be as buoyantly happy as she was and seems to be more introspective somehow. I cannot imagine what ails the girl, but if her mood doesn't improve over the next week or so, I will ask her what is worrying her. I don't imagine there is anything seriously wrong, and Tompkins is certainly not worried about anything. I'm reminded of the old cliché about a dog with two tails whenever I see him.

One day soon, I must go and see Millie and start some serious planning for our wedding. Some days ago, Lady Mary happened to mention in passing that all the Russells have been married in the local church. I contented myself with a non-committal, "That's very interesting, Lady Mary," and we talked of other things. I assume you will not wish to break with tradition, my love, and the local church will be very acceptable to me. In all honesty, my dear, where we marry is less important to me than being your wife, and if you decided to marry over the anvil in Gretna, I would stand proudly by your side.

You must have been in Cairo for more than a week now, husband-to-be, so it is reasonable (at last) to haunt the letter box in anticipation of your first letter from the embassy.

All my love, my dearest man

Sabrina

***

British Embassy

Cairo

Egypt

20 September

My darling wife-to-be,

At last, I have stopped travelling and can relax in familiar surroundings for at least a few days.

I hope my lady will have posted a letter shortly after I left Brantley because if she did, I can expect to receive it quite soon. I fear I will soon make a nuisance of myself in the mail room as I enquire for a letter every time I pass the door. And that is quite a frequent event at present.

We were very lucky that we were delayed only a matter of hours due to the accident to our passenger as our captain had predicted that our arrival in Cairo would be delayed by several days. The change in fortune was brought about when a Royal Navy destroyer caught up with us in the early morning and the destroyer captain expressed his willingness to take the injured man from the 'Golden Star' and let the navy doctor examine him before taking him on to Gibraltar.

The actual transfer was quite enthralling to watch. The liner, 'Golden Star', and the destroyer were sailing directly into the swell side by side and very close together. There was a whooshing noise, and a rocket trailing a light line flashed across the gap between the ships. Very quickly, our sailors used the light line to pull a much heavier cable across the gap, and this was fastened to the mastheads on both ships. A running block was mounted on the cable and pulled across to us. The invalid was strapped onto a stretcher, and then the stretcher was slung below the running block. Some sailors on the destroyer pulled on a line attached to the running block, and it started to move, with the stretcher slung below it, out over the water and onto the deck of the destroyer. It was a breathtaking display of seamanship and co-ordination such as I have never witnessed before. Within a few minutes, everything had been dismantled and the destroyer started to accelerate. As soon as she was clearly ahead of us, our ship turned across her wake and reversed course to head for Cairo once more.

I have informed the High Commissioner, as I had done previously with Sir William, that I intend to return to England in six months in order to marry a beautiful lady called Sabrina. Neither has raised any objection, so I anticipate a long leave and then a return to duty somewhere in this part of the world. But in the meantime, I have to deal with the task set me by Sir William Ellis. It may be classified as a secret in London, but fortunately, the High Commissioner has been informed and we have had a very useful discussion about it. The High Commissioner agrees with my contention that there is little chance of achieving the result desired by the Colonial Office committee and an alternative solution will be required.

What may be of great value is that the High Commissioner has advised the British Resident in Aden that I will be in the protectorate but, due to the nature of my assignment, will not call to pay my respects as an embassy official would normally do. I regret that I cannot be more explicit, my love, but you can be assured that it is _important for our country_.

(Here, Sabrina had underlined 'important for our country' on the original and written in the margin 'and therefore dangerous'.)

I plan to remain in Cairo for the next five days and then take passage on a ship southbound through the Suez Canal and down the Red Sea to Aden. As I will have to report to Sir William through this embassy and receive his instructions by the same route, I will arrange for our letters to be treated similarly. It will mean that our correspondence will take longer to pass between us, but there should be no interruption in the interchange of news.

As soon as my mind is free of embassy work, I start to wonder how you are, my darling, and how the alterations are progressing and so on. In truth, Sabrina, you are in my thoughts for close to one hundred percent of my unoccupied time, and I miss your company and good sense more than I can express in words.

I must close this letter now so that it will go on tonight's boat.

Take care of yourself, my love,

James.

***

My dearest Sabrina,

I was called to the High Commissioner before I could dispatch the letter I wrote yesterday, and I was extremely annoyed by this chance event. Sending you a letter by each homeward-bound English ship is, I believe, extremely important as I want you to know that you are not forgotten.

On the other hand, it gives me a chance to tell you that I was thrilled beyond description when your first letter was placed on my desk.

I carry it everywhere. I read and reread whenever I have the opportunity, and as a result, the paper is starting to disintegrate due to constant unfolding and then refolding in our rather humid climate.

Perhaps I should answer it before I wear out the print.

You are correct, my dear. Like you, I will never be comfortable when we are apart.

I would never have expected Tompkins to take the motor car without my permission, but since the outcome is what we hoped for, I will do nothing to spoil his happiness, except to pull his leg a little next time I see him.

About 'bang, crash' – I'm sure you will find that Charlie will soon start on reconstruction and the noise level will then reduce dramatically.

I am afraid that I will leave Cairo before your next letter can arrive and then it will have to be sent on to Aden after I have advised the embassy of my new address. I will write from Aden as soon as I am able, my wife-to-be.

All my love, my dearest

James.

***

Some days later, Sir James packed. He left the embassy with the High Commissioner's good wishes ringing in his ears and took a carriage to the quay where he boarded a steamer for Aden.

It must have been an exceedingly tedious journey as Sir James' journal records on each day were very little beyond, 'I arose at six and walked the deck until breakfast. Read until lunch and then snoozed in a steamer chair for an hour or so. I walked around the deck until it was time to change for dinner, and then after dinner walked around the deck again until I could decently retire for the night'.

When the ship arrived at Aden, Sir James went ashore immediately, using one of the ship's boats. He hired a carriage and drove to a villa in Crater, occupied by an army officer he had served with in France. He knew from his previous visit to Aden that once again he would be welcomed by Brigadier James Cartwright like a long-lost brother, and also that he would be able to stay at the villa for as long as he desired. Brigadier Cartwright was not at home when Sir James arrived, but the Brigadier's batman, a corporal who introduced himself as Tucker, showed Sir James to a spacious and comfortably furnished room at the back of the villa. Tucker called a young, dark-skinned, turbaned servant boy and instructed him to unpack Sir James' bags.

"If you would like to have lunch, Sir James," Tucker said, "please come to the mess whenever you are ready and I will get you something to eat."

"Thank you, Tucker, I'll be five minutes."

"Very good, Sir James," Tucker responded as he smartly about-turned and left the room, looking every inch a soldier, although he was in civilian clothes.

True to his word, Sir James went to the mess, where he enjoyed an excellent but solitary meal, and then followed the local practice and retired to his room for a siesta.

In the late afternoon, feeling refreshed after a short sleep that was, for the first time in a while, undisturbed by the motion and noise of a ship on the high seas, Sir James reclined on a deck chair on the balcony outside his room with his feet propped up on a stool. He pondered over his problem and considered how he should progress the task he had been set in London.

Clearly, it would be next to impossible to verify the position of the boundary and by so doing ensure that the mineral deposits were on, or more accurately, *under* English territory. He had explained this to the Colonial Office committee, although he was not at all sure that they had understood what he had described to them.

The High Commissioner in Cairo had known exactly what Sir James meant when they'd discussed the issue and had agreed with his conclusions. Unfortunately, he was unable to offer any suggestions about a modus operandi Sir James could follow.

As Sir James sat and mused, his thoughts started to gel into at least a preliminary plan of action. It would be necessary to determine as quietly as possible the position of the boundary, but at the same time it really seemed essential to find out how much Jalal Al Hafrey knew about the mineral and then whether he really understood the value of it in the long term. If he was as knowledgeable as Sir James believed him to be, the next logical step was to find out how Al Hafrey intended to exploit the deposits and with whom.

After that, of course, it would be necessary to consider how best to proceed on the basis of knowledge and not simply conjecture.

But where was he to start? That was the burning question of the moment.

That evening, when he sat down to dinner with an unusually silent Brigadier Cartwright, Sir James had the good fortune to discover the answer to one of his questions without asking directly for guidance. This was a great relief to Sir James as it would have been difficult to use the Official Secrets Act to mask the reasons for a question if an old and trusted friend like the Brigadier had asked for an explanation.

Between mouthfuls of food, the brigadier had said with some heat and apropos nothing, "I am sick to death of border disputes."

"Why is that, Brigadier?"

"There are no written records here. They don't even know when they were born, so why do we think they would know and be able to prove the boundaries of the land they think they own? I have a small army of clerks looking for specific deeds and they can find nothing. Even within the city, the chances of proving land ownership are remote, and the further you are away from Crater, the more your chances of success reduce."

"So, if I had done something wrong and decided to flee from Aden to find sanctuary in an adjoining land, I wouldn't know when I had crossed the border?" Sir James asked rhetorically.

"Well, you probably would," Brigadier Cartwright responded cynically. "As soon as you crossed what was considered to be the border by the local tribe, they would put a bullet in you."

"Which would not be much help if you intended only to escape," Sir James commented grimly as he realised that one way to verify the boundary position would be to ride towards where it was believed to be. Accidentally!

Accidentally on purpose that is.

For a few minutes, there was only the sound of cutlery on crockery.

"Does anyone go into the interior?" Sir James asked, and then added, "For example, Brigadier, are there no archaeological expeditions?"

"There are a few people who go and grovel about in the heat and dust," the brigadier commented disparagingly. "And they come back with shards of pottery and other artefacts, which they are convinced will give an insight into past civilisations. That may be so in a purely cerebral sense, but put into the context of the Great War, what have we learnt from history? Nothing at all! Segments of mankind still go out and inflict their views on the weakest vessels in their area just as they have done quite pointlessly for millennia."

Sir James, who didn't exactly agree with the brigadier's point of view and knew when he was about climb onto one of his hobbyhorses, adroitly changed the subject.

"Do you know a local man called Jalal Al Hafrey, Brigadier?"

"I wouldn't say I know him, but I have met him in the course of my duties," Brigadier Cartwright responded. He paused to load his fork with food before asking, "Why?" then put the forkful in his mouth and started to chew industriously.

"I saw him at a reception on board HMS Neptune last year and heard afterwards that he had gone to Oxford. He must have been very well educated, as well as intelligent, to be accepted by an Oxford college, and I was a little intrigued by the man. I'm sure you will agree, Brigadier, that it is quite unusual for the son of a local sheikh to go to Oxford."

"First of his kind, but not the last I suspect," the brigadier commented.

They finished the main course, eschewed the sweet, but helped themselves to a large brandy each before resuming their conversation.

"I have an invitation to a reception Al Hafrey has organised," Brigadier Cartwright said. "It clashes with a prior engagement, and I was just about to politely decline, but perhaps you would like to go in my place, Sir James?"

"That's a very good idea, Brigadier. When is the reception?"

"It's the day after tomorrow at eight in the evening. I'll send a note to Al Hafrey first thing in the morning," the brigadier replied.

After dinner, Sir James said goodnight to the brigadier and retired to his room, where he sat down to and wrote his first letter to Sabrina from Aden.

**

c/o Brigadier James Cartwright

Post Office

Aden

29 September

My very dear Sabrina,

As you can see, I have safely reached Aden after a short but exceedingly boring voyage, during which I could do nothing more than eat, sleep, and exercise. The only enjoyable element of the journey was that I had many free hours, during which I could indulge myself in joyful recollections of the exceedingly happy weeks we spent together.

I miss you more than I can express in words and look forward to the arrival of your next letter. Unfortunately, that is a delight that will have to wait until it is forwarded from Cairo and I return from a journey into the interior of the country and can receive it. Likewise, my next letter to you must wait upon my return from my journey, so do not be alarmed if you do not receive a letter for several weeks after you receive this one.

I have no interesting news to impart. In my defence, I can only write that I haven't been here long enough to meet any of my fellow countrymen, except the brigadier, and so have no knowledge of the trials and tribulations they are overcoming in this far away and barren land.

Tomorrow, I must start the assignment the government has given me and do so with a little apprehension as I know next to nothing about this locality.

I send you my love, dearest lady,

James.

***

Early next morning, and smartly dressed in civilian clothes, Sir James left the brigadier's villa and walked down to the port, where he hoped to renew his acquaintanceship with the Harbour Master, Captain Raj Shah.

Captain Shah, who had retired from the Indian Navy following a long and successful career, came to Aden to take up the vacant post of Harbour Master and had lived in Crater for some years. As one of the senior officials in the protectorate, he had met a large number of people in the course of his duties, and as a result, he was quite well informed about the important members of the populace, and also about local culture.

It was this knowledge that Sir James hoped to explore without giving any hint of his real interests.

It was some time since they had last met, and Sir James was very pleased to see the friendliness in Captain Shah's eyes as he emerged from the Harbour Master's Office and feel the welcoming grip of his hand.

"Sir James, come in, come in!" Captain Shah said as he led his guest inside the small office and gestured towards a chair opposite his desk. As he took his seat, Sir James glanced out of the large window at the bustling harbour and wondered how Captain Shah managed to keep track of the multitude of different vessels that continually came and went from the port. The Captain continued to speak as he cleared a space among some of the charts and assorted papers strewn across the desk, " This is an unexpected honour. When did you return to Aden?"

"Yesterday, during the late morning, Captain," Sir James responded.

"And as I am the first person you have visited, you must need some information. Just like the last time. Is that not so, Sir James?" he asked astutely.

"Yes, you are, and yes, I do," Sir James said with a grin.

The door opened and a servant walked in carrying an Arabic coffee pot in one hand and a small stack of tiny ceramic cups without handles.

"Gawa?" Captain Shah asked.

"Yes please," Sir James responded and watched with awe the accuracy with which the servant directed a stream of coffee from the bird's beak mouth of the coffee pot into the cup. The pot was in his left hand at head height and the cups in his right hand at waist level and not a drop was splashed or spilled. Sir James accepted his cup and drank it with relish.

"You like the coffee, Sir James?" Captain Shah asked.

"Very much, Captain," Sir James responded. "I think it must be the cardamom that gives it the special flavour. I enjoy watching your man pour it, as well, of course. His skill is phenomenal."

Sir James accepted a second cup without thinking. He tasted it and savoured the aroma and said, "Mmm!"

"Did you enjoy your leave, Sir James? I remember that you were not very enthusiastic about returning home when your tour of duty came to an end."

In a very serious tone of voice, Sir James said, "As you say, Captain, I didn't want to return to England. There seemed to be no point, but I decided that I should make the effort if only to see my mother, and in the end, it proved to be the best decision I have ever taken in my life."

They accepted another cup of Gawa each as Captain Shah asked, "Why was that?"

"I met a young lady who has promised to be my wife," Sir James said proudly. "And this time, I'm impatient to return home so that we can be married."

With a big beaming smile, Captain Shah stood and held out his hand as he said, "Please accept my congratulations, Sir James. I hope you and your future wife will be very happy."

"Thank you, Captain. I'll tell Sabrina what you said, and I'll send you an invitation to our wedding. It's a long way to travel, but I hope you will be able to attend."

"I'll certainly try, but it will depend on circumstances here, as I am sure you will understand," Captain Shah responded.

"Absolutely," Sir James answered, and both men shook their empty cups from side to side to signify that they wanted no more of the Arabic coffee.

When the servant had collected their cups, he left the room, and then, very aware of the old adage that walls have ears, Sir James said circumspectly, "I hear that there are some archaeological expeditions based in Crater?"

"That's correct, Sir James. One is German and the other is French. I didn't know you were interested in archaeology?" he added, curiosity apparent in his voice.

"Not many people do," Sir James responded. "I was reading archaeology at university, but I gave that up to be a soldier and have never gone back. I still have a passion for the subject, and as I am here and have time, it would be of interest to talk to the archaeologists and possibly visit one of the digs."

"I recommend that you talk to Hans Richter," Captain Shah said immediately. "He is the leader of the German expedition and speaks excellent English. I'll give you a note of introduction if you wish?"

"Yes please, Captain," Sir James replied.

"Can I help you with anything else, Sir James?" Captain Shah asked as he wrote the introduction.

"Do you know a local man called Jalal Al Hafrey?"

"Naturally, I've met the man in the course of my duties, but I wouldn't say I know him," Captain Shah said, accidentally echoing Brigadier Cartwright's response as he said it. "Why do you ask?" Captain Shah asked.

Intentionally using the comment he had made to Brigadier Cartwright the previous evening, Sir James said, "I saw him at a reception on board HMS Neptune last year and heard afterwards that he had gone to Oxford. He must have been very well-educated, as well as intelligent, to be accepted at such a prestigious college, and I was a little intrigued by the man. I haven't had the pleasure of meeting him yet, but I expect to tomorrow evening. I think it would be useful to know something of the man before we meet."

Captain Shah sat in thought for several minutes, and after he had assembled his thoughts, he said, "There is fact and there is conjecture. I'll start with the little factual information I have. Jalal Al Hafrey is the eldest son of Sheikh Mohammad Al Hafrey, who is the ruler of a big tract of barren desert north of here. When his father dies, Jalal Al Hafrey will be the next sheikh and inherit responsibility for his people, but he will have no money with which to improve their standard of living. I know he went to England for his senior education as I have seen him on a number of occasions when he embarked on a ship and when he came home. He lives in quite a large house and entertains lavishly. Do you wish to hear the conjecture as well, Sir James?"

"Naturally," Sir James responded.

"It is rumoured that he receives a very good monthly stipend from a foreign government, and that would certainly account for his ability to live like a rich man rather than an impoverished local. There are also rumours that he is a very short-tempered and vicious man. I must emphasise, Sir James, that these are not facts, but it would be as well to bear them in mind if you meet him."

Captain Shah finished writing the letter of introduction to the archaeologist, and after stamping it, scribbled his signature and handed it to Sir James.

"I must thank you for your time and knowledge, Captain. I am very appreciative of both and will call and see you again before I leave Aden."

With that, the two men shook hands. Captain Shah returned to his desk, and Sir James went in search of a gentleman called Hans Richter.

CHAPTER FIVE
Exposed

Crater wasn't a large town, and it didn't take Sir James very long to walk along a sand track and past a small mosque to the location he had been given by Captain Shah. As the captain had said, there were several walled villas there.

They were all of typically Arab construction, and he stopped at the fourth, past the mosque.

High, plain, plastered mud-brick walls surrounded and protected whatever was built inside the enclosure. There was a large entrance closed with two big doors of sun-bleached carved timber studded with square-headed iron nails. In one entrance, there was a small wicket door. If Captain Shah had not described the distinctive carving in the middle panel of the wicket, Sir James would have been unable to distinguish which of the half dozen or so residences in the area was the one he wanted. The dusty fronds of several date palms drooped over the wall and rustled occasionally when a short-lived current of hot air stirred them into motion.

There was no knocker or bell rope, and Sir James had to make do with his fist. He tried rapping the door with his knuckles, but it was so heavily built he made an insignificant amount of noise and hurt his knuckles as he rapped. The side of his clenched fist made a more satisfactory thudding noise, and after banging for some minutes, he heard the metallic scraping and rattle of a bolt being withdrawn on the other side of the gate. The door creaked partially open, and a wizened brown face surmounted by an untidily wound, off-white turban peered out.

He opened his mouth, exposing a few brown teeth and a great deal of pink gum and said something unintelligible in an old and quavering voice.

"Sabaah al khayr, *Good morning*" Sir James said quietly, "Ismi James Russell *I am James Russell.*"

There was no verbal response, and the old man simply stood in the gap of the partially open door and stared at Russell.

Sir James said, "Uriid atkallam ma' ya sayyed Hans Richter*I would like to speak to Mr Hans Richter.*"

The man stood and stared a moment longer, then stepped back and closed the door. Sir James heard the bolt squeak back into place, then there was silence and he could do no more than stand in the sun on the sand outside the gate, feeling like a beggar.

Sir James made a careful inspection of the construction of the gate, but after several minutes of this pointless time-filling activity, he began to wonder if he should leave and try again another day. Just as he was about to turn away, he heard the scraping rattle of the bolt and the wicket opened again. This time, it opened wide, and framed in the opening was a blond-haired, blue-eyed European man dressed in a khaki bush shirt and jodhpurs. The tops of a pair of highly polished riding boots were visible above the threshold of the opening.

The blue eyes quickly examined Sir James, and a cultured voice stated, "You must be English. My name is Richter, Hans Richter."

Sir James extended his hand as he said, "My name is Russell, and I have a short note of introduction from Captain Shah." He passed the note to Hans Richter, who took it and quickly read it.

"Please come in, Mr Russell," Richter said as he stepped back from the wicket door. Sir James had to bend his head low and step over a high threshold to enter and realised as he did so that the old-fashioned design was quite a good defence. It would have been impossible for a normal-sized man to attack through the opening with a sword.

Once inside, he straightened himself and realised that he was a good head taller than the German archaeologist, although Russell noted that he moved like an athlete. The courtyard was such a contrast to the sandy street outside that Sir James could not prevent an involuntary gasp of pleasure as he took in the cool verdant expanse of flowers and shrubs surrounding the tiled courtyard.

"What a lovely place to live," Sir James said admiringly.

"It is, and the credit must go to Ali Mohammad, who is the gardener here," said Richter as he pointed to the man who had answered Russell's knock on the gate. Ali Mohammad recognised the surprised pleasure in Sir James' expression and smiled broadly in turn.

"Ali Mohammad cannot speak," Richter said apropos of nothing. "He was on the wrong side of an argument and had his tongue cut out."

"I wondered why he didn't respond when I spoke," Sir James said in a matter-of-fact way, and then when the fact of the mutilation registered, he added with a real note of horror in his voice, "When did it happen? I thought that sort of barbarism had died out hundreds of years ago."

"No!" said Richter without elaboration. "Some people still do it as a warning to others."

"I cannot imagine anyone so depraved," Sir James exclaimed with revulsion.

"You were in the war?" Richter asked, and when Russell nodded, he went on. "Then you must know that quite normal people carry out the most brutal acts at times."

"Yes," said Russell, "In the heat of the moment, that is true, but what was done here was deliberate brutality. Do you know who it was?"

Richter chose not to argue the point and simply answered the question. "Yes, of course I know who wielded the knife. I think I know, but what I cannot prove, is who ordered the man with the knife to use it. Exacting revenge on the servant will not stop his master ordering someone else to do the same thing on another occasion, and stopping the master is important."

"I see," said Sir James, who looked as if he intended to pursue the subject until Richter said, "In any event, that is not your problem, Mr Russell, so how can I help you?"

"I was in university and had started studying archaeology when I became involved in the war."

Richter interrupted, "Officer Class," he said, "Not cannon fodder." They were statements, not questions.

"Yes, I was an officer," said Sir James Russell. "But that didn't stop me being shot at by your countrymen."

"How do you know it wasn't me, Mr Russell?" Hans Richter asked cheerfully.

"I don't," he answered tartly, then after a second or so said with a grin, "But I'm very pleased you were such a rotten shot."

"Come and have a coffee, Mr Russell," Richter said cheerfully. "And you can tell me how I can help you."

"Thank you, Herr Richter," Sir James responded as he followed his host into his living quarters.

Several hours and many coffees later, Sir James set off on the walk back to the brigadier's compound, pleased that he had been able to persuade Hans Richter to show him one of the digs later in the week. As he walked, he reflected on the fact that the two people he had shared with coffee today had been sworn enemies just a few years before and had been trying desperately to kill each other. *I'm pleased we were unsuccessful,* he thought, *Hans Richter is quite a pleasant man.*

How he was going to persuade Richter to lend him a horse or a camel he didn't yet know, but he was certain a solution to that problem would present itself when the time was ripe.

Sir James had dinner with the brigadier and told him what he had been doing with his time during the day, more to punctuate the rattle of knives and forks on ceramic plates than from any strong desire to hold a conversation.

"Jalal Al Hafrey has agreed to you attending the reception in my place," the brigadier announced as he reached for the brandy decanter. After Sir James had refused, he poured himself a large measure and sniffed at it appreciatively.

"You should have one, Sir James," the brigadier boomed. "Good for the digestion, you know."

"So I have heard," Sir James agreed. "But tonight, I don't think I will join you."

"All the more for me, then," the brigadier said as he downed the last of the first brandy and poured a second just as big as the first.

After a decent interval, Sir James retired for the night.

***

Sir James presented himself at the main entrance to Jalal Al Hafrey's residence at the time indicated on the invitation and was directed across a large, tiled courtyard towards a wide doorway leading into the majlis by a servant. He took off his shoes outside the door and lined them up against the wall beside the many pairs of sandals that had been abandoned to the right of the opening.

He stepped inside and immediately understood what Captain Shah had meant when he said Al Hafrey lived like a rich man.

The floor was covered with large thick carpets that Sir James thought were Persian. There were many richly-covered cushions in reds and greens laid out against the two side walls in horizontal and vertical rows where the guests who had already arrived reclined at ease and drank gawa from small, decorated ceramic cups passed to them by attentive servants. At the end of the majlis opposite the door, the floor level had been raised to form a carpeted dais on which the cushions were thicker and covered with a golden material. There was a pattern on the cushions that Sir James believed to be woven from gold thread by the way it shimmered in the light from the candles that illuminated the room. Two men reclined on the cushions on the dais. One was clearly an Arab and the other was, with equal certainty, a European. They were deep in conversation as Sir James entered.

The Arab was Jalal Al Hafrey, and he hadn't noticeably changed in appearance since Sir James had last seen him. He was a dark-skinned, bearded young man dressed in traditional Arabic clothing. Sir James noted that he was wearing a Bisht in dark brown cloth, trimmed with gold lace.

Al Hafrey noticed the new arrival and stood up slowly, rising from the cushions with the fluid ease of an uncoiling snake. He was quite a slim young man and about a head shorter than Sir James. The European on the other hand was a much more heavily built man and struggled to get up from the floor, eventually untangling himself from the sumptuous cushions with some difficulty. He was not quite as tall as Al Hafrey and stood sweating beside Al Hafrey in crumpled clothing that was completely unsuitable for the climate. Sir James was unable to identify anything in the clothing that gave a clue to the man's origins, and as he didn't deign to greet Russell, there was no accent he could use for identification.

"Sir James Russell, I imagine?" Al Hafrey said in public school English.

"That is correct, sir," answered Sir James, assuming that 'sir' would be a sufficient honorific for the son of a sheikh.

It wasn't, and Al Hafrey responded sharply and immediately with, "I prefer 'Sheikh', Sir James. 'Sir' doesn't adequately describe my status."

"I beg your pardon, Sheikh," Sir James apologised, knowing that he had been wrong-footed by his host.

"Come and sit down, Sir James," and Al Hafrey gestured towards the cushions on the dais.

"Thank you, Sheikh," Sir James said politely and subsided quite gracefully on to the cushions for a big man. Al Hafrey's European companion, on the other hand, plumped down on the cushions with all the grace of a collapsing sack of potatoes.

Al Hafrey stared at his new guest for a few moments with an expression on his face that reminded Sir James of a hunter appraising a prize stag. A servant offered a ceramic demitasse of coffee and hovered nearby waiting to refill it after Sir James had drunk the first one.

"Major Sir James Russell MC, DSO," said Al Hafrey, "I wondered when I would meet you."

Sir James was momentarily nonplussed by the inference that Al Hafrey had known for some time that he was coming to Aden and drew the only possible conclusion.

"I assume the brigadier told you something about me?"

"Dear me, no," Al Hafrey exclaimed with a short, mirthless laugh, in which his companion joined. "It would be interesting to toy with you, Sir James, but I will not put you in an invidious position and ask you pointed questions to which you can only reply with half-truths or lies. I have known for some time that Sir William Ellis had sent you to meet me, and I know also the reason why your government is interested in a dialogue between us. You are too late. I have a satisfactory agreement with the government this gentleman represents and have no desire to change anything now."

Sir James said nothing.

There was nothing for him to say.

The secrecy with which his assignment had been veiled had clearly been ineffective. The truth was known, and that was the end of the matter. As a soldier, he had learned when to stand and fight and also when a strategic withdrawal was a more appropriate course of action.

"I cannot deny the accuracy of your statements, Sheikh. If you have already concluded an agreement with this gentleman's government. there is nothing for me to do. If you will excuse me, I will take my leave."

"I can certainly understand your desire to leave, Sir James, and I have no objection," and he started to turn towards his companion in an obvious and deliberate gesture of dismissal. Then he turned back, and the expression on his face was unmistakeably malevolent as he said harshly, "Do not meddle in my affairs, Major. If you ignore my warning, you will regret your temerity when you discover that your fiancée will not have much use for a eunuch." And this time Al Hafrey did turn and present his back to Sir James.

Sir James couldn't prevent an involuntary shudder of horrified revulsion passing through his body, but then he steeled himself, rose to his feet with commendable suppleness, and walked from the majlis into the moonlight with his head held proudly erect.

Sir James walked briskly along the sandy streets and passageways that led towards the brigadier's villa, and as he walked, he reviewed the unexpected events of the evening.

Fortunately, he was not so deeply immersed in his thoughts that he was unaware of his surroundings, and when he heard an unexpected sound behind him, he turned towards it and dropped into a defensive crouch. The figure that had launched itself at Sir James' back was taken by surprise and tripped over his shoulder to lie sprawling in the dust. Sir James immediately turned again, dived onto his assailant, and was in turn thrown to one side, and the wind was knocked out of his lungs as he landed awkwardly on his back. Sir James could see his attacker kneeling in the sand a few feet away and could also see the moonlight shine on the blade of the wicked-looking knife he held firmly in his hand. Sir James was unarmed and knew his life was in extreme danger but could do nothing about it as he was still gasping for air.

He saw the knife curve up and back as his attacker prepared to stab down into his chest as he struggled ineffectually to move. He knew his last seconds had come, and he felt suddenly so sad that he was going to die so pointlessly in this small, dirty town.

"No, you don't," said a voice. Then there was a noise like two pieces of wood being smacked together, and Sir James' attacker collapsed into the dust.

A strong pair of hands caught hold of his shoulders and pulled Sir James to his feet.

"Are you hurt, sir?" Tucker asked.

"No! Thanks to you. Another few seconds and he would have probably murdered me. How did you happen to be here?"

"Brigadier sent me to escort you home, sir, but you left the reception earlier than the brigadier expected," Tucker explained.

"It was rather earlier than I expected," Sir James said but didn't elaborate.

"It's just as well you came back by the most direct route, sir," Tucker said simply.

"I agree," said Sir James. "But what do we do with him?" he asked gently, prodding his assailant with the toe of his shoe.

"Leave him there, I think, sir. He'll wake up in a while with a bad headache and then go back to the hole in the rocks he calls home, I imagine. I expect he'll try to rob someone else tomorrow night."

Sir James decided to leave the matter there, but he wasn't at all convinced that his attacker had been a robber. It was too soon after leaving Jalal Al Hafrey for him to be convinced that there was no connection between the sheikh's warning and the attack, but he couldn't be certain.

Back at the villa, Sir James asked Tucker to arrange for him to see the brigadier in the morning and then went to his room, where he examined his bruises and thanked his lucky stars that he didn't have a big hole somewhere in his body. Before retiring for the night, Sir James carefully thought over what had happened, decided what his course of action had to be, and also decided that he would take the brigadier into his confidence and no one else.

With that, he went to bed and, quite remarkably, slept like a baby.

After breakfast, Sir James joined the brigadier in his meeting room cum office, and after they were both seated, he said, "I would like to take you into my confidence as I think it important that someone in authority knows what has occurred. Is that acceptable to you, Brigadier?"

"Yes, of course," he said.

"Very well," said Sir James, and he described in some detail the meeting he had attended at the Colonial Office in London and the great emphasis that had been placed on secrecy.

Sir James went on, "Clearly there was someone at the meeting who is in the pay of a foreign government."

"A confounded spy," the brigadier interrupted.

"Exactly so," Sir James agreed and then continued. "And clearly that spy has passed on the details of my mission to Al Hafrey and his supporter. Do you have any idea who the man with Al Hafrey could be, Brigadier? He wasn't introduced to me but was clearly a European. He was a dark-haired man of medium height and heavy build."

"The man who is most often seen with Al Hafrey is Luigi Stromboli from the Italian Embassy in Cairo. He would fit your description," the brigadier said.

"Thank you, Brigadier," Sir James then, then resumed his explanation. "I can do no more here as Al Hafrey has made it quite clear that an approach from our government will not be welcome. To my mind, it is very important that I return to England as quickly and quietly as possible to alert Sir William Ellis that he has a spy in his group. Do you agree with my conclusion, Brigadier?"

"Yes, most definitely," the Brigadier responded. "And if anyone asks about you, they can be told that you are in the interior for a few weeks."

"Thank you, Brigadier," Sir James said. "Now all I have to do is get on a ship back to England as soon as possible."

"That's easy to arrange, I think, as I know there is a ship from P&O passing through here this afternoon. I'll send Tucker to the agent to arrange for you to have a passage on her and then he can pack your things and escort you on board."

"Thank you, Brigadier," Sir James said. "And perhaps Tucker could deliver a note to Hans Richter for me after I have left?"

"Of course," responded Brigadier James Cartwright.

And so, a little more than three days after arriving in Aden on a next to impossible mission, Sir James left for England, hoping that he was taking the correct action.

There had been no time to write to Sabrina and indeed there had been no point. He would be in England as quickly as a letter and seeing her in person was infinitely better than pen, ink, and paper.

CHAPTER SIX
Dismissed

Twelve days later, Sir James disembarked at Southampton and caught the boat train into London, where he alighted at Waterloo Station and hired a cab. Thirty minutes later, he had settled into his room at the Bertram Club.

His first priority was to arrange a private meeting with Sir William Ellis at a venue remote from the Colonial Office. He settled down to write a letter that was going to have a fundamental effect on his life and future career.

***

Bertram Club

15 October

Sir William Ellis

Colonial Office

London

Dear Sir William,

I have arranged for this letter to be delivered to you in person and not to your secretary as is customary, as I believe it is essential that the content of the letter and the identity of the author should remain confidential until after we have had the opportunity to meet. When I have imparted the information that I have gleaned during my short time in Aden, you will be able to decide on an appropriate course of action.

Until we meet, I will only say that your plans have been seriously compromised.

In order to maintain an appropriate level of confidentiality, I respectfully request you to come on your own to the Bertram Club as soon as possible.

Yours sincerely

Signed: Sir James Russell.

Russell went downstairs with his carefully addressed and sealed letter and arranged for the Chief Porter to send one of his staff to the Colonial Office to deliver it.

"He is to give the letter to Sir William Ellis and no one else. Is that clear, Giles?" Sir James instructed.

"Perfectly clear, Sir James," the Chief Porter responded.

"Please advise me as soon as your messenger returns after delivering the letter."

"Yes, Sir," Giles said.

Sir James Russell returned to his room to wait. And he had to wait quite a long time before there was a knock on his door, and when he opened it, he was astounded to see Sir William Ellis standing on the threshold.

"Good afternoon, Sir William," Sir James managed to say as he recovered from his surprise. "I'm very pleased to see you. Please come in."

Sir William walked into the room and sat on the chair indicated by Sir James.

"I have come like a thief in the night in response to your summons, and I hope you will be able to justify the secrecy you have insisted upon," Sir William said angrily.

"You will be better able to make a judgement when you have heard what I have to relate, Sir William, and I would remind you that I am not known for wasting the time of government employees."

"Really," Sir William said in an unfriendly tone. "There is always the first time. Well? What have you to tell me?"

Sir James started with his arrival in Aden and his discussion with Brigadier Cartwright that led to the chance to meet Al Hafrey at his reception. He relayed what he had learnt about Jalal Al Hafrey from Captain Shah and the financial aid he was rumoured to receive from a foreign government that supported his lavish lifestyle. Russell described his meeting with Hans Richter and the arrangements he had made to go into the hinterland to try to locate the boundary by using the archaeological expeditions as a cover.

"I was convinced that I had attracted no undue attention and no one could possibly have known that I was acting in secret under your direct instructions, Sir William."

"The committee's instructions," Sir William corrected as he sought automatically to minimise any risk to himself by dividing responsibility amongst the other committee members.

Sir James ignored the comment and continued, "I went to Al Hafrey's reception with an easy mind, expecting to meet a man socially that I hoped to do business with. I was received cordially enough, but it soon transpired that Al Hafrey not only knew who I was but also why I was in Aden, and then he named you, Sir William, as the man who had sent me. He also made it abundantly clear that any overtures from our government would be unwelcome as he was quite content with the arrangements he had negotiated. Clearly, Sir William, the veil of secrecy with which you tried to conceal my venture has failed entirely. That means that a member of the committee you promulgated or someone in the Colonial Office who has access to secret discussions is a spy for a foreign government. I returned in secret to London, Sir William, and insisted on a private meeting with you, because I believe there is a better chance of catching the spy if our discovery of his existence remains a secret for as long as possible."

"I cannot believe it. You must be mistaken!" Sir William blustered. "I know all the men appointed to the committee. I handpicked most of them and no one has put a foot wrong since they joined the Colonial Office."

"Spies, who are wrong-footed, Sir William, rarely survive long as spies. In my opinion, you need to take immediate steps to isolate everyone who was at that meeting to prevent any collusion and then appoint someone to check each man thoroughly. I am quite prepared to be examined if that should be considered necessary."

Sir William had become very pale as the implications of Sir James' revelations registered, and unusually for him, he was also speechless for a few minutes as he saw himself standing on the brink of a personal disaster if one of his appointees proved to be working for a foreign power. He would be considered culpable and would be extremely lucky to retain his position. He racked his brains, trying to find a way out of the dilemma Sir James had presented. His immediate reaction was to try to find a way to blame Russell, but he soon realised that he would not be able to achieve that very desirable aim on his own.

He had accepted Sir James' request for a meeting away from the FO and now realised that in so doing, he had separated himself from all the resources and trappings of power that his office gave him. Consequently, he would have to appear to be cooperative until he could see how the matter could be resolved, but by then, Sir William knew, matters could be very different.

He couldn't reject Sir James' advice to examine each man individually, although he desperately wanted to, but if he accepted it, whom could he appoint to conduct the enquiry in sufficient secrecy?

It had to be someone who was not employed by his department so that no one could charge him with manipulating the truth to protect a crony. He could think of no one who was independent enough, and was at the point of asking Sir James if he could recommend someone when Sir William had an inspiration.

"The person who examines the committee members," he said to Sir James. "He has to be a man of standing and also outside my department. As you indicated, Sir James, the enquiry has to be conducted in secrecy to avoid alerting the spy. If a government official with sufficient standing to conduct such a delicate enquiry suddenly disappears from his office, tongues will begin to wag, and that would be most undesirable, as I'm sure you will agree?"

"Indeed I do, Sir William," agreed Sir James, wondering where this analysis was leading.

He was not left in doubt for very long.

"The only person I know who meets all my requirements is you, Sir James. You are not a member of my department. You are a man of impeccable integrity, and as you are officially in Aden, no one knows you are here. You are the ideal person to conduct the enquiry in the shortest possible time, and I entreat you to accept the responsibility and rid our country of a traitor."

"I must give the matter some thought, Sir William. It is an honour to be asked ,but it is also a very onerous task, particularly as I will feel responsible for the execution of the man who is found guilty. In war, the death of an enemy spy is a regrettable expedient, but in peace, the death of a countryman, even if he is a traitor, is quite another matter. Please come back in an hour, Sir William, and I will give you my answer."

Sir William stood and started to walk toward the door. When he reached it, he stopped with his hand on the door handle and stared back at Sir James, who was still in his seat.

"I'll return in an hour, Sir James," he said cooperatively then added pompously, "And I hope you will find it in your heart to take on this unpleasant duty for the sake of our country."

Sir William opened the door and then closed it after he was in the corridor.

Sir James didn't move. He continued to sit as Sir William had last observed him and tried to decide between duty and personal desire. Should he accept and find the traitor or should he decline and return to Brantley Manor and Sabrina? He decided first one way and then equally strongly the other. He was still oscillating between the two extremes when Sir William tapped on the door and re-entered Sir James' room.

"Have you decided?" Sir William enquired anxiously.

"Yes, I'll conduct the enquiry," Sir James exclaimed, although a millisecond before he spoke, he was quite certain he would decline.

"I'm very relieved," Sir William exclaimed and then asked, "Have you decided how to conduct the enquiry and where it will be held?"

"No, not yet. First of all, Sir William, I need to examine the personal files of all the people on or below your grade who attended the meeting. You can arrange to have them sent here by special messenger in the morning, and I'll make my initial review here in my room."

"Certainly, Sir James," Sir William agreed with relief apparent in his voice. "I'll arrange that immediately." As he turned to leave the room to return to the Colonial Office, he said, "I cannot believe one of my staff is responsible, Sir James, and if you have no objection, I will return here in the morning and we can perhaps review what you have discovered over a cup of coffee."

Sir James thought *why is coffee important?* as he said, "I think it will be difficult for you to be seen to be impartial if you come and review the evidence, Sir William, but you would be welcome to join me for a coffee."

"You are correct, of course," Sir William replied and once more turned towards the door.

"Wait, Sir William," Sir James exclaimed as the reason why coffee seemed important flashed into his mind. "There were caterers serving coffee and other refreshments between the meetings of the committee at the Colonial Office. I want their personal details as well, but if you are as certain of the probity of the men you have appointed as you say, you had better send me the details of the catering staff involved first."

"That's a brilliant thought, Sir James," Sir William said in a honeyed voice whilst he ground his teeth together in vexation at being given orders by such a junior diplomat. "I'll ensure you receive all the records you have asked for as quickly as possible in the morning."

"Thank you, Sir William," Sir James responded. "And please do not speak about this matter to anyone."

"Naturally," Sir William said but sounded more than a little huffy as his desire to appear cooperative started to wear a little thin.

Sir James ate a good dinner and retired to bed quite early, which proved to be a mistake as his thoughts prevented sleep for a long time. He wanted to do his duty and he wanted to go to Sabrina at the same time, and he went around and around the conflicting desires, unable to find a solution. In the end, he slept and dreamt improbable dreams of courts of enquiry and executions, and all the time, Sabrina in various roles flitted in and out of the dreams. He woke in the early hours bathed in sweat and just able to recall that in his last nightmare he had put duty above all else and shot the traitor only to find that he had executed Sabrina by mistake.

He didn't sleep again and in the morning was relieved to get up and start a new day.

Still affected by his dream, he didn't have an enjoyable breakfast, and when he returned to his room, the arrival of a messenger from the Colonial Office with a pile of manila folders did nothing to lift his spirits.

The messenger also delivered a note from Sir William confirming that he had supplied the files for all the committee members, going on to explain that the files for the catering staff would be delivered later in the morning as they had to come from a different department.

Sir James settled himself at the desk and started to read through the personnel files that had been delivered. As he read each file, he started to make brief notes about education, income, appointments, membership of political or other clubs, and so on. He wasn't searching for a specific characteristic but hoped to find something that marked out a particular person as different and worthy of further examination.

At the end of some hours of concentration, he had been struck only by the strong similarity between the records he had been studying. He leant back in his chair and thought about what he had read. They all had the same sort of background, education, and position on the Colonial Office pay scale, but there were no private details that could hint at financial or other difficulties that could lead a man to betray his country.

The messenger from the Colonial Office returned with another bundle of manila folders, and shortly afterwards, Sir William arrived. Sir James sent for coffee, and then he and Sir William sat in chairs on opposite sides of the desk with the two piles of manila folders between them.

As he put his hand on the larger of the two piles, Sir James said, "These are the personal files of the committee members, and I have read through all of them. There is nothing in any of them that would indicate that one of these men has led anything but a blameless, professional life."

A smile spread across Sir William's face, and he released a big sigh of relief at Sir James' words, but his pleasure was short-lived as Sir James went on. "However the records provide no information about the private lives of any of these individuals. We do not know if they have financial or other problems that would leave them vulnerable to blackmail by a foreign government, for example. All I can say is, so far so good. Now that I have the records of the catering staff, I will examine them next and see what I can discover."

"I hope you can discover something soon, Sir James. I cannot conceal this disaster from my superiors for much longer."

"I understand, and will do my best to resolve the matter as quickly as possible," Sir James said, although he didn't feel as confident of a quick resolution as he sounded.

Sir William departed as soon as he had drunk his coffee, and Russell set to work on the records of the catering staff and took notes of the salient features, as he had done before. Not unexpectedly, there was almost no similarity between the six men who had served the refreshments that day.

They had experienced different levels of schooling. Most had gone to an elementary school; one had completed an apprenticeship in a tailor's shop; and one had managed to almost completely avoid the statutory education. They came from different parts of the British Isles and had the sort of nondescript surnames that fill large sections of a telephone directory. As with the committee members, there was nothing in the records that gave a lead to the private lives of the six men.

Rather disconsolately, Sir James started to look at the documents again, and as he hadn't bothered to look at them previously, he started to read the Christian names, and they seemed to be as nondescript as the surnames. There was David, Michael, Maurice, John, Alex, and another David.

Nothing remarkable there, he thought, *except there was something about Alex that tickled my memory.*

Sir James looked at the Jones folder again and found, just as his memory said it would, that the Christian name was written as 'Alex'. There was another name written in parentheses immediately afterwards. Now 'Alex' is usually the abbreviation for 'Alexander', and in a way, this was correct as the name in parentheses was 'Alessandro', which, Sir James knew, was the Italian equivalent of 'Alexander'.

Now that's an unusual Christian name for someone from this green and sceptred isle, Sir James thought and then sat bolt upright in his chair as the connection sent a shock through his body. Al Hafrey's confidante was Italian and suddenly there was an Italian Christian name turning up in London in the middle of a search for a spy in the Colonial Office.

Coincidence? Sir James wondered.

Probably, he thought, *but it's the only lead we have at present, so we have to follow it. But how do we follow it?*

Sir James decided that he needed to consult Sir William Ellis and was about to ask the Chief Porter to send someone to Sir Williams' office when that worthy arrived. Ellis was far too anxious about his future wellbeing to sit calmly in an office and pretend that his world was not about to collapse around his ears.

He had barely sat down before he said quickly, "I hope you have some good news for me, Sir James?"

"I have discovered a possible and very fragile link between one of the catering staff and the country that supports Al Hafrey," Sir James said carefully.

"Give me his name," Sir William demanded, "and I'll have him arrested immediately. Quickly now, there is no time to lose."

What Sir William meant was that no time should be lost ensuring that he was blameless, and consequently, Sir James' next comment came as something of a shock.

"Certainly not, Sir William," Sir James said. "We do not know enough to be able to arrest the man and keep him in prison for any length of time. In any event, we can learn far more if we allow him some freedom of movement and study what he does and who he meets."

"I must report to my superiors, Sir James. But what can I tell them?"

"Only the truth, Sir William; the simple, plain, and unvarnished truth," said Sir James.

"That's very easy for you to say, Sir James," Sir William said, and the concern he felt about his future made his voice tremble from the tension. "If the government's policy fails, then a scapegoat is sought, and at the moment, I will be seen as the sacrificial lamb."

"Perhaps I should come with you, Sir William, as I am able to brief them first-hand about events in Aden and the research I have been doing."

As his spirits rose for the first time that day, Sir William quickly said in agreement, "A very good idea," as he assumed that Sir James hadn't realised that his presence would deflect interest from himself and onto Sir James.

His spirits fell again as Sir James said, "As you are the chairman of the committee, I have to report to you, Sir William, and I believe it's necessary to support you as far as I am able. But with your experience, you must surely understand that the ultimate responsibility remains with you."

Probably for the first time in his professional life, Sir William was speechless. He could think of nothing to say that would refute the statement he had just heard, and his spirits sank even lower.

Sir James piled up all the manila folders and put them in a drawer, which he then locked. He stared at Sir William for a moment before breaking the lengthening silence.

"Tomorrow is Friday, and it will be difficult for you to arrange a meeting during the day. Consequently, I plan to return home in the morning and come back on Monday. I recommend that you arrange a meeting on Monday afternoon with the minimum possible number of senior people. I further recommend that the venue for the meeting is outside the Colonial Office so that no one is alerted to our current predicament inadvertently. Is that acceptable to you, Sir William?"

"Yes," Sir William agreed unhappily, as he would have preferred the meeting to be held immediately. But he knew better than most that it would be next to impossible to arrange a meeting at such short notice without everyone assuming there was a much worse crisis. Sir James' proposal would bring everyone together quickly enough and, more importantly, calmly.

"Very well, Sir William, I will return here before midday, and you can leave a message for me with the Chief Porter, giving the time and place for the meeting."

Sir James studied his companion for a few moments then said, "I do not think you should be overly concerned, Sir William. If the waiter proves to be the culprit, you can hardly be blamed for the results of his espionage. You did not employ him."

"Thank you for those words of support, Sir James. I will bid you goodnight and hope you have a very pleasant few days at home."

"Thank you, Sir William," Sir James responded as he showed his companion to the door and let him out into the corridor, saying as he did so, "Until Monday, Sir William," then closed the door on a retreating and despondent back.

Sir James had dinner and retired to bed. After a good night's sleep, he arose early and set off for Paddington Station before it was properly light. At the station, he had to wait twenty minutes for a train and alighted at Taplow station. He wondered if he should go immediately to Sabrina's home but decided it would be more sensible to get a horse cab to Brantley Manor, have breakfast, change, and then drive to Taplow in the Bentley.

Then I can give Sabrina a lovely surprise, he thought as he embarked on a daydream full of romantic and rosy feelings for the lady who would soon be his wife.

Consequently, a little more than an hour and a half later and still quite early in the morning, Sir James stopped the Bentley outside the Severn's house. He knocked on the front door, and when Elsie opened it, he held his forefinger across his lips to signify silence. Elsie complied, but a big smile of pleasure spread across her face.

He leant forward and whispered, "Is Miss Sabrina up?"

Elsie nodded vigorously and beckoned.

Sir James followed Elsie along the corridor towards the closed door to the room in the back of the house on tip toes. She knocked, stood back to allow Sir James to enter, which he did soundlessly, then followed him into the room and stood to one side.

Sabrina was sitting at the desk writing. Perhaps more accurately, she *had* been writing, but was now sitting with an exasperated expression on her face, staring out of the window as she tapped her teeth and sought inspiration.

Without turning around she asked, "What is it, Elsie?"

Elsie had entered into the part of Sir James' co-conspirator and said calmly, "You have a visitor, miss."

"I don't want to see anyone this morning," Sabrina said. "Please send whoever it is away."

"I cannot do that, miss," Elsie said cheerfully.

"Why can't you?" and Sabrina sounded quite angry but didn't turn away from the window.

"Surely you don't want me to send Sir James away, Miss Sabrina," Elsie said.

"What foolishness is that, Elsie?" Sabrina said sharply, and as she turned away from the window, she accidentally dropped her pen on the table with a clatter and caused a stream of ink blots to splatter all over her letter. She looked towards the doorway and saw a man standing beside Elsie. She thought, *That's James,* and then, *it cannot be James. He's in Aden. Isn't he? What's happening to me? Have I gone mad?*

Her face had gone quite pale, and with her hand on her heart, she managed to say, "Are you real?"

"Yes, Sabrina," Sir James answered. "I'm not a ghost. I'm really here, but I wish I hadn't given you such a shock," and he started to move across the room towards her.

She jumped to her feet and her chair clattered across the floor as she threw herself into his arms.

As he wrapped his arms around her shoulders, she managed to say, "My dearest man, you're really here. How marvellous! I cannot believe it! Do you have to go back?" Then her arms twined around his neck and further comment was prevented by a long and lingering kiss that was only momentarily disturbed by the sound of the door closing as Elsie discretely left the room.

Their embrace was disturbed a few moments later by a knock on the door, and as they moved slightly apart, Sabrina called, "Come in," and a visibly excited Mrs Severn rushed into the room.

"Sir James," she cried, "what a lovely surprise. But what has happened to bring you home so much earlier than you expected? Are you in good health? I do so hope that you will not have to return to those heathen lands," and she paused for breath.

Sir James said calmly, "Perhaps we should sit down, Mrs Severn, and I can tell you and Sabrina a little of what has occurred to bring me back to England."

"That's a very good idea.. Sabrina, please ring the bell and we will have some tea."

"No cake today, Mrs Severn?" Sir James teased gently.

"It's not fresh, Sir James," Mrs Severn said seriously.

"Oh, Mother!" said Sabrina. "You baked it yesterday, and I'm sure it will be just as delicious today."

"Indeed," Sir James agreed. "And it will be even more delicious as I haven't had a slice of your cake for months, Mrs Severn."

"Oh! Very well then," Mrs. Severn said, and Elsie was duly dispatched for tea and cake.

They sat down around the coffee table, and Sir James told the two ladies that his original mission to Aden had been unsuccessful, and he had thought it prudent to return to the Colonial Office to obtain further instructions in person.

Then Elsie brought in the tea and cake and there was a little general conversation about the weather and so on whilst Elsie was in the room.

"You shouldn't have worried, Mrs Severn," Sir James said after eating a mouthful of fruit cake, "It's as delicious as I expected."

Sabrina supported her future husband with, "There you are, Mother, I told you so," and gave her mother a hug.

Once Elsie had left the room, Sir James told Sabrina and her mother about his journey to Cairo and then onwards to Aden. He described the bustling activity at the ports, the sights and smells of the towns and the beautiful garden at Hans Richters residence. He also mentioned, although without going into any details about the reason for his visit there, the sumptuous décor at Al Hafrey's residence. The two ladies exclaimed over the extravagance of having real gold thread in cushions on the floor.

"Oh James, what an extraordinary place!" said Sabrina. "I can scarcely imagine it. I do hope that once we are married, I will have an opportunity to accompany you on your travels and experience it for myself."

"I would like that very much," he replied. "It is an interesting part of the world and their customs and traditions are very different to our own", *which can make my job somewhat trying at times,* he thought.

***

When he announced that he would return to London for a conference the next Monday, Sabrina was most displeased.

"You have only just come home after an absence of several months, James, and I don't want to lose you again so quickly. I need your help with the alterations in the West Wing. I could have managed if you had remained in Aden, but now you are home, your assistance will be invaluable."

"I do understand, Sabrina," Sir James said calmly. "But I have to resume my assignment as soon as possible and I am expected at the Colonial Office next week. I don't expect to be away more than a day or so After all, I should still be in Aden in all reality."

"Sorry, James," she said contritely. "I was being selfish and not thinking."

"Don't worry, Sabrina, I don't want to be away from you longer than duty demands. Would you like to come to Brantley Manor and show me how Charlie Hod is getting on?"

"Yes, very much," she said.

Ten minutes or so later, Sir James escorted Sabrina to the Bentley and helped her into the front passenger seat as he was driving and then held the rear door open for Elsie to get in.

He suddenly remembered Sabrina's letter and said, "I'm very sorry, Elsie, I should have congratulated you on your engagement! I hope you and Tompkins will be very happy when you set up house together, but I imagine that it will take some time to get everything in order. Do you have any idea when you and Tompkins will marry?"

Sir James was thinking in terms of nine to twelve months hence and was visibly surprised when Sabrina said from the front seat, "Actually, James, they will be married a week on Sunday."

Sir James said thoughtlessly, "My word, that's soon," and was going to add something more, but Elsie's face had turned such an uncomfortable shade of red that he understood the situation that had developed in his absence and said nothing. In fact, he could think of nothing to say that comfortably fitted the situation and mitigated the embarrassment he had unwittingly caused, except to say quietly, "Sorry, Elsie."

He walked to the front of the motor car, started the engine, climbed in, and they drove to Brantley Manor in an uncomfortable silence. When they arrived, Elsie went around to the servants' quarters and Sir James and his fiancée climbed the front steps and entered the main hall, where they were greeted by Benson.

"Where is my mother, Benson?"

"She's in the morning room, Sir James."

"Thank you, Benson," he said.

Sir James explained, "My mother was still in bed when I was here earlier this morning, Sabrina, so we must see her first and then go to see the alterations."

Sabrina nodded her agreement, and hand-in-hand, the couple went to the morning room to greet Lady Mary.

Sir James hoped that this first meeting with his mother could be kept short as he desperately wanted to talk privately to Sabrina, but Lady Mary would not be put off. She wanted to know in detail everything that her son had experienced since he had left Brantley Manor and, carefully folding the newspaper she had been reading and placing it on the table next to her, she started to question him. However, in response to his extremely vague replies that often verged upon monosyllabic, she said wryly. "Ever the diplomat, James. It is clear you are keeping your own counsel on this occasion. I'm sure you will enlighten us one day."

With that, she picked up the paper and shook it open again. .

The couple politely excused themselves and left Lady Mary to her morning paper.

As they walked towards the west wing, Sir James suddenly stopped and turned to his fiancée, put his arms around her, and held her close to his chest. They kissed then kissed again.

Slightly breathlessly, he said, "When we became engaged, Sabrina, I thought I would be away for about six months and we planned to marry when I came home from Aden. I have returned much sooner than I expected, and I can see no reason why we should postpone our wedding until spring, as we first planned. I would marry you tomorrow if that was humanly possible to arrange, but would you be prepared to marry me sooner than we first planned?"

"Today is too soon? Yes please, as soon as possible," said Sabrina with a beaming smile of pleasure. "What a superb idea, husband-to-be," and she threw her arms about his neck and kissed him with more passion than she knew she was capable of demonstrating.

A cough caused them to move quickly apart again.

Lady Mary said sternly, "It's time you young people were married, and then I wouldn't have to chaperone you." But she couldn't help smiling at their obvious happiness.

Sir James said, "We have just talked about that, Mother, and as I've come home early, we will marry sooner than we first planned. There has been no time to decide when and where yet, but we will tell you what we decide."

"I assume you will follow Russell tradition and marry in our local church?" Lady Mary said.

Sabrina decided to take the initiative and said quickly, "Being your wife is more important to me than anything else, James, so where we marry is a secondary consideration. If you would like to follow the Russell tradition, I have no objection to being married in the local church. Perhaps we should go and see the church and meet the vicar? We will have to set a date for the service and arrange for the banns to be read anyway."

"Banns!" exclaimed Sir James. "So much for my idea of a wedding tomorrow. I had totally forgotten about the Banns, and they will have to be read in your parish church as well, Sabrina."

"Of course," she responded, "and as they have to be announced on three consecutive Sundays, it will be four to five weeks before we can actually marry. That's a terribly long time to wait," she said sadly.

"November is not the best time to marry," said Lady Mary, "It's bound to be cold and probably raining as well."

"You really are a pessimist today, Mother," Sir James said chidingly.

"No," Lady Mary responded. "I am simply being realistic, and talking about realism, where are you going to live? The alterations to the west wing aren't nearly finished. Weren't you about to inspect them?"

"We were, Mother, but became distracted."

"So I noticed," Lady Mary commented dryly then added, "May I come with you or would you like to go on your own?"

"Please come as well, Lady Mary," Sabrina said and linked arms with the older woman so that they could walk comfortably together.

After a long and careful examination of the amount of work Charlie Hod had accomplished, all three of them went to the library for refreshments and to discuss how to proceed.

Sir James summed up the situation clearly and succinctly.

"We gave Charlie Hod six months to complete the alterations, and he thought that would be difficult to achieve. He has done a great deal in two months, but he cannot complete what's left by the time we marry in about a month. My mother's question of where we are going to live was more apt than I realised when she asked it."

"There is plenty of room in my mother's house, and I'm sure she would be delighted if we stayed for a month or two," Sabrina offered.

Not to be outdone, Lady Mary countered with, "As you know, we have room here also, James."

"We do not need to solve the problem of accommodation for several weeks yet, but it's nice to know we will not start our married life in a haystack," Sir James said with a laugh. He continued, "I think we should let Charlie Hod continue as we planned and move into the west wing when it is finished. I don't think there is anything more we can do here today, so if my fiancée is willing, I suggest we go and find the vicar of Brantley Parish Church and start making arrangements for our wedding. Do you agree, my love?"

"Definitely," said Sabrina as she stood up. "Please excuse us, Lady Mary?" she added.

"Of course," Lady Mary responded, and after a moment asked, "Should I arrange lunch for you?"

Sabrina and Sir James exchanged glances, and then the latter said, "Please excuse us, Mother, but we will go to Upton when we have seen the Vicar of Brantley and will probably have a meal in the inn there if we will inconvenience Mrs Severn too much."

After saying goodbye, Sabrina and Sir James went out to the Bentley and had driven most of the way to Brantley Church when Sabrina remembered Elsie. Sir James turned the motor with difficulty and drove back to the Hall, where they collected Elsie and set off once more for the church.

Sir James parked the car beside the gate into the churchyard and all three of them walked along a well-kept gravel path to the main door of the church, which Sir James tried unsuccessfully to open.

He looked at his watch and said, "It's after twelve so I expect Reverend Wilson will have gone home to lunch. I think we had better go on to Upton, have lunch, see your vicar, and then return here. By the way, Sabrina, what's the name of your vicar?"

"Gwynn," she said. "Actually, he's from a place in Northwest Wales called Llanberis." Then she added, "Someone in the village had spent some time in Wales and remembered the way they used to refer to people as 'Jones the milk' or 'Evans the fish', and one night, he referred to our vicar as 'Gwynn the hymn' and the name has stuck, in private at least."

"Does he know?" Sir James enquired through his laughter.

"No idea," said Sabrina, "but I shouldn't think so. I certainly hope not as he is a very nice man."

"Shall we go to Upton, Sabrina?" he asked.

"I think we should," she responded.

***

The weekend quickly passed in a whirlwind of meetings and discussions, planning and compromise, and all too soon, it was time for Sir James to return to that other world of intrigue and possible danger. The calm sadism of Al Hafrey's threat made Sir James shudder when he thought about it. He tried not to do so, but the subject returned unbidden to his mind at inappropriate moments, such as when he kissed Sabrina goodnight, but fortunately, she did not notice his reaction.

Tompkins drove Sir James to London and dropped him at his club before embarking on the return journey to Brantley Manor. Sir James enjoyed a tasty dinner in the club and retired for the night and slept dreamlessly.

Before anyone else was about in the morning, he was dressed and had eaten breakfast, simply to be able to respond to Sir William's instructions as quickly as possible. If Sir William had arranged a meeting of senior Colonial Office mandarins, it would be bad for his reputation if he was late. Whilst he waited, he wondered where the meeting would be held and who would attend, and, quite naturally, Sir James hoped that the outcome would do him credit.

A little after nine, the Chief Porter knocked on Sir James' door and delivered an envelope.

The message Sir James read after he had extracted a single sheet of Colonial Office headed notepaper from the envelope was insultingly brief. After the addresses and salutations, it said simply,

'Come to my office at ten'.

It was signed by Sir William Ellis.

It was not at all what Sir James expected after his last discussion with Sir William, and a shiver of apprehension tickled his back as he wondered what had happened to make him change his mind.

Sir James walked to the Colonial Office from his club and then up the main staircase to the floor, where Sir William's office was situated. He was a little early and didn't mind waiting in the anteroom for a few minutes, but when ten o'clock passed and he continued to wait, he did start to care and his irritation mounted with each passing minute.

About fifteen minutes after ten, the inner door opened and Sir William's secretary came into the anteroom.

"Good morning, Sir James," the secretary said without apology, "Sir William will see you now."

Sir James suppressed his annoyance and said, "Thank you," politely and walked into Sir William's almost palatial office.

At the far end of the thickly carpeted room, Sir William was seated behind a large mahogany desk with a leather top. In front of the desk were two mahogany chairs for visitors that had leather upholstered seats. To the left of the room was a mahogany conference table of a comfortable size for about twelve people with armchairs that matched the table. There were several large oil paintings on the walls that looked as if they could have been Old Masters.

It was an overpowering room redolent with supremacy and wealth. Sir James walked the length of the room and sat in the chair indicated by Sir William. They exchanged polite good mornings and then there was a short silence that Sir James decided to break.

"I assume there has been a new development, Sir William, as you have decided to hold a meeting in your office and not at another location as we had agreed."

"Yes, you're correct," Sir William said bluntly and recalled coming back to sit in his chair in this office a very angry individual only a few days before. The way Sir James had assumed control of the security problem as if he had a right to do so was a bitter memory made even more galling by the fact that he, Sir William Ellis, had found it necessary to kowtow to this young upstart in order to buy time and prevent a scandal. But he was on home territory now, and in his discussions with his superiors, he had taken steps to denigrate Russell and the story he had brought to London.

Sir William said, "I think you will agree, Sir James, that you were given a specific task by the committee."

"Yes."

"Have you completed it?" was the next question.

"As you know –" Sir James started, but he was quickly interrupted by Sir William.

"Just answer yes or no, Sir James."

Unwillingly, Sir James complied and said, "No."

"Did you have permission from this office to leave Aden, Sir James? Yes or no?" Sir William asked forcefully.

Again, Sir James had to answer in the negative.

Sir William said, "To summarise, Sir James, you have failed to complete the task you were given and you have left your appointed station without permission. My superiors view such dereliction of duty very seriously indeed and considered putting you in prison. Naturally, I interceded for you and suggested that you be dismissed instead. They agreed to my recommendation, and consequently, you are no longer a member of His Majesty's diplomatic corps. Good day, Sir James."

Sir James remained seated, momentarily stunned into silence by this unexpected turn of events.

Sir William's words echoed in his ears. Determined not to show the despair that was washing over him, he stood up abruptly.

"What about the spy we were looking for?" Sir James managed to say as his thoughts of a glowing career as a diplomat crumbled to ashes.

"Oh, that," said Sir William in an offhand way. "We consider that was just a story you fabricated to provide a reason for leaving Aden. In any case, it is of no concern to you now." He reached out, pressed a button on his desk, and the secretary entered the room. "Wilson will show you out." He then picked up a file of papers and started to read them with a satisfied expression on his face. Clenching his fists in an effort to control his mounting anger Sir James had no option but to walk out of Sir William's office and allow the secretary to escort him from the building. On the pavement, the secretary turned on his heel and, without a word, hurried back through the main entrance of the Colonial Office.

The good reputation he had fought so hard to acquire had been destroyed in one swoop by a frightened but clever man and he didn't know what he could do now to correct the damage Sir William had done.

Sir James simply stood in stunned silence in the middle of the pavement, impeding the passage of men and women alike, until he was confronted by a nurse pushing a Silver Cross perambulator. The nurse was a determined lady, as they often are, and the pram too big to be easily ignored.

Sir James stepped to one side and said, "Excuse me," to the nurse, who sailed past with her nose in the air and a disdainful sniff for *men who have nothing better to do than get in the way of an honest working girl,* but it broke the spell and restarted a numb brain. The child riding in the pram also caught Sir James' attention. He wasn't sure if it was a boy or a girl, but it had bright blue eyes and a mop of golden curly hair. The baby was sitting up, and Sir James approved of the padded leather harness the child was wearing to prevent it falling over if the perambulator moved unexpectedly.

We must do that, he thought as he anticipated marriage and parenthood, and the thought brought him back to reality with a bump. Clearly, he could not go back to Sabrina and admit that he had been disgraced.

Whether it was fair or otherwise was now not important.

If he wanted to hold his head up and be an influential member of society, he had to clear his name. How was another issue, and he wouldn't solve anything standing in the street outside the Colonial Office getting in everyone's way, so he walked back to the club, desperately trying to find the key to his dilemma.

As he entered the main door of the club, the porter left his desk and hurried to greet him.

"Good day, Sir James. You have a visitor, sir. He's waiting in the morning room and gave his name as Captain Caruthers. Shall I tell him you're here, sir?"

The last thing Sir James needed at that moment was a protracted session of wartime reminiscences, but at the same time, he couldn't bring himself to the point of rudeness where he would ignore a visit from a close friend and battlefield comrade.

"There's no need to announce me," he said to the porter, "I'll go in immediately. Has he ordered coffee?"

"No, sir"

"Then bring coffee for two, please."

"Yes, sir," the porter said and saluted Sir James' departing back.

Sir James pushed open the door of the club's morning room and let it swing closed behind him as he walked in. His old friend was sitting in one of the leather wingback chairs, avidly reading a newspaper.

So avidly in fact that he was unaware of Sir James' presence until he heard a voice say, "Still reading, I see."

Caruthers dropped his newspaper as he leapt to his feet.

"James," he said loudly as he quickly scanned his friend's features. "Still living in hot countries, I see."

"Yes, indeed, and I have only recently returned so your visit is exceedingly well timed, my friend"

"You look well, and I hope you are."

"I was better a few hours ago," Sir James answered, and then, using his friend's nickname, he added, "But how are you, Carrie? And what brings you to find me today of all days?"

"Chance," he said, then asked, "But why is today such a bad day for you, James?"

"I have done nothing wrong, but I have been summarily dismissed from the Colonial Office," Sir James said bitterly.

"Surely not! Can you tell me about it?," his friend asked..

"All I can say is, on my recent posting I discovered evidence that there may be something untoward occurring at the Colonial Office. However, rather than sharing my concerns it appears that my superior would rather the problem simply disappeared," Sir James said. "Sir William dismissed me this morning, just days after my return from Aden, thus preventing any meaningful investigation." As he continued talking, giving Caruthers a brief summary of the meeting that morning, he felt the sheer injustice of his treatment burning anew

"A very bad business, James. I wish there was something I could do to help you, but unfortunately ... " Carrie spread his arms wide apart to demonstrate his inability.

"I don't expect anyone can help," Sir James responded glumly. . "Whatever happens, I must find a way to clear my name before I can return to my fiancée. I cannot expect her to marry me and share my disgrace. Anyway, that's enough of me for one day, so now please, tell me what you have been doing since the war ended."

They chatted on for another hour and drank several more cups of coffee, but at the end of it, Sir James had no clear idea who Caruthers worked for or what he did. It seemed to be something secret, but that was only a feeling Sir James developed from what was not said rather than an explicit statement.

In any event, the friends parted on the best of terms after agreeing to meet again in the next week or so.

Sir James spent the rest of the day in his club and went to bed after dinner as usual, but didn't sleep.

He lay in his bed for most of the night, wide awake, going over and over the events of the day and imagining what he could or should have done differently.

But each repetition of each cycle of thought led him back to the unalterable conclusion that he had been ruined by Sir William Ellis so that Sir William could continue to live in the manner to which he had grown accustomed. And he grew quite sick with his pent-up anger at Sir William's iniquitous behaviour.

He went to breakfast in a sombre mood and ate very little as his mind still sought for a way recover his lost reputation.

Later, as he sat at the desk in his room, he remembered that he still had all the personnel files that Sir William had sent to him and realised that he should make arrangements to return them. He noticed that the top file happened to hold the personal details of Alex Jones, and seeing it made Sir James realise that the problem of a spy in the Colonial Office had not been resolved. Sir William had skilfully concealed the possibility by denigrating him and then having him dismissed.

Should I continue the investigation? Sir James wondered. *If I could find the spy, perhaps Sir William's superiors would see that they had been deceived and reinstate me?*

Sir James quickly realised that action was much better than moping in his room and decided to make some discrete enquiries about Alex Jones. First of all, he would go to Somerset House, where he should be able to find details of his birth and parents, and then he would go to the home address given in his file to find out what his neighbours thought of him. After that, he didn't yet know, but hoped the initial enquiries would give him a lead.

Sir James left the club shortly afterwards.

He took a cab to Somerset House, where he found that his title was of considerable benefit when it came to opening doors and dusty old records but of no value at all when the records didn't have any mention of an Alex, Alexander, or Alessandro Jones. There were lots of Jones' of approximately the correct birth date to accord with the details on Alex Jones' personal record but none had a first or second Christian name that could be twisted to fit no matter how hard Sir James tried.

"That's a pity," said Sir James when all possible records had been explored without success. "Do you often find that someone's details are missing?"

"No, sir," said the old clerk who had been delegated to assist Sir James. "We do occasionally find a gap in our records, but I imagine that's because the parents forgot or didn't bother to have the child registered. Failing to register a birth is not as common now as it used to be, but it still happens. I'm sorry, Sir James, but I cannot help you further."

Sir James thanked the old man and gave him a good tip to reward his diligence then walked out of Somerset House and hired a cab to take him to Kilburn, where, according to the records, Alex Jones lived and in his early years went to school. As the cab entered Kilburn on Edgware Road, Sir James saw a middle-aged policeman walking his beat with slow strides and observant eyes.

"Stop just beyond the copper," he instructed the cabby.

With the Jones Manila folder grasped firmly in one hand, Sir James jumped from the cab on the corner of Brondesbury Road and walked back towards the policeman.

"Good afternoon, officer," Sir James called as soon as he was close enough.

"Good afternoon, sir," responded the policeman.

"I should be grateful if you would direct me to Millison Street."

"In Kilburn?" the policeman responded, looking and sounding puzzled.

"Yes," said Sir James, opening the folder and checking the address again. "Yes, that's what it says here. Number twenty Millison Street, Kilburn."

"I'm sorry, sir," he said, "But there's no Millison Street in Kilburn. Who are you looking for, sir?" the policeman asked. "I may know the person and where he lives."

Their conversation was interrupted by a sudden volley of gunfire. It sounded quite close, and Sir James asked, "Army?"

"No, sir, it's the local militia. There's a rifle range just beyond those houses," and he gestured along Brondesbury Road.

"Thank you," Sir James said then opened the folder again before saying, "His name is recorded as Alex Jones."

The policeman thought for a few moments and then said, "I don't know anyone of that name sir, but it sounds familiar," and he looked worried by his inability to place the name. "If you give me your address, I'll certainly inform you if I remember."

Sir James gave him one of his business cards.

He read the card and said, "Thank you, Sir James," without a change of expression or intonation but privately noting the fact that he was having a conversation with a knight.

A strange odour that Sir James found unpleasant drifted past them on the breeze and he asked, "What's that smell?"

"It's the smell of the hops from Kilburn Brewery, sir."

"It's a good thing beer doesn't smell like that," Sir James remarked, and the policeman chuckled.

"Indeed, sir," he agreed.

"Good day, officer, and thank you," Sir James said and returned to his cab. He had climbed more than halfway through the door when he had an idea and backed out onto the pavement.

"Another question, if I may, officer?" he asked.

"What's that, sir?" the policeman responded.

"Where is St. Edward's School?" Sir James asked.

"There is no school of that name here, sir," said a policeman who was becoming increasingly suspicious of Sir James' motive for asking all these unanswerable questions.

Sir James sensed the policeman's feelings and said in explanation, "It's really very odd, officer. I have here the personal details of a man employed by a catering company working at the Colonial Office, and with your help, I have discovered that he has given false information about his home address and school, and earlier in the day, I found that he didn't have a birth certificate either. I wonder what his story is."

"It's certainly very odd sir, as you say. But if you will excuse me, I must complete my beat."

"Of course," said Sir James and climbed into the cab again, instructing the driver to take him back to his club.

Sir James enjoyed his dinner in a rather less pessimistic mood than when he had picked at his breakfast. As he ate, he mulled over what he had learnt.

What he *hadn't* learned would have been a more precise description. The whole business was more than a little suspicious, but that was as far as it went. There was nothing tangible, and the only way he could improve his knowledge was to follow the man and see firsthand what he did and to whom he spoke. It was actually a little more difficult than it appeared.

How do you follow someone when you have no idea what he looks like nor where he is likely to be?

A problem for tomorrow, Sir James decided. He went to bed, put his head on the pillow, and slept like a stone.

In the morning over breakfast, his thoughts returned to the unanswered question from the previous evening, and the more he thought about it, the more impossible a solution appeared to be without hiring a detective to do the investigation for him.

On the periphery of his vision, as he attempted solving the apparently insoluble, he noticed the Chief Porter gesturing in his direction and realised he was about to have an uninvited visitor.

The man who weaved in and out between the tables as he hurriedly crossed the breakfast room looked vaguely familiar, but it was not until he was only a few yards away from his table that Sir James recognised him. It was Sir William Ellis's secretary. He was red-faced and panting, and Sir James wondered if he had run all the way from the Colonial Office.

Without the benefit of a preliminary and polite good morning, he said bluntly, "Sir William wants to see you in his office immediately."

Sir James said pointedly, "Good morning, Mr Wilson. When you go back to your master, please inform him that I am no longer employed at the Colonial Office and I am not obliged to obey his instructions."

Wilson smirked and said, "Sir William expected you to say that and he has instructed me to tell you that you have been reinstated, and he expects you to go to him immediately."

"I don't accept the reinstatement," Sir James said calmly. He poured himself another coffee then held the coffee pot over an empty cup and added politely, "Would you like a cup, Mr Wilson? It's very good coffee."

Wilson shook his head, clearly unsettled by Sir James' attitude.

Sir James was supposed to be doing as ordered and hurrying to the Colonial Office, not sitting calmly at his breakfast table offering cups of coffee.

Wilson said, "What do you mean 'you're not accepting your reinstatement'?"

"My statement seems to be crystal clear to me, Mr Wilson, but for your benefit, let me add that I do not intend to accept any offer of employment with the Colonial Office again, no matter how attractive your masters make it."

Sir James beckoned to the Chief Porter who had remained in the breakfast room near to the door.

"Yes, Sir James?" he said when he reached the table.

"Please show this gentleman out, Giles," then to Wilson he said, "Tell your master that he can come here at eleven if he wishes to have a meeting. Good morning, Mr Wilson."

Sir James resumed his interrupted breakfast and Giles gently grasped Wilson's upper arm and guided him out of the breakfast room.

A little more than thirty minutes later, Giles carried a small silver tray into the breakfast room, walked to Sir James' table just as the latter was about to start reading The Times, and delivered a letter. Sir James folded the paper carefully and laid it on one side. He then opened the envelope with the silver paper knife the Chief Porter had thoughtfully placed on the tray and extracted a single sheet of poor-quality paper.

Sir James started to read, and as a frown of bewilderment creased his forehead, he turned the sheet over to find out who had written the letter. He found it was from someone describing himself as Constable Drew of Kilburn Police, and suddenly the text of the letter started to make sense. After the usual salutations it said,

'After you left, I continued to wonder why the name Alex Jones sounded familiar and eventually spoke to the desk sergeant about your visit. He remembered immediately that Alex Jones had disappeared suddenly some years ago. He's still listed as a missing person. The house he lived in became progressively more derelict after he disappeared and was eventually pulled down as it was becoming dangerous.'

That doesn't help Sir James thought. *It simply complicates the matter. Why should someone disappear and later reappear at the FO as a caterer? What had he done to cause him to disappear in the first place, I wonder?*

Further musing was prevented by the reappearance of Wilson, who looked even redder and more out of breath than he did on his previous visit.

Before he could speak, Sir James asked in a considerate tone, "Have you had to run all the way to the Colonial Office and back again, Mr Wilson? May I order you some refreshments?"

Wilson nodded then shook his head.

Sir James waited patiently.

Eventually, Wilson's breathing slowed enough for him to say, "Sir William insists that it is your duty to attend at his office when he calls for you, as he is a government officer and you are a member of the general public. If you do not come voluntarily, he will send the police to arrest you and take you there."

"And on what grounds will he arrange for my arrest?" Sir James asked.

"I have no idea, Sir James," Wilson responded. "But Sir William has a wide experience and will certainly think of something that will satisfy the police and seriously incommode you. He is quite sure that you wouldn't wish your fiancée to find out that you have been expelled from the FO one day and arrested the next."

"That's blackmail, Wilson," Sir James exclaimed angrily and forcibly pushed his chair back with a protesting screech as he jumped to his feet and headed for the door. Wilson, who had jumped back in alarm when Sir James leapt up, suddenly found himself running to catch up with a very angry man. Along the main road they hurried, and to casual bystanders it must have looked like a race, Sir James out in front, striding along with his coat tails flapping, and Wilson panting and red-faced, trailing along behind. At the Colonial Office, Sir James took the stairs two at a time and had disappeared into the main corridor before Wilson had reached the first landing.

Outside Sir William's office door, Sir James stopped to compose himself before politely knocking on the door and walking in.

He was halfway to Sir William's desk before the incumbent realised he had a visitor, and it was another few seconds before his eyes focused and he recognised who his visitor was.

Sir William stood up quickly, his face white except for red blotches of anger on his cheeks. His voice steadily rose in pitch and volume as he said, "So you have deigned to come at last, have you? Why did you do it? I'll sue you for defamation and take every penny you possess. I'll teach you to try to humiliate me," and he collapsed back into his chair, gasping for air.

"Have you taken leave of your senses? What are you talking about?" Sir James shouted in turn.

Wilson, who had entered the office during the exchange between the two knights, waved a newspaper in front of Sir James' face and shouted in turn, "It's the lies you've written in here."

"Are you both mad?" shouted Sir James in a voice that was developing parade ground volume and must have been audible at the other end of the building, "What in the name of all the furies are you two shouting about?"

"It's your article in The Times," said Wilson in a more normal voice.

"It's your *fantasy* in the Times," Sir William screeched.

"What article? I haven't written an article for 'the Thunderer' or any other newspaper," Sir James said in bewilderment.

"Here, look," Sir William shouted as he slammed his fist down on the open newspaper lying on his desk. He scrabbled the newspaper up and thrust it into Sir James' chest.

"I repeat," said Sir James, "I haven't written an article for theTimes and I do not know what you are talking about."

"Read it," Sir William ordered. "You are the only person with the knowledge to write this article. My superiors are furious because they have found out through a newspaper about matters I thought better they didn't know."

"Like the possibility there's a spy, for example?" Sir James asked bluntly.

Sir James sat down, opened the newspaper on Sir William's desk, and smoothed out the wrinkles before starting to read the article that Sir William had indicated.

It was on the leader page and was headed,

COLONIAL OFFICE FOLLY

by

Martin Alison - Deputy Editor

Sir James said immediately, "I know no one by the name of Martin Alison. As a matter of fact, I know no one who is connected with The Times or any other newspaper."

Sir James turned his attention back to the newspaper and started to read the article.

'In the Colonial Office, occupying a palatial office, is a civil servant whom I shall refer to as Mr Little. He is a man who entered government service about forty years ago, and as far as is known, he has served the crown loyally for the whole of that time. Unfortunately, the information that has come to our knowledge recently suggests that self-interest is more important than loyalty and honesty, and it appears that Mr Little has been somewhat economic with the truth he has disseminated to his superiors.

One suspects that the reason for this sudden change in morality may have something to do with Mr Little's impending retirement. He wouldn't wish to do anything, or be responsible for anything, that could jeopardise his pension and elevation to the peerage.

The information that has come to this office is that another civil servant, and I will refer to him as Mr Knight, has just returned from a secret mission that proved to be far from secret. Mr Knight returned immediately to London so that he could inform his superiors confidentially that it is possible a spy is active in the Colonial Office.

One would imagine that Mr Knight would be rewarded appropriately for his foresight and responsible actions, but regrettably, he received not a commendation for his courage and devotion to king and country, but summary dismissal.

To discover a reason for this extraordinary turn of events, one must look at the actions of Mr Little and our statement that he had been economic with the truth. The truth is that he told his superiors that Mr Knight had returned to London without permission and before completing his assignment. Both facts are true, but unfortunately, he forgot to mention the reason for Mr Knight's unexpected return, and in consequence, Mr Knight was dismissed for dereliction of duty.

So, Mr Little preserved his position and the spy is free to do his worst as there is no one looking for him. Perhaps someone at the Colonial Office should investigate the folly of Mr Little's behaviour.

***

Sir James straightened up in his chair and stared at Sir William. "I didn't write the article and I certainly didn't speak to the newspaper, but what has been reported is essentially true, so you cannot expect me to deny it. You had no compunction when you arranged for my dismissal, Sir William, so you cannot expect me to show you any pity."

Sir William collapsed back into his chair, a broken and defeated man. Wilson slunk out of Sir William's office and could be seen through the half open doorway, sat at his desk with his face buried in his hands.

Sir James stood up, turned away from the desk, and started to walk to the door. After a few strides, he stopped, turned back, and rested both hands on the surface of the desk so that he could bend forward and look Sir William in the eyes.

"Come with me," he said.

"Where to?" asked Sir William faintly.

"To the Foreign Secretary, where you will explain the whole truth and ensure that my unwarranted dismissal is reversed."

"That will ruin me."

"You are already a ruined man. The newspaper has seen to that. Come with me, Sir William."

One hour later, Sir James walked from the Colonial Office without a stain on his character and looking forward to starting his new career running the estate at Brantley Manor. He had been reinstated by the Foreign Secretary and had then immediately resigne d as he had no wish to work with the likes of Sir William Ellis again. He made arrangements with Wilson to return to the Colonial Office in due course to liaise with his successor and to hand over the files he still had at the Bertram Club.

Wilson provided the link between Sir William and 'Mr Little' when he was asked.

"His name is William Edward Ellis," he said. "When the initials are written together, they spell 'wee', which means small or little."

"I never knew Sir William had a second Christian name, let alone what it is," said Sir James.

"Which simply reinforces your statement that you did not write the article in The Times," Wilson said. "I wonder who supplied the story to Alison?"

"In my opinion, I don't imagine we will ever find out," Sir James commented, but he was wrong.

Some hours later, when Sir James came down for dinner, he found Captain Caruthers waiting for him.

He said, "Come and join me for dinner, Carrie. I have a great deal to tell you."

"Gladly," Captain Caruthers responded cheerfully, "and I have a great deal to discuss with you as well, but first, a question if I may?"

"Please sit, Carrie, and ask as many questions as you wish," Sir James said cheerfully.

They both sat down, ordered the food they wanted from an extensive menu, and accepted a glass of Bristol Cream sherry from the wine waiter. After an appreciative sip, both men relaxed in their chairs and enjoyed the anticipation of the good meal to come.

Captain Caruthers asked quite neutrally, "How is Sir William?"

"Clearing his desk, I should imagine," Sir James answered. "The Foreign Secretary's condemnation of Sir William's conduct was scathing to say the least. I had no reason to like the man after the way he treated me, but I did feel some sympathy for him. He's lost everything he's worked for and tried to preserve, including his reputation. He went too far and was exposed by The Times. Have you read it?"

"No," said Caruthers, "I didn't buy a newspaper today."

"That's a pity, Carrie. Whoever wrote it must have known Sir William quite well to have been able to use 'Little' as a pseudonym for him."

"Martin Alison knows Sir William much too well. He has followed Sir William's ascent through the corridors of power with careful attention, hoping that one day he would be able to repay him in kind for destroying his own father's career. Alison senior took his own life shortly after Sir William had him dismissed for a crime someone else was later found to have committed. A pardon is not of much value when one is dead," Caruthers added sadly.

"How do you know about that, Carrie?" Sir James asked.

"Martin is my cousin," Carrie responded. "The family were horrified by Alison senior's death but were unable to get redress as every line of enquiry was blocked by the phrase 'Official Secret'."

"I wondered why you were so attentive when I told you what Sir William had done to me. I suppose you told Alison what I said and he wrote the article?"

"Indeed. I have to say, you didn't give me much to go on, but I was very pleased at the amount of detail I retained. Martin was able to enhance the article using his extensive knowledge of the Colonial Office and of the methods with which Sir William operates," Carrie said cheerfully. "And I was even more pleased by the outcome. It was a just retribution."

"I hope that will be the end of the matter," said Sir James.

After that, conversation between the two men was reduced to the bare minimum, allowed by the polite consumption of a substantial five course meal, and when they had finished eating, each of them enjoyed a cigar and brandy and talked of inconsequential matters for fifteen minutes or so.

They parted with tentative and well-meant promises to meet again quite soon.

Next morning, Sir James returned to Brantley Manor by train and horse cab as he had done a little more than a week before, and for the next three weeks, Sir James and Sabrina were engaged almost full time on the exhausting business of organising their wedding and arranging where to live after their marriage.

CHAPTER SEVEN
Abduction

One moonless evening, after they had been to visit Millicent to discuss some detail of coordination between Sabrina's wedding dress and Millicent's bridesmaid dress that Sir James didn't really understand, they drove back to Brantley Manor. Sir James stopped the Bentley close to the foot of the steps below the main entrance, and as he always did, he got out of the motor car so that he could walk around the front of the car to help Sabrina alight.

As Sir James closed the motor car door, he heard something crunch the gravel behind him. As he turned toward the sound, something slammed into the side of his head, and searing pain flooded his brain as he collapsed, unconscious.

Sabrina heard and saw nothing untoward, and as she always did, she started to turn in her seat towards the door as it opened. She felt a hand grasp her arm just above the elbow and was vaguely conscious that it seemed bonier that her fiancé's and the grip harder than she was accustomed to, but as she always did, she allowed the hand to support her and assist her to stand beside the car.

Fractions of a second later, she was grasped from behind and something was forced against her face. She tried ineffectually to pull it away and recognised the smell of ether as she collapsed unconscious into the arms that encircled her.

A little while later, Benson, who had heard the car arrive, came to see why Sir James had not come in to the Hall. He looked over the balustrade opposite the main entrance but could only see the Bentley in the light spilling out of the open door. He walked down the steps and peered through the window on the driver's side. No one was visible, and he assumed that Sir James and Sabrina had decided to go for a walk in the grounds and started to walk back towards the steps, leading up to the main entrance.

Why would anyone want to go for a walk in the dark at this time of night? he mused.

As Benson mounted the first step, he paused as he thought he heard something behind him. He stood absolutely still, listened with all his concentration, and heard a faint groan from the passenger side of the car. Benson rushed back to the motor and was horrified to see Sabrina lying motionless on the gravel beside the open front door.

Benson's natural first instinct was to go to help the young lady, but common sense and training quickly replaced this impulse, and instead he ran to the steps, shouting for assistance. A servant materialised through the doorway like a jack in the box.

Benson, in a much louder voice than he would have normally used, shouted, "Steven. Send someone for Elsie, then come down here and help me. Quick as you can, lad. And bring a lamp with you."

After what seemed a lifetime to Benson, but which was in reality only a few minutes, Steven came rushing down the steps and ran to where Benson was just visible beyond the motor car. He was on his knees beside Sabrina and carefully examining her prostrate form. Her eyelids flickered, and she groaned. Then there was inert silence again.

"I can't see anything wrong with her," he said to Steven. "But we must get her inside as soon as Elsie comes and can help us lift her up."

Shortly afterwards, Elsie arrived, and the three of them carried the prostrate form of Miss Sabrina Severn up the steps and into the Hall, where they laid her gently on a couch near the fire.

With a gentle touch, Elsie carefully examined Sabrina and said, "She doesn't appear to be injured, but there is a strange smell," and she bent forward to examine Sabrina's face more carefully as she groaned again. Elsie sniffed then sniffed again.

"That's ether," she exclaimed. "Someone's put her to sleep. Where's Sir James? He should be told about this immediately."

"My son should be told about what immediately, may I ask?" said Lady Mary severely. "And what's the matter with Miss Severn?"

"We don't know, my lady," said Elsie. "Mr Benson found her outside, lying unconscious by the Bentley, and we have just carried her inside and laid her down. Someone has administered ether to her."

"Benson," instructed Lady Mary. "My son and Miss Severn were coming to see me this evening and Sir James was driving the car; therefore, my son must be here somewhere. It is inconceivable that he would allow Miss Severn to be ill-treated without making an attempt to stop the attack, so he may be outside somewhere injured. Take some of the servants, give them lights, and search the area around the car as quickly as possible, then come back to me."

"Yes, my lady," Benson responded and hurried outside, calling for Tompkins and several more of the estate's male employees as he went.

Sabrina suddenly became the centre of attention when she sat up, opened her eyes, took a big gulp of air, and opened her mouth to scream. Fortunately, what her eyes could see was recognised by her brain and the panic subsided a little.

"Where's James?" she asked when she couldn't see him in the crowd surrounding her.

Lady Mary naturally adopted the role of spokeswoman and said candidly, "We don't know, Sabrina, but we are looking for him in the grounds. What happened?"

"I don't know," she cried out. "I thought James was helping me out of the car as he always does, then someone, but definitely not James, caught hold of me, put something over my mouth that reeked of ether, and now I'm here. I must find James." She sounded panic-stricken, tried to get up, and would have fallen flat on her face if Elsie and Steven had not contrived between them to catch hold of her and prevent it. They pushed her back onto the couch.

Elsie said, "You must lie still until the effect of the ether wears off, Miss Sabrina. Benson and some of the men are looking for Sir James, so there is nothing we can do except wait for news."

"Did you see or hear anything, Sabrina?" Lady Mary enquired.

"Nothing at all. Your son always helps me alight from the motor, and I expected my door of the motor car to open, and it did. It was dark, and I expected a hand to help me get up, and that was what happened. Then another hand held a cloth over my face. I smelt ether and tried not to take a breath but couldn't stop myself. The next thing I knew, I was lying here."

She turned on her side, and with her face pressed against the back of the couch, she started to weep, and no one could do anything practical to comfort her as they didn't know what had happened either.

They could only stand and stare.

Benson came back looking very grave, and Lady Mary took him away to one side so that they could converse without Sabrina overhearing.

"Have you found Sir James?"

"No, my lady," Benson responded. "We have looked very carefully all around the car, and there is no sign of him. There are two furrows in the gravel leading from the car near the driver's door to the grass at the edge of the drive. Beyond the bushes there are the hoof prints from several horses and a heap of fresh dung. We can only imagine that Sir James was rendered unconscious, perhaps like Miss Sabrina, and then dragged across the gravel to the horses and carried away. Though why anyone should want to kidnap Sir James is beyond my understanding."

The expression on Lady Mary's face had become more serious by the moment, and she said quickly, "Send Tompkins to get the Rolls. I'll go and see the Chief Constable. He'll know what to do, particularly as my son has been employed by the diplomatic corps and the Colonial Office."

"Yes, my lady," Benson replied and went to do his mistress' bidding.

Lady Mary went back to Sabrina, who said immediately in a tense and worried voice, "Where's James? How is he?"

"We don't know where my son is, Sabrina. The evidence suggests that he has been abducted, and I can only assume it has something to do with his recent activities in Egypt or Aden. I will go to the Chief Constable immediately and get his advice. You had better stay here tonight as the police may wish to talk to you."

"Yes, Lady Mary," she said, and once again, her emotions overflowed into floods of tears, accompanied by sobs of fear and anguish.

***

As Sir James started to regain consciousness, he could feel hands under his shoulders and hear his heels dragging in the gravel. There were horses nearby, and as he started to struggle, he was dropped unceremoniously onto the grass at the side of the drive. A hand clamped something across his nose and mouth, and he recognised the smell of ether, and although he tried not to inhale, his involuntary intake of breath after about half a minute couldn't be prevented. His world became black again.

He remembered struggling back to consciousness on a number of occasions, but each time, as soon as his captors detected a movement, they administered another whiff of ether and put him back to sleep again.

***

Lady Mary returned after about an hour with a man she introduced as Detective Inspector Martin Judd to Benson at the door, and to Sabrina, who was too apprehensive to stir from the couch in the hall.

As Sabrina sat up to return Judd's deep voiced greeting, her first impression was that he looked less like a policeman and much more like her idea of a villain. D. I. Judd was a big, square-shouldered man with thick, curly black hair and an equally thick black beard and moustache. Shrewd green eyes peered out from under thick bushy eyebrows, and what little could be seen of his face seemed to be deeply tanned. Sabrina privately revised her impression from villain to pirate captain.

As she dabbed her eyes with a sodden handkerchief, she said politely, "Good evening, Chief Inspector. I hope you can find my fiancé quickly."

"I'll do my best, miss, but first perhaps you can tell me as much as you can remember of the events of this evening before I go outside to look around."

Judd took out a notebook, and as Sabrina spoke, he wrote frequent shorthand comments in a well-schooled hand. When she had finished her narrative, he questioned her to clarify any points he was not sure about and then started to gently probe Sabrina's memory for anything that Sir James might have said that could have indicated a problem.

Sabrina told him that most recently, prior to his resignation, Sir James had been working with Sir William Ellis at the Colonial Office. . Sir James' visits to Aden and Egypt were also recounted, although in far less detail. Sabrina described as much as she could remember of Sir James' social interactions with Hans Richter and Al Hafrey; but as Sir James had been intentionally vague about his dealings in the Middle East and hadn't mentioned Al Hafrey's threat the possible involvement of a distant Arab was not given much credence.

At the end of the interrogation, Judd said, "Thank you, Miss Severn. I have no more questions at present, but I may have to come back to ask you more in the light of future developments." He got up from the chair he had used and walked to the entrance, where he spoke briefly to Benson, and then the two of them went outside.

As they started to walk down the steps, Judd said, "Show me the tracks in the gravel first, please."

"Of course," said Benson as he led the way towards the driver's side of the Bentley. "They start here and go that way towards the shrubbery," and he pointed.

Judd had a very powerful torch, and it lit up the area as if it was daylight. They followed the tracks across the gravel and through the shrubbery to the point where the horses had been hitched to convenient trees.

Judd swept the area the torch and said, "Look there. See the wheel tracks? They had a light cart. I wondered how they were going to get an unconscious man as heavy as Sir James onto the back of a horse and keep him there. They just bundled him into the back of the cart and drove away. No one would have heard a thing whilst they stayed on the grass, and if one of the horses had neighed, no one would have considered it at all odd out here in the country."

He turned towards Benson and said, "I'll follow these tracks to see if I can find anything, but I suspect they will return to the drive before long. You can go back to the Hall, Benson, and ask Lady Mary if she would be kind enough to see me when I return."

"Very good, Chief Inspector," Benson said and walked towards the Hall.

Thirty minutes later, Chief Inspector Judd returned to the Hall and was met at the entrance by Benson, who helped him remove his overcoat.

"Lady Mary will see you in the library, Chief Inspector. If you will follow me, sir?" Benson set off towards the library with Judd a few paces behind as he had stopped momentarily to see if Miss Severn was still occupying the couch.

"Miss Severn is with Lady Mary, I assume?" Judd commented.

"No, sir," Benson responded, "She's gone to her room. Lady Mary managed to persuade her that she should rest as she could do nothing practical to help find Sir James. Do you need her?"

"No, not tonight," Judd said after a moment's thought.

Benson knocked on the library door, and after a slight pause opened it and announced the Chief Inspector.

Lady Mary remained seated and said, "Please sit there, Inspector," and indicated to Judd that he should take the chair on the opposite side of the fireplace.

Lady Mary pre-empted any questioning by asking, "It's quite late, Chief Inspector. Would you like me to arrange for you to stay at Brantley Manor tonight or would you prefer Tompkins to drive you home?"

"I would prefer to go to my office, if that can be arranged. I must start a full-scale search for your son."

"Do you wish to have some refreshments or ask any questions, Chief Inspector?" Lady Mary enquired.

"I need nothing to eat or drink, thank you." Chief Inspector Judd took out his notebook again and looked at some of his previous entries in order to confirm the accuracy of his memory.

"When your son was in London, he had some meetings at the Colonial Office. Do you know where he stayed in London, Lady Mary?"

"At his club, I imagine. I think he would have mentioned it if he had stayed somewhere other than the Bertram Club."

"Did he happen to mention anyone he met whilst he was there, apart from the officials at the Colonial Office?"

"Yes, he mentioned that he had dinner with a Captain Caruthers. Christopher Caruthers, I believe. He was one of my son's fellow officers."

"A final question, if I may." Lady Mary dipped her head to signify her assent as Judd asked, "Did your son say anything that made you consider that he was worried about anything?"

"Apart from getting everything ready for his wedding in four weeks' time, he didn't seem to have a care in the world," Lady Mary responded. As Judd stood up and slipped the notebook into an inside breast pocket in his jacket, she rang the bell for Benson.

Judd said goodnight and was driven to his office in Maidenhead.

***

Sir James started to regain full consciousness after what seemed a very long time, during which he partially woke to hear strange noises, like a railway train, and then sank back into oblivion. The smell of ether had seemed to be a constant companion since he had been attacked.

With his brain still muzzy from the effects of the soporific, he managed to think, *Where's Sabrina?* and a long time later, *I must see if she's alright.* He knew he was lying down and tried to move but couldn't. His muscles seemed to work, but no matter how hard he strained, he couldn't sit up, nor could he turn to the side. He could move his head, but his arms and legs were immoveable, and then he realised that he couldn't see. *Am I blind or is it just dark?* He couldn't hear anything either. *Have I gone deaf as well?* he wondered.

Although he tried to control his emotions, his brain took the little pieces of sensory information that it had assembled and conjured up a picture that fitted the perceived facts.

He had been buried.

Alive!

He screamed in frantic, absolute panic, then shouted, "Help me," at the top of his voice and heard his voice rebound off something.

He immediately realised that he could hear an echo from his voice. Taking a deep breath, he set his intellect to work in order to deduce what he could from what he could sense and at the same time try to control the panic invading his body.

Clearly, he was lying down.

It was too hard to be a bed, so possibly it was a bench. He could feel his legs and muscles reacting to his desires to move, so he knew his limbs were still functioning. If he couldn't move, then he had been tied or strapped down onto the bench. Why that should be, he didn't know. There were too many possibilities to make a conclusion.

At least he had solved the problem of hearing, and he half-grinned with embarrassment at the remembrance of his earlier shout of panic.

His sight was another matter. He didn't think he had suddenly become blind, so it was either very dark or his eyes were covered. After a little concentration, he was reasonably certain there was nothing around his head, so it must be dark.

I hope Sabrina is unharmed, he thought, *but I can do nothing to help her except shout and swear at present.*

I have a terrible headache, he thought, *and I'm dreadfully thirsty.*

Then the effects of the ether re-established themselves and he lapsed into unconsciousness again.

***

Chief Inspector Judd's reputation as a detective was second to none, and he had achieved it by virtue of consistent, methodical, painstaking elimination of impossibilities, no matter how plausible or implausible they appeared to be at first glance. And this was due in no small measure to his ability to think imaginatively.

He sat as his desk in his office in the police station and thought about the strange disappearance of Sir James Russell. He decided that the obvious local enquiries could be delegated to his assistant, Detective Constable Martin, and he would go to Sir James' club first thing to see what he could discover there. Then he tried to imagine what the people who had abducted Sir James would do.

They wouldn't have gone to the trouble of abducting him if they intend to murder him, so I don't need to look for a body. Not yet, anyway! They could have hidden Sir James in one of the villages in the area surrounding Brantley Manor, but I wouldn't expect them to as Sir James is too well known a figure here. Moving an unconscious man from place to place in public without attracting unwanted attention would not be too easy to organise, either. How would I do it?

Two possibilities occurred to him immediately. *They could pretend to be undertakers and move Sir James in a coffin,* but he immediately rejected that idea as no one ever moved a coffin about at night. Except when the police had someone exhumed of course. The other idea was more plausible on the face of it. *The abductors could pretend to be doctors taking a very sick patient to hospital. They could be absolutely open about their activities, and if they hinted about a contagious disease, they would be left completely alone. And if I wanted to move a long way quickly, I would use the train.*

Chief Inspector Judd had no need to spend more time thinking as he had a plausible idea to follow up. He reached for a pad of paper and wrote in a row across the top of the page the names of his assistants in order of seniority and underneath the tasks he needed them to perform.

The most important he gave to DC Martin and the local enquiries to Martin's assistants. Martin's task was quite simple. Starting at the nearest railway station to Brantley Manor, he was to find out if an invalid had been escorted onto one of the late evening trains by one or more 'doctors', and if so, where their tickets would have them travel to. Martin was then to travel to the same destination and find out if the medical party had alighted, and if so, try to find out where they had gone.

Judd pillowed his head on his arms and had an hour's sleep leant over his desk. The duty sergeant brought him a large mug of strong, sweet tea at six and shook his Chief Inspector awake.

Judd drank his tea in the tiny washroom alongside the toilets as he shaved in a cracked mirror and washed as best he could in a miniscule hand basin. He blessed his wife for the umpteenth time as he took a clean collar out of the emergency bag she maintained for him in a drawer in his desk, fitted it to the collar studs, and folded a neat knot in his tie.

Wishing he had time for breakfast, Judd put on his jacket, picked up his overcoat, and left the office. He stopped at the duty sergeant's desk to tell him what he wanted done and to leave the notes he had written for DC Martin on his desk before heading for the station and a train to London.

Sir James surfaced through an ether-induced haze and realised that light was percolating into the room he was incarcerated in through a small opening set high in one wall. He scanned as much of his surroundings as the movement of his head and eyeballs permitted and saw nothing else of note. There was no other window and no door within his field of view.

Just bare stone walls, and he imagined that it was a basement room set largely below ground level. That would certainly account for the lack of external noise.

He raised his head as far as it would move and looked along his chest. He could just make out the edge of a thick leather strap across his upper chest. If there were similar straps across his hips and legs, it would explain his inability to move.

Why have they done this to me? he thought, and a combination of fear and the indignity of his position caused him to start shouting with the maximum power he could squeeze from his lungs.

He had only shouted two or three times before he heard the click of a door opening behind him, and once again, an ether-soaked cloth was pressed to his face and he collapsed into an unconscious state once more.

***

Chief Inspector Judd went directly to the Bertram Club and displayed his warrant card as he introduced himself to the Chief Porter.

Giles said, "Perhaps you would like to come into my office, Chief Inspector? We can talk privately there."

Judd agreed, and when they were both seated, Giles asked, "How can I help you, Chief Inspector?"

"Sir James Russell was abducted from Brantley Manor, and his fiancée was given ether and left lying on the drive beside their car. It was obviously a carefully planned attack, which suggests that Sir James' activities have been observed quite closely over a period of at least some days to understand how he behaves. One of my officers is making enquiries around Brantley Manor, but I wonder if you have noticed anyone loitering here when Sir James was in residence?"

"How appalling, Chief Inspector! I trust his fiancée was otherwise unharmed?"

"She was very shaken by the experience but fortunately nothing worse. However she is understandably distraught and anxious for Sir James' swift and safe return. As am I."

"I'm sorry, Chief Inspector," Giles said after a pause for thought. "There have been no untoward happenings that I can think of. I can ask the porters if you wish, but I doubt if they have any information as they would automatically alert me if they were unhappy about anything."

"Thank you, Mr Giles," Judd responded. "But perhaps you can tell me where I can contact Captain Christopher Caruthers. I understand he met Sir James whilst he was here."

"That's correct, Chief Inspector. In fact, he came twice, and he gave me his visiting card the first time in case Sir James didn't return before he had to leave. I have it here somewhere," and he started to rummage through the top drawer of his desk.

Judd interrupted the search by asking, "May I look at Sir James' room?"

"Yes, of course," Giles responded. "I'll take you up and unlock the door and then come back and find that visiting card."

The two men went upstairs and parted at the door of Sir James' room.

It didn't take Chief Inspector Judd very long to inspect the contents of the room as he had only left a change of clothes in the wardrobe and a razor, soap, and so on in the bathroom. Judd checked the drawers of the desk, and except one, which was locked, found that they were all empty. Judd was just about to go out to find Giles when the Chief Porter arrived with a beaming smile of triumph on his face and a small oblong of card in his hand.

"Here's the card, Chief Inspector," Giles said as he handed it over.

"Thank you," Judd responded automatically, then asked as he pointed to the desk. "Do you have a key for that drawer? It's locked but all the others are unlocked and empty."

"Yes, I have duplicate keys for all the locks. I'll go and get it," and Giles hurried off.

Judd sat on the edge of the bed and waited about five minutes. He stood up again when he heard Giles' footsteps in the corridor and walked to the door to meet him.

He took the key and said, "Thank you, Mr Giles. Now if you will excuse me," and Judd gently closed the door, leaving a rather surprised and disappointed Chief Porter standing in the corridor.

Judd crossed the room, sat at the desk, and opened the drawer. He took out and placed on the desk a heap of brown manila folders with a leatherbound volume on top. He looked at the coat of arms and thought, *that must be Sir James' personal diary*, and put it to one side to look at later if need arose.

He took the top folder, opened it, and realised he was looking at someone's personal file. He put it down and looked at the next with the same result and put it on top of the first. He quickly scanned the other folders and found that they were all personal files and placed each one on top of its predecessor in the pile.

What in the world is Sir James doing with a pile of personal records? Judd wondered.

He picked up the top folder, opened it again, and noticed that a handwritten note had been pinned to the inside of the front cover. Judd quickly opened the diary and verified that the note had been written by Sir James. He read 'No evidence . No private or financial information.' He noted that the file was marked confidential and was for a high-ranking civil servant. He quickly went through the remaining files and found that all except the last six were for civil servants and had the same note as the first. The last six were from a catering company, and these all carried the same note except the sixth and last. where Sir James had outlined in his note what he had failed to discover about Alex Jones. The letter from Constable Drew was also pinned to the inside of the cover.

What on earth is all this about? Judd wondered.

He picked up the diary and looked at it thoughtfully as he debated mentally whether he should pry into a man's private records. *It could be a daily journal for work and very relevant or it could be personal, but there's only one way to find out,* he thought.

Judd opened the diary, and starting on 1ˢᵗ January, he scanned the first lines of each day's entry for several weeks and quickly verified that it didn't seem to contain any very personal observations. Nothing that the writer would be embarrassed about if he knew a third party had read them, in any case.

Judd knew from his conversation with Sabrina when Sir James had sailed for Egypt and turned the diary pages until he found the relevant entry. It took him about an hour to read the remaining entries, and by the end, he knew about the Al Hafrey threat, the suspected spy, and the problems with Sir William Ellis.

Chief Inspector Judd leant back in his chair, folded his arms behind his head, and emitted a short whistle of amazement. All of a sudden, he realised the magnitude of the problem he faced, but he also knew he wouldn't solve it sitting where he was.

He put the diary and all the other records back in the drawer, closed it, and then locked it.

Downstairs, he found the telephone and rang the number on Caruthers' visiting card. Someone picked up the telephone receiver so quickly that he must have been within arm's reach of it.

A cultured male voice said, "Hello?" in an interrogative way.

"Can I speak to Captain Caruthers?" Judd asked.

"I am Captain Caruthers," responded the voice cheerfully.

"Good," said Judd and added without elaboration. "I am Chief Inspector Judd of the Metropolitan Police."

"How can I assist you, Chief Inspector?" Captain Caruthers asked, but he sounded a little less cheerful than he had before his caller had identified himself with his rank in the police force.

"Can you come to the Bertram Club? I need to talk to you as soon as possible but do not wish to discuss the matter over the telephone."

"I'll get a cab and come straight away, Chief Inspector," said Captain Caruthers in business-like tones.

Thirty minutes later, he was shown into the dining room where Chief Inspector Judd was just finishing the substantial early lunch he had ordered to compensate for his missed breakfast and the anticipated missed dinner.

After mutual introductions, Judd immediately informed Caruthers that Sir James had been abducted.

"That's dreadful news, Chief Inspector. Who could have done such a thing?"

"I don't have any idea yet, but we are pursuing several lines of inquiry at present," Judd said and then asked, "Please tell me everything you can remember of your recent meetings with Sir James."

"Certainly," he said.

Judd took out his notebook and listened intently to everything that Caruthers could tell him. The Chief Inspector made several notes during Caruthers' description, but there was no new information and Caruthers' account simply confirmed what Judd had learned from the diary.

Judd said, "Thank you for your time, Captain," and stood up to signal the end of the discussion. "Perhaps you would contact me if you think of anything relevant?" he added.

"You can be certain that I will, Chief Inspector," Caruthers said as he shook Judd's hand and then walked from the room.

For his part, Judd collected the folders and diary from the desk in Sir James' room and returned to his office by cab and train to collect the reports from the detectives he had sent out to look for evidence in the villages in the area surrounding Brantley Manor.

Detective Constable Martin had not returned, and the other detectives had discovered nothing that could be of value to Judd's investigation.

***

Sir James partially woke as someone released the straps that were restraining him. Two people grabbed him by the shoulders, levered him up, and twisted him off the platform he had been lying upon and let go. Sir James' legs failed to support

160

him, and he thudded onto the floor at the men's feet. One of them kicked him in the ribs, and Sir James cried out from the pain and clutched his side. His assailant would have kicked him a few more times if he hadn't been pushed away by his companion.

In silence, they dragged him across the floor to the wall and stretched him out beside it. A broad leather strap with a steel ring at each end was passed around his waist, and then the rings on the strap were secured to the ring at the end of a chain with a padlock. One of the men pocketed the key. Sir James was just conscious enough to see that the other end of the chain terminated in another ring, through which a horizontal steel bar passed. The bar was secured to the wall at each end. The arrangement was intended to allow limited movement to the left or right. The men gave Sir James a jug of water and a bucket and left without speaking a word, and he heard through the waves of nausea and sleepiness the bolts being slammed home.

He tried to stand but toppled over and landed on the floor in a nauseous, heaving heap. After some minutes, he tried again, and this time managed to stand up. He swayed like a tree in a strong wind and had to grab hold of the rail his tether was fastened to in order to stay upright. As the minutes passed, he became progressively more stable and started to take stock of his surroundings. Not that he could see anything that really attracted his interest.

In shape, his prison was almost a cube. It had a floor of brown quarry tiles and the walls and ceiling were unpainted plaster. A door was set in one wall, and opposite the door was the small window he had noticed earlier. The sun was shining through the window, and from the position of the bright patch of sunlight on the floor, he guessed that it was probably late afternoon. After using the bucket and then drinking some water, he sat on the floor with his back against the wall and wondered if his captors ,whoever they were, would bother to feed him. The thought made him feel even more ravenous than before, but there was nothing he could do except sit still, keep calm, and hope for the best.

***

Judd had to wait more than one and a half hours longer before he had a telephone call from Detective Constable Martin.

When he heard DC Martin's voice, Judd asked, "Where are you?"

"I'm in Cambridge, sir."

"I see. Please report."

"Yes, sir," DC Martin answered and took a deep breath before launching into his report. "I went to Upton station as you directed and was just in time to see a wagon and a pair of horses being unhitched from a lamp post. I stopped the driver and asked him if he knew who owned the conveyance.

"'I do,' he said rather angrily, 'I 'ired the cart and horses to a foreign looking cove yesterday afternoon and 'e was supposed to return them to my stable by six last evening. I've been looking for it for hours.'

'Who did you hire it to?' I asked.

'Funny name 'e 'ad,' the driver said. 'Never 'eard the name before. 'e said 'is name was Shake.'"

Martin continued. "I went into the station and the ticket clerk checked the sales for the previous evening. Someone had bought six first class single tickets to Cambridge, but he couldn't tell me more and directed me to the Station Master. The night ticket clerk had left a note for the Station Master, and I was permitted to read it. It said,

'Sir, at three minutes to eight o'clock, a man dressed in a long white coat like a doctor came to my window and asked for six first class tickets to Cambridge. He spoke English but he had a funny accent.'"

Judd interrupted, "That description could apply to half the people living in England."

"Yes, sir," Martin agreed without comment.

"Well go on, then," said Judd after a few moments of silence.

"Yes, sir. The clerk wrote, 'I issued the tickets and received payment for them and then the man went out of the station into the street.'"

"Martin," Judd interrupted, "Was this a long note?"

"Yes, sir."

"In that case, save the details for your written report and tell me briefly what you have done."

"Yes, sir," said Martin. "I assumed they had actually gone to Cambridge and came here myself. I went to see the ticket collector who was on duty at the main station in Cambridge last night, and he confirmed that they alighted from the train here. After he had taken their tickets, he sat down in his ticket booth. As there had been no one else on the train, he was able to watch them carry the stretcher along Station Road and turn into one of the villas about halfway along on the right. Salisbury Villas, he says they are called."

"Very good work, Martin," Judd said. "I'll get a car and join you at the railway station as soon as possible."

Judd called the duty sergeant and told him to arrange a car and a driver to take him to Cambridge and then telephoned Chief Inspector Milligan of Cambridge Police to inform him about the abduction and advise him why he was interested in Salisbury Villas.

Milligan was very cooperative and agreed to find out who lived in the villas and to meet Judd at the Railway Station when he arrived.

***

Due to the lingering effects of multiple applications of ether, Sir James was still not fully in possession of his faculties when something hit his shin and caused an involuntary groan to escape from his lips. He opened his eyes, managed to focus on the gloating face of Jalal Al Hafrey, who was staring down at him, and wished he had kept his eyes shut. The threat Al Hafrey had made rang in his ears, and as the reason for his abduction became clear, he cringed in anticipation of the pain of castration and the natural fear any male experiences when he contemplates his future life as a gelding.

"I can see you haven't forgotten my promise," Al Hafrey said in educated and conversational tones as if he was discussing the weather. "You were warned not to interfere in my affairs, and as you have taken no notice, you must pay the penalty."

Al Hafrey laughed, and the mirth was so evil that Sir James, brave soldier though he was, suddenly knew the truth of the much-used phrase 'his bowels turned to water'.

He did his best to sound brave.

"I have done nothing to thwart your plans, Al Hafrey. Since I returned, I have been too busy with other matters."

"Looking for a spy in the wrong place," Al Hafrey sneered, then said, "No matter if you had looked in the right place, we have plenty of sources of information. Losing Alex Jones would not concern us."

"Thank you for confirming what I suspected, Al Hafrey," Sir James said calmly.

"Don't call me Al Hafrey. I am Sheikh Al Hafrey."

"Your father is Sheikh Al Hafrey and an honourable man. You are merely his son and not at liberty to use the title."

Al Hafrey's voice screeched up several octaves, and he kicked Sir James' shin hard as he demanded once again that Sir James address him as 'Sheikh', but his demands were ignored.

Sir James said, "How do you expect to avoid the police?"

"Ha!" he said derisorily. "Your wonderful policemen are still plodding about looking for clues at Brantley Manor. If I had painted big 'This way' signs on the gate, they wouldn't be able to find you, so don't expect to be rescued before my knife removes your virility."

After standing and gloating over his prisoner, he added viscously, "I hope you enjoy your last night as a man, Sir James Russell, because tomorrow morning at ten, I'm going to enjoy converting you into a eunuch."

Al Hafrey turned and walked out of the little cell and slammed the door shut behind him.

Sir James sat with his back to the wall, pulled his knees up, rested his folded arms across his knees, and lowered his head onto his arms. He tried not to give way to his fears or to think about his future life if Al Hafrey had his way.

But it was very hard maintaining the traditional stiff upper lip when there seemed to be nothing to stop Al Hafrey carrying out his threat.

Judd, Chief Inspector Milligan, and DC Martin met in the ticket hall of the small station building and prevailed upon the Station Master to go home and let them make use of his office for a private conversation.

After quickly giving his companions a reprise of Sir James' probable abduction as a drugged and defenceless person on a stretcher, and the research he and his detectives had carried out, he said, "There is one name that has occurred twice. Miss Severn mentioned him last night, and there was quite a lot about him in Sir James' journal. He sounds a nasty piece of work, and I would like to know where he is, as he has threatened Sir James with emasculation." Milligan and Martin couldn't help an involuntary shudder of horror at the thought as Judd added, "I wouldn't like to think of any man in that barbarian's hands."

"What's he called?" Milligan demanded.

Judd took out the notebook to confirm the name and said, "Al Hafrey was the name in Sir James' journal."

"I know about him," Milligan almost shouted with enthusiasm. "He's a cruel and sadistic little man. There have been many complaints about his cruelty, but we have been unable to find enough proof to be able to prosecute. One of the Salisbury Villas is owned by an Arab called Sheikh Al Hafrey, and it's probably the same man who abducted Sir James." He gestured over Judd's shoulder and said, "The villa is about halfway down Station Road on the right."

"According to the ticket collector on duty last night, the stretcher was taken into a villa about halfway down on the right," Martin exclaimed.

"If we're correct, I don't think much of Sir James' chances of returning to the bosom of his family in one piece if we don't do something very quickly," Judd said, articulating what his companions were thinking.

"The first thing we need is a search warrant. Can you help with that, Mr Milligan?" Judd asked, and when he received an assenting nod, he continued. "Then we need to know the layout of the house and have enough men to ensure surprise and make a quick and thorough search. It would be a pity if Sir James lost his testicles because we were unable to take full advantage of the surprise our unexpected attack will cause."

Milligan and Martin nodded their agreement.

"As this is my area," said Milligan, "I will arrange the warrant, and if you have no objection, Chief Inspector Judd, I will take charge of the operation. I suggest we meet here in two hours' time. The extra constables we require will be here by then, and I will brief everyone on the layout of the building at that time."

Judd didn't like to hand over control of his investigation to another officer, no matter how competent he was, but he needed Milligan's whole-hearted support and said, "As you say, Milligan, this is your area, and your proposal is acceptable to me. We will meet here in two hours."

Two and a half hours later, it was nearly midnight as nine solidly-built policemen quietly filed out of the station ticket hall and walked softly along the right-hand side of Station Road and stopped at the entrance gate to the premises. It was chained shut, but that didn't provide much of a barrier as the gate could be lifted from its pintles. The two leading constables simply lifted the gate and moved it out of their way.

They walked in two silent columns along the path and stopped just short of the front door. One of the constables walked forward and examined the door with a quick flash of light from his torch. He walked back and exchanged a few whispered words with the constable leading the other column and Chief Inspector Milligan.

Milligan raised a hand in the air, looked around to make sure he had everyone's attention, then shouted, "Now!" as he brought his hand down.

The two leading constables launched themselves at the door and hit it with their shoulders with a combined weight of twenty-eight stone. The hinges and door lock broke to pieces under the impact and the door crashed to the floor about halfway along the hall. As agreed at the briefing, Judd and Martin headed for the stairs to the basement, assuming that Sir James would be kept in one of the cellars.

***

Sir James was standing up straight and staring angrily at a gloating Al Hafrey when they heard the front door crash down, followed by footsteps running down the stairs.

"I'll still finish you," Al Hafrey screamed as he pulled a wicked-looking dagger from his belt. He launched himself across the room with the blade aimed directly at Sir James' genitals just as Judd crashed the cellar door open.

With considerable presence of mind, Sir James leant back against the wall and grasped with both hands the bar to which he was tethered. With his right leg bent at the knee, he raised it as high as he could and then straightened it forcibly, deliberately aiming his size eleven brogue at Al Hafrey's face. Al Hafrey couldn't avoid the collision, and the impact forced his head back so violently that there was a sharp crack as his neck fractured. His dagger clattered across the floor moments before Al Hafrey's body landed with a thud at Sir James' feet.

Judd, Martin, and Sir James stared down at the lifeless figure then looked at each other.

Judd summed up their feelings succinctly when he said simply, "Poetic justice."

"Does he have the key to that belt, Sir James?" Judd asked, pointing at Al Hafrey's body.

"I don't think so," Sir James responded shakily. "One of the other men had it."

To DC Martin, Judd said, "Go up and ask Chief Inspector Milligan if he has found a padlock key, and if he hasn't, ask him to search his prisoners for it. Ask him to send it down here so that we can release Sir James."

Five minutes later, Milligan came down to the basement himself. He gave the key to Judd and then looked at the body lying near Sir James' feet as Judd started to release him.

"Who's that and what happened to him?" he asked of no one in particular.

Judd chose to answer, "That's Al Hafrey. He broke his neck when he collided with Sir James' foot."

"I'm not surprised," he said as he looked down at Sir James' shoes.

As soon as he was free to move away from his tether, Sir James' resolve broke and he was unable to prevent himself from heaving dryly over the bucket. After a few minutes, he swallowed a little water then wiped his mouth and straightened his back.

With commendable calm, he said, "I can only thank you for rescuing me, gentlemen. You obviously know who I am, so perhaps you would be kind enough to introduce yourselves."

This was quickly done, and Sir James had the pleasure of thanking both of the Chief Inspectors in turn for their part in his rescue and warmly shaking their hands.

Judd beckoned to DC Martin, and when that gentleman was standing by Judd's side, he said, "This morning, I gave Detective Constable Martin a pointer, Sir James, but it was his devotion to duty that led us to Cambridge and your rescue."

"In circumstances such as these, it is difficult to know what to say. Thirty minutes ago, I thought I was doomed to be a eunuch, but thanks to you, Detective Inspector Martin, and these other gentlemen, I can look forward to holding in my arms a child I have fathered. Thank you seems to be a very inadequate recompense for your expertise, but it's all I can say," and he shook Martin's hand very warmly indeed.

Milligan said, "If you would like to take Sir James home, Chief Inspector, I'll ensure everything is cleared up here and send you a copy of my report for your records."

"That's very acceptable, Chief Inspector, and I'll ensure you receive a copy of Sir James' statement as soon as it's been prepared. Thank you for your cooperation tonight. I doubt if the outcome could have been so successful without your unstinting support. Goodnight, Chief Inspector."

"Goodnight, Mr Judd," Milligan said as he started to organise the removal of the prisoners and the body.

As Judd started up the stairs to the ground floor, Sir James shook Milligan's hand warmly again and said, "Thank you, Chief Inspector, and goodnight," then followed Judd up the stairs and out into the fresh air. They walked back to the railway station and in the yard climbed into the waiting police car.

Judd said to the driver, "We're going to Brantley Manor to take Sir James home, but go through Maidenhead so that we can drop DC Martin back at the station."

"Yes, sir," said the driver.

"Thank you, sir," said Martin gratefully as he would get home to his bed some hours earlier as a result.

"When will you want to take a statement from me, Chief Inspector?" Sir James asked.

"I'll come over to the Hall late tomorrow morning if that will be convenient for you, Sir James?"

"Perfectly convenient, Chief Inspector," Sir James responded.

The three men lapsed into silence as the driver demonstrated his extensive knowledge of the road network in his area as he worked his way across country on the minor roads. In Maidenhead, DC Martin was again thanked profusely by Sir James for his part in affecting his release, and then they set off on the final stage of the journey to Brantley Manor.

At the Hall, Judd refused to come in.

"I think it better for you to have your reunion without a policeman watching. Please tell Lady Mary that I will see her tomorrow, Sir James," and with that, he climbed back into the motor car and was driven away, leaving Sir James standing on the driveway. Sir James climbed the steps up to the front door like a geriatric and found that it was locked, which he realised wasn't very surprising when one considered that it was about four in the morning.

I should have asked Judd's driver to switch on the bell when we came up the drive, Sir James thought, *and then everyone would be awake by now.* He reached for the bell pull at the side of the door and pulled it. He pulled again and again for several minutes and then retired to sit on the balustrade to see if anyone would answer his summons.

There was a long period with no sound of activity, and it was much longer than Sir James would have expected or liked.

Someone only had to pull on a pair of trousers, light a candle, and crawl down the stairs, after all.

He was desperately tired, ravenously hungry, and in great need of a bath and clean clothes and no one was taking any notice. He'd been drugged and abducted, kicked, threatened with mutilation, and it appeared that no one seemed to care one jot.

Sir James jumped to his feet, stamped in fury to the front door, and started to assault the bell pull so violently that in retrospect, he was amazed that he hadn't pulled it out of its socket.

He was so intent on making the maximum possible noise with the bell and his voice that Benson's calm voice saying, "Good morning, Sir James," into his ear was a considerable shock, as he hadn't heard the bolts being pulled or noticed the door opening.

Sir James took a very deep calming breath and firm control of his irritation before saying, "Good morning, Benson," in exceptionally polite tones.

"I'm very pleased to see you, Sir James. We have been so worried about you. You are unharmed, sir?"

"Thanks to a very intelligent police officer, I have not been mutilated as my captor intended. If Chief Inspector Judd and his colleagues had been a few hours later, my condition would have been irretrievable and marriage impossible."

Sir James saw the expression of horror growing on Benson's face as he worked out what his master was alluding to and ordered, "Forget that I said that, Benson."

"Yes, sir," he said dutifully, but he shuddered all the same.

They walked into the main hall, and Sir James stood with his back to the fire for several minutes whilst Benson relocked the front door.

"Is my fiancée here?"

"No, Sir James. She decided to go back to her mother this afternoon."

"I see, and obviously my mother has not been disturbed by my door knocking activities."

"Normally, I think she would have heard you, Sir James, but Lady Mary has been so worried about you that she intended to take a sleeping draft when she went to bed," Benson confided then asked, "Can I get you something to eat, Sir James?"

"Yes please, Benson. I haven't eaten since before I was abducted, so please call cook and ask her to prepare breakfast for me. Whilst she prepares the food, I will bathe and change my clothes."

"Very good, sir," Benson said and immediately went to do Sir James' bidding.

Sir James stood warming himself at the fire for several more minutes, contemplating how extremely fortunate he had been, and then went to his room to bathe and change.

Standing in front of the mirror in his dressing room, he examined the slowly darkening bruises on his legs and torso. *I've had worse from falling off a horse*, he thought. He was nursing a constant headache, though, from the after-effects of the ether, which made sudden movements inadvisable. Turning away slowly he ignored the gathering stiffness in his ribs and began dressing.

Thirty minutes or so later, he came back downstairs and went to the breakfast room where Benson served him a very hearty breakfast.

When he was replete, he walked around to the back of the house, climbed carefully into the Bentley, and set off for Taplow.

As he pulled up outside the Severn's house, he realised suddenly how very early it still was. There was no sign of life, the curtains were still drawn, and there wasn't even a wisp of smoke from one of the chimneys to indicate that one of the servants had started work. He realised that he would have to postpone his reunion with Sabrina for a little longer and decided to sit in the car until he could see some activity in the house. He settled back in his seat, closed his eyes and tried to ignore his throbbing head. In no time at all he was sleeping soundly.

In the servant's quarters, Elsie woke up in her small single bed, threw back the covers, and got up to start another day. *I hope there's good news about Sir James today*, was her first thought as she hurriedly dressed and then went into the kitchen to boil water for morning tea. Whilst the kettle boiled, she laid the tray and then took two cups of tea and two small plates of digestive biscuits upstairs.

She knocked on Mrs Severn's bedroom door then went in and put her tea and biscuits on a side table. Elsie went to Sabrina's room next, and after putting the cup and biscuits down, she went to the window, pulled the curtain, and looked out.

She gasped, turned back towards Miss Severn, and said quickly, in a voice that was high pitched from excitement, "The Bentley's outside, Miss, and there's someone sitting in it."

"What?" Miss Severn said as she bounced out of bed and rushed to the window, pulling a dressing gown on over her nightclothes as she went. "You're right!" she cried. "Perhaps there's news of James?" She unfastened the casement and pushed the window wide open with a bang.

"Tompkins," she called, then again, "Tompkins," as she tried to attract the attention of the person she could see indistinctly in the car.

The figure moved, looked up at the house, then the door of the motor car swung open and she stood in suspended animation as the unmistakeable form of Sir James stood in the road looking up at her.

He waved, and that broke the spell.

Sabrina said in a quiet, almost disbelieving voice, "James?" Then in the same moment, and at twenty times the volume, she shouted, "James!" again, turned on her heel, and rushed from the bedroom and down the stairs with Elsie close behind.

Sir James waved, heard Sabrina call his name, saw her disappear from the window, and assumed she was coming downstairs. He rushed around the car, vaulted over the gate, and started to run up the path to the front door. As the door opened, he stopped and looked with awe at the barefoot vision of loveliness framed in the doorway.

Then Sabrina was in his arms and they were hugging each other as tightly as they could. He kissed her on the top of her head as her face was buried in his shoulder and stroked her hair gently, enjoying the faint trace of her perfume as he did so.

After a few moments, she said indistinctly, "I have prayed for your safe return,

James, and now you are here. I'm so happy." Then she pushed herself a little away from his shoulder and said in a worried tone, "You haven't been hurt, my love?"

"No, Sabrina. I wasn't harmed thanks to Chief Inspector Judd. A few hours later and it would have been a different story, but this time there's a happy ending."

Elsie, who had been enraptured watching the young couple's reunion, suddenly remembered her duty and said in a mock scolding voice, "Miss Sabrina. If your mother could see you standing in the garden in your night attire, she would be very distressed and extremely worried about what the neighbours might say if they see you. I think you should go upstairs immediately. Sir James will not disappear whilst you are getting dressed."

"I'm sorry, Elsie," Sabrina said contritely. "You are right, of course," and then said but only half in jest, "Please guard him, Elsie, and make sure he doesn't disappear again," as she released her hold on Sir James and went quickly back to the house.

Elsie said, "I'm so very pleased you have returned safely, Sir James. This house will be much happier now. Please come this way, sir," and she led Sir James into the sitting room at the back of the house. "I'll just go up and see if Miss Sabrina needs anything," and as Elsie turned away and walked from the room, Sir James noted that the girl appeared a little thicker around the middle than he remembered

Not very long afterwards, Sir James jumped to his feet as a fully dressed Sabrina came into the sitting room, threw propriety out of the window, and herself into her fiancé's arms and hugged him tightly again.

"Darling James," she said into his shoulder. "I was so worried about you."

"As I was about you, Sabrina, when I was conscious long enough to think about anything. I didn't know if you had been hurt or abducted, and what was far worse was the knowledge that I was powerless to come to your aid. It was a dreadful feeling."

Although she revelled in the comfortable feeling of James' arms warmly surrounding her body, the practical side of Sabrina's persona took charge.

"It's very early. Have you had breakfast yet?" she asked.

"Yes," he said, then explained. "I was very dirty when I was released, so I washed, changed, and breakfasted at Brantley Manor before I came here. And that reminds me. My mother wasn't awake when I was at the Hall, so I wonder if my lady will allow me to drive her to Brantley for breakfast? I really ought to see my mother."

"Of course, James," Sabrina agreed. "I'll just see if my mother will be dressed and able to see you before we go," and she detached herself from Sir James' embrace and moved gracefully out of the room and disappeared up the stairs.

Ten minutes later, and after receiving Mrs Severn's heartfelt congratulations on his unscathed return, Sir James escorted Sabrina from the house and helped her into the front seat of the Bentley.

At Brantley Manor, they went directly to the breakfast room, where Benson had said Lady Mary was enjoying a good meal after a total loss of appetite following Sir James' abduction.

Lady Mary saw Sir James as he ushered Sabrina into the breakfast room, and in her haste to greet him managed to drop her knife and fork onto her breakfast plate with a terrible clatter as she suddenly stood up.

So that she wouldn't offend against the rules she had learnt as a child and speak with her mouth full, she hastily swallowed what she had been chewing and said, "This has been a dreadful business, James, and I'm so pleased you have come home unharmed. It must have been an appalling experience for you."

"It was, Mother, but it's over now. I must meet Chief Inspector Judd this morning and make a statement. Then I hope we will be able to live in peace."

"I agree with that wholeheartedly," answered Lady Mary, who suddenly realised that she had totally ignored her future daughter-in-law and said, "I'm very sorry, Sabrina, I haven't even wished you good morning yet. Good morning, Sabrina," Lady Mary said, then, with a masterful piece of understatement, added, "I expect you are as relieved as I am."

"Good morning, Lady Mary. I'm extremely relieved and very happy to be reunited with James again. The last few days have been a nightmare."

"Please help yourself to breakfast, Sabrina, then come and sit down. Will you have something more to eat, James?" Lady Mary enquired.

Sir James nodded as he said, "Several days without food has sharpened my appetite, so I think I will have a little more." He liberally helped himself to a substantial plate of bacon, eggs, and toast and sat down beside Sabrina to eat.

When all three of them had finished, Sabrina asked, "Can you tell us why you were abducted, James? From my own point of view, it's extremely worrying to be attacked on one's own front doorstep, and doubly so when my future husband is suddenly spirited away."

"I was abducted by an Arab called Jalal Al Hafrey. He is the son of a sheikh who rules a poor area some distance inland from Aden. Al Hafrey thought I was meddling in his affairs and decided to make an example of me. Fortunately, Chief Inspector Judd found me in time."

Lady Mary asked, "Where is Al Hafrey now? He's in prison, of course?"

It was one of the questions Sir James had been dreading as he had no idea how his fiancée would react to what he had done.

He responded simply, "Actually, he's dead."

"What happened?" asked Lady Mary. "Did he commit suicide when he was caught?"

"In a way," Sir James answered truthfully but unhappily.

Lady Mary looked quizzically at her son. Normally, his explanations of events were quite comprehensive, but here he was being exceptionally coy about what had happened, and she knew he was hiding something.

"James," Lady Mary said bluntly, "I'm your mother, don't forget, and I know when you are avoiding an issue. I think you should tell us exactly what happened without cutting corners."

"Yes, I suppose so," said Sir James unhappily as he couldn't foresee how his revelations would be received. He took a deep, calming breath before admitting, "Unfortunately, I was responsible for his death." He then explained the circumstances of his incarceration and what Al Hafrey had intended.

White-faced from the shock of Sir James' explanation, Lady Mary gasped in a shocked and outraged voice, "The man was a barbarian! He deserved to die if he intended such an act."

Sabrina said nothing immediately but sat clutching her fiancé's hand, lost in the horrors of what she had just learnt and wondering if she would have had the courage to marry James if Al Hafrey had not been stopped.

After a little thought, she said vehemently, "You acted to defend yourself, as you have every right to do, James. I'm very glad you did and cannot criticise you for ridding the world of such an evil man."

"I agree," Lady Mary said.

There was a long silence as they contemplated the horror that could have been perpetrated and its effect on them individually as well as collectively, and they were all quite relieved when there was a knock on the door and Benson came in.

"Chief Inspector Judd has arrived and would like to see you, Sir James," he announced.

"Thank you, Benson. I'm expecting him. Please take him to my study," Sir James said as he stood up.

"Yes, sir," Benson responded as he left to carry out Sir James' instruction.

"Please excuse me, Sabrina, Mother. I have to write a statement for the police, but I shouldn't be very long," and with that, Sir James also left the breakfast room.

A few minutes after Sir James sat down at the desk in his study, Benson showed Chief Inspector Judd and another man into the room. Judd introduced his companion to Sir James as Superintendent White of Special Branch.

"When we have finished, Sir James, Superintendent White would like to ask you some questions, if you have no objection."

Knowing that a representative of Special Branch could only want to see him about the Colonial Office spy, Sir James agreed immediately.

Superintendent White sat down beside Judd, and whilst Judd organised his notebook and pencil, Sir James quickly scrutinised his unexpected other visitor. Superintendent White was as nondescript in appearance as his name suggested, and Sir James supposed that being unobtrusive was a useful attribute for someone who was trying to catch spies.

As soon as he had his notebook and pencil ready, Judd asked Sir James to describe everything that had happened to him from the time he had been attacked. This Sir James did, and Judd wrote comprehensive notes as he spoke. After asking several questions to clarify points that were not completely clear, Judd said, "Thank you, Sir James. I don't think there is any more I need to know, so I'll have the statement typed out, and if it will be convenient for you, I will bring it tomorrow for you to check and then sign."

"That's quite acceptable, Chief Inspector," Sir James said to Judd, and then to Special Branch officer, he added, "Before I answer your questions, Superintendent, I would like to know why the Special Branch is suddenly interested in me."

"Our interest originates with a report that Chief Inspector Judd submitted to us yesterday after he had read the notes you attached to the personnel files you left in your room at your club."

Sir James looked enquiringly at Judd, who explained what he had read and why.

"Very well," Sir James said. "And what do you wish me to tell you, Superintendent?"

"I would like to know if you have found out any more since you wrote your notes," Superintendent White asked.

"I did learn one thing," Sir James said and went on to relate Al Hafrey's boastful claim about other spies being available if Alex Jones was unmasked. "He did sound very confident when he made the claim," Sir James concluded.

"Pity you killed him," Superintendent White said sadly. "It would have been instructive to question him."

"I didn't kill him," protested Sir James. "I was trying to defend myself from a man with a knife and he broke his neck when he collided with my foot. Isn't that so, Chief Inspector?"

"Absolutely correct, Sir James. Clearly, you were only intent upon defending yourself."

"It really doesn't matter either way, " Superintendent White said bluntly. "If Sheikh Al Hafrey finds out that you were the cause of his son's death, however unwittingly, he will think only in terms of an eye for an eye. You know the Arab world, Sir James, and you know what I'm saying is fact."

"Indeed I do, Superintendent."

There was an awkward silence for a few moments, which Sir James broke by asking, "Do you have another question, Superintendent, or is that all?"

"No, that's all, thank you."

"Then I'll bid you both good day," Sir James said, and he tugged on the bell pull as he stood up.

Benson entered the study quickly, and Sir James said, "These gentlemen are leaving now."

"Very good, sir" Benson responded, and as Judd and White stood up, Benson said, "Please come this way, gentlemen" and ushered them from Sir James' study.

Soon after he had been left alone, there was a light knock on the study door, and Sabrina entered the room in response to his, "Come in, please."

"I noticed Chief Inspector Judd leaving with another man. Was he a policeman as well?" she asked, as she sat on the visitor's side of the desk and reached across to take his hand in both of hers.

"In a way, but a specialised one. He is from Special Branch."

"What's that?" Sabrina asked as he knew she would. Sabrina had an enquiring mind and always asked about the things she didn't know about.

Sir James said, "To combat the Irish terror campaign in 1883, the Metropolitan Police established a small group in the criminal investigation department and called it the Metropolitan Police Special Irish Branch. Over time, the Irish part of the name was dropped as the group took responsibility for countering a wide range of extremist activities, and it is generally known as Special Branch today. The man with Judd was Superintendent White, and he is interested in the Colonial Office spies."

"Spies?" she queried. "I thought there was only one."

"Unfortunately, that may not be so. Al Hafrey was quite boastful about other spies being in the Colonial Office. But that is now White's problem, I'm very pleased to say."

"And I am very pleased to hear you say it, husband-to-be. I think you, all our relations, and I have had enough to worry about during the past two days to last us all a lifetime. I really hope we can enjoy a more peaceful life from now on."

"As do I, my dearest," he agreed.

CHAPTER EIGHT
Marriage

The remaining days before their wedding passed in a flurry of activity as Sabrina and Sir James planned and re-planned, with little to distinguish one day from the next. The weather made its own unwelcome contribution to the sameness of each day by being consistently grey, wet, and chilly.

Almost every morning, Sabrina and Sir James sat at the desk in his study to read through the mail that had arrived for them by the first delivery. Before they arrived in the study, one of the servants had sorted the correspondence into three distinct piles. One each for Sir James and Sabrina and then another pile for letters addressed jointly. Usually, they dealt with the joint correspondence first and then opened the privately addressed envelopes.

One grey, wet morning after reading through a dozen or so letters accepting the wedding invitation, Sir James picked up and opened an official-looking letter. He read through it quite quickly then looked out of the window for a moment.

"On a morning like this," he remarked to Sabrina, "It is difficult not to immediately say 'Yes please!' when one is told that one is to be invited to go to a sunnier country."

"What is it about?" asked Sabrina, indicating the letter Sir James held in his hand.

"It's from the brigadier. Would you like to read it or … ?" She shook her head and he continued. "After the usual greetings, including good wishes to you, Sabrina, the brigadier wrote that he was recently in Cairo and in the course of conversation learnt that the High Commissioner wants me to go back and rejoin his staff. There is an official letter in the post, apparently."

"Will you go back, James?" she asked a little apprehensively.

"Much as I would like to be in a warmer place at present, it will be much too hot in a few months to be pleasant," he commented a little flippantly. In a more serious tone, he said, "More important is that we will shortly be married, and as the High Commissioner will find out when he writes, I am no longer at the beck and call of the Colonial Office and do not have the slightest interest in becoming so."

"I'm relieved to hear that, although some warmer weather would be quite pleasant," and after a few moments of silence, Sabrina added, "I hope the weather will be kinder on our wedding day."

"I'm sure it will be," Sir James said with his fingers firmly crossed .

A few days later, the anticipated letter from the High Commissioner arrived, and after reading it, Sir James didn't require a great deal of time in which to write a polite 'Thank you but no thank you' letter that was dispatched by return.

And there the matter rested as they had more important issues to resolve.

It was an unfortunate but inescapable truth that a week before the day of the wedding, Sabrina still didn't know whether her Uncle Bertram would be available to give her away. Worse was the fact that Sabrina had no idea who else she could ask if Uncle Bertram declined.

Sir James was in a similar position with regard to his best man. Christopher Caruthers had said he would be honoured to be best man when they had spoken about it in London, but as he hadn't acknowledged the invitation, Sir James didn't know if he had even received it.

Sir James attempted to gloss over the situation by saying to Sabrina one afternoon in joke, "If the worst happens, *I* will escort you down the aisle and *you* can be my best man." However, this simply provoked a tetchy reply.

"Don't be ridiculous, James," his future wife said, as she failed to see anything remotely humorous in the situation.

Two days before the great day, Caruthers arrived in the early evening.

Sir James said, "I was becoming a little concerned as I hadn't heard from you, Christopher."

"You shouldn't have worried, James. When you asked me, I said I would be honoured to be your best man, and you saw me make a note in my diary to arrive this evening. What was there to worry about?"

"Nothing really, I suppose. It's just that it's such an important day for Sabrina that I worry something will be forgotten."

"And it's not an important day for you as well?"

"Well, yes, of course it is," Sir James responded. "But doubly so for my future wife."

"Well, you don't have to worry about me now, and I'll try to ensure that nothing is forgotten," Caruthers said cheerfully. "Where are you going for your honeymoon?" and then he added, "When will I meet your fiancé?"

"Why not come and meet her now before I take her home?" Sir James suggested, and as they walked to the library where Sabrina was reading, he answered the previous question.

"We have decided to postpone our honeymoon until the spring when the weather should be a little better, and then we will make a tour of the capitals of Europe. In the meantime, we will live at Sabrina's home whilst the alterations in the Hall are completed."

"That's a sensible plan," Caruthers said approvingly, then asked, "Are you planning to be a man of leisure now that you've left the Colonial Office?"

"I haven't decided anything about the future yet," Sir James said. "I had an offer from the High Commissioner in Cairo but I've turned that down."

Caruthers whistled in surprise but didn't comment further as they had reached the library, and he had been rendered speechless by his first encounter with Sabrina's beauty and happy smile of welcome. He was smitten at first sight, and although he tried to hide the fact, his eyes kept returning to gaze on the beautiful young woman he had just been introduced to as if they were attached to her body with springs. Sabrina noticed, of course. Whilst she was mature enough to recognise that men found her beauty attractive, and be quietly pleased by the unspoken compliment this implied, she could detect the hungry look in Christopher Caruthers' eyes and thought that his attention was bordering on objectionable. She was very relieved that Sir James seemed not to notice.

I must be quite sure I am never alone with Christopher Caruthers, she thought, *as I am not at altogether sure he would behave as a gentleman should.*

The following morning, Uncle Bertram arrived at the Severn's home and was verbally chastised by Mrs Severn for not answering the invitation.

"But I did," he said vehemently. "I posted it last week." He handed his coat to Elsie to hang up.

Elsie folded the coat over her arm, and as she did so, a letter dropped out of a pocket onto the floor. Uncle Bertram bent down, picked it up, and became suddenly very red in the face.

"I'm extremely sorry, Sabrina," he said, holding the letter out. "I really did think I had posted it."

***

The day of the wedding could not have had a worse dawn.

There was no wind, and rain poured in a torrent from a layer of thick black clouds that seemed to be anchored to the tops of the surrounding trees. At eight in the morning, it looked as if Sabrina's wedding would surpass a record for the most rain-sodden celebration of all time. At nine, the rain had eased a little, and by ten, the calm had been replaced with a stiff breeze that seemed to be blowing the clouds away.

When Sir James drove to the church with Christopher Caruthers, the rain had eased and they managed to walk to the porch with only a minor sprinkling of raindrops on their shoulders.

They exchanged pleasantries with the ushers, and then side by side they walked with echoing footsteps towards the altar and sat in the first pew on the right-hand side to wait for the ceremony to begin. As they sat, they heard the rattle, squeak of the door, then the footsteps and muted comments of the guests as they came into the church and were guided to a pew by one or other of the ushers. Just before the ceremony was due to start, Sir James noticed that Mrs Severn had arrived, and they exchanged polite greetings before she took her place in the front pew on the bride's side of the aisle. He half turned in the pew in order to cast a quick glance along the length of the aisle and saw that the little church was completely full of guests, and he noticed that the vicar and the choir boys were all assembled at the church door, together with a radiant Millicent Malcolm in a long rose-coloured dress and two fidgety flower girls.

Only his bride was missing, but he could do nothing but sit still, control his nerves, and hope the wait would soon be over.

After ten nail-biting minutes, there was the sound of a motor car arriving outside the church.

Millie slipped through the door and out into the porch to make any necessary last-minute adjustments to Sabrina's dress. "You look lovely", she said, as she swished the soft silk of the train and it settled in gentle folds at her feet, "and so happy."

"I have truly never felt happier" replied Sabrina, "and it is all thanks to you, my dearest Millie. If you hadn't agreed to accept a lift home from London with James after the train crash, I would never have met him."

Millie gave her best friend a heartfelt hug, before checking the delicate crystal tiara that Lady Mary had insisted Sabrina wear for her 'something borrowed' was still firmly fixed in place. As Uncle Bertram stepped alongside and offered his arm to Sabrina, Millie went back into the church to await their arrival.

The squeak of the door was followed instantly by the rustle of anticipation as the congregation turned to try and catch their first glimpse of the bride. Footsteps could be heard entering the church, followed by a low-voiced conversation between the bride and the vicar, then silence.

Caruthers nudged Sir James in the ribs, and they moved from the pew to stand in the nave just in front of the altar.

The organist started to play one of Sabrina's favourite hymns, and Sir James could trace Sabrina's progress down the aisle by the "Doesn't she look beautiful?" and "Every happiness, dear," comments he could hear the congregation making as she passed.

Then Sabrina was standing at his side; a veiled vision in white silk. He reached out and took her hand just as she was suddenly illuminated by a beam of sunlight that shone through one of the windows like a spotlight in a theatre.

He managed to say in a voice that was taut with emotion, "You look beautiful, Sabrina," as he gently squeezed her fingers.

The wedding service was performed faultlessly by the vicar, and at its conclusion, he led the newlyweds into the chancel to sign the parish register. After the ceremony, Lady Sabrina and Sir James Russell walked down the aisle behind the vicar, smiling and acknowledging the good wishes and congratulations that were showered on them from estate tenants, friends, and relations alike.

As they paused momentarily in the porch with the intention of saying a few words of thanks to the vicar, they heard two or three loud-voiced commands, followed by the rattle of steel on steel. The vicar urged them onward, and they stepped out of the church and found themselves walking between two lines of uniformed army officers who were holding their drawn swords out to form a shining arch over the path.

Sabrina said, "What a lovely idea, James."

"It is," he responded. "I had no idea this would happen, so I imagine we must thank Christopher for arranging it."

"Yes, we must," said Sabrina. "He has been a good choice as best man, James," she said, then thought, *It is a pity I dislike him so much. He is quite a thoughtful man when he isn't staring at me so hungrily.*

The wedding breakfast at Brantley Manor, the toast to the bride and groom, and the various speeches passed off faultlessly, and then suddenly the celebration was all over and the greater majority of the wedding party started to disperse. Sir James and Sabrina went up to one of the guest rooms and changed out of their wedding finery into everyday clothes. By five in the afternoon, they were ready for Tompkins to drive them to the Ritz in London, where Sir James had booked the bridal suite for a three-day honeymoon as a surprise for Sabrina. Just before the newlyweds were due to leave, the remaining guests and the staff at Brantley Manor congregated on the steps to wish the young couple well as they walked down to the motor car in a shower of confetti. Tomkins stood by the open rear door of the Bentley and gave a salute that a guardsman would have envied as Sir James helped his wife of a few hours into the back seat.

As the car set off down the drive, Lady Mary turned to re-enter the Hall and found she was looking directly at Christopher Caruthers. He was staring after the motor car with the sad expression of a child that had just seen an irreplaceable possession spirited away.

"Is something wrong, Mr Caruthers?" Lady Mary asked.

"No, Lady Mary. Nothing's wrong," he responded. He mentally composed himself and managed to say, "It has been a most enjoyable day," as if he really meant it.

"Indeed, it has," Lady Mary responded with a smile. "If you will excuse me, I'll go to my room. Perhaps I will see you at breakfast?"

"I'm sorry, Lady Mary, but I will return to London this evening as I have business to attend to early tomorrow morning." As he said it, he knew he was simply escaping from Brantley Manor in order to go to his rooms and use alcohol to blot out the thought of Sabrina in his best friend's arms. For all his internal confusion, he managed to add genteelly enough, "But before I leave, I must thank you for your unstinting hospitality to a stranger."

Lady Mary held out her hand for Caruthers to shake and said, "Not at all, Mr Caruthers. Thank you for supporting my son so ably," as she thought charitably, *I wonder what he's hiding. Perhaps it's something to do with the war? War is simply beastly.*

They shook hands and went their separate ways.

***

At the end of an idyllic start to their life as husband and wife, Tompkins drove the ecstatically happy couple back to the Severn's house, where Sabrina and Sir James moved into their temporary private quarters on the first floor of the house. Compared with the space they would have in the west wing of the Hall, their temporary home could only be described as bijou, but as they spent most of their time no more than an arm's length apart, they had no imperative need for additional space.

Their lives as a newlywed couple quickly developed a simple routine.

After breakfast, the couple drove to the Hall, where Sir James immediately busied himself with the business of running the estate. Whilst her husband was occupied with the problems of farm management, Sabrina spent time her time either getting to know her mother-in-law or, if Lady Mary was occupied, selecting a book from one of the shelves in the library and immersing herself in it. After lunch at the Hall, they would normally exercise two of the horses, and then late in the afternoon, they would be driven to the Severn's house where they had dinner before retiring for the night.

***

The alterations in the west wing of the Hall were progressing steadily, and the newlyweds made several excursions to the big stores in London to purchase furniture and fittings for their home.

It was a time of great excitement but also of immense contentment for both Lady Sabrina and Sir James Russell as they indulged in the age-old imperative of nest building. There wasn't the smallest cloud on their blissful horizon and nothing appeared likely to change that idyllic state, until an official government messenger arrived unexpectedly at the Hall early one morning.

He was shown into the library, where Sabrina and Sir James were reading their correspondence. He handed Sir James a letter as soon as he had been introduced and then insisted that Sir James sign a receipt book to prove he had received it. As soon as the formalities had been completed, he was escorted from the Hall by the butler.

Sir James examined the envelope. As he slit it open, he said to Sabrina, "It's from the Colonial Office," and then he read it.

He laid the letter carefully on the table in front of him. To Sabrina, he said, "It's from the Foreign Minister's private secretary. I am requested to go to the Colonial Office and see the minister at my earliest convenience."

"Will you go?" Sabrina asked. "I mean, as you are no longer employed by the Colonial Office, why should they ask you to go and see them?"

"I have no idea why they should want me to go there, unless it has something to do with the spy. I will have to go sometime," he admitted. "One cannot completely ignore a summons from a senior civil servant, but I'm enjoying married life far too much to suddenly rush up to London simply because they say to come. Perhaps next week we could combine my visit to the Colonial Office with some shopping and a visit to the theatre?"

"What a good idea," Sabrina agreed. "I do like to make an asset out of a chore. Would you mind if Millie comes as well , James? She will be company for me whilst you are at the Colonial Office."

"I think that's a capital idea." Sir James said cheerfully.

***

And so, a little less than a week later, Tompkins set off for London with three passengers, dropped Sir James at the entrance to the Colonial Office just before eleven, and then took the two ladies to Knightsbridge, where he stopped at the main entrance to Harrods and helped them alight. After they had disappeared into the store, Tompkins drove the Bentley to the hotel where Sir James had reserved rooms for the party and made sure the luggage was unloaded and sent to the correct rooms.

In the meantime, Sir James had climbed the main staircase and located the office of the secretary who had written the letter. Five minutes later, he was ushered into an office that was far more imposing than the one Sir William Ellis had occupied before his fall from grace.

The little gold plaque on the door had the words 'Sir Michael Marshall' engraved upon it in a Gothic script, but apart from the name, gave no other clue as to the official position of the current incumbent.

The secretary led Sir James into the room and said by way of introduction, "Sir James Russell to see you, Sir Michael," then immediately turned to leave the office. He closed the door quietly as he passed into the ante-room.

"Took you long enough to respond to my request," Sir Michael said bluntly, but to minimise the effect of his brusque words, he stood and offered his hand to Sir James.

"Please sit down," he said, indicating one of the leather-clad visitors' chairs and sat down behind his desk once again.

Sir James sat down, nonchalantly crossed his legs as he leant back in his chair, and quickly passed a glance of assessment over his host. He saw a tall, white-haired, impeccably dressed, elderly man who looked every inch a career civil servant and who had the air of confident superiority of one who expected to rise inexorably to the top of the tree.

Sir James said quite calmly, "Your secretary's letter asked me to come at my convenience, and I have done so. Now I am here, Sir Michael, may I ask why you have requested my presence? You must be aware that I have resigned from the Colonial Office and why."

"Yes of course, and also that you have declined the High Commissioner's request that you join him in Cairo again. Why was that?"

"For three reasons, Sir Michael. My initial reason is that I no longer work at the Colonial Office. Secondly, because of the way I was treated by Sir William Ellis. I was exceedingly fortunate that someone took my part and enabled me to leave here with my reputation intact."

Sir James paused as he thought back over recent events and realised how very different his life could have been without the support of the 'Thunderer'.

"And what is the third reason?" Sir Michael asked impatiently.

"I have just had the extreme good fortune to marry a very beautiful young woman and I have no desire to leave her in England whilst I go and endure the heat of Arabia."

"Take her with you, Sir James. The ladies are never bored in these foreign countries," Sir Michael said as he tacitly ignored the first two reasons and focussed on the third, hoping that Sir James would do the same.

"You sound as if you have firsthand experience," Sir James responded and then said, "Where were you stationed?" After the briefest of pauses, he added, "Since you and your wife have both been to Egypt, perhaps my wife could meet Lady Marshall and have the benefit of her firsthand advice?"

Sir Michael squirmed on his seat with embarrassment.

"I'm not married, and much as I have desired to experience other countries, I have never had the opportunity to travel to foreign climes," Sir Michael said in a rather strained and almost aggrieved voice as if it was Sir James' fault he had stayed comfortably in London. He then added pompously, "I have never been able to free myself of my duties here," as if serving in a foreign country was a bit of a holiday for those fortunate enough to be selected.

Sir James smiled but chose not to comment. He said only, "The other reasons are just as important to me, so if there is nothing else, Sir Michael, I'll wish you good day." He stood up.

"Please sit down, Sir James," Sir Michael said with concern evident in his voice. "You haven't heard what the High Commissioner needs."

"I thought his letter was reasonably explicit," Sir James responded. "And after reading what he wished me to do, I had no difficulty declining his request, although it was a considerable honour to be asked. I'm sure there are many able men in the government's service who could carry out the High Commissioner's wishes just as well as me, if not better."

"That is not our opinion, of course," Sir Michael said, and he just managed to keep out of his voice the relief he felt when Sir James sat down again. He had really thought that Sir James was about to walk out, and that would have been disastrous.

Sir Michael thought for a moment and decided that it was important to keep Sir James talking as there was always the possibility that he would change his opinion if the subject was broached properly. He needed a plausible delaying tactic, and after a few seconds thought, he had a sudden inspiration.

"Perhaps I could order us some coffee, Sir James," and he pulled his pocket watch from his waistcoat pocket, opened the lid, and examined the face intently before adding, "It's already well past the time for elevenses."

"That is a welcome suggestion, Sir Michael. We left quite early this morning."

Without showing the relief he felt at his guest's agreement, Sir Michael pressed the bell push on his desk, and when his secretary hurried into the office, he was instructed to arrange coffee for the two of them.

Sir Michael reviewed Sir James' last statement and said, "I had assumed you came alone this morning, but from your use of the plural, you clearly had company."

It wasn't really a question, but Sir James treated it as such and explained.

"My wife and her best friend came with me. We have to finish furnishing our apartments at Brantley Manor, and my wife decided that a trip to London was too good an opportunity to miss. I imagine that Harrods has a lot less stock than it had two hours ago."

Sir Michael laughed and said cheerfully, "That's a very ungallant statement, Sir James."

"You are correct, of course, Sir Michael. It was a flippant comment that has no basis in truth. My wife knows she can buy whatever she desires, but I am certain that she will buy only what is required and at the same time make sure she gets good value for money."

"Your wife sounds a very competent lady, Sir James."

"She is not only competent but also intelligent and beautiful," Sir James said proudly.

"You're a very lucky man," Sir Michael said seriously.

The coffee arrived and there was a pause in the conversation whilst the secretary poured them a cup each and then passed milk and sugar.

After the secretary left the office, Sir Michael decided to try a different tack.

"Where did you go for your honeymoon, if I may ask?"

"We had three days at the Ritz after our wedding, but we have decided to postpone our honeymoon until the spring, when the weather is more suitable for travelling. We plan to do the Grand Tour," he added in explanation.

"Your wife likes to travel?" Sir Michael asked.

"Yes of course, and she has read so much about Paris, Rome, and Venice that she would love to experience the ambience of such romantic places," Sir James said, and his pride in his new wife was almost palpable.

"I think it would be an honour and a pleasure to meet your young wife, Sir James, but I doubt if that will be possible as I imagine you will return to Brantley Manor tonight."

"In fact, Sir Michael, we plan to stay in town tonight and go to the theatre, so if you would care to join us for dinner, you would be very welcome."

"Thank you, Sir James. I should be delighted to join you."

With the reason for Sir James' visit apparently forgotten, the two men shook hands and said cordial goodbyes and parted. Sir James went to his hotel to be reunited with Sabrina, and Sir Michael went to the Foreign Secretary to report his progress, or as his leader described it, 'the total lack of it'.

When Sabrina and Sir James were in their room changing before dinner, their conversation quite naturally concentrated exhaustively upon Sabrina's activities and what she had purchased for their new home and why she had chosen this article in preference to that one. Just before they went downstairs, she remembered the primary reason for their visit.

"I'm sorry, James," she said. "I have been prattling on about shopping and I haven't asked what happened at the Colonial Office."

"Nothing, really," Sir James responded. "Sir Michael Marshall started by trying to persuade me to join the High Commissioner, and then when we had coffee the subject just fell off the table. By the way, he's coming to dinner tonight."

"Why is that?" asked Sabrina.

"I explained that we are going to make a tour of Europe in the spring as a belated honeymoon, and he seemed quite interested in meeting you. I hope you don't mind, but there was no possibility of consulting you beforehand."

"Don't worry, James. I don't mind and will only complain if he makes us late for the theatre. What did you get tickets for?"

"It's the London production of a play by Noel Coward called 'The Young Idea'. Apparently, he has just returned from America and plays one of the leading roles," Sir James said enthusiastically.

"That sounds interesting," Sabrina responded, and they collected Millie from her room as they went to dinner.

Sir Michael had already arrived when they reached the dining room, and after he had been introduced to both ladies, they went to the table Sir James had reserved, sat down, and enjoyed a pleasant meal that Sir Michael enlivened with entertaining tales of his youth.

Just before they were due to separate, so that Sir James' party could go to the theatre, Sir Michael said out of the blue, "I understand, Lady Sabrina, that you and your husband are going to Europe for a delayed honeymoon. You wish to absorb the atmosphere of all those historic places, I imagine?"

"That's correct, Sir Michael," she responded.

"Are you interested in history?" he asked.

"Yes, of course, but why do you ask?"

Sir Michael ignored the question and asked, "Wouldn't you like to *make* history?"

"I don't understand you, Sir Michael," Sabrina said, and she sounded a little annoyed as well as puzzled.

"It's quite simple really, Lady Sabrina. If your husband accepted the High Commissioner's offer, you could help your husband shape history. Is that not worth the minor discomfort of life in a foreign land?"

Sabrina and Sir James were speechless with surprise. Looking at each person in turn, Sir Michael said, "I have enjoyed your company enormously this evening and I hope you enjoy the play. Coward is a strange man, but if you ignore that, you will find that he is a very good playwright and actor. I look forward to your answer, Sir James. Goodnight."

CHAPTER NINE
Cairo

Sir James was not entirely certain how it had happened, but within a very short time, it appeared that his enthusiastic rejection of the High Commissioner's offer had suddenly turned into an equally eager acceptance of it, and he had his wife's whole-hearted support as well.

And that's why we are pitching and rolling across the Bay of Biscay in a full-blooded gale on this so-called passenger liner, Sir James thought savagely as he was sick for the umpteenth time. He was normally a good sailor but something he had eaten had conspired with the weather and reduced him to a weak, sickly shadow of his normal self.

And adding insult to injury was the fact that his wife was enjoying the best of health and treated the gyrations of the ship as if she was walking in the park on a spring day.

And that's the other problem, he admitted to himself, *my blonde-haired, beautiful, young wife has an ability to attract men of all shapes, sizes, and descriptions from every corner of the ship like moths to a naked flame or iron filings to a magnet.* There was nothing in her behaviour that he could take exception to, as she treated all the admirers with equal impartiality, but he admitted he was as jealous as it was possible to be and would be heartily relieved if all of them went over the side on the next wave. *If only I could be well again* he thought and vomited weakly into a strategically-placed bucket once more.

Why didn't I insist we went on an aeroplane? he thought. *We could have flown from Croydon on Imperial Airways and been in Cairo long before now.* Then he remembered that they had decided to travel by ship in order to give Sabrina a little more time to acclimatise to the much higher temperatures of the Middle East, and he felt guilty as well as sick.

But as usually happens, the storm and the illness waned, and it was only a day or so longer before Sir James was restored to full health and became once more his wife's protector from the temptations of the world. But of course, his presence at Sabrina's side didn't completely prevent his wife's male admirers displaying their interest in the politest and least offensive manner possible.

It was bad enough seeing Christopher Caruthers' infatuation, he thought to himself more than once. *But at least I know something about him and can expect him to behave like a gentleman. I know nothing about any of these other people.*

Sabrina, on the other hand, continued to be a smiling and radiant young woman, but she was clearly far from oblivious to the affect she was having on the men with whom she had unwillingly come into contact. On the first morning that Sir James escorted her for a walk on the promenade deck, she took his arm, hugged it, and said, "I'm so pleased to have you well again, husband. It was becoming exceedingly tedious being polite to all those obnoxious men."

It is fair to record that Sir James' health improved quite remarkably from that moment on.

In Cairo, just before midday, one or two of the male passengers disembarked without a backward glance, but the majority watched enviously as Sir James assisted his wife down the gangway and into the carriage that the High Commissioner had sent for them.

As they were driven across Cairo to the villa that had been assigned to them, Sabrina had her first sight of the town where she was going to live and later recollected the scenes she had viewed as if they were a series of isolated pictures concentrating on different impressions. There were no paved roads, only tracks in the beaten sand between the walls surrounding buildings. Sabrina assumed they were homes for some of the people but couldn't be sure. She saw only two motor cars, and they were covered in dust and looked abandoned. There were lone donkeys laden with bags and packages trotting through the dust at the urging of their drivers. She saw several trains of loaded camels walking majestically along the same street. There were many people about, and they all seemed to be wearing long dresses. As she looked more closely, she realised the figures wearing the light-coloured gowns had beards and must be men. The people with dark clothes were veiled or had some sort of mask covering their faces, and Sabrina realised she was looking at female Egyptians for the first time. Some of the women had small children cavorting in the dust around their feet. There were many smells floating on the air, ranging from the mouthwatering scent of roast mutton to the nose-wrinkling odour of an overfull cess pit. In one open space, there was a large dark green tree. Sabrina thought it might have been a thorn tree, but what attracted her attention particularly was the way the bottom of the foliage had been neatly trimmed off parallel to the ground, as it was such a contrast to the unkempt and dusty appearance of the foliage above.

Sabrina drew her husband's attention to the tree and asked, "Do the local people prune the tree like that?"

"No, it's the goats. Look, Sabrina, there's one now," and he pointed.

Sabrina was fascinated to see a big goat standing on its hind legs and stretching its neck up as far as it could reach in order to bite off a small piece of twig. As she looked, she realised that there were quite a number of goats all performing the same acrobatics and easily understood how the tree had been shaped by numerous hungry teeth.

As they drove on towards their villa, she saw palm trees with bunches of dark brown dates hanging down. But the overriding impressions that Sabrina recollected and described to her mother were the unbearable heat of midday coupled with the blinding quality of the sunlight as it reflected back of every surface and the multitude of flies that assaulted them from every direction.

They drove through the main gates and up to the front door of their villa. They were met at the entrance by Frobisher, the household's senior steward, and after mutual introductions, Lady Sabrina and Sir James adjourned to their room for a siesta during the worst heat of the day.

At four, Sir James went to the High Commission to introduce himself, and whilst he was so engaged, Lady Sabrina had a long discussion with Frobisher about how the household was to be organised for her husband's benefit. Fortunately, they saw eye to eye about everything except a few minor issues, and when they parted, Lady Sabrina believed she had established a good working arrangement with the leader of the domestics.

The Russells soon established a daily routine, which revolved around Sir James' attendance at the High Commission each morning whilst Sabrina dealt with domestic matters, read, or wrote letters, and then after their siesta, Sir James returned to his office whilst Sabrina visited other wives or entertained them.

During the weekends, when the weather was not too unpleasantly hot and humid, the young couple spent their time at the polo club. Sabrina joined the other spectator wives, and Sir James, who was already an accomplished horseman, very soon became a skilled player and the number two in the first team.

It was a comfortable if unexciting life, and if they saw no sign of the chance to shape the history that had brought them to Egypt in the first place, they didn't discuss the matter.

The first tiny ripple that ruffled the tranquil surface of the Russells' marriage actually occurred one afternoon at the polo ground.

The final chucker had just finished, and the lady who had been accompanying Sabrina had gone to correct her makeup before meeting her husband. Sabrina sat quietly in her chair looking out over the polo ground and admiring the sunset until she became aware of someone standing beside her.

She looked around and saw a male figure standing unacceptably close to her chair. Her eyes rose quickly to his face, and the angry comment she was about to utter died when she recognised the man's face.

"Christopher," she gasped. "What in the world are you doing here?" she asked and immediately wished she hadn't when she heard him say,

"I wanted to be near you, Sabrina."

Sabrina blushed as the implications of his comment registered, and she said angrily, "That's ridiculous, Captain. As you well know, I'm a married woman. You were my husband's best man, after all, so you of all people should know my situation. Does my husband know you're here in Cairo?"

"No, not yet," he said miserably. "I'm sorry I offended you, Sabrina. Seeing you sitting there alone and looking so beautiful … my feelings overcame good sense."

"And your sense of propriety," she said acidly. "Before my husband comes and asks what has brought you to Cairo, you had better go and think of a better reason for your presence than the one you gave me." Sabrina sounded very angry, and her cheeks had flushed with her emotion.

"Yes, Sabrina. I'll leave immediately if you say so, but I will be able to see you again, won't I?"

"I do not expect so," she said discouragingly. "And certainly never alone. Good evening, Captain." She heard him move away as she turned back to the sunset. But it was no longer as beautiful as it had been, and she wondered what she should tell Sir James about the incident.

"Sorry I've been so long," a lady's voice broke into her introspection, and Sabrina turned back towards the room again. "Are you feeling alright, Sabrina? You look quite flushed. I thought it was the sunset making you pink, but it isn't. Can I get you something?"

"No thank you, Mrs Davies. I do have a headache, and when Sir James arrives, I will ask him to take me home."

That night, Sabrina slept very little as she tried to decide whether to tell her husband about Christopher Caruthers' unexpected appearance or not, and if she did mention it, whether she should relate what had been said. The indecision lasted all night and extended through an unusually silent breakfast, and then Sir James went to the High Commission and Sabrina's opportunity to inform her husband was gone.

At lunch, Sir James said cheerfully, "I had a visitor today. I'm sure you will never guess who has arrived in Cairo."

"No, I'm sure I won't," Sabrina answered, knowing what the answer would be and rather dreading what Sir James would say Christopher Caruthers had told him.

"Christopher Caruthers arrived in Cairo yesterday and came to greet me this morning. He sends his respects to you of course, Sabrina."

"Thank you, James," she responded and then couldn't stop herself asking, "What has brought him here?" and sat in fear of the answer for what seemed to be a very long time whilst Sir James consumed a large forkful of food.

"He asked the FO if he could be posted to Egypt, and when it became known that he had been the best man at our wedding, they decided to send him here as my assistant. I need someone I can trust, and Caruthers is ideal. Isn't that good news?" he finished enthusiastically.

"Yes, indeed," Sabrina said with contrived enthusiasm. "You certainly need someone you can trust," and she wondered as she said it if men had different meanings for the word 'trust' depending on whether one meant at work or socially with other men's wives. Having led quite a sheltered life until her marriage, Sabrina was beginning to find the affect her beauty had on the men she met rather disturbing and uncomfortable and wished it didn't happen.

Sir James was prattling happily on, and Sabrina suddenly started to pay more attention when she caught the words "... invite him to dinner when the Davies come over next week. Perhaps he would like to join the polo club. I'm sure he must be able to ride. What do you think, Sabrina?"

"It's a very good idea, James, and it will help Captain Caruthers settle in if he meets people like the Davies and the Edgars," she agreed with as much eagerness in her voice as she could feign.

Nothing more was said on the subject, and after they finished their lunch, they had their customary siesta.

Routine day followed routine day, and then suddenly a whole week had passed and it was the day of the dinner that Captain Christopher Caruthers would attend.

It was an event that she had viewed with eager anticipation until Caruthers had arrived on the scene and made his unfortunate and unwelcome advance. Sabrina was honest enough to admit that it was flattering to be admired by another man, but at the same time, she wished he would find another focus for his ardour and hoped desperately that he wouldn't say or do anything during the dinner party to cause embarrassment or worse.

Having ensured when she arranged the place settings that Captain Caruthers would be sitting as far as possible from her own seat and when they enjoyed their pre-prandial drinks that he couldn't speak to her alone, Sabrina almost enjoyed her first experience as a hostess in Egypt.

After their guests had departed, she said to Sir James, "I think our first dinner party was a reasonable success, don't you?"

"Yes, very much so," Sir James said. "All the credit is yours, my lady wife."

On that self-congratulatory note, they retired to bed and slept the sleep of the innocent, but it is probable that they would not have slept so well if they had overheard the conversation between Mr and Mrs Davies as they drove home in their carriage.

"Did you see that Captain Caruthers eyeing Lady Sabrina?" Mrs Davies asked her husband indignantly.

"I couldn't help noticing," Mr Davies responded. "You kept poking me in the ribs to make sure I did. Perhaps someone should douse him in cold water?" he added half humorously.

"Where will you find cold water in this country?" she asked scathingly. "Perhaps you should have a quiet word with him."

"Indeed, Mrs Davies," he responded, then leaned back and let the good food and better brandy work its soporific best.

Over the following weeks, Sabrina did not have the misfortune to meet Caruthers again, and she largely forgot her initial uneasiness at his presence in Egypt. Not that she had any reason to feel anything at all, she reasoned. He had been a friend of her husband's before she'd married, and now, he was for her, no more than a casual acquaintance. It had been an unwelcome surprise to discover that Caruthers' infatuation had driven him to Cairo to be near the object of his desire, and she had to admit, it was a considerable concern. She realised that her concern stemmed not from anything she might herself do but from the possibility that Sir James might hear or see something and misconstrue it.

Fortunately, it was very unlikely that Sir James would have noticed anything at the time, as he was very busy preparing for a meeting to ensure that acceptable arrangements had been made for an international conference to be held in London to discuss the Balfour Declaration. Sir James had made a point of reading the declaration and found that it supported the idea of a Jewish state in Palestine and recognised that there was much more to be read on the topic if he was going to make a useful contribution in London.

As Sir Michael Marshall had intimated to Sir James, he was being involved with the formulation of history and finding out firsthand that it was a very busy and time-consuming occupation. And since Sir James was busy, Caruthers, who quickly proved to be a very able assistant, was busy as well, but that didn't stop him dreaming about Sabrina whenever he was free to think private thoughts.

As he had promised his wife he would, Mr Davies took Caruthers on one side at the Polo Club and had a private, well meant little chat about the inadvisability of coveting other men's wives. However, Davies' words were too obscure for his homily to have any effect on Caruthers, even if he had understood that the warning was meant for him.

There were no more dinner parties as Sir James was far too busy to spend time on entertainment, and consequently, Caruthers had to endure a continuing separation. Even through his partial insanity, he knew that he could not make an attempt to meet Sabrina accidentally without hurting his cause more than he would advance it, but his jealousy, when Sir James left his office to return to Sabrina, was difficult for him to hide. As the weeks and months passed, his infatuation strengthened into an obsession, and impractical schemes to eliminate Sir James as Sabrina's husband started to ferment in his brain.

CHAPTER TEN
Betrayed

It is probable that the outcome of this sorry affair would have been quite different if Caruthers had not been involved with the arrangements for the conference in Cairo and more unfortunately chanced upon some information that resonated with something he had been told in London.

He had found a list containing the names of Prince Faisal's delegation and had casually scanned it. It was a long list of sheikhs from different tribes, and one name leapt out at him.

It was Al Hafrey.

Caruthers cast his mind back to a comment made by one of the senior civil servants at the FO when they had discussed his desire to go to Egypt as an assistant to Sir James, and the perfect plan for removing his rival without risk to himself or his desires leapt into his mind.

And in less than two days, his waiting would be over.

Caruthers knew that the Arab delegation would arrive late on the day before the conference, and he made sure he knew where Sheikh Al Hafrey would stay the night.

Late in the afternoon, he sat in his office and, after a little thought, wrote the following note:

'Sir James Russell, the man who killed your nephew, Jalal, will attend the discussion tomorrow as part of Mr McMahon's delegation'.

He didn't sign the note. He carefully folded it, placed it in an envelope, and, after sealing it, sent it to Sheikh Al Hafrey. To ensure it was delivered to the correct person, Caruthers paid one of the High Commission messengers a hefty fee for his services.

Caruthers spent most of the remainder of the day trying not to let the big happy smile of anticipated triumph remain too long on his face.

The next day, all the delegates attending the discussion congregated at the High Commission, and Caruthers found himself sitting several rows back from the conference table. In front of him, Sir James was sitting several seats to the right of Sir H McMahon at the conference table. Opposite were the Arab delegates, and by careful reference to the seating plan, Caruthers was able to identify Sheikh Al Hafrey.

As the discussion progressed through the day, Caruthers noticed that there was no sign of animosity between Sheikh Al Hafrey and Sir James when they conversed. On the contrary, they were polite and respectful, almost friendly towards each other, and Caruthers started to wonder if his note had not been delivered.

It was the only reason he could imagine for the unexpected behaviour of the two men. Not that he really knew how he expected them to behave. He didn't really expect a pitched battle at the conference table, but when he considered the matter, some sign of enmity would not have been amiss.

At the end of the day, Caruthers was so concerned at the apparent failure of his plans that he sought out the messenger he had dispatched with the note and was assured that it had been delivered into Sheikh Al Hafrey's hands in person.

Caruthers was absolutely crestfallen. He had not expected Sir James to survive the day, yet here he was, full of life. He thought sadly, *Life can be so unfair at times.*

Caruthers walked out of the High Commission and went to his lodgings, where he tried to drown his sorrows with most of a bottle of whisky and succeeded only in producing the worst headache he had ever experienced when he woke from his drunken slumbers the next morning. Somehow, he managed to get himself out of bed . He ignored breakfast but drank a large quantity of water before walking to the High Commission with the sun beating down on his throbbing head and glaring into his eyes.

His hope that he would be able to reach the sanctuary of his office, lock the door, and rest his aching head were dashed just as he reached out for the door handle.

Behind him, the voice of the Deputy High Commissioner said, "Have you seen Sir James this morning, Caruthers?"

"No, sir," he answered truthfully. "I haven't seen him since yesterday."

"It's very disturbing," the DHC said seriously. "No one has seen him since the conference finished yesterday, and this morning, we have received a message from Lady Sabrina saying that he didn't go home last night."

"That's really very strange," Caruthers said, and he had great difficulty suppressing a smile as he said it. *Perhaps my plan worked after all,* he thought.

"We have notified the police, of course, but if you think of anything that might indicate what has happened, please tell me immediately."

"Yes, sir," said Caruthers, who had no intention of offering advice of any description.

Caruthers opened his office door, entered, locked the door after he had closed it, and danced with joy all the way to his desk, his hangover miraculously cured. *Perhaps I should go and visit Sabrina later,* he thought happily.

Much later in the day, when Caruthers had recovered from the effects of too much alcohol, he decided to leave his office in order to visit Sabrina.

He knew that he should commiserate with her about the 'unexpected and unexplained' absence of her husband and hoped he would be able to maintain a sufficiently po-faced expression whilst he did so. He would have to try very hard. Much harder than in the office, where a great and uncontrolled grin of happiness would spread over his face whenever he wasn't distracted by everyday events.

Caruthers was just locking his office door when the DHC happened to be passing.

"Did you remember anything, Caruthers?" he asked.

"What about, sir?" Caruthers asked enquiringly, then remembering the role he was supposed to be playing added, "Sorry, sir! That was stupid of me! You mean about Sir James, of course. No, nothing, I'm sorry to say. I was just going to see if I could offer my condolences to Lady Sabrina."

"Condolences?" said the Deputy High Commissioner sharply. "Sir James is not dead yet. He's only missing. You would be better to express your sympathy and hope he's soon returned, young man." With that, the DHC turned away and stamped off in disgust, muttering about the lack of education these young diplomats seemed to have. *The idea!* he thought. *Giving her his condolences at a time like this. The last thing we need is an unnecessarily panicked young wife at present.*

Then he stopped as he remembered he hadn't passed on some information.

"Caruthers," he called after the departing figure.

"Yes, sir," said Caruthers and walked back.

"I forgot," the DCH said. "I have been informed that the last person Sir James was seen talking with was Sheikh Al Hafrey just after the conference ended. Goodnight, Caruthers."

"Goodnight, sir," Caruthers responded and managed to contain his grin of happiness at the news.

From the office, he took a cab directly to the villa where the Russells lived. He knocked on the door and gave one of his visiting cards to the maid as he was invited into the hall to wait. He was so certain that he would be able to see Sabrina and feast his eyes on her beauty that it was a considerable blow to his self-esteem when he found he could not.

Frobisher said as he handed back the card, "I'm sure you will understand, sir, that Lady Sabrina is far too distraught by the disappearance of her husband to wish to see anyone today. She asks for your understanding, sir."

Caruthers was momentarily speechless, then said, "I'm an old friend of Sir James and know his wife quite well. Are you sure Lady Sabrina knows it is me, Christopher Caruthers, calling?"

"Yes, sir, I'm quite sure," said Frobisher and then added firmly as he opened the front door again, "If you will excuse me, sir, but I have to return to my duties." Suddenly, Caruthers was once again outside the house and no nearer to seeing his heart's desire.

As he walked back to his accommodation, he tried to develop a plan for seeing Sabrina again, but his ideas were being muddled by a parallel train of thoughts that tried to understand why she had declined to see him. Didn't she realise he was devoted to her? Was someone deliberately trying to keep them apart?

When he reached his room, the first thing he saw was the nearly empty whisky bottle he had left on the sideboard when he'd collapsed into bed in his despair the previous evening. He decided not to have a large whisky immediately but wait until he had decided what to do. Not that he had a great deal of choice. He had to go to his office and play the role of a friend and colleague worried for the safety of Sir James Russell. The difficulty was hiding the pleased smile that kept creasing his lips as he thought about his rival's predicament. He desperately wanted to bask in Sabrina's company but couldn't imagine how that could be achieved if she refused to meet him if he went to the villa again. And she was unlikely to go to the polo club, he realised. He hadn't even begun to resolve his problem, but he reached for the whisky bottle anyway and poured himself a large measure.

Perhaps a drink will help me think, went through his mind, and he chuckled over his unexpected rhyme.

He poured himself another large measure, downed it, then poured another for luck and drank that. He threw the empty bottle into a corner, where it landed with a resounding crash, and then dumped himself fully dressed onto his bed and heard the tortured screech emitted by overstretched bed springs.

***

Sir James was sitting on the deck of a dhow, trying by turns to find a comfortable position and also some shade from the big lateen sail that was driving the craft steadily in a southerly direction from Suez. The sun was really too high for there to a big patch of shade, and what there was moved erratically about the deck as the dhow heeled and changed course to suit the vagaries of wind and sea.

Sir James eventually gave up and moved to a position where he could sit and lean against the gunwale, and then, when he was as comfortable as he could manage, he thought back over the past hours.

He had escorted Al Hafrey from the conference room and they had stood at the top of the steps outside the building exchanging views about various subjects relating to the conference with every sign of mutual respect whilst Al Hafrey waited for one of his tribesmen to arrive with a carriage.

Being interested in all things to do with the Arab world, Sir James said, "If I may ask you, Sheikh, can you tell me what route you will take to return to your homeland?"

"I will go back the way I came."

"May I ask what that was, Sheikh?" Sir James asked.

"We travelled by camel train west from our homeland, which is to the north of Aden on the edge of the Rhub Al Khali, until we crossed the trade route that lies beside the Red Sea. We turned north and passed through Jeddah on the way to Mecca, where we performed Umrah."

"I understand that Umrah is not as important as the Haj. Is that so, Sheikh?" Sir James asked.

"That is correct, Sir James. Umrah can be performed at any time of the year, but the Haj starts only on the eighth day of Dhu al-Hijjah and is an obligation that every Muslim must fulfil once in his lifetime if he is fit and can afford to make the pilgrimage."

Sheikh Al Hafrey paused, and Sir James said quickly, "Perhaps you would continue with the description of your journey, Sheikh."

"Very well," he said, although he didn't sound very interested in the subject. "After performing Umrah, we travelled on northwards until we were three or four days to the East of Aqaba. Here we made a camp at an oasis and left some of our followers there to guard it. My half-brother then continued north to Amman in order to meet his uncle, and I came to the conference. I had a choice, Sir James; I could either ride under the sun across the open desert to Suez and Cairo, which would have taken me about two weeks and require setting up camp each night, or ride to Aqaba and take a dhow around to Suez. I chose to take my ease and travel by dhow. It's a much greater distance, of course, but a dhow is quicker than a camel and doesn't have to stop for food and rest. At Suez, I simply arranged for someone to drive me to Cairo in a motor car. As I said before, Sir James, I will simply go back the way I came."

As Al Hafrey stopped speaking, Russell noticed a carriage stop at the foot of the steps. At the same time, he realised that Al Hafrey's bodyguards were standing behind and on either side of him and heard Al Hafrey's voice say, "You'll die if you try anything, Russell. You will come with me on your feet or as a corpse. It is no concern of mine which you choose."

Sir James forced himself to relax. Opposed by three strong men, he couldn't hope to prevail, and being conscious and unfettered was better than the alternative. Consequently, he allowed himself to be propelled down the steps to the carriage without trying to raise the alarm.

He had been taken in the carriage to the Nile, together with Al Hafrey and his two bodyguards, and then on a felucca across to the other bank. Once they had disembarked from the felucca, they were driven at breakneck speed through the moonlit desert to Suez by a young Arab who spoke to the motor car as if he was talking to a favourite camel. At Suez, just after dawn, they boarded a waiting dhow, and it was immediately poled away from the shore. As soon as they were clear, the sail was set by sweating, chanting locals, and in a very few minutes, the sail stopped flapping and filled with wind. Not long afterwards, he noticed the land was slipping away behind them at quite a good rate.

Poor Sabrina, he thought, but there was nothing he could do to alleviate her concern when she eventually found out about his abduction.

He noticed the crew casting surreptitious glances in his direction and wondered why. He was on his own and posed no threat to a group of tough and agile sailors, and it was unlikely to be due to the colour of his skin. Sailors were more likely to have come into contact with foreigners than anyone else, so that couldn't be the reason. Anyway, whatever it was that interested them eluded him, and he hoped he might get an answer before the voyage finished. Not that he knew with certainty where the dhow was headed, except that it was to somewhere outside the Gulf of Suez on the east side of the Red Sea. The only port he had heard about was Jeddah, but that was so far away, it would take more than a week to get there on a sailing dhow, and that assumed a steady wind.

He would just have to wait and see.

At the stern, Sheikh Al Hafrey reclined on thick, brightly-coloured cushions on a large predominantly red Persian carpet. He looked as if he was asleep. His bodyguards sat quite close to the sheikh, and whilst they were without the benefit of cushions and carpet, they shared the shade from an ample awning that had been stretched across the stern. The guards were definitely not asleep and cast a speculative eye in Sir James' direction every so often.

Sir James continued to wonder what there was about him that excited the interest of the sailors and guards and could only assume that they knew about Jalal Al Hafrey's death. *I suppose they are wondering how I'll conduct myself when I meet Jalal's father. Just as well this sheikh is the half-brother or I might already be dead,* he thought.

He was disturbed by a shadow moving across him and looked up to find one of the crew holding out some food.

Sir James said, "Shukran, *thank you*" and the sailor replied with, "Afwan *you're welcome*" and that was that. Sir James ate dates and rice, drank some tepid, brown water, crossed his fingers to ward off illness, and then tried to sleep whilst the dhow shouldered its way through the rolling seas as it continued its southerly course.

***

Next morning, Caruthers didn't have a hangover of quite the same severity as the previous day, but he was still far from his normal self. He was quite convinced his ruse for disposing of Sir James had worked, and that made the thumping headache much worse when he realised that he had no idea how he would manage to meet Sabrina. How could he support Sabrina in her grief and start gaining her affection if he couldn't find a way to be with her in the first place?

He managed to wash, shave, dress, and find his way to his office in a state of thirst and hunger. He sat at his desk for most of the day, and his thoughts travelled around in circles as the papers he was supposed to deal with accumulated upon his desk.

Late in the day, the Deputy High Commissioner sent a messenger with a note for Caruthers, instructing him to come to the DHC's office immediately.

He did as he was instructed.

The DHC said, "Everyone is upset by the sudden disappearance of Sir James Russell, Caruthers, and as you have been so close to him, it is understandable that you would be affected more than most. However, you must put personal feelings behind you and deal with your work with due diligence."

"Yes, sir," said Caruthers in penitent tones. "I certainly will."

"Good," said the DHC. "You may leave the office now, and as you have been a family friend of Sir James and Lady Sabrina, I would like you to deliver this note of sympathy to Lady Sabrina on your way home."

Caruthers couldn't believe what he had just heard and said, "I'm sorry, sir, would you say that again? I don't think I heard correctly the first time."

"I said, 'Please take this note of sympathy to Lady Sabrina'. Is that clear now, Caruthers?" the DHC sounded quite irritated at Caruthers' obtuseness.

"Oh, yes, sir!" Caruthers responded. "Quite clear now, sir."

He accepted the letter from the DHC and managed to walk from his office with a suitably dignified gait. But once safely locked in his own office, Caruthers danced around his desk and let a big grin of happiness spread over his face.

In the end, all his worrying had been pointless as the DHC had solved his problem for him.

Caruthers left his office as quickly as possible but decided to go back to his accommodation in order to shave and change his clothes before calling on Lady Sabrina as he wanted to make as good an impression on her as he could.

An hour later, he presented his card to the maid who answered the front door at the Russells villa and said, "I have a letter for Lady Sabrina from the Deputy High Commission."

The maid said, "If you would like to give the letter to me, sir, I'll deliver it to Lady Sabrina immediately."

Caruthers, who could see his opportunity slipping away, had an inspired thought, and with no regard for the truth at all, said quickly, "That will not be possible, I'm sorry. The Deputy High Commissioner instructed me to place his letter in Lady Sabrina's hands. Perhaps you would be kind enough to inform your mistress of that."

"Yes, sir," the maid said. She opened the door of a small reception room beside the front door and indicated that Caruthers should enter as she said, "Please wait in here and I'll inform my mistress immediately." With that, she left the room and closed the door behind her.

Caruthers waited. As time passed, he became increasingly impatient as he felt he was being expected to wait rather longer than was polite, and totally ignoring the fact that he had betrayed Sir James Russell in a most cold-hearted fashion, he thought, *I'm a family friend, after all, and entitled to preferential treatment. I shouldn't be expected to wait like this.*

Consequently, when the maid eventually returned, Caruthers' wounded pride provoked harsh criticism.

He said, "About time you came back, my girl. Did you get lost? I'm not accustomed to being kept waiting, and I'll make sure your mistress knows about your dilatory behaviour when I see her."

The maid, however, had been well trained and, apart from a slight increase in the pink of her cheeks, gave no other sign of her feelings at Caruthers' ungallant behaviour.

She ignored his comment and said sweetly, "If you would be kind enough to follow me, sir, I'll take you to my mistress now."

She left the room and led Caruthers to another larger room at the back of the villa, which had windows that looked out towards a glorious, glowing, colourful sunset largely made up of pinks and reds with a little shading of blue and green. Sabrina was standing near the window with one hand resting on the back of a chair, staring out at the ever-changing colours of the sunset when Caruthers was brought into the room and announced.

Her duty done, the maid slipped out and closed the door behind her.

"Good evening, Captain Caruthers," she said. "My maid told me you have a letter for me. I hope it's good news."

Caruthers passed the letter over and said, "I don't know if it's good news or not, Sabrina, as the DHC didn't confide in me. But if there is any new information, I do not know it."

"I see," she said coldly. "Please sit down," and she indicated a chair some distance from where she was standing.

Caruthers did as he was told and rejoiced that he had been placed where he was able to enjoy Sabrina's shapely curves in silhouette against the light. His joy was short-lived, however, as she quickly moved to a side table set almost behind him, slit the envelope open with a swift movement of an ivory-handled paper knife, and extracted the contents.

Sabrina carefully scanned the letter then replaced it in the envelope and placed both the knife and the letter on the side table.

She said, "There will be no reply, Captain Caruthers. In the letter, there is only an expression of sympathy and an offer of support if such should be needed. It is silent on the subjects I most wish to know about."

Caruthers said nothing.

His reticence was due in the first place to the fact that he actually knew nothing about Sir James' situation and secondly because he didn't want to attract attention to himself and precipitate his dismissal from Sabrina's presence. For the moment, he was ecstatically happy to be in the same room as the woman he yearned for during every conscious moment.

The silence lengthened, as did the shadows, as the light from the sunset faded and Caruthers sought in vain for a subject he could speak about that would not immediately invoke memories of Sir James.

But he waited too long.

"What do you know about my husband's disappearance, Captain?" Sabrina asked suddenly, and her natural concern imbued the simply worded and quite reasonable question with undertones that shook Caruthers' self-control to its foundations.

Has she heard something? he thought in a sudden panic.

"Why should I know anything?" he asked, and it was a good thing that it was too gloomy for Sabrina to detect the guilty look that passed across Carruthers' face, although she did notice how he shifted uneasily in his chair.

"You are my husband's assistant and attended the conference with him. Did you see or hear anything amiss?"

"No, nothing" he responded truthfully. "Everything passed off calmly."

"Who attended the discussions at the High Commission?" she enquired. "From the other side, I mean," she clarified.

"The Arab delegation was quite small, and only one person spoke for them, and that was a man called Sheikh Al Hafrey."

Sabrina gasped in shock as she coupled together her husband's disappearance with the Al Hafrey name.

"That's very bad news, Christopher," she said, forgetting in her distress that she wanted to keep this man at arm's length. "Was there any animosity between Sir James and the sheikh?" she asked.

"No, nothing," he responded truthfully, and he remembered his disappointment at the almost friendly relationship they had displayed as they discussed the arrangements for the planned international conference in London.

"Does Sir Henry know about Jalal Al Hafrey?" she asked in a worried tone.

"Who's that?" Caruthers asked, deciding on the spur of the moment that it would be better not to admit his knowledge.

Sabrina explained quickly, and Caruthers did his best to look shocked at the thought that his friend and employer might be facing death at the hands of a vengeful Arab.

"Perhaps you should write to Sir Henry and tell him what you know. I can wait if you want to write now and I can deliver your letter in the morning." For a moment, Caruthers had a rosy dream of another hour in Sabrina's company, but it was quickly shattered.

"Wait until morning?" Sabrina's voice had risen considerably in volume as she finished her first statement and continued to rise as she went on. "My husband may be facing death and you think the matter to be so unimportant that my letter can wait until tomorrow. You insensitive …. Words fail me!" and she stamped her foot on the floor in her irritation.

She hurried to the corner of the room, pulled the bell cord, and at the same time called "Fatima!"

"Yes, my lady," said a pleasant female voice, and to Caruthers' intense surprise, as he had believed that he was alone with Sabrina, a pretty young woman came towards Sabrina from a side room just as a maid knocked and came into the room from the main part of the house.

"The electricity has failed again. Shall I light the lamps in here, my lady?" the maid asked.

"No, thank you, Zahra, I'll go to the study. Please ask Mr Frobisher to meet me there."

"Yes, my lady," she said and left the room.

Sabrina turned to Fatima and said, "I want to send a letter to Sir Henry McMahon. Is your typewriter in the study?"

"Yes, my lady," she responded.

"Good," she turned to Caruthers, who was still sitting in his chair, wondering how he would make amends for his stupid insensitivity. He should have realised that Sabrina would find Sir James' disappearance a little more distressing than he did himself. *Hopefully time will help her forget,* he thought.

"Thank you for bringing me the letter from the DHC, Captain, but there's no need to wait as I'll send Frobisher to Sir Henry with my letter as soon as it's ready. Goodnight, Captain. Come along, Fatima," and she turned and whisked out of the room.

Moments later, the maid Zahra re-entered the room, politely escorted Caruthers to the front door, and, restraining her impulse for more violent action, managed to gently close it behind his retreating back.

***

Sir James woke with the dawn and stretched his back and legs before rising and making his way to the stern to use the 'thunder box' that was slung out over the wake. After a rudimentary wash, he walked back to where he had been sleeping and sat down again on the gunwale. He had discarded the remnants of the dress uniform he had been wearing when he was captured and was wearing a thobe and ghutra like Al Hafrey and his guards. From a distance, he supposed he must look like an Arab, but up close, his colouring would give him away immediately. As the sunrise brightened the sky, he realised that the dhow had altered course and was now heading much more to the east than when darkness had fallen last evening, and he assumed that they were now in the Red Sea. Sometime later, they turned onto a more north easterly course, and Sheikh Al Hafrey pointed out over the bows.

He said, "We will be in Aqaba in two days," and Sir James understood as never before the phrase, '*Time passed on leaden feet*'.

***

Caruthers didn't sleep much that night as he was too busy wondering what he could do to make amends for the unfeeling behaviour that had upset Sabrina so badly the previous evening. He had hoped to make a good impression but seemed to have done the exact opposite on the few occasions that he had been in her company. *What can I do to persuade her that I'm a worthy replacement for her husband?* was the thought buzzing around in his head as he arrived at the High Commission.

He was very late getting to his office and hadn't had time to walk from the door to his desk before a messenger arrived.

"Sir Henry wishes to see you immediately, Captain. He's been asking for you every few minutes for one and a half hours and becoming crosser at your non-appearance every time. I hope you have a good excuse ready, Captain."

Unfortunately, the distance Caruthers had to walk between his office and Sir Henry's was far too short for Caruthers' tired brain to the formulate a good excuse for his tardiness, so he walked into Sir Henry's presence without one.

Sir Henry sat in the centre of a long table with a number of his senior aides, including the DHC on either side of him.

Caruthers was ushered to the single chair that had been placed on the opposite side of the desk from the High Commissioner and directly in front of him.

Before attempting to sit down, Caruthers said, "I must apologise for being so late arriving, gentlemen. I overslept."

"Worrying about Sir James, I've no doubt," someone said, although the sarcasm in the voice was lost on Captain Caruthers.

"Exactly so, sir," he responded, grateful for the suggestion.

Sir Henry said politely, "Sit down, Captain."

"Thank you, sir," he said as he subsided gratefully into the chair.

"Last night, I received a letter from Lady Sabrina, and what she has told me puts a new and worrying complexion on Sir James' disappearance. She believes he may have been abducted by the Al Hafrey family in order to exact revenge for Jalal Al Hafrey's accidental death. Lady Sabrina says she asked you about this matter as you are a close friend of Sir James, but you denied all knowledge of the affair. Is that correct, Captain Caruthers?"

"Yes, sir," Caruthers said.

"How very strange," Sir Henry remarked obscurely. "Don't you think so, Deputy?"

The Deputy High Commissioner simply nodded his agreement as he stared at Caruthers with an expression that was cold and unfriendly.

In fact, Caruthers was uncomfortably aware that everyone was staring at him, and their expressions were not as friendly as he was accustomed to seeing.

Sir Henry continued, "I received another letter this morning. It's from one of the participants at the recent meeting here and explains where Sir James will be taken and why. The writer was Sheikh Al Hafrey. He also returned a note that was written by someone in the High Commission and delivered to him by one of the messengers the night before the conference commenced. The messenger had no difficulty identifying you, Captain, but to be doubly certain, we have compared the handwriting on the note to a known example of your own. Sheikh Al Hafrey doesn't like a Judas any more than we do, Captain Caruthers, which is why he returned your note so that we could take appropriate action."

As Sir Henry paused for breath, the DHC said, "You told Lady Sabrina you knew nothing about the Al Hafrey affair, which means you are a liar as well as a traitor, Captain, but lying is a mere bagatelle in comparison with the cold-blooded betrayal of your friend and colleague. Why did you do it, Captain? What possible motive could you have had for your actions?"

There was a long silence as everyone at the table stared at Caruthers and waited for him to answer. For his part, Caruthers sat stiffly in his chair and contemplated the life he now faced as a disgraced man. He would be stripped of his commission, blackballed at his clubs, if he didn't resign first, and become a pariah in society.

Eventually, Caruthers cleared his throat and said, "I cannot answer that."

"Cannot or will not?" the DHC asked sternly.

Caruthers again didn't answer. He just sat and stared at the table.

After a long pause, one of Sir Henry's assistants – Williamson by name – said, "My wife and I had the pleasure to dine with the Russells one night when Caruthers was also present. My wife commented on the way Caruthers kept eying Lady Sabrina, and I can think of only one reason for Caruthers to behave as he has. He wants Lady Sabrina for himself, and he can only achieve that if Sir James is disposed of."

Everyone on Sir Henry's side of the table stared at Caruthers with disgust and loathing competing with anger on their faces.

Caruthers sat staring at the table, and eventually, Sir Henry broke the silence.

He said quietly, "As you have not denied what has been said, Captain, I assume it is true."

"Yes, sir," Caruthers said in a whisper.

"What absolutely despicable behaviour," Sir Henry said, and his voice was much louder now. "And you are supposed to be an officer and a gentleman," he thundered, and the sound of his anger echoed back from the high ceiling. He went on, "I would court martial you if we were bound by military law, but as we are not, you must leave Egypt today. I will not have you defiling this country with your presence for a moment longer than is unavoidable," and he rang the bell on his desk. When the Sergeant at Arms entered the room, Sir Henry said, "Higgins. Escort this ...ah! gentleman to the side room there." Sir Henry pointed and then continued, "Lock the door and guard it until eleven o'clock."

"Yes, sir," he responded.

Higgins marched smartly to Caruthers' side and, holding tightly to his arm, ushered him to the side room. He opened the door, pushed Carruthers inside, then closed the door again and locked it. He stood on guard just to the side of the door.

***

Sir Henry pushed his chair back from the table.

He said, "DHC, please send a telegraph message in my name to Suez and find out when Sheikh Al Hafrey sailed from there, then return to my office."

"Yes, sir," the DHC said and quickly left the room.

Sir Henry turned to another of his colleagues and said, "Duncan, I would like you to go to the Garrison Commander. Tell him what we know and ask him to meet me here at noon with plans for sending an armed force to save Sir James."

"Yes, sir," he said, and his chair scraped across the floor as he pushed it back. He stood up then hurried from the room after the DHC.

Higgins watched silently as Sir Henry and the remainder of his aides left the conference room.

***

Caruthers stumbled into the room, and when he recovered his balance, he found it was bare except for a table and a chair. There was a standard service revolver on the table, and he knew exactly what Sir Henry expected him to do at some convenient time during the next hour. Caruthers walked to the table, picked up the revolver, and opened the magazine. As he expected, he found only one cartridge. It was usually sufficient, but Caruthers wasn't about to expunge his guilt by putting the gun's barrel in his mouth and pulling the trigger. Many men before him had chosen death before dishonour, but he, Caruthers, had too much to live for and wouldn't conform to that pattern.

I don't have a family to worry about, so why make the ultimate sacrifice? he thought.

He sat on the chair, put his feet on the table, and wondered idly what Sir Henry would say when he discovered he was still alive.

At eleven exactly, Sir Henry strode into the conference room and beckoned to Higgins, who reported in a quiet voice that there had been no sound from the side room where Caruthers was incarcerated.

Sir Henry frowned.

He had never known of an instance when an officer had not taken the opportunity to save his family from disgrace by ending his life when given the chance. It meant that Caruthers was not only alive but in possession of a loaded gun and could kill someone if he decided murder couldn't make much difference to his position.

"Sergeant," Sir Henry asked. "Are you armed?"

"Yes, sir," he responded crisply.

Sir Henry pulled his own revolver from its holster, checked that it was loaded, and took his place in front of the door.

"When I say, now, Sergeant," he said quietly, "I want you to open the door, but keep to one side. If he shoots me, shoot back and don't miss."

"Yes, sir," the sergeant responded.

"Now!" said Sir Henry.

The sergeant unlocked and pushed the door open. Sir Henry stepped into the room with his pistol raised and ready to fire.

Caruthers didn't move and he didn't speak.

Sir Henry gave a short sigh of relief before collecting the revolver and then said to Higgins, "Bring him out, sit him down, and guard him well."

"Yes, sir," he responded.

***

At midday, Sir Henry joined his aides and Colonel Smythe, the Garrison Commander, in the conference room. He didn't sit in his place but stood and stared down at the man sitting in the chair opposite.

Sir Henry said, "Stand up, Carruthers," and when Carruthers had complied, he continued, "You have behaved in the most treacherous manner. You are a cowardly individual and your loathsome actions were intended to result in the death of a brave and decent man.. You have declined the opportunity to end this matter with some dignity, and consequently, I will have you returned to England in the gaol of the first ship that sails from here. "

There was silence after Sir Henry finished speaking, and Carruthers simply stood and stared at the table, knowing that every eye was examining him with anger mixed with disgust.

Sir Henry turned to his deputy and said, "I think Carruthers should be kept in this building until we have secured a passage for him, but we cannot expect Sergeant Higgins' men to mount a twenty-four-hour guard. If he gives his word not to try to escape, do you think he will keep it?"

"I don't think we have a choice, really, Sir Henry. We don't want the local police involved in this scandal, if at all possible," the DHC responded.

Sir Henry turned his attention back to Carruthers and asked, "Will you give me your word that you will not try to escape?"

"Yes, Sir Henry," Carruthers said clearly. "I will not try to escape."

To the Sergeant at Arms, Sir Henry said, "Sergeant Higgins! Escort this person," and he pointed at Carruthers, "Down to your office in the basement. As you know, he is not to leave this building."

"Yes, sir," said Higgins. He moved to stand beside Carruthers, who stood to attention as if on parade, looking directly at Sir Henry.

Carruthers opened his mouth as if to speak and then closed it again. What could he say to atone for the actions he had taken, except to apologise? Although, an apology would be treated as hot air by these worldly-wise people.

Silently, Captain Carruthers turned and marched with his escort to the door and disappeared from view.

As Higgins and Carruthers left the conference room, Sir Henry turned to Colonel Smythe and said, "I think Duncan has briefed you on the circumstances of Sir James' abduction, Colonel, and as you will be aware, my immediate concern is to arrange for you to send a suitable force out into the desert to rescue him from certain death at the hands of Abdulla Al Hafrey. We know that Sheikh Mohammad Al Hafrey has boarded a dhow at Suez. Sir James was with him and appeared to be unharmed, but that's all we know. We assume that Al Hafrey will go to Aqaba, because he came from there, and then rejoin his half-brother at their camp somewhere to the East of that town. What have you been able to arrange, Colonel?"

"By the greatest good fortune, Sir Henry, we have a mixed company of about two hundred men in a camp near Suez, including a platoon of riflemen with their camels. The bulk of the men are foot soldiers with their arms and equipment on donkeys. The remainder of the company is made up of an artillery battery with their draft horses. They were preparing to deploy into the desert to the west of the town for training as a lot of the men are new to this part of the world. I have sent the commanding officer fresh orders by telegraph, instructing him to move all his men and equipment across the canal, except for the artillery. The riflemen with their camels should have crossed the Suez Canal by now and will be awaiting further orders. The remainder of the men with their arms and equipment on mules will follow as quickly as they can and set up a base camp before deploying east. The artillery with their horses will remain in the camp west of Suez until they receive further orders, although I cannot imagine we will need heavy guns to rescue your man. Now that I know Sir James is likely to be taken through Aqaba, I will order the Company Commander to start searching for him to the east of the town as soon as I get back to my headquarters."

Colonel Smythe stood up and said, "Please excuse me, Sir Henry, but the sooner I can send new orders, the better it will be for Sir James."

Sir Henry nodded, and Colonel Smythe marched from the room.

Sr Henry said, "Now that we have spoken to Colonel Smythe, and provided that no one has a better solution, I propose to visit Lady Sabrina this afternoon to tell her what we know and what we are doing."

No one spoke, so Sir Henry said, "In the absence of an alternative suggestion, I will arrange to go in about an hour's time."

Williamson said, "If you will excuse me, Sir Henry, but it might be prudent if one or two of our wives made themselves available to stay with Lady Sabrina until her ordeal is over."

"That's very sensible, Williamson. Will you arrange that for me?"

"Certainly, sir, and if you will excuse me, I'll start arranging that straight away."

"Yes, of course."

"Very well, gentlemen." Sir Henry turned his attention to affairs of government once more.

***

Whilst Sir Henry consulted the Garrison Commander, Carruthers walked meekly beside Higgins to the marble staircase that led to the lower floors. Although he had told Sir Henry he wouldn't try to escape, he had no intention of honouring that commitment if an opportunity for escape presented itself. Close to the top of the first flight of stairs, Carruthers hesitated slightly with the result that Higgins was suddenly half a pace ahead as they reached the top step. As Higgins started down, Carruthers gave him a violent push in the back that made him stumble and then fall. He hit the stairs face-first about halfway down the flight and then tumbled to the bottom, where he slammed into the wall at the back of the landing.

He lay on the floor in a crumpled, silent heap.

Carruthers didn't hesitate.

Without a sideways glance at Higgins as he passed his recumbent form, Carruthers ran quickly and quietly down the remaining flights of steps. He walked calmly out of the building into the sunshine before anyone noticed Higgins' body lying on the landing and raised the alarm.

***

In the middle of the afternoon, Sir Henry McMahon arrived outside the Russell villa in his coach, and by the time he had alighted, the gate and front door had been opened and an unsmiling Frobisher was on the threshold to welcome a most distinguished and unexpected visitor.

"If you will come this way, Sir Henry, I will escort you directly to my mistress," said Frobisher, and he led the way into the house.

Frobisher knocked on the door to the sitting room and opened it.

"Sir Henry McMahon to see you, my lady," Frobisher said and immediately left the room as Sir Henry entered.

Lady Sabrina saw Sir Henry, lost all colour from her face, and sprang to her feet.

With her hand on her heart, she cried out, "What has happened?"

Sir Henry hadn't anticipated such a reaction from Lady Sabrina and wished he'd had the foresight to ask his wife to accompany him.

He said in as calm a voice as he could manage, "Please do not distress yourself unnecessarily, Lady Sabrina. I haven't brought bad news."

Sabrina immediately assumed that the news was good and jumped to the hoped for conclusion. "James is safe," she said. "That's wonderful," and she hurried across the room and took Sir Henry by the hand.

"I'm sorry to have misled you, Lady Sabrina," he said quickly. "We have no news about your husband yet, but there has been a development that I believe I should tell you about directly, so as not to let the information reach you through the back door."

They sat down on opposite sides of a small mahogany table, and Sabrina, who was still white-faced, managed to ask in a remarkably calm voice, "Please start at the beginning, Sir Henry."

"Thank you, Lady Sabrina," he said, impressed by the rapidity with which she had regained her composure..

"First of all, you were correct to bring my attention to the Al Hafrey incident, and we know now that Sir James has been taken by Al Hafrey. We believe they are heading into the desert east of Aqaba. As a result, a large army contingent has been sent in pursuit."

"When do you think the army will meet up with Al Hafrey?" she asked, hoping that her husband's ordeal would be short -lived. She had no doubt that it would be an ordeal for him if the father was anything like Jalal Al Hafrey. She tried not to think of the possibility of his murder.

"Unfortunately, it will take them several days to reach Aqaba, and then they have to find Al Hafrey's trail and track them into the desert. We cannot estimate how long it will be until we have some idea of where they are heading."

"I see. Is there more to relate?" Lady Sabrina asked, and Sir Henry noted approvingly that her colour had improved and her voice was stronger.

"Yes," he said. "The worst news of all."

"Go on," she said. "Nothing can be as bad as my husband's abduction and possible death."

"I imagine so!" Sir Henry said and paused for a moment before adding, "I am sorry I have to tell you this, but Sir James was betrayed by Christopher Caruthers."

Sabrina gasped and said, "I can't believe that, Sir Henry. Captain Caruthers was here only last night and seemed to be genuinely concerned about my husband."

"I'm sorry, Lady Sabrina, but we have the note Caruthers wrote to Al Hafrey, and I doubt if Al Hafrey knew about a connection between your husband and Jalal's death until he received it."

"That's dreadful news, Sir Henry. What possible motive could he have had for taking such dastardly action?"

Sir Henry had hoped Sabrina would not think to ask such a question, and once again, he wished he'd had the foresight to bring his wife.

Sir Henry took a deep breath and said, "The answer is quite simple but rather shocking. Carruthers has tried to eliminate your husband so that he could have you for himself."

Sabrina flushed red with anger and embarrassment as the full implications of Sir Henry's blunt statement registered.

"How could he think such a thing?" she asked in a furious tone. "He was my husband's friend and only an acquaintance as far as I was concerned. I have never once given him any sign of encouragement. In fact, since he arrived, I have done my best to *dis*courage him. I didn't like the way he regarded me, but he was James' friend and assistant, and I assumed he was trustworthy. I know James thought he was."

She stopped and dabbed delicately at her eyes.

"What has happened to Carruthers?" she asked.

"I told him this morning that he would be sent home on the first available ship and he gave me his word that he wouldn't try to escape from the High Commission building whilst we arranged his passage. He broke his word almost immediately and seriously injured one of our attendants whilst escaping into Cairo. Obviously, we are searching for him, but he hadn't been located by the time I left my office to come here. I must say, Lady Sabrina, that you do not need to be concerned for your safety as Mrs Williamson will stay with you tonight and keep you company."

"That's very thoughtful of you all," Sabrina said gratefully. "I will be pleased to have company tonight. When will she arrive?"

"Very soon now," Sir Henry said as he stood up. "If you will excuse me, Lady Sabrina, I must return to my office."

"Of course, Sir Henry," and she stood also and tugged on the bell pull.

Moments later, Frobisher arrived and escorted Sir Henry back to his carriage.

***

After Caruthers left the High Commission, he walked dejectedly back towards his accommodation with his head down. He hadn't expected Al Hafrey to return his note to Sir Henry.

That had spoiled literally everything.

Life is so unfair, he thought as he mooched along. *All I wanted to do was be with Sabrina and James Russell had been in the way. I was so clever to get Al Hafrey to take poor old James away, and then Al Hafrey had to be clever and spoil it. And now I'm a ruined man … although no one knows except me and the High Commissioner, of course,* he remembered. He also remembered what Sir Henry had said. "Stay in the High Commission building until we have arranged a passage home for you." Not until he had seen Sabrina once more.

With that resolution made, Caruthers straightened his back and started to march along as if he didn't have a care in the world. Without conscious thought, he took the direct route to the Russells' villa and arrived outside the main gate just in time to see Sir Henry entering. He realised immediately that any possibility of seeing Sabrina by walking up to the front door and asking, "May I see Lady Sabrina," had disappeared, so to avoid drawing attention to himself, he continued walking until he had passed the gate.

It was not long before he realised that he had circled the grounds, and as he approached the property for the second time, Caruthers could see that the watchman was no longer guarding the gate. Without thought, he crossed the road so that he was on the same side as the villa. As he walked past the first gate post he angled himself slightly so that he was aiming diagonally into the garden. Without altering his pace he walked purposefully across the driveway and by the time he reached the next gatepost he was just inside the grounds. . He didn't attempt to approach the villa but simply disappeared into the vegetation, and as he did so, he heard the slap, slap of sandals approaching from the house. He didn't stop to see who was coming but walked quietly along, just inside the boundary wall, looking for somewhere to hide until dark. He found a small summer house on the edge of a big area of lawn, and inside it were half a dozen or so deckchairs and each had a brightly-coloured, striped canvas seat. He unfolded one of the chairs quietly, set it down behind the door so that he wouldn't be seen unless someone came right into the summer house, and sat down to think. He noticed that he could see the veranda and some windows and a glazed door at the back of the villa through a grille set in the summerhouse wall but couldn't tell what the room was used for.

He had no idea what he would do when the occupants of the house were asleep because he was reacting to events as they happened and had no time to make plans, but he was sure he would think of something when the time came.

He heard the departure of Sir Henry in his carriage and a little later the arrival of another carriage and then Frobisher welcoming Mrs Williamson.

Then silence.

And in the warm gloom of the summer house, lulled by the buzzing of distant insects, he dropped off into a peaceful sleep.

When he woke, it was dark, and he noticed as soon as he opened his eyes that the lights had been lit in the room opposite and it was immediately apparent that he was looking into one of the bedrooms. In order to get a better view, he carefully carried his deckchair over to the grille and adjusted it so that the back was as nearly upright as possible. Caruthers was very pleased to find that he could sit down and, with his head leant back against the seat, still look into the bedroom through the bottom of the grille. He noticed that the glow from a crescent moon gently illuminated the grass area between the summer house and the villa and realised that it would help him when he decided to enter the villa.

Because that was what he knew he must do if he was to see Sabrina again. He was quite sure he would be welcomed when she overcame her surprise.

So, he sat quietly in the dark and watched the lights come on and go off in the various parts of the villa he could see as the occupants readied themselves for bed. Eventually, only the light in the room opposite remained on, and when Sabrina appeared near the partially-opened French window, Caruthers had great difficulty restraining himself. More than anything he had desired in the world before, he wanted to rush across the grass and throw himself at her feet and only restrained himself with great difficulty.

As he regained his composure, he realised that Sabrina was talking to someone, and his fevered mind immediately conjured up a picture of a rival, but before he could do anything, he saw that Sabrina was talking to another woman.

Mrs Williamson, he assumed, and he calmed down again.

The two ladies talked for a little longer, and as they did so, they steadily moved away from the window into the back of the room, where he couldn't see them clearly. After another five minutes or so, the light went out, and he assumed that Sabrina had gone to bed in the room just opposite where he was watching.

He waited another ten minutes or so to let everyone go to sleep, then, as quietly as possible, he left the safety of the summer house and slipped across the moon-glowing grass in his stocking-clad feet and stepped up onto the wooden veranda.

It complained under his weight with a squeaking, groaning sound that should have woken the watchman but didn't, and he started to breathe again.

Caruthers moved across the veranda to the French window with extreme care, fearful that there would be another badly fixed board to announce his presence, but he reached his objective without another alarm.

He stopped by the opening and listened intently. He could hear someone breathing regularly but wasn't sure she was asleep until a gentle snore disturbed the silence.

Caruthers grinned as he thought, *Who would have imagined that someone as ladylike as Sabrina would snore?* as he stepped over the threshold into her bedroom.

He stopped momentarily to let his eyes become accustomed to the reduced level of light and then tiptoed to the bed, where he could see Sabrina lying under the mosquito netting.

She was sleeping on her back under a very light cover that didn't completely hide the curves of a beautiful young woman.

Caruthers lifted the netting, passed it over his head, and then let it drop behind him as he sat on the edge of the bed.

After a few moments, during which he allowed his eyes to admire the young woman spread out before him, he took her hand and squeezed it.

Trying to keep the passion he felt out of his voice, he said, "Darling Sabrina, you must wake up."

Sabrina stirred and half opened her eyes, saw what she wanted to see, and said, "Oh James, you're safe," and clutched the hand that was holding hers.

Caruthers was rather offended and said roughly, "It's not James, it's me, Christopher."

Sabrina's eyes opened wide at that, and as soon as she recognised who it was sitting beside her, she erupted out of bed on the opposite side with a banshee scream, grabbed the bed clothes around herself, and huddled in the corner of the room as far away from Christopher Caruthers as she could manage.

Caruthers was still sitting on the side of the bed, stunned into silence at his welcome, when Mrs Williamson arrived. She took in the scene with a glance, grabbed the first available object, which happened to be a very nice brass vase, and hit Caruthers a good, hard blow on the head. It made a very satisfactory 'boing' noise, and Caruthers collapsed on the floor.

Moments later, the room was full of jabbering male and female servants and order wasn't restored until Frobisher appeared and took charge.

***

Several hundred miles away, Sir James was being woken up by one of the crew after an uncomfortable night on the deck of the dhow. They had reached Aqaba and the captain of the dhow wanted to get rid of his passengers as soon as they could be put ashore, even though it was only just dawn.

As Sir James straightened his aching back, he noticed Al Hafrey and his two bodyguards walking towards him from the stern.

Al Hafrey said, "I have left you unfettered on the dhow, Sir James, because you know as well as I that there was nowhere for you to escape to. You could have jumped over the side, but you would have had no chance of avoiding the sharks and swimming to shore. But we are leaving the dhow now and you have a choice. Either you give me your word that you will not try to escape or we will tie you up to make sure you cannot. Which will it be?"

"I have done nothing wrong, Al Hafrey, so I do not need to escape. I took no action against Jalal except to defend myself when he attacked me."

"For your sake, I hope my half-brother believes you," Al Hafrey said, and he stepped toward the steep, narrow plank that stretched precariously down between the side of the dhow and the shore. Al Hafrey stepped up onto the gunwale and then onto the plank, which bent a little under his weight, but as he stepped carefully along it towards the shore, it flexed more and more at each step until he was having some difficulty maintaining his balance. Al Hafrey managed to remain upright but reached the shore at an unceremonious pace and just managed to avoid tripping and falling onto the sand. Both the bodyguards gasped with relief when they saw their sheikh safely on dry land.

One of the guards went next, and he was obviously accustomed to traversing such a flexible gangplank as its movements did not seem to cause him any difficulty at all. The remaining guard pushed and prodded Sir James until he climbed onto the plank.

Sir James managed to reach halfway without too much difficulty, but then the movement of the plank started to destroy his balance and he chose to jump into the water rather that fall in. He landed in the water feet first with an enormous splash that generated great hoots of laughter from the crew on the dhow, and then he waded from the sea, soaked to the waist.

Once he was out of the water, he turned and waved to the men on the dhow, who responded this time with a cheer, and then he walked with squelching boots to a grinning Al Hafrey.

"You will soon dry out, Sir James," he said encouragingly as the water drained out of his clothes and momentarily darkened the parched sand with moisture.

"Indeed I will, Sheikh ," Sir James said politely.

"Tell me, Sir James, how did you manage such a dignified fall?"

"I had a choice, Sheikh. I could either wait until I fell off ignominiously or choose to jump whilst I still had some control. I chose to jump."

"Very wise, I must remember your example."

"It would be better to ensure a stronger gangplank, Sheikh," Sir James said seriously, "then you would have no problem at all."

"True," he said as an enormous splash and another cheer echoed through the anchorage. Sir James turned and was just in time to witness the reappearance of the second guard as he surfaced close to the side of the dhow, where the water was much deeper.

He had clearly fallen in almost as soon as he had stood on the plank.

Someone on the dhow shouted a few angry words of command and a rope was thrown to the floundering, spluttering guard. When he caught it, one of the sailors ran down the gangway as if it was as solid as iron and pulled the guard towards the shore. As soon as the guard was able to stand up, he let go of the rope and the sailor ran back up the gangplank, pulling the rope after him. The dhow was already being poled away before the sailor reached the deck, and there was another angry exchange between the sailor and the dhow captain as the former had to scramble up the rapidly increasing slope of the gangplank to get back onto the dhow.

One dry and one exceedingly wet guard came and stood to attention either side of Sheikh Al Hafrey and waited for the sheikh to speak.

Sheikh Al Hafrey gave his instructions in Arabic, assuming incorrectly that Sir James knew nothing of the language.

In fairness to the sheikh, it was most unusual for a European to know any Arabic and Sir James had given no hint that he understood a word. Up till now, their conversation had been entirely in English, and Sir James had no intention of altering his captive's knowledge until it suited him.

Consequently, Sir James knew exactly where they were going but waited for the sheikh to address him in English before reacting in any way.

Al Hafrey said, "We are going to meet my half-brother. It will take three days' hard riding to get there. As you know, Sir James, it's a barren desert. If you wish to drink, ask Mustafa as he will carry your water supply. If you escape, we will not look for you. Without water, you will be dead very quickly."

"As I said before, Sheikh, I have no need to escape as I have done nothing wrong."

"Perhaps my half-brother has a different interpretation," Sheikh Al Hafrey said indifferently. "After all, he has put a price on your head and demanded your capture. I imagine he wants the pleasure of ending your life himself. I shall just deliver you and collect the reward."

"What reward?" Sir James asked. "Your half-brother doesn't have enough money to pay his guards, so he certainly won't pay you anything, Sheikh."

"I am confident my half-brother will keep his word," Al Hafrey said angrily.

"In three days, you will know who is right, Sheikh." Sir James responded.

"And you will be dead." Al Hafrey answered.

"Where are the horses, Sheikh, or do you intend to walk?" asked Sir James.

"We will use camels. You have ridden a camel?" the sheikh asked.

"Me?" he responded. "Ride a camel?" he added in a rising tone of voice that suggested incredulity at the idea and not a little apprehension at the prospect. "I only ride thoroughbreds," he said untruthfully but in as superior a voice as he could manage. Sir James wondered how he would be able to conceal the fact that he knew how to ride a camel and hoped he could remember the mistakes he had made when he'd first tried.

"You'll have to learn something new, then," Al Hafrey said. "A horse wouldn't survive where we are going."

"What is your half-brother doing in a camp north of Medina when his land is far to the south?" Sir James enquired.

"He's been on the Haj, visited his uncle in Amman, and is on his way home. He is only waiting for me to report the result of our meeting in Cairo. You will be an unexpected bonus." He laughed mirthlessly, and a shiver of apprehension tickled Sir James' spine at the sound.

Al Hafrey turned to one of his guards and told him to collect the camels and bring them to the shore then squatted on his heels whilst he waited. Sir James sat cross legged on the sand, and the remaining guard stood conspicuously between his master and Al Hafrey's prisoner and fingered the haft of the dagger stuck in a scabbard attached to his belt.

Although his position was extremely precarious, Sir James couldn't stop himself admiring the intricate silver wire decoration on the scabbard and the hilt of the dagger.

The camels arrived and knelt obediently to the guard's command. Al Hafrey mounted with the ease born of life-long practice and instructed Sir James to mount as well. Sir James did as he had been instructed but slowly and ungracefully and then, much to Al Hafrey's amusement, nearly fell off again as the animal lurched back onto its feet. Al Hafrey urged his camel forward, and in a ragged line, they started trekking eastwards as the sun started to rise over the horizon.

Several dusty hours later as the heat of the sun started to strike down on the small caravan, Al Hafrey stopped for a few minutes and drank sparingly from the goatskin water container he had slung on the saddle in front of him. The two guards also drank, but when Sir James held his hand out for his water bottle, the guard called Mustafa knocked his hand away and rode on, laughing at the Englishman's discomfort.

Sir James rode after him, but as he had the slowest of the available mounts, he had no chance of catching up with any of his captors and failed to do so until they stopped for the night. By the time Sir James reached the camp, they were comfortably ensconced on rugs in front of a fire and eating some food they had brought with them.

By this time, Sir James was not only extremely thirsty but also very, very angry.

Not that it showed as he climbed stiffly down from the camel's back and hobbled it as he had been shown in the morning. He straightened up, stretched his back, and walked across to the three Arabs, then picked up one of the discarded water skins and drank for several minutes.

To an uncomprehending Al Hafrey, he said, "If I die of thirst before you reach your half-brother, you can wave goodbye to your ransom."

Then he bent down, took a firm two-handed hold on Mustafa's thobe, and lifted him to his feet as if he had no weight at all. Then before any of them could comprehend what he was about to do, Sir James drew back his fist and unleashed a punch to Mustafa's face with all his angry strength behind it. Mustafa flopped onto the sand like a partially filled sack of grain and lay inert. The other guard started to pull out his dagger as he scrambled to his feet. He rushed at Sir James with his knife already raised to strike, but at the last minute, Sir James stepped to one side and thrust out his leg as the guard passed.

The guard tripped and sprawled onto the ground. Moments later, he received the full weight of Sir James' muscular mass on his back and had the wind knocked out of him. Sir James picked up the dagger and was back on his feet before Al Hafrey realised the danger he was in.

His ignorance was short-lived as Sir James quickly pressed the point of the dagger up into the flesh under Al Hafrey's chin by the Adam's apple and said, "Lie down."

Al Hafrey complied, and Sir James ordered, "On your stomach," and withdrew the knife from under his chin and pressed it into the side of his throat. Al Hafrey complied, and seconds before his head touched the sand, Sir James struck him a full-blooded blow on the side of the head with the butt of the dagger. Al Hafrey collapsed.

Well! That's a sudden change of fortune, Sir James thought as he quickly surveyed the three recumbent Arabs.

He quickly went back to the guard he had only winded, used the butt of the dagger to knock him out as well, and then cut a good yard from the bottom of the guard's thobe. This he tore into strips about two inches wide. The guard's hands were bound firmly together with one strip and his feet with another. Then to further immobilise the man, he pulled hands and feet and tied them together as closely as he could and left him lying on his side. The second guard, Mustafa, had started to moan but was treated in exactly the same way as his companion, as was Al Hafrey a few minutes later.

Now that he felt safe from attack, Sir James gathered some food and water and settled down to a meal and to recover from the exertions of the last quarter of an hour or so.

As he sat and ate, he started to wonder what his best course of action would be. *One thing's certain*, he thought, *I won't throw myself on the mercy of old Abdullah Al Hafrey. He may not be as fair and merciful as I would like to believe he is, so continuing eastwards is not an option. If the boot were on the other foot, Mohammad Al Hafrey would abandon me here and ride on into the sunrise, but I cannot do that. At the same time, I do not want to release him or his guards and risk recapture.* Sir James realised it was a problem he would have to find a solution to by morning and then turned his attention to the possibility that the High Commission would attempt his rescue by sending troops after him. It was probable, he conceded, and since Al Hafrey had made no attempt to cover his tracks, it was likely the army would know he had been brought through Aqaba and the direction they were travelling in. They should be somewhere behind him to the west, but how many days behind was a major problem as there was very little water available.

He decided he would think more clearly after the exertions of the past day had been overcome with a few hours' sleep, so after building up the fire and checking his captors were still firmly bound, he lay down. Within minutes, he was asleep.

He awoke in the morning to the groans and complaints of his captives. He took a water skin and poured water into each open mouth in turn and was reminded of chicks receiving food from the mother hen as he did so. He checked that they were still firmly bound then ate and drank sparingly. A plan for dealing with his prisoners had been in his mind when he woke, and he reviewed it as he ate. He couldn't find a fault with it and proceeded to put it into action.

He rounded up the camels, selected the two best beasts for his own use, and allowed the other two to roam freely again. As he didn't want Al Hafrey and his men pursuing him, he assumed shortage of food and, more particularly, water, would discourage them from making the attempt. Consequently, he packed three quarters of the water and all the food on one of the camels he was going to take with him. He estimated that there would be enough water to keep the three Arabs alive for about two days, particularly as they would only have two camels between them and might have to take turns walking. He quickly revised that opinion. Sheikh Mohammed Al Hafrey would ride and the least favoured guard would walk. He put a saddle on the camel he had selected and then tied a halter between the two beasts. A separate rope was tied to the pack camel, and the free end pulled back into the camping area and dropped on the ground near the second guard. Mercifully, he took the water skin around the three captives and allowed them to drink as much as each could consume, and after covering the heads of Mustafa and Al Hafrey with their ghutras, he walked back to the other guard and tied the rope to the man's belt. He quickly cut the bindings around the guard's legs and then walked to the camel he had selected and climbed on with a practised ease that he had carefully hidden the day before.

In a few moments, the camels had moved far enough for the rope attached to the guard to tighten and drag him across the sand. After a few yards, Sir James stopped the camel to allow the guard to climb to his feet and then started the camel forward again at an easy pace and started to head in a roughly north-westerly direction, which would eventually lead him to Amman.

With his hands tied behind his back, the guard was unbalanced and fell often, but Sir James would stop long enough for him to regain his feet and then set off again. Sir James drank water when he had the need but deliberately ignored his captor's pleas for a drink as he wanted him to be so thirsty when he was released that his only thought would be to reach the camp he had left that morning as quickly as possible.

In the middle of the afternoon when the guard had fallen yet again and was lying inert in the sand, Sir James dismounted, untied the end of the line attached to the guard's belt, coiled the rope, and tucked it into the food bag on the pack camel.

He remounted, called out, "Ma'a salama , *goodbye*" and rode on, leaving the Arab lying on the sand.

A little later, Sir James stopped to drink a mouthful of water, looked back to see if the guard had recovered, and was relieved to see him on his feet and scrambling back along the track he'd made earlier.

Sir James was quite pleased that his plan to escape from Al Hafrey and lay a false trail had succeeded, but he continued along in the same direction until he was confident that the guard could no longer see him. Then, following the plan he had conceived based on the assumption that the army would follow the track Al Hafrey had made from Aqaba, he changed direction until he judged he was travelling roughly south-west. He intended to follow this course until he crossed the old track and then turn west in the hope that he would meet the army patrol before he ran out of water.

He rode on until the moon was setting, then hobbled the camels, ate and drank a little, and then lay down to rest until morning.

In the first light of dawn, he remounted and continued to trek south westwards. After a few hours of riding across the empty, barren, almost featureless desert, looking fruitlessly ahead and to left and right for a sign of the path, he was beginning to believe he must have crossed it in the night. Then he looked down to rest his eyes from the sun's glare and saw the tracks under the camel's pads. He stopped and looked to his right and could immediately see the faint traces their passage had left in the sand two days before. He drank a little water and, with a much more cheerful demeanour, started to follow the path back towards Aqaba, blessing the luck that had made him look down at that crucial moment.

Sir James had expected to meet the force he was sure the army would have sent after him before he reached Aqaba, but when he was able to see the settlement and no soldiers in the hazy distance a day later, he was forced to reconsider his plans. Either the army had not sent a force or they had gone a different way.

There was no sense in simply going on as he could be riding into danger as easily as he was riding away from it, so he stopped and made camp a good distance from the track he was following. He hobbled the camels in a hollow surrounded by low dunes and made camp in the same area. He decided to light a fire and have some coffee to drink. It was still daylight, so the light from the fire wouldn't give him away, but the smell of the smoke could. After some thought and careful examination of the surrounding desert from the top of the highest sand dune he could find, he decided it was a risk he could afford to take. There was no wind and he hadn't seen a living creature for days.

Fifteen minutes later, after eating some unsatisfying stale food and drinking a tin cup of good coffee, he snuffed out the remnants of the fire and leant back against the dune where he was camped and wondered what he should do next. Riding into Aqaba didn't seem sensible as Al Hafrey could have supporters there. If he did decide the risk was worth it, getting a boat from Aqaba back to Suez, even if one was available, seemed a rather long-winded way to return home to his wife. A better solution, provided he could find food and water, might be to change direction a little and head for Suez and then Cairo across the desert.

He knew something of the area from his previous tours in Egypt and estimated that it was about one hundred and fifty miles to Cairo. He had two camels that had done very little work over the past few days, and if he rode them alternately, they would last far longer than he would himself. Another advantage was that the closer he approached Suez, the more likely he would be to find a motor car he could hire and considerably reduce the journey time.

And that would be a very desirable occurrence, as seven or eight days on camel back was not appealing.

He decided to sleep on it. If it still seemed to be a good idea in the morning, he would act upon it immediately. And that was what he did.

During the morning and well north of the seaport, he crossed the track that led from Aqaba to Amman. He saw no one, and if anyone saw him in the distance, he would have been ignored as he looked from a distance just like an Arab riding one camel and leading a second. It was such a commonplace occurrence, it would not have been remarked upon.

When he was a good distance to the west of Aqaba, he came across a small settlement where he was able to water the camels and fill his water skins without having to communicate with anyone. Food was a different proposition, and Sir James was still reluctant to draw attention to himself as he recognised that he was alone and extremely vulnerable.

Consequently, with his stomach growling from hunger, he resolutely remounted his spare camel and continued his journey westward until late in the afternoon when he stopped to rest for a few hours. He was too hungry to sleep, so after a few hours, he gritted his teeth against the hunger pangs and mounted the camel that had rested since morning. The camels plodded on through the eerily quiet moonlit desert and Sir James stirred himself from his lethargy periodically to check his direction against the stars.

Even though his stomach was so painfully empty, the shear fatigue of continuous travel started to make him feel sleepy, and several times he almost dozed off. As a precaution, and whilst he was still half asleep, he tied the leading rein to his wrist as he didn't want to go to sleep, fall off, and be unable to catch his mount when he woke up. But in the end, common sense made him stop, hobble the camels, and lie down for what he expected would be an hour or so but what actually became half the night as he was woken by the first rays of sun breaking over the horizon.

Annoyed with himself for sleeping when he could have been reducing the distance between himself and his beloved Sabrina, he simply had a quick mouthful of tepid water, prepared the camels, mounted, and set off.

After a while, he became aware of a dust cloud on his horizon and wondered idly who could be leaving Suez in such a hurry as to raise so much dust. He rode wearily onward, conscious that the dust cloud was getting steadily closer but not really taking much notice of it, and before long, he had been lulled to sleep by his extreme weariness and the motion of the camel.

He started to wake up when his camel changed the rhythm of its movement and suddenly jittered sideways, and became fully awake when something hard hit and stung his arm. An English voice shouted rudely in an unmistakeable Brummie accent, "Wake up, you stupid, dozy Arab! Where do you think you are going?"

There was some jeering from a few yards away, and Russell realised he was surrounded by armed men dressed in Egyptian Army uniforms who were riding camels. He returned to full consciousness very quickly.

He looked intently in the direction from which he had heard the voice and saw a soldier wearing the stripes of a sergeant on both sleeves. He had a whip in his right hand and was raising it with the obvious intention of striking Russell again.

In a much stronger voice than he expected to produce, Sir James said, "If you hit me with that whip again, Sergeant, I'll have you court-martialled for striking a senior officer. What is your name and who is in charge here?"

The sergeant's face was a confusion of emotions as he tried to understand how this camel-riding individual, who was dressed in a scruffy, dirty dish-dash, could command such perfect officer English. The hand holding the whip was quickly lowered, and his back stiffened as he said quickly, "Giles, sir. I am in charge of this platoon, sir."

"What are your orders, Giles?" Sir James asked.

"I am ordered to take my platoon to Aqaba and search in the desert to the East of the town for a group of Arabs who have captured someone from the High Commission. The rest of the company are following."

"Is that all, Sergeant? Do you know the name of the person you are supposed to find or what distinguishes this group of Arabs from any other? What are you supposed to do after you have found this group of Arabs?" Sir James asked.

"The person we are supposed to look for is Sir James Russell, but my orders didn't cover anything else, sir," the Sergeant responded.

"I see," Sir James said. "Well, you do not need to search any further as *I* have found *you*."

Sergeant Giles was not the quickest thinker in the British Army, and his puzzlement was plain to see.

Russell waited a few moments then said quietly, "My name is Sir James Russell, Sergeant, and I managed to escape from my captors a few days ago. I haven't had food for several days, so I suggest you make camp here so that I can have something to eat whilst I brief you on what has happened."

"Yes, sir," he responded, and less than ten minutes later, they were all squatting on the sand and Sir James was eating dates and unleavened Arabic bread. These he washed down with copious drafts of water. Shortly afterwards, one of the Egyptian soldiers brought a coffee pot and a stack of cups and served Gawa to the whole party. In a disengaged part of his brain, Sir James noted that the orderly's ability to pour coffee was far below the standard set by the servant who attended Captain Raj Shah, but the taste and aroma were just as good.

As soon as he had finished his impromptu meal, Sir James decided to deal with the question of the sergeant's lack of orders.

He said, "As your orders do not cover the present situation, Sergeant, I intend to fill that void with my own orders, and I will relay them to your Commanding Officer as soon as I return to Cairo."

"Yes, sir," the Sergeant responded happily, pleased to know that someone would do the thinking for him.

"I require two of your men to escort me to Suez and help me find transport to Cairo. Once that has been achieved, they can come back and find you East of Aqaba. I want you to take the rest of your platoon and pick up the trail of the Arabs who captured me." Sir James described in detail what had happened between his capture in Cairo and his escape and stressed that Al Hafrey and his guards would leave a distinctive trail comprised of two sets of camel tracks and one set of footprints. "I want you to pick up Al Hafrey's trail and follow it without being seen until you can locate the oasis they are using as a base. You must then move back towards Aqaba and make camp until the rest of the company reach you. You must all remain in camp until new orders reach you. Is that clear?"

"Yes, sir," Sergeant Giles confirmed without moving.

"Then let's get on with it," Sir James said a little impatiently.

Sergeant Giles stood, saluted, and in a few minutes, all the platoon were mounted and two soldiers had been selected to escort Sir James back to Suez.

***

Late the next afternoon, just outside Suez, Sir James realised that the route they were following was converging with a track that was frequently used by wheeled vehicles pulled by horses, although he couldn't understand why, as there was nothing to the east of his location that would attract such traffic.

Perhaps the army has been using it for manoeuvres? he thought. *They certainly look like the tracks made by artillery.*

Sir James turned onto the track and, with his escort behind him, headed for Suez. Sir James had reached the Suez Canal before he saw something on wheels, and that something was an army staff car. It was waiting at the top of the quay and waiting to board the ferry that was about to dock. Russell could hear that the car engine was running and realised that some decisive action was required if he was to stop the car driving onto the ferry. Dismounting and rapping on the window to attract attention was unlikely to be effective as the driver would only see someone dressed in scruffy Arabic clothing, assume he was a beggar, and drive away.

Sir James ordered his escort to block the staff car from moving forward or back and stopped his camel just beside the door. Predictably, the driver started to sound his horn, and when the soldiers showed no sign of moving, the driver's door was pushed open and a small bare-headed man in army uniform climbed out and straightened up. He took two small, wary steps towards the front of the staff car, but Sir James spoke first.

He said severely and in unmistakeable English Officer tones, "You're not properly dressed, Corporal. What is your name?"

"Martin, sir," the corporal said automatically, then his mouth dropped open as he realised that the scruffy Arab sitting on the camel had spoken to him in impeccable English. There was something not right here, and Corporal Martin, born coward that he was, started to retreat to the illusory safety of his driving seat.

Sir James had already noticed that the car had no visible senior office insignia and asked, "Who's your passenger, Corporal?"

Corporal Martin responded to the voice, not the appearance, and said, "It's Captain Williams, sir."

"Please tell Captain Williams that I am Major Sir James Russell from the High Commission and I require transport to Cairo."

"Yes, sir," he responded and bent down to speak to the passenger on the back seat.

The back door of the motor car opened and a young officer stepped out into the sand, pulling on his cap. He didn't salute but walked to Sir James, looked at him closely, and said politely, "How do I know you are who you say you are?"

Sir James realised that there was nothing to be gained by demanding cooperation and decided it would be better to be conciliatory. "My wallet is some miles that way with an Arab called Sheikh Al Hafrey," he pointed back into the desert. "I will be unable to satisfy your reasonable suspicion until we reach Cairo and meet someone who knows me. Perhaps you would be kind enough to take me there."

Captain Williams thought it over for a second and assumed it would be sensible to do as asked, just in case he turned out to a major after all, but he wasn't going to start saying "Sir" and saluting until he did know.

"Very well, I'll take you to Cairo. Please move those animals and get in," he said.

"Thank you, Captain."

He gave the leading rein of his camel to one of the escorts and ordered the men to go back to their platoon. They saluted and rode back into the desert.

Sir James walked to the car and climbed into the back beside Captain Williams, who sniffed the air and wrinkled his nose.

Sir James noticed and said, "Sorry, Captain, but it's not easy to get a bath in the desert."

Captain Williams got out of the car and said, "I'll travel in front with Corporal Martin. You smell a little too ripe for my delicate nose." But he didn't sound too offended.

Four hours later, Sir James, feeling refreshed after sleeping for the entire journey, climbed out of the car outside the entrance gate to his villa and was followed a few moments later by Captain Williams.

Whilst Captain Williams waited by the side of the motor car, Sir James walked through the entrance with the intention of going to his front door, but he didn't get very far. The gate guard saw a large man dressed in a very soiled thobe coming through the entrance and sprang out of his little gatehouse to stop him. He wasn't going to allow some dirty and probably smelly Arab to walk up to the front door unchallenged. It was more than his job was worth.

In Arabic, the guard said, "Who are you and what do you want?" and he peered under the edge of the stranger's ghutra at the dirty-bearded face and thought, *I know you from somewhere.*

Much to the gate guard's surprise, the Arab said in English, "Have you forgotten me already, Abdullah?" and he took off the ghutra as he said it.

Abdullah took one long look at the bearded face and called out at the top of his voice, "Welcome sir, welcome," and completely forgetting he had a weak leg started to dance with joy and had to be caught by Sir James as he started to overbalance.

Sir James turned and beckoned to Captain Williams and said, "As you can see, my gate guard recognises me. I must thank you for your kindness this morning and hope you are satisfied that I am Sir James Russell."

"Indeed I am, Sir James. I'm pleased I was able to help you this morning."

Further conversation was prevented by the arrival of Frobisher, who was closely followed by Sabrina, who threw herself into Sir James' arms as she said loudly, "Thank God you are home and in one piece!" As she smelt the odour from his unwashed body, she released herself and said practically, "Obviously there were no facilities for bathing where you've been, James."

He held her slim, rounded shoulders in his hands, but at arm's length, and said, "I do so want to hold you in my arms, my darling , but you're correct. I need a bath," and he released one of her shoulders and scratched his stubbly chin and added, "and a shave also."

Sabrina said, "I'm desperate to know what happened to you, my love. Can you postpone your bath for ten minutes and tell me?"

"Yes, of course I can," he said, realising as he said it that he was so relieved and pleased to be with his lovely young wife again that he would done anything if she had asked.

He turned to Captain Williams. "Perhaps you would like to join us and listen and then assist me again by going to the High Commission to tell them I'm safe?"

"I should be delighted, Sir James," he said.

Sir James said, "I don't think we should go into the villa to talk, so perhaps we could use the summer house?" Then he turned to Frobisher and said, "Bring some drinks to the summer house, and then when Captain Williams has gone, send out a hip bath and plenty of soap and hot water. I'll wash there and then these dirty clothes need not contaminate our rooms."

"Certainly, sir," said Frobisher before walking back to the house.

With his wife at his side and Captain Williams a discrete step behind them, they walked along the lawn and went into the summer house. Sir James noticed that there was a deck chair in front of the grille and wondered why someone had been sitting there but didn't comment. He moved the chair further into the room, and Captain Williams opened two more of the deck chairs and they all sat down after Sir James had checked which way the wind was blowing and made sure he was down wind.

Without preamble, Sir James said, "I was standing on the steps outside the High Commission after the conference, talking to Sheikh Al Hafrey, when I realised that his two bodyguards were standing close behind me. Al Hafrey gave me a choice. I could go with them voluntarily or be taken by force. Either way, I would be taken to his half-brother, who is Jalal's father. There was no one about, so I couldn't shout for help, and I decided that being an uninjured prisoner was the better option. I cooperated and, as a result, retained freedom of movement."

Sir James then relayed everything that had happened during the past days, and at the end there was a long silence. Sabrina looked apprehensive but didn't immediately speak.

Captain Williams had a definite air of hero worship and said, "What an amazing story. You are to be congratulated upon your courage and resourcefulness, Sir James."

"Thank you, Captain," he responded and leaned back in his chair as the efforts of the past days started to affect him.

Eventually, Sabrina said, "And so, my dearest husband, you now have two Al Hafreys looking for vengeance."

"So it would appear, my love."

Sir James turned to Captain Williams and said, "Now that you have heard what has happened, I should be grateful if you would call at the High Commission and inform Sir Henry that I have returned safely and will report to him personally as soon as I can. You have heard what I have related to my wife, so you will be able to answer any immediate questions he might have."

"Certainly, Sir James," he said and left the summer house.

Sabrina called Frobisher, and then Sir James was able to start cleaning himself up and once again dress in freshly-laundered clothes and re-enter his home. With his wife on his arm, he surveyed the familiar objects of his home and couldn't help exhaling a sigh of relief that he was able to do both.

CHAPTER ELEVEN
Resolution

That same evening after dinner, Sabrina returned to the subject that was causing her most discomfort. "James," she said, and her voice had lost its customary cheerful lilt.

"Yes, Sabrina?" Sir James responded, laying to one side the newspaper he had only just picked up.

"I am extremely concerned about the danger you are in," she said. "For the second time in half a year, your life has been in put in danger by Arabs with a grudge. The police managed to save you from a terrible disfigurement before we were married, and this time, you managed to outwit your captors yourself. But what will happen next time? I don't want our child to grow up fatherless." She stopped speaking suddenly and put her hand to her mouth.

A beetroot red blush suffused her cheeks, and through her embarrassment, she managed to say, "I'm truly sorry, James. I have been so overjoyed to see you again and so worried about the danger you're in, that I forgot to tell you the most important news. I think, no I'm sure, you will be a father soon. In about seven months, I believe. Isn't that marvellous?"

Sir James rose to his feet and folded his wife into his arms and kissed her tenderly.

Full of emotion, he managed to say, "I'm going to be a father? I can't believe it," and he hugged Sabrina again. He went on, "You couldn't have given me better news, my dearest. I'm so happy for you, and for us. Your mother will be ecstatic when she hears the news." Then assuming the role of worried father-to-be, he added, "When should we return home?"

"For the sake of our child, not for several months yet, but to keep you out of Al Hafrey's clutches, I think we should go as soon as it can be arranged."

"I can't run away, Sabrina" he said seriously. "What would people think?"

"I don't care what other people think, James. You must think of your responsibilities as our child's father." Sabrina sounded just as serious as her spouse.

Sir James said, "I'll talk to Sir Henry tomorrow morning and see what can be arranged. But I can't promise anything, Sabrina," he warned.

"I understand, my love," she said and then added invitingly, "It's already late and my bed has been very lonely whilst you've been away," and she took his hand and gently pulled him towards their bedroom.

***

Next morning, the young couple breakfasted together and then parted until lunchtime. Sabrina adjourned to the small room beside their bedroom that they used as a library so that she could write to her mother, and since she was quite certain that her husband would never think of it, also to Lady Mary.

Sir James went to the High Commission, but long before he reached his office, he found that he had acquired a comet's tail of enquirers and well-wishers who would have crammed, chattering like a flock of birds, into his office behind him if he hadn't had the foresight to open the office door just enough to slip through and then firmly shut the door in their faces, that is.

Sir James sat at his desk and listened to the diminishing chatter outside his door, and eventually, it became quiet. He wasn't sure whether to wait for a summons to Sir Henry's office or just go in the hope that he was free and prepared to see him, but the decision was taken for him.

There was a sharp knock on the door and a messenger sidled into the room and said, "Sir Henry would like to see you at your convenience, Sir James," which Sir James mentally interpreted with a grin as diplomatic speak for, "Come at once if you're breathing."

"Is anyone outside?" Sir James asked.

The messenger looked puzzled but said calmly enough, "There was no one there when I arrived, sir."

"Good! Thank you. I will go to Sir Henry immediately." Sir James stood up and walked to the door, opened it a little, and to the messenger's surprise and alarm, peered out into the corridor and listened intently. The crowd had gone, and Sir James walked briskly through mercifully empty corridors to Sir Henry's office. Here, he was greeted with enthusiasm by Sir Henry's secretary and, during the few seconds it took to traverse the office, was plied with more questions about his exploits than he could have answered in several hours.

Sir Henry was effusive in his welcome but restricted himself to questions about Sir James' health, and when he was satisfied about that subject, he enquired about the beautiful Lady Sabrina. Obviously, she had made a considerable impression on him.

Sir James was ushered to a central place at the big conference table, and by the time he had sat down, the other officials Sir Henry had ordered to attend had arrived and found their seats on the opposite side.

Fortunately, he didn't know that Caruthers had sat in exactly the same seat not many days before and confessed to his duplicity.

At Sir Henry's invitation, Sir James described everything that had happened since his betrayal. He spoke in the calm, considered tones of a trained and experienced officer. When he finished his history and leant back in his chair, he was enthusiastically congratulated by all present on his courage and intelligence.

Sir Henry allowed the outflow of praise to continue for a few minutes, then after a sharp rap on the table to get silence, said, in unconscious mimicry of Lady Sabrina, "Now that you have upset two Sheikh Al Hafreys, Sir James, how do you suggest we deal with it?"

There was a long silence whilst Sir James stared at the table, deep in thought, and the other participants looked at each other, exchanged worried glances, and tried not to be the first to catch Sir Henry's eye as he looked around the table.

Sir James was the first to break the silence.

He asked, "What happened to the army?" and there was a long pause whilst everyone tried to impose a sensible meaning upon words that didn't make immediate sense.

"What do you mean?" asked Sir Henry eventually, wondering why Sir James should ask such a question, then said in explanation, "Nothing has happened to the army, Sir James."

"No! No!" said Sir James. "I assume you sent a small army force to rescue me. Am I correct?"

"Yes, of course," Sir Henry responded warmly. "You wouldn't expect us to abandon you, would you?"

"No, I didn't think you would," Sir James said, "but what I want to know is quite simple. Where is the rescue party now?"

"No idea," Sir Henry admitted. He turned to one of his colleagues and said, "Duncan, please find out from the garrison commander exactly where his force is," and then, to the amusement of everyone at the table, said, "You can also tell him to stop looking for Sir James as he has come home without the help of the army." To everyone else, he said, "I imagine the soldiers are somewhere between Aqaba and Sheikh Al Hafrey's camp by this time. They were instructed to proceed cautiously as we hoped to surprise the Arabs and release you unharmed."

Sir Henry studied Sir James for a few moments then asked, "What have you in mind, Sir James? You wouldn't ask for the location of the army patrol without a reason, I'm quite sure."

"That's correct, Sir Henry, and your comment about the Al Hafrey's requires some serious consideration as I don't wish to go through the remainder of my life looking over my shoulder for an assassin."

"Quite so," Sir Henry answered and waited for Sir James to continue.

"From what I have heard said about him, I believe Sheikh Abdullah to be a decent man, and if he knew the truth about his son's death, he would probably not perpetuate his vendetta against me."

"Even if that were true," the man called Duncan interrupted, "What do you plan to do? Invite him around for tea and cucumber sandwiches?"

"No, invite myself," Sir James responded.

"I don't have time for riddles," Sir Henry said with a note of irritation in his voice. "Please explain what you propose."

"Yes, Sir Henry." Sir James answered politely. "What I propose is this. I'll go back into the desert to meet our patrol, and then with their active support, I will simply walk into Al Hafrey's tent and ask him to listen to what happened to his son. If he's as honourable as I believe him to be, he will accept my explanation."

"Sounds very hazardous to me," Sir Henry commented to a chorus of agreement from his colleagues. "And what happens if he doesn't accept your explanation?"

"Then nothing has been lost and the army will have to help me leave again."

"What about the Sheikh's half-brother, Sir James?" someone asked. "He cannot be very happy with you, either. If you had knocked me on the head then tied up me up and left me in the desert, I would be very angry with you."

"Compared with what was planned for me, I think he was treated lightly, particularly as he was able to go home with his body and soul intact. He lost face, to be sure, but I don't believe I treated him badly enough for him to start a vendetta. But I'll just have to wait and see."

Sir Henry said in summary, "What you wish me to do, Sir James, is to authorise the army to escort you into Al Hafrey's camp and then bring you home in one piece. Is that correct?"

"Yes, sir."

Sir Henry sat in thought for a few minutes whilst his colleagues fidgeted and Sir James tried to retain a calm demeanour as the natural desire to avoid danger clashed with a desire to do his duty as an officer.

Sir Henry broke the silence with a sudden cough that made some of his audience jump at the unexpected noise.

"It is my opinion," he said, "that the risks of taking no action outweigh the risks of following Sir James' plan. It would not be sensible to let Al Hafrey feel he can kidnap and threaten one of His Majesty's subjects with impunity. Immobilising Al Hafrey and his followers in his camp will demonstrate his impotence and then releasing them unharmed will show we are essentially humane and peaceful. Hopefully, it will be an appropriate lesson."

He paused and then turned to look along the table.

"Duncan," Sir Henry said calmly. "Please go to the Garrison Commander and tell him what I wish to have done and arrange for Sir James to be escorted out to the army's camp."

"Yes, sir." Duncan responded and left the room immediately.

Sir Henry stood up and reached across the table to shake Sir James by the hand. "I'm very pleased to see you here in one piece, Sir James, and I hope that you will be in the same state next time I see you. Please give my regards to your wife. I have to say, I found Lady Sabrina a most competent and charming young lady."

"And very beautiful," said an envious voice, not quite sotto voce enough, and Sir Henry glared at the speaker.

"Thank you, Sir Henry," Sir James said as he ignored the interruption. "I will certainly pass on your felicitations to Lady Sabrina." Then he remembered his private news and added, "I'm very pleased to be able to tell you, Sir Henry, that I will be a father soon."

"That's truly very good news, Sir James," said he replied as he warmly shook Sir James' hand once again. All the other members of Sir Henry's group crowded around and offered congratulations and handshakes, and a few remembering what Sir James was about to undertake wished him Good luck as well.

"When will Lady Sabrina need to go home?" Sir Henry enquired thoughtfully.

"Not for several months, I believe, Sir Henry," Sir James answered, hoping that his planned excursion to Al Hafrey's camp would allow him the freedom to choose.

"I had it in mind to take you with me to the conference in London. You have been involved with the preliminary discussions already so you would be a useful assistant. You could escort Lady Sabrina home when we go to the conference. What do you think, Sir James?"

"It's a capital plan, Sir Henry, and I approve, as I'm sure Sabrina will when I tell her."

"That's settled, then," Sir Henry said with a smile then added, "I'll send Duncan to tell you what arrangements have been made, Sir James."

"Thank you, Sir Henry."

"Very well, gentlemen, that will be all," and Sir Henry turned and went back to his desk and was immersed in official papers before everyone had left the room.

Sir James walked back to his office, and as he was unable to settle down to the paperwork that had accumulated on his desk during his absence, he decided to return home early for lunch.

Sabrina was extremely curious about the outcome of the meeting Sir James had attended, and as soon as he arrived home, she took her husband by the hand and led him to their little library so that they could converse privately.

Sir James first explained what he had agreed with Sir Henry about meeting Al Hafrey.

Sabrina immediately recognised the risk her beloved husband would run but could think of no better solution. Clearly doing nothing was a potentially disastrous option, so she said simply, "Take care of yourself, my dearest man. I shall be on pins the whole time you are away."

"I'll have the army to look after me, so you should try not to worry. If all goes according to plan, there will be no need for conflict."

"I'm pleased to learn that there *is* a plan," said Sabrina, but she sounded a little sceptical. After a pause whilst they simply enjoyed being in each other's company and looking at each other, Sabrina remembered the other issue that Sir James was to discuss with Sir Henry and asked, "Did you talk to Sir Henry about returning home, my love?"

"I did," said Sir James and teasingly said no more.

Sabrina said a little crossly, "Tell me," in a tone that allowed for no further delay.

"I'm sorry, Sabrina," he said contritely. "Sir Henry wants me to attend the conference in London with him and suggests I escort you home then."

"When is the conference?" she asked.

"Not for several months yet, so there will be plenty of time to arrange passages. I must write to Charlie Hod and make sure he has the alterations completed by the time we get home. Sir Henry sends his best wishes to you."

"That's nice of him," Sabrina said with a smile, then returning to the earlier topic, her smile disappeared as she asked, "When will you go to find Al Hafrey?"

"I don't know yet. Duncan has gone to the garrison commander, so I'll know when he returns. Soon, I hope. I would like to get it over and done with as soon as possible so that we can get on with our life without a threat hanging over us."

"I agree, James," she responded. "The sooner the better."

And with impeccable timing, they heard the gong sound for lunch and walked hand-in-hand to the dining room and enjoyed a pleasant meal together.

Duncan arrived just after they arose from their siesta, and thirty minutes later, Sir James, dressed in civilian clothing ,climbed into the back of an army motor car and set off to join the force poised about twenty miles from Al Hafrey's camp.

***

As he sat in the back of the car as it sped through Cairo, he had time to reflect on the pain of his sudden separation from Sabrina.

When Frobisher knocked on the sitting room door and announced that the car had arrived, Sir James realised that it was exactly on time and, on this occasion, cursed military punctuality.

Sabrina had said calmly and quietly, "I'll just accompany you to the door," knowing as she said it that she did not want to let her man out of her sight because he was going into danger.

At the front door, she put her hands behind his head, and as his arms folded around her, they kissed and he said, "I must go, my love," but she didn't release her hold on his neck.

She said nothing. Indeed, she didn't need to say anything as they were of the same mind. She didn't want him going into danger and he didn't want to risk losing his life and a happiness he had never previously known.

But he had to go. So, slowly and carefully, he forced her hands apart and stepped back.

"I would give anything to stay here with you, my dearest lady, but I must go. As you know, I must." He turned away, and with his emotions carefully hidden, marched down the drive every inch a soldier.

Internally, he felt as if parting from Sabrina was tearing him apart.

Captain Williams broke into Sir James' unhappy silence by saying, "You smell a little sweeter tonight, Sir James."

"What?" he said. "Oh, yes, I expect I do. Haven't had time to get smelly yet," Sir James added in an effort to improve his sombre mood, then asked, "What time do we arrive?"

"About nine, I expect, if we don't have too many punctures. I have the written orders for Major Jarvis, the force commander, and I expect he will want to talk to you tonight so that he can brief his subalterns in the morning. Essentially, Sir James, we plan to enter the camp tomorrow evening."

"I'm pleased we will move quickly," Sir James commented and then lapsed into silence as he really wasn't in the mood for idle chit chat.

Some hours and four punctures later, they drove into a low-lying area between two sand dunes and alighted from the motor car. With Captain Williams leading the way, they stumbled and slipped through the loose sand until they came to a small, tented encampment. Sir James was surprised that there were no sentries but felt that it was not his place to comment on how the army conducted its affairs in the field.

They went directly to Major Jarvis's tent where Captain Williams saluted and handed over the major's new orders and then introduced Sir James. The major waved the newcomers to folding chairs whilst he slit open the envelope and read the instructions he had been sent.

After a few moments, he said, "Seems quite straight forward on the face of it. Take you in and bring you out without killing any of them or any of us."

"Sounds quite easy said like that," Captain Williams said cheerfully.

Major Jarvis ignored the remark and asked, "What exactly do you wish to do, Sir James?"

"Talk to Al Hafrey without being killed," Sir James said bluntly.

"Why should he want to kill you?" Jarvis asked reasonably, and Sir James explained everything that had happened.

"I can see why you need to have a little support," he said when Sir James had finished. He then added, "Is that why we were sent to get you back from Al Hafrey's clutches?"

Sir James simply nodded his agreement.

"I don't understand why you have arrived by road from our rear when you are supposed to be a prisoner twenty miles east of here?" Jarvis said.

"I escaped." Sir James said without elaboration.

"It's a marvellous story," Captain Williams said enthusiastically. "A real 'Boys Own Paper' adventure."

Sir James glowered at Captain Williams, but at Major Jarvis' insistence told the latter what had happened.

"That *is* quite a story," Jarvis exclaimed when Sir James had finished and then added, "We probably saw Al Hafrey and his two guards pass a few days ago. It's not certain, of course, but there were three men and only two camels and they were going in the right direction. It would be stretching coincidence a little too far to expect two groups identical to the one you have described."

Sir James said, "Yes, it would," then asked, "If you saw them, they presumably saw this camp."

"Yes, definitely," Jarvis said. "They were too close to miss it."

Sir James tried not to show the concern he was starting to feel.

"Have you discovered anything about Al Hafrey's camp yet, Major?" Sir James asked.

"Yes, of course," Major Jarvis responded with a certain air of pride. "We know the exact location of all the guards they set at night."

"And how is that, Major?" Sir James asked.

"Naturally, we have had the Al Hafrey camp under observation each day, hoping to see some sign of you, and we have observed the guards going to their positions each night at sunset before we have withdrawn from the area."

"And you haven't been observed?"

"I don't believe so. None of the Arabs in the camp have given any sign that they knew we were observing them. Several camel riders have passed here quite closely, going both towards the camp and away from it, but none of them has spoken to us or taken any interest in what we are doing."

"Where do you observe the camp from, Major, if I may ask?" Sir James was very polite and conciliatory; simply an ex-soldier asking how a colleague was dealing with a problem.

"There's some high ground to the south that gives a clear view into the camp," Major Jarvis said.

"And you are confident that you have amassed sufficient data to get us into the camp and safely out again." Sir James said; a statement, not a question.

"Of course," Major Jarvis exclaimed a little angrily. "I wouldn't risk the lives of my men if I didn't."

"Naturally, you wouldn't risk your men if you could avoid it," Sir James said quietly. "But let me propose a different scenario to you. May I?"

"Go ahead, Sir James. I should be happy to listen to you and then knock down your ideas." Major Jarvis sounded quite confident.

It wasn't what they were expecting, and both Captain Williams and Major Jarvis gasped with surprise when Sir James said, "Why is it that you have no sentries to protect your camp, Major? The locals may have people watching this camp and one of them may have seen me arrive. If Al Hafrey chose to attack you tonight in an attempt to recapture me, you would know nothing about the assault until Al Hafrey appeared in your tent with a sword and a gun."

Jarvis went red in the face with suppressed rage. "Don't try to tell me how to organise my command," he said in furious tones. "I will decide when and where I need sentries. In my opinion, Al Hafrey's men would be no match for my soldiers, and I doubt they would be stupid enough to attack my camp. Please keep your opinions to yourself, Sir James."

"Certainly, Major," Sir James agreed as he mentally kicked himself for being less than tactful. "If you will excuse me, I will go to my tent."

"A good idea, Sir James." Major Jarvis said bluntly.

Sir James bent to pass under the tent flap and then walked quickly to his tent. He was pleased to see that there was just sufficient moonlight to be able to walk around without tripping over tent pegs and guy ropes. Once in his tent, he let the flap fall into place behind him. After his eyes became accustomed to the gloom, he stepped over to his camp bed and pulled it away from the canvas wall of the tent. He crawled into the space between the bed and the tent wall then took out his clasp knife and quickly cut a two-foot-long horizontal slit in the canvas. He quickly squeezed through the hole and then reached back into the tent so that he could pull the bed back into place to conceal the hole he had made. He was just about to crawl away when he remembered that there had been dark-coloured blanket on the bed, so he turned again, reached into the tent, and grabbed it. Then, as quickly as he could wriggle on his belly, he crossed the sand between the tent and the nearest dune. No one moved or shouted, so Sir James assumed that no one had seen him, and he proceeded to climb until he was just below the top of the dune. Very slowly and carefully, he raised his head until he could see the next dune, and after satisfying himself that there was no one in sight, he quickly wriggled over the summit and lay down on his back in a shallow depression he found just below the crest.

Sir James stared up into the cloudless night sky and marvelled at the display of stars displayed before his incredulous gaze. He didn't think that he had ever seen so many stars in his life before and hoped he would live long enough to bring Sabrina into the deep desert to show her the wonders in the sky. And with Sabrina's name and form in his mind's eye, he suddenly felt very sad.

After a few moments, he suppressed his emotions and put his brain to work. He had left the camp secretly, simply acting on an impulse, and realised that good fortune had placed him on the side of the army camp furthest away from Al Hafrey. He had experienced a premonition of danger born from Major Jarvis's overconfident lack of precaution and moved without stopping to analyse his feelings.

I'm going to look very foolish in the morning if nothing happens, he thought as he turned over to lie on his stomach and wriggled back up the slope until he could look down into the moonlit camp. He covered himself from head to foot with the blanket and hoped he would be invisible if anyone passed. He relaxed for a few minutes, with his head resting on his arm, then peered out from under the edge of the blanket and inspected the moonlit camp.

Nothing had changed.

Every five minutes or so, Sir James repeated his inspection, and as time passed, the heat from the sand started to warm the front of his body as quickly as the clear night sky abstracted heat from his back. The desire to turn over and reverse the effects of the heating and cooling became ever more urgent, but he was able to resist the temptation as he didn't want to risk attracting attention to himself.

The possibility of an unwelcome knife in the ribs was a sufficient deterrent.

And then he heard a noise from below and knew he didn't have to keep still any longer.

He pulled himself up and looked over the crest of the dune into the moonlit valley and watched the Arabs flood down the dunes on the opposite side of the wadi and into the unsuspecting camp.

Clearly, Al Hafrey did not intend to start a major conflict with the British army. The Arabs simply entered each tent and herded the occupants out into the open, where they were forced to lie down on the sand, wearing those parts of their uniform they had chosen to sleep in. Those who made a noise or were otherwise uncooperative were simply knocked on the head and dragged out and dumped unceremoniously on the sand beside their compatriots.

Major Jarvis came out of his tent and was goaded across the sand towards a small group of white-bearded Arabs, with a sword point scratching his back. He tried to be dignified, but the attempt was rather spoilt by the shirt tails flapping around his painfully thin, hairy legs.

There was no sign of Captain Williams, and Sir James hoped he had driven back to Cairo.

When Major Jarvis reached the leaders of the raiders, he was held firmly by the arms whilst he was questioned. When Jarvis gestured towards the tent Sir James was supposed to be sleeping in, several Arabs were sent to it. They disappeared inside and rapidly came out again, empty-handed. Following a few shouted words, the guy ropes near the entrance were slashed apart and the tent pushed over, leaving the camp bed exposed in the pale moonlight. Two of the Arabs picked up the bed and threw it onto the collapsed canvas of the tent, where it landed upside down.

Sir James was very relieved to see that the slit he had made in the canvas was no longer visible so the raiders had no immediate indication as to which way he had gone and consequently no idea where to search for him.

One of the senior Arabs shouted something that Sir James did not hear clearly, but Major Jarvis and two other men were moved to one side and surrounded by armed Arabs. After a few more shouted commands, the whole of Al Hafrey's force moved away from the camp site and started to climb the dunes. Jarvis and the other captives were herded along with them. Some of the braver soldiers started to get up, but after a few well-directed shots whistled over their heads, they threw themselves down again, and no one moved until the last Arab thobe and ghutra disappeared over the crest.

Sir James remained in his refuge and watched the scene below.

Initially, all was a confusion of milling, shouting soldiers, but one of the Non Commissioned Officer s soon realised that all his superiors had disappeared and took charge. Very soon, the confusion was replaced with order as the soldiers rushed to their tents for their clothes and weapons and equally quickly returned and formed up in their platoons and waited for further orders.

The NCO was obviously an experienced man as he deployed all the men in the first platoon as sentries around the area, pointing out to each man as he was selected where he should take up his position and which sector he should observe.

Sir James thought sourly, *Locking the stable door and all that,* realising as the thought entered his mind that his present situation would have been much less dangerous if Major Jarvis had possessed as much sense as one of his NCOs.

Once all the sentries were in place, the second platoon was designated as the next set of sentries and then dismissed to go to the mess tent with the remainder of the force.

As soon as the soldiers had disappeared into the mess tent, Sir James assumed that all the sentries would be looking away from the camp in order to detect approaching locals and decided it would be safe to leave his hiding place. He wanted to find the NCO who had assumed command before too many of the soldiers came out of the mess tent. Sir James slid down the steep lea side of the dune and slithered across the flat area to one of the tents, where he stood up and looked around.

As far as he could detect, no one had seen him.

He walked boldly out into the open area between the tents and looked around. He saw a man who looked like the NCO he had watched from the top of the dune and walked directly towards him. The NCO was now fully dressed, and Sir James noted that he had the three stripes of a sergeant on his sleeves. He was sitting on a bench and so deep in thought that he didn't realise he had company until Sir James spoke.

"Good morning, Sergeant. I am Major Sir James Russell and the reason you were raided last night. What's your name?"

"Evans, sir," he said as he jumped to his feet, then added, "Good morning, sir," and relapsed into silence as he wondered if he should salute and call this stranger in civilian clothes 'Major'.

"Well, Sergeant Evans, you dealt with an unprecedented situation very skilfully this morning. Well done. I will see that you are commended when I return to Cairo."

"Thank you, Major," Sergeant Evans said, then added, "Will you take over the company now, sir?"

"Will you accept my orders, Sergeant? I'm attached to the High Commission in Cairo, so I'm not on active duty, but we must do something to get Major Jarvis and the other men back." Sir James said.

"Yes, sir," he responded, and the relief he felt now that someone else was taking responsibility was evident in his voice.

"How many NCOs are there?" Sir James asked.

"Three corporals and myself, sir."

"Good men, Sergeant?" Sir James queried.

"Two are very good, Major, but the third has only just been promoted and lacks experience. He's keen enough, sir."

"Very well, Sergeant. I'll use Major Jarvis' tent as my headquarters. Send someone with something to eat and drink. Order a full parade in two hours and then come to me for further orders."

"Sir," Sergeant Evans responded, then gave a crisp salute, about turned, and marched away.

"Sergeant," Sir James called.

"Sir?" he responded and doubled back to Sir James.

"Major Jarvis said he has had men watching the Arab camp. See if you can make a sketch of the layout and bring it with you."

"Yes, sir," he said as he saluted and about turned again.

Sir James walked slowly to Major Jarvis' tent and sat down on the edge of the bed. He rested his elbows on his knees, his chin in his hands. He was desperately tired, and it seemed only seconds later that he woke up as he landed on the sand beside the bed. A mess orderly came with some food and a jug of coffee, and these had the effect of reviving Sir James' flagging spirits, at least temporarily.

Sergeant Evans came after about forty minutes and handed over a sketch of the Arab camp, complete with the positions about where sentries were posted day and night. It was much more detailed than Sir James could have hoped for.

"This is very good, Sergeant. Did you make it?"

"Yes, sir," he said.

Sir James studied it carefully. There were only three guards shown, but they were on the highest dunes in the area of the Arab's camp and each commanded a view over a considerable distance. He noticed that one of the guard positions had been crossed through.

"Why has this been altered, Sergeant?" he asked.

"This guard has moved closer to the camp," and Sergeant Evans pointed at the new location with a grimy-nailed forefinger. "The two dunes are about the same height, so the guard can see just as far. Perhaps they didn't want to walk further than necessary."

"Possibly so," Sir James answered. "But it presents an interesting possibility that could be to our advantage."

"Sir?" Sergeant Evans asked in a puzzled voice.

Sir James took a sheet of paper and drew a horizontal line across the sheet. He then drew two semicircles to represent the dunes and, on the top of the right-hand semicircle, a small stick figure as the guard. From the guard's head, he drew another line that sloped down and just brushed the top of the right-hand curve.

"This is the guard keeping a good lookout," Sir James said, pointing at the stick figure. "And he can see nothing below that line. Therefore, if we stay below his line of sight in the valleys between the dunes, we can bring our soldiers right up to here," and he indicated the left-hand semicircle.

"Yes, sir, but how do we get past the guard without him raising the alarm?"

"We need a diversion. Do you have any riding camels here?" Sir James asked.

"Yes, sir. We have six camels," and it was clear from the puzzled frown on his face that Sergeant Evans was having some difficulty reconciling the request for camels with the previous discussion.

"If you were the guard and someone approached on a camel, would you look at the rider or continue to watch the surrounding sand dunes?" Sir James asked.

"Watch the rider, sir."

"Exactly so," Sir James said, "and while he is watching the rider and then speaking with him, two of our men can quickly climb up the dune behind him and knock him on the head."

"It's a good idea, sir, but I don't think any of the soldiers can ride a camel and none of them speaks any Arabic." Sergeant Evans responded.

"But I can do both, sergeant." Sir James said calmly.

The two men then settled down to the detailed planning of their assault on the Al Hafreys' camp on the assumption that Sir James' diversion would allow the troops to take up offensive positions on the face of the dune immediately above Al Hafrey's tent.

One hour later, Sir James inspected the soldiers and then told them what they were going to do and, more particularly, why he needed to meet Al Hafrey. Two hours later in the midday heat, they started to move in an easterly direction cross-country towards the Arabs' camp. They proceeded with caution and several times had to back track and find an alternative route as they were able to see the distant guard through the gaps in the ranks of dunes. Looking into the sun as the guard was, he probably would not have seen them, but it was not worth taking a chance when there was an alternative route.

Not long before they reached the last few lines of dunes, Sir James mounted his camel and rode off in a southerly direction, taking great care that he stayed out of sight in the valleys.

After several hours, he turned towards the east and an hour later to the west and headed for Al Hafrey's camp from what he hoped would be an unexpected direction.

Everything now depended on his ability to attract the guard's attention and keep him occupied until he could be incapacitated.

***

As Sir James rode away, Sergeant Evans beckoned his three corporals to come to his side.

When they were standing in a rough semicircle in front of him, he said quietly to each man in turn, "You know your orders. Do you have any questions?"

All three said, "No, Sergeant."

"Very well," Sergeant Evans continued. "From now on, there must be no talking. We will advance in single file, keeping close to the base of the dune. Return to your men."

"Yes, Sergeant," they answered.

The sergeant returned to the head of the column and signalled to his troops to advance. After several hours of steady walking, they reached the base of the dune directly west of the guard and Sergeant Evans signalled the column to halt. As far as he could tell, they had not been seen. One of the corporals climbed up the face of the dune at the south end until he was just below the crest and had an interrupted view to the south. From this position, he would be able see Sir James approaching without being seen by the guard. After quite a short wait, he signalled to Sergeant Evans that Sir James was in sight and signalled again when Sir James was about fifteen minutes ride from the guard.

When he saw the second signal, Sergeant Evans moved cautiously around the northern end of the dune. In his planning, Sir James had expected the guard to be so bored with watching a hot, barren, featureless, and empty desert that his curiosity about an approaching rider would make him turn towards the rider and watch him instead.

He was right.

When Sergeant Evans peered circumspectly around the edge of the dune, he could see that the guard had turned his back on his responsibilities in order to watch the approaching rider. The sergeant beckoned, and two of the soldiers came and stood behind him. One was a big burly man and similar in stature to the sergeant. The other, who was wearing a thobe and ghutra, was shorter and slimmer.

Whilst his back was turned to them, they crossed the narrow valley between the two dunes, and as soon as the guard was out of sight again, they headed for the southern end of the dune he stood on. About halfway along, the sergeant stopped and carefully climbed the face of the dune until he could just make out the top of the guard's ghutra. Satisfied that the guard was still facing away from them, he estimated how much further they would need to go and then slid down to join his comrades. All three men moved further along the dune and then started to climb it.

***

Sir James rode steadily towards the Arab camp and was pleased to see that the guard on the south side had started to watch his progress. As he approached more closely, he guided his camel so that it would pass close to the foot of the dune the guard was standing on and was pleased to note that the guard had lost interest in his primary responsibility and was watching him with great interest.

Sir James stopped at the foot of the dune below the guard and called out, "Salaam Aleikum , *hello*."

The guard was just opening his mouth to respond when the heads and shoulders of two men appeared behind the guard's feet. With impeccable timing, they each grabbed an ankle and violently pulled him up and back. The guard fell flat on the sand with a thud and a humph of expelled air as his chest hit the sand, and he disappeared from view to be replaced moments later by his soldier substitute.

It had happened so quickly and silently that Sir James was certain that no one had noticed, but he slowly looked around to make sure and was relieved that everything remained calm.

In a voice intended to carry no more than twenty yards, Sir James said, "Well done," and then turned his camel towards the tents that were grouped under a small plantation of date palms. He assumed it must be a small oasis and wondered if it appeared on the army's maps.

As he approached closer, a man walked out of the biggest tent and stood watching him. He was a man of medium height and was barefoot. He was wearing an off-white thobe and the red and white check ghutra common to the Nejd. He had a dagger at his belt, but as far as Sir James could see, he didn't have a gun anywhere near, so he wasn't expecting any trouble. Not that a lone man presented much of a risk.

Sir James made the camel kneel and then slid down onto the sand and started to walk towards the tent.

When he was close enough, he said, "Salaam Aleikum, *hello*" and received the appropriate reply and a polite enquiry about his health, which he answered equally politely.

Continuing in reasonable Arabic, Sir James asked, "Are you Sheikh Abdullah Al Hafrey?"

"No, he is inside with his half-brother."

"My name is James Russell. Please ask Sheikh Al Hafrey to come out and speak to me. As you can see, I am unarmed."

The man's eyes had widened in surprise at the name 'James Russell', and he said, "He'll kill you when he sees you." He didn't seem to be very concerned about the impending death of a non-believer.

Sounding much calmer and more confident than he really felt, Sir James said, "Please tell the sheikh that an honourable man will hear what I have to say before he exacts misplaced vengeance."

The man hesitated, and Sir James injected a note of command into his voice when he said, "Tell the sheikh what I said."

Stung by the tone of voice, the Arab turned on his heel and shuffled away into the gloom of the tent.

Sir James didn't hear the first exchanges in the conversation, but the incredulity and then increasing anger of one of the speakers as he questioned the messenger didn't sound very reassuring.

Suddenly, three men erupted from the tent.

Leading the trio was a man Sir James assumed to be Sheikh Abdullah Al Hafrey. He was followed by Mohammad Al Hafrey, and trailing a little way behind was the messenger.

Sheikh Abdullah had a rifle, which he aimed directly at Sir James' heart. As Sheikh Abdullah started to pull the trigger back, Sir James realised that he had badly misjudged the hatred this man felt and then closed his eyes and prayed for a quick death.

A shot rang out, and in the sudden silence, Sir James heard a thud as something fell on the ground, followed by someone cursing fluently in Arabic, and opened his eyes again. Sheikh Abdullah was as pale as a dark-skinned person can be. He was holding his shattered right hand with the left and blood dripped steadily onto the thirsty sand at his feet. The broken rifle lay on the ground beside him.

"You are as stupidly bloodthirsty as your son, Sheikh," Sir James almost shouted. "You would murder an unarmed man just like Jalal would maim a man who is tied up. What has happened to Arab masculinity and bravery?"

Al Hafrey didn't immediately answer, and then it was too late. Sir James realised that the gunshot from the dunes above them had attracted attention from all around the encampment and the area in front of the tents was rapidly filling with armed agitated men.

He said, "You have a choice, Al Hafrey. You can either order your men to go back to their tents or watch them die. Which do you prefer?"

Al Hafrey said, "You cannot enforce your threat, Russell, so why should I listen to you?"

"Look to your right, Sheikh," Sir James responded as he lifted his left hand.

The sheikh looked and gasped as he saw the number of armed men on the dunes above his camp and realised how many rifles were pointing at him.

"If you make the wrong decision, Sheikh, you will be the first to die, and you will have more holes in your body than a colander," Sir James said conversationally.

Sheikh Al Hafrey decided that losing a little face by capitulating was preferable to being dead and ordered his men to go back to their tents. As soon as the area was clear, Sir James made another signal, and the soldiers withdrew, leaving Sir James and the sheikh glowering at each other.

Sir James took the initiative. "I came here voluntarily, Sheikh, believing that I would meet an honourable man who would listen to what I had to say, but instead I have had the misfortune to meet a vindictive old man who believes what he wishes to believe." Sir James went on to describe in some detail Jalal Al Hafrey's lifestyle and the support he received from a foreign Government. Sir James' capture and Jalal's accidental death were also detailed. The sheikh didn't interrupt and when Sir James had finished speaking sent a messenger hurrying away.

After a silent wait that was only about five minutes in duration but seemed much longer, the messenger returned with two men, who hurried up to Sheikh Al Hafrey without bothering to look at the foreigner who was standing before him.

The sheikh glared at the two men, and then losing his temper, he shouted in a voice audible for at least fifty yards. "After my son's death, you, Hassan, and you, Jamil, came to me and told me what had occurred. But you lied to me. My elder son wasn't murdered by the Englishman, as you claimed. I have wasted much money and effort trying to find my son's murderer based on your story, but now I know the truth. Jalal's death was accidental and occurred when he attacked a man who was chained up. That's the truth. What do you say now, you traitors?"

"Why would I lie to you, Sheikh?" Hassan started but was interrupted.

"Because you are a fool," Sheikh Abdullah shouted.

"He's worse than that," Sheikh Mohammad stated in an equally loud voice.

Hassan took a deep breath, obviously intending to defend himself, but he was pre-empted by Jamil.

"May Allah forgive me, Sheikh, but I lied to you. I only agreed to support Hassan's story because he threatened to kill me if I didn't. I didn't dream another life would be threatened by our story."

"Not only threatened," Sheikh Abdullah almost screamed. "I tried to kill this man." He gestured at Sir James. "Only someone shot me before I could," and he waved his mangled hand in the air and spattered his blood all over them.

Spotted with Sheikh Al Hafrey's blood, both Hassan and Jamil looked around, and their faces registered shock as they recognised their former captive. They knew they had been found out. Jamil fell on his knees, grabbed the sheikh around his legs, and started to plead for mercy. Hassan simply stared at Sir James with an inexpressive face, and it was clear that he knew his hours were numbered and pleading for mercy would only cause him to lose more face; if that was possible.

Sheikh Abdullah said to his half-brother, Mohammad, "Take them away and tie them up. I'll deal with them later," then allowed his servant to wash and bandage his hand.

Sir James said, "You should come to Cairo and have your hand treated by a surgeon before it's too late."

"No one will be interested in an old Arab," Sheikh Abdullah said quietly, and Sir James could see from the man's demeanour that he was in considerable pain.

"I think you're wrong, Sheikh, but you will never find out if you just sit here. I will return to Cairo tonight, and you are welcome to join me," and Sir James waved up to Sergeant Evans, who was sitting on the crest of the dune watching the events unfurl below.

The sergeant disappeared down the windward side of the dune and a few minutes later appeared at the south end at ground level. He marched smartly across to Sir James and saluted.

"Sir?" he asked.

"Who fired?"

"I did, sir. It was all I could do. I couldn't let him shoot you," Sergeant Evans said a little anxiously, as he had received explicit instructions not to open fire unless fired upon.

"I thought my last moment had come when I heard the shot. It was a great relief to know that it hadn't been Al Hafrey who had fired. That was very well done, sergeant."

Although he didn't say anything, Sir James was very pleased that Sergeant Evans had read the situation so accurately and had possessed the courage to ignore his orders.

"Where did you learn to shoot like that?"

"Shooting rabbits on a big estate near my parents' home, sir," he answered.

"You must have been very successful," Sir James said.

"The head gamekeeper said I had shot myself out of a job, sir. That's when I decided to join the army. No option, really," Sergeant Evans said with a grin, which Sir James accompanied with a smile of his own.

"There is nothing more for us to do here, Sergeant. What are your orders for returning to camp in Cairo?"

"Don't know, sir. Major Jarvis did not tell me," the sergeant replied.

"Good Lord!" Sir James exclaimed. "I had forgotten all about the major," and he turned to the sheikh and said, "Where is Major Jarvis, Sheikh? He must be released immediately, together with the other men you captured."

Sheikh Al Hafrey gave the necessary orders, and within a few minutes, the major was escorted directly to Sheikh Abdullah, his two junior officers trailing a few yards behind. The major was very angry, and as he was staring directly at the sheikh as he marched along, he failed to notice that Sir James and Sergeant Evans were also there.

As soon as he reached the sheikh, and before the dust stirred up by his angry footsteps had had time to settle, Major Jarvis launched his verbal attack.

But he didn't get beyond an angry-sounding, "I am Major Jarvis of the Guards and I protest–" But what he was about to protest died unspoken when he heard a familiar voice behind him.

"Be quiet, Major," Sir James ordered. "You would not be in this predicament if you had been a more conscientious officer. A ring of sentries around your camp last night would have prevented Al Hafrey's successful assault and your subsequent incarceration."

"What right do you have to question my actions?" Jarvis shouted. "When we return to Cairo, I'll have you locked up."

"When you return to Cairo and the events of the past day are known, Major Jarvis, you will be lucky to retain your commission. But I am quite certain that you will not retain your command. Your commanding general will never allow you to hazard your men again."

Major Jarvis became suddenly quiet as the truth of Sir James' assertions registered.

Sir James said, "At present, you still have command, Major, and I suggest you carry out your orders. For my part, I wish to return to Cairo as soon as it can be arranged. When is Captain Williams due to return here?"

"He is due back this afternoon to collect you, Sir James."

"Very well, I'll return to the camp and wait for him. Will you come to Cairo with me, Sheikh, and get your hand treated by an expert?"

"I believe I must ," he said, and it was not long before Sir James Russell and Sheikh Abdullah Al Hafrey rode away to the army camp on camels. For Sir James, it was a comfortable ride, but for Al Hafrey, every jolt was an agony that he carried unflinchingly. When they reached the camp, they found that Captain Williams was already there, waiting impatiently for someone to arrive and tell him what had happened. In the car on the way to Cairo, Sir James gave Captain Williams a full account of events in the past hours.

"I'm very happy to say," Sir James concluded, "that Sheikh Al Hafrey has accepted that I did not murder his son, as Jalal's servants had alleged, so the vendetta is over." Then after a few moments, he added, "What will you do with Hassan and Jamil, Sheikh?"

"They have been punished according to our laws.," Sheikh Al Hafrey said, and when he could see that Sir James was about to question him further, he added, "I will not say more. We have rules of conduct, just like you, and we expect them to be obeyed." He said no more, but the increasing paleness of his face was a mute testimony to the pain he was suffering as the motor car bounced and swayed along the rutted dusty track and the fractured bones in his shattered hand were subjected to constant movement.

Like good things, all nightmares come to an end eventually, and this drive for Sheikh Abdullah Al Hafrey was no exception. They arrived in Cairo and the better road surface reduced Al Hafrey's distress in proportion. They arrived at the main hospital, and Sir James escorted Al Hafrey through the corridors to a surgical ward where he knew that a surgeon friend from his army days in France was in charge.

Doctor Michael Halliday gave Sir James a perfunctory greeting and immediately started to undo the bandages on Al Hafrey's right hand. For a big man, he was remarkably gentle, and he very quickly exposed and cleaned the damaged hand and examined it with great care.

"I have seen worse damage, Sheikh," he said, using the title as a courtesy as he hadn't given Sir James time to introduce his companion. "But I cannot begin to repair your hand if you are conscious. It would be too painful for you. And brave as you are, you will be unable to prevent involuntary movement and that will make the operation much too difficult for me. If you want my help, I will have to give you something to make you sleep for several hours. Do you agree, Sheikh?"

Sheikh Al Hafrey looked first at Sir James, who nodded his head in agreement, then at Halliday, who simply stared back.

The pain was becoming unbearable and the possibility that it might stop for a few hours was too attractive to resist.

"Please help me, doctor," was all the sheikh said.

It was all he needed to say, in fact, as he was lying on a bed and only half-conscious within ten minutes.

As soon as the sheikh was sleeping, Sir James left the hospital and went directly to his home, where Sabrina threw her arms around her husband's neck and wept copious tears of joy and relief and thanked God for her husband's safe return.

"It is a joy to see you, my darling. I was so afraid our child would grow up without knowing his father. I'm very pleased the army's plan worked."

"I'm afraid the army's plan failed dismally and I'm only alive and holding you in my arms because the army recruited a man who shot rabbits in his former life." The stress of past weeks suddenly took its toll, and he couldn't stop himself weeping as the tension oozed away. Sabrina cradled his head against her breast and comforted her man, not realising as she did so that she would make the same gesture of love and support for their child on many future occasions.

Eventually, he managed to say, "It's all over. We no longer have to live in fear of Sheikh Al Hafrey."

"Thank heaven for that, James. One day, you must tell me what happened, but for now, having you restored to me is sufficient."

***

Next morning, Sir James went directly to the hospital to see Sheikh Al Hafrey and was pleased to see him sitting up in bed, looking a great deal less racked by pain than he had the previous evening.

As soon as he saw his visitor, the sheikh said, "Doctor Halliday is hopeful that I will be able to use this hand again. I must thank you. You were very considerate to a man who was trying to kill you, and I am in your debt."

"There is no debt, Sheikh, but when you are better, there is something I would like to talk to you about."

"Why not talk now? It was only my hand that was injured and not my brain."

"Very well, Sheikh," Sir James said as he rapidly put his thoughts into order and related everything that had occurred from the meeting at the Colonial Office to his capture by Jalal Al Hafrey.

Sir James concluded by saying, "If you would be willing to consider the possibility, Sheikh, my government would be interested in a formal treaty that would allow us to mine the minerals that lie in the mountains on the southern border of your lands. In return, we would pay you for the minerals removed. It could make you a rich man and help your people enormously."

There was a long silence as Sheikh Al Hafrey considered the ramifications of Sir James offer.

Then he said, "At present, we can only speak in general terms and about principles, but I would be interested to know more of your government's intentions."

"I'm pleased to hear that, Sheikh, and I will speak to the High Commissioner this morning and seek his advice."

The two men exchanged cordial Arabic pleasantries, "Ma'a salama, *goodbye*," and Sir James left the hospital in order to go to the offices of the High Commission.

Half an hour later, Sir James walked into the High Commission and was a little surprised to reach his office without seeing a single person, as the building was usually a hive of activity. As soon as he was sitting at his desk, he reached for a sheet of paper and, after thinking for a moment, dipped his pen in the ink well and wrote to the High Commissioner, requesting an appointment.

A messenger came in response to Sir James' enthusiastic tug on the bell rope and took Sir James' request to the High Commissioner's private secretary. Half an hour later, he returned with a note from the High commissioner, requesting Sir James' presence in his office thirty minutes later.

***

Punctually, Sir James knocked on the door of the High Commissioner's office and then opened it and entered the room.

When the High Commissioner saw Sir James, he stood up and beckoned to him. But before Sir James was twenty feet from his desk, the High Commissioner was on his feet with a big smile of welcome on his face.

He said, "I have been asking for news of you for hours, but no one knew anything. Then your note arrived asking for an appointment to see me, so I did at least know you were alive, when I expected to hear you had been murdered by the Al Hafreys. I expected you to arrive in my office showing some signs of the trials you have been subjected to and decided to see you alone to save you discomfort. Clearly, my precaution was unnecessary as you look as if you were about to go on parade. I wish to hear the whole of your story, Sir James, but before I do so, I will call the DHC and several other senior staff together so that we can all hear your story at the same time. Please sit down, Sir James."

He pointed to a comfortable chair near his desk and then tugged on the bell pull.

A messenger arrived in response to the bell and received his instructions from the High Commissioner. After a short wait, the messenger returned, and they followed him to the main conference room, where Sir James informed all the senior High Commission staff what had happened since they had last sat there. He concluded with the news about the mining agreement he had provisionally arranged with Sheikh Abdullah Al Hafrey and was overwhelmed by the strength of the congratulatory comments he received.

*****

At the end of a memorable day, Sir Henry McMahon returned to his wife of thirty years and, over dinner, explained in detail everything that had happened to the Russell family and in particular what Sir James had achieved on his own. Her advice was cogent and chimed melodiously with her husband's own conclusions.

As a result, Sir James was summoned to the High Commissioner's office the next morning. Sir Henry stood, shook his visitor's hand with enthusiasm, and said, "Please sit, Sir James," and indicated a chair opposite his own. When they were both seated, Sir Henry said without preamble, "After the ordeal the Al Hafreys have put you through, Sir James, I have decided to send you home on leave for three months. At the end of your leave, I wish you to take charge of arrangements for the London conference. You will be my official representative and have an office and staff commensurate with the tasks you will have to undertake. Do you have any questions?"

"That is very generous, Sir Henry. A period of rest and relaxation would be very welcome, I must confess. And I have no questions at present," Sir James managed to say as he recovered from his surprise. "But I expect there will be some in due course."

"I expect so as well, Sir James. Now, if you will excuse me, I have some urgent dispatches to deal with."

"Certainly, Sir Henry," Sir James said as he stood up to leave. "And on behalf of Lady Sabrina and myself, I must thank you for your thoughtfulness."

Sir James left the High Commissioner's office and returned to his villa in order to tell his lovely wife about the momentous changes that had occurred since breakfast and to start planning their future.

It would be a busy future, of that there could be no doubt. There was a new home to organise, a son or daughter to nurture, and an international conference to arrange.

"Shaping history," as Sir Michael Marshall had intimated.

THE END

EPILOGUE

It was a typically unpleasant January day and almost two years to the day since Russell had driven Miss Sabrina Severn along this same route. Russell, or, more accurately, Sir James Russell, slowed his nearly new, dark green Bentley and turned off the main road. He drove through the same imposing gateway and along the well-maintained gravel drive between rows of imposing and mature beech trees. In the car, sleeping in the corner of the front seat and leaning against him, was his wife.

Sir James stifled a cavernous yawn and prayed for the moment when he would be able to stop and switch off the engine. He drove around a long right-hand bend, and suddenly, the driveway opened out and Sir James brought the big car to a gentle halt at the foot of an imposing flight of steps. He switched off the engine and, sighing with relief, climbed out and walked around to the passenger's side of the motor and helped his wife to alight. The front door opened and the figure of Benson appeared as a backlit silhouette. He hurried down the steps to meet the travellers.

"Good evening, Sir James," he said. "Good evening, my lady. Welcome home. I hope your journey has not been too taxing?"

"Good evening, Benson," she answered a little sleepily. "The journey has been long and tiring. It has been particularly so for my husband, who has had to drive so far today. It was thoughtful of you to ask."

"Not at all, madam," Benson responded.

"Benson," said Sir James. "Would you please call Edith? She can help my wife."

An hour later, Sir James Russell and his wife met in the library, and after he had poured them each a brandy, he raised his glass and said, "I hope for a less hazardous existence for myself and a more happy and relaxed life for you, my lady."

"My sentiments entirely, my dear," she said. "But now, I think we should retire for the night."

"Quite right as always, my love." he said. "We need some rest, and tomorrow,

I might start going through my diaries. I feel a compulsion to write a history of the two years since we met whilst all the problems with the Al Hafreys are still clear in my mind."

"Well, my dear," she responded. "Apart from running the estate, you have no other commitments at present and the library will be a peaceful haven for you to work in."

In the morning, after a substantial breakfast, Sir James then went to the library, unlocked a cupboard, and took out notebook after notebook and stacked them on an adjacent desk, together with the three volumes he had carried from Egypt. He organised the individual volumes into chronological order and checked to ensure that all the records were there. Each black leatherbound volume was embossed with the family coat of arms. It was foolscap size and about three quarters of an inch thick. As Russell had filled a volume on average every month, he had twenty-four volumes of notes to examine. He settled down in a comfortable armchair, cleared his mind of extraneous thoughts, and started to concentrate on the diaries that outlined his recent life.

What you have just read was compiled from the detailed notes that Sir James wrote at that time.

About the Author

John Milton Langdon is a Fellow of the Institution of Civil Engineers. He has a master's degree in maritime civil engineering. Langdon retired in 2005 after an active and rewarding career as a civil engineer and became a professional author. Initially, he worked in Britain, but from 1975 he dealt with project development in Bahrain, Iran, Iraq, Saudi Arabia, the United Arab Emirates, and Nigeria. He now lives in Suffolk, UK.

Other books by John Milton Langdon

Against All Odds

Telegraph Island

Full Circle

Ring of Gold